THE STALLION

Hasan heard them. His head came up. His nostrils flared. His eyes went wide and bright and wild. He burst into the sunlight, a creature all of fire and swiftness, defying them with every line of his body.

"See," said Al'zan, "he has both lightness and brilliance. And temper—of that, altogether too much. We shall teach him to master it."

"Will he let us?" asked Zamaniyah.

"With time and patience. And love; that, too."

They watched the stallion dance his hatred. Rearing, wheeling, slashing the air with hoofs and teeth; striving to spring upon them, high though they stood, and railed in stone.

"He is like a wind of fire," Al'zan murmured.

"A *khamsin*," said Zamaniyah. "The wind out of the desert, that burns as it blows, and scours the flesh from bone. Khamsin," she said, naming him. "Khamsin."

He stood still below them. His sides heaved, but his head was high, his tail a banner over his back.

"You are Khamsin," she said to him, "and I am Zamaniyah. We shall be friends yet, you and I."

Hasan turned his back on her.

A WIND IN CAIRO

Judith Tarr

SPECTRA

BANTAM BOOKS
TORONTO • NEW YORK • LONDON • SYDNEY • AUCKLAND

A WIND IN CAIRO

A Bantam Spectra Book / March 1989

ISBN 0-553-27609-3

Published simultaneously in the United States and Canada

PRINTED IN THE UNITED STATES OF AMERICA

O   0 9 8 7 6 5 4 3 2 1

To
Alex and Galina

and to
Sheiky

Acknowledgments

Many people have lent aid and comfort, in many ways, to the writing of this book. Most especially:

My agent, Jane Butler, who asked for a book about horses; Susan Shwartz, who put together horses and Arabian Nights, thereby inspiring a short story and a novel (and who provided the novel with a title); and Lou Aronica, Amy Stout, and the staff of Bantam Spectra, who helped to turn the idea into reality.

Sandra Miesel, whose assistance in research has been beyond price; Rob Dean, who found a book with just exactly the right pictures; and Elizabeth Moon, for sending me in the right direction at the right time.

A lifetime's worth of teachers both human and equine, and most especially Alex and Galina Vukolov, masters of the art; and their descendant of the *saqla* mare, Sheik Nishan, who is our own Khamsin.

In the Name of Allah, the Beneficent, the Merciful.
By the snorting coursers,
Striking sparks of fire
And scouring to the raid at dawn,
Then, therewith, with their trail of dust,
Cleaving, as one, the center of the foe,
Lo! man is an ingrate unto his Lord
And lo! he is a witness unto that;
And lo! in the love of wealth he is violent.
Knoweth he not that, when the contents of the graves are
    poured forth
And the secrets of the breasts are made known,
On that day will their Lord be perfectly informed concerning
    them.

The Koran, *Sûrah* 100: ''The Coursers''

1

"And she was shaped *just* so," said Hasan, miming beauty in the air.

"Melons," sighed Rashid, who had already had as much wine as was good for him. "Pomegranates." He staggered. The others propped him up. People, passing, disapproved.

Hasan smiled sweetly at them. "And a fine day it is, good sirs. Such a lovely cloud of dust in our enchanted streets. Such a ripe reek of offal." He sniffed delicately. "Ah. Camel dung. The finest vintage, my friends. The very finest."

His companions applauded. He saluted them with graceful extravagance. A waterseller jostled past him, goatskin sack about his neck, copper cup swinging from his belt, crying his wares.

"Water!" Daoud was disgusted. "Wine for me. Sweet wine, lovely wine, wine of Cairo, wine of Alexandria, wine of Damascus . . ."

"Wine of Paradise," hiccoughed Rashid.

Hasan shook his head sadly as they paused before his father's gate. "No wine there, alas. Only milk and honey."

They groaned in chorus. He bowed and bade them a fond farewell.

It was cool under his own roof, quiet after the clamor of the street, fragrant with roses and citron. As he turned the corner into the first shaded court, servants came running to greet him. They brought water for his feet and his hands and his sweating face; a fresh robe, light and cool, and soft slippers; a cup of sherbet to cool his throat. "Young master," they murmured. "Young prince."

He smiled at them. It was a joyous world he lived in. Good wine warming his middle, fine friends newly parted from, and the whole small kingdom of his father's house devoting itself to his pleasure.

There was a shadow or two on his bliss, to be sure. A little matter. A wager lost. Or two. Or maybe three. He shrugged, sipped the last of the sherbet, turned toward the inner stair.

"Young master."

He paused. Kemal abased himself as only Kemal could, with perfect correctness but with most imperfect servility. "Young master," the old man said, "your father commands your presence." He spoke of Hasan's father as a proper Muslim would speak of the Prophet.

Hasan regarded him with distaste and his message with disfavor. But even Hasan knew better than to ignore the summons of Ali Mousa Sharif. In as good order as he might, he went to face his father.

When Ali Mousa was pleased with his son, he waited in the garden under the lemon tree. When he was not pleased, he waited in the court of the white fountain. Now Kemal led Hasan through the empty court, where the fountain played all alone; passed the door which led to the garden; and ushered him into a high cool chamber with tiles the color of the sky. White daylight poured from louvers in the roof to illumine Ali Mousa's face; a fan swayed slowly, languid as the slave who wielded it.

Hasan had been more puzzled than perturbed. Looking into his father's eyes, he began to be—not afraid. But apprehensive: yes, he could admit to that. He bowed low, kissed the carpet between his hands. But it was not in him to grovel at anyone's feet, even Ali Mousa's. He raised himself, sat on his heels.

Ali Mousa looked at him. Hasan knew what he was seeing. Handsome Hasan whose mother had been a Circassian slave, whose father was of the lineage of the Prophet. Hasan who was beautiful and knew it, who could widen his fine dark eyes and flash his fine white teeth and charm his way out of anything. Even, he was certain, this. He armed his eyes. He readied his smile. He ventured a flicker of both.

"I presume," said Ali Mousa, "that you have an explanation to offer."

Hasan offered innocence. "Explanation, Father? What is there to explain?"

"The Pearl of the Desert," said Ali Mousa.

Hasan gaped like an idiot. This was not like his father at all. This was as direct as a Frankish charge.

"Nine mares," said Ali Mousa. "Nine daughters of the east wind. Nine elect of the elect of Arabia, and each in foal to a prince of stallions. And above them all, the beautiful, the incomparable, the Pearl of the Desert, mother of nine champions, bearer of the heir of my beloved lost prince. Ten perfect jewels adorned my stable; and this morning one came to take them away. They were his, he told me. He had won them. He offered proof. *I,* said the document he carried, *Hasan al-Fahl Sharif ibn Ali Mousa ibn Abd al-Mahdi ibn Suleiman al-Qurayshi of the blood of the Prophet, upon whose name be prayer and peace, having wagered at backgammon the ten mares who are mine to wager, do hereby surrender into the hands of this my creditor—*"

With each word Hasan sank down farther, until he lay upon tiles as cold as his heart. But he was still Hasan. He raised wide brimming eyes. "Father," he said. "Oh, Father. I was winning. The luck was with me. I was going to win the emir's whole harem. But then—but then—"

For all the heed Ali Mousa took of him, he might never have spoken at all. "When you roistered yourself into the public prison, I dismissed it as mere youthful exuberance. When you cut a swath through the daughters of Cairo, I called it but manhood waxing the hotter for that you were early come to it. Even when you were brought to law for dyeing the Imam Masoudi's beard green while he slept in his own garden, I confess, I found myself more amused than not; I resolved to forgive you. You are my only son, and young, and possessed of more than your share of high spirits.

"But this," said Ali Mousa, "this passes the bounds of simple mischief. I have paid your fines, defended you in court and before a succession of outraged fathers, and satisfied your swarm of creditors. Never to my knowledge have you lied; have you wagered away that to which you have no right; have you wagered it in backgammon, which every school of law has condemned as the creation of Iblis."

"I swear," cried Hasan. "I swear I won't do it again!"

"So have you always sworn. And, to do you credit, kept your word. Only to advance to a sin which as far exceeds its predecessors as the Pearl of the Desert exceeds the waterseller's donkey. To what will you rise now? Rape? Murder? Apostasy?"

Hasan pressed his forehead to his father's foot. "I promise. I promise. No more."

"And for how long? How long before the wine rises in you, or your companions incite you, or your own demon pricks you to some new outrage?"

Hasan lay on the floor and wept. Ali Mousa neither moved nor spoke. Hasan, wept dry, hiccoughing, lifted his head. His father's face was set in stone. He had never seen it so implacable; so utterly unmoved by his tears. "What can I do?" he cried.

"Obviously," said Ali Mousa, "you cannot be your own master. My fault. I have not raised you as a father should. I have indulged you to the point of folly; I have spoiled you to ruin. But that is done. I have failed in my office. I shall surrender you now to one who may be stronger than I, and sterner."

Hasan rose to his knees, too shocked yet to understand.

"It is an old custom. Cruel, I thought once; antiquated. Yet my kindness has begotten only pain. We shall see if the old way does not prove best. Tomorrow," said Ali Mousa, "you depart from Cairo. My servants are bidden to conduct you to the one who will be your father henceforward until he judges you worthy of your name: to him who was my own father in more than blood, the Sheikh Uthman of the Banu Faisal."

Hasan sank back upon his heels. Sheikh Uthman. That terrible old man, that hawk of the desert, that Bedouin bandit who alone in the world had ever been impervious to Hasan's eyes or his smile. Hasan had heard him once when he brought his reek of camels and the desert into Ali Mousa's clean house: "That's a fine lily of a boy you have, young Ali. Lovely as his mother, and with her red hair, too; and as spirited as one of my young stallions. All he needs is a dose of the lash, to teach him submission."

Hasan's tears burned away in a fire of anger. "How can you do this to me? How can you cast me out?"

"Better now and by my own will, than later and by the will of the city's tribunal. I have been a fool, but I am not blind. I see that there is no hope for you while you dwell in my house. In Sheikh Uthman's tent, among his sons, perhaps you will learn to be a man."

"It will kill me."

"Allah forbid," said Ali Mousa. "But if He so wills, then so He wills it. He is the Merciful, the Compassionate. He is the Lord of the Worlds."

Hasan would not bow his head to piety. He was too far gone in outrage. "What have I done to deserve exile? Punishment, yes, gladly I will bear anything, even the lash. But to be flung into the desert, cast among the sons of camels, turned into a filthy Bedu dog—"

Ali Mousa struck him. He reeled more with astonishment than with pain. "You will not speak ill of my kin and yours. My father sent me as now I send you; and I was younger, no more than a child, and I had done nothing to earn his wrath, but he was adamant. The desert is the forge of men. So shall it forge you."

Anger shattered. Tears sprang anew. True, this time; piteous. Hasan flung himself upon his father's knees. "Please, Father. I'll do anything. I'll be your slave, your servant, anything. Only let me stay with you!"

Ali Mousa never moved. "Tomorrow," he said, "you go."

"I'll kill myself!"

"Tomorrow," said Ali Mousa. "I have decided. It is settled. After this night, until Sheikh Uthman sends you back to me, you are no longer my son."

The harem was closed against Hasan. His mother would not speak to him. When he forced his way to her door, he found

it barred, and silence within for all his hammering and
shouting and tearful beseeching.

He retreated at last, shaking, drawing back to the haven of
his own chamber. But there was no haven left. Everything in
it that had been his own was gone, save for one pitifully small
bundle laid by the door. The lone servant who would come to
wait on him was his father's, the one of them all whom he
could be said to respect, the tall dour soldier-slave Mahaut
who had taught him what he knew of the arts of war. Mahaut
did not know the meaning of pity. He stood with folded arms
and watched Hasan fling himself from wall to wall, weeping,
raging, wreaking havoc with what few furnishings his father's
wrath had left him.

The storm passed as swiftly as it had come. Hasan sank
down, empty. Mahaut was silent. Hasan swallowed. His
throat was raw. "It's a game," he said hoarsely. "Isn't it? A
show. To shake me to my senses. Tomorrow I'll beg him to
be merciful, and he'll let me win him over. Won't he,
Mahaut? He loves me. He can't bear to be parted from me."

Mahaut's blue Frankish eyes rested on him. Measuring
him. Bare feet, torn robe, discarded turban. But no bruises on
his precious white skin, no mark on his cheeks where the red
down was just beginning to thicken. Even his passion was a
pretense. There was no more to him than a pair of eyes and a
famous smile. Mar one or both, rob him of his vaunted
beauty, and what would he be? Nothing. Nothing at all.

He scrambled up. "There is more to me than that. There
is!"

Mahaut raised an ironic brow.

"I'll show you. I'll show you all." Hasan kept saying it.
Mahaut said nothing at all. He was simply there, inescapably,
wherever Hasan turned.

Hasan knew the taste of prison. It was bitter, and it was
cold. Anger warmed him little in it.

"I'll show you," he whispered. He stood still in the
middle of his emptied floor. Mahaut watched him tirelessly, in
calm that was too perfect even to be contempt. Hasan was no
match for Frankish muscle, nor ever could be.

His shoulders drooped. His head sank in dejection. He
drifted, stumbling, toward the bundle and the door. Mahaut
did not move.

Hasan snatched, leaped, bolted. Full under his jailer's hands, the wind of them chilling his nape as he darted beneath. They caught his gown. He twisted viciously. The fine linen tore. He burst out of it, all but naked in drawers and shirt, and running all the lighter for it.

The Frank knew his master's house, but Hasan knew every cranny in it, and every smallest bolthole. He laughed even as he fled, white wild laughter, fierce with mockery.

The last he knew of Mahaut was the thudding of feet and the snarl of a Frankish curse. Then he was over the garden wall, bundle slung behind him, the crowds and clamor of the city before. They parted: shocked eyes, startled faces, a flicker of laughter.

He halted in an alleyway, gulping air, grinning like a mad thing. After a moment he remembered what he carried. He lowered it, spreading it open on the ground; and laughed aloud. Fine robes for the desert, these; princely fine. Under the interested eye of a small grey cat, he put them on, winding the turban, hanging from his belt the weight that had been the heart of his booty. A very heavy weight, jingling musically.

He laughed again, lighter now, freer. "Oh, surely, God is with me!" The cat yawned and flicked her tail. "I'll show them," he said to her. "I'll win back everything I ever lost. I'll win it back a hundredfold. And then I'll be perfection itself. They'll see. They'll see what I am, by Allah, by every saint and prophet."

Rashid and Daoud were there in Faranghi's, waiting as they always were, with the shifting crowd of others who always came to the scent and the sound of princely largesse. The sun went down in prayer. The night fell in wine and roistering. The luck was on Hasan. He could feel it. Tonight would be his triumph. Tomorrow. . .

"I'll go," he said. "He thinks I'll beg and grovel and cry to be set free. I'll show him. I'll go to the old monster in Arabia. I'll be the greatest desert raider who ever was."

They cheered. They called him by the name which Sheikh Uthman had given him, which for bright defiance he had taken for his own. "Al-Fahl! Al-Fahl! Al-Fahl!" The Stallion tossed his haughty head and bade the wine go round again.

Music, song, bold and wanton women falling helpless before his eyes. The luck was singing in him.

Tonight, no backgammon. "Law," he explained with care round the sweet stammer of the wine. "Law says no backgammon. Bones, O my beloved. Bones that dance and sing."

They danced for him. Gold heaped for him. His hands were charmed tonight. They could not cast awry.

The emir was there, sweet sacrificial lamb. Dark oily slant-eyed Turk, soft prey for the Prophet's child on whom were prayer and peace and precious, precious luck. Ten mares, he wagered. Double or none. On all that Hasan had. Poor victim. Hasan stroked his dancing beauties; crooned to them; laid his will upon them.

"*Allahu akbar, Allahu akbar:* God is great, God is great! There is no god but God, and Muhammad is the Prophet of God. Come to prayer, O ye Muslims; come to prayer. Come to prosperity, come to prosperity. God is great. God is great. There is no god but God!"

The muezzin's wail shattered Hasan's spell. In the tavern was sudden silence: prayer rugs spread, heads bowed, backs bent toward Mecca. Infidels looked on, bored or interested or infernally amused. "Allah," prayed Hasan with the dice in his hand. *"Allahu akbar."* He cast. The dice rattled as they fell. Rolled. Settled in the stillness of the hour of prayer.

Eyes stared up at him, mocking him. Serpent's eyes. Defeat; disaster. He saw his hand creep out. One touch while all eyes bent in worship. One small encouragement, for his own salvation.

His hand froze. An inch more, only an inch. There was no one to see.

Only God.

He turned as all the others turned. He had nothing to pray for, except despair. But perhaps, afterward—one loss, one only. The luck would come back.

Fortified with prayer and wine, he was magnanimous in defeat. "Another cast?" he said. "In God's name?"

The emir likewise could be generous, for a Turk. "Another cast," he agreed. And another, and another. Hasan won a little. He lost rather more than a little. The next cast surely, or the next . . .

* * *

In the end they left Faranghi's. They had drunk all the wine he would let them drink. Faranghi the miser, Faranghi the fool. They found a more generous seller. His wine was stronger. It made them wild. Hasan had lost his embroidered coat, his belt of gold set with lapis and silver, his dagger with the emerald hilt. His purse was thin and frail. They were drinking it dry, his fine friends, his brothers in the blood of the vine. Their faces blurred. Their names were all one. *"Thirst,"* he said to them. "I name you *Thirst.*" They laughed. Good fellows. They always laughed at a prince's jest. Even a prince whom luck had made its fool. "Sharif, I am," he sang. "Sharif, sharif, blessed and beloved, scion of the Prophet's tree. A sharif should be above reproach. A sharif should be a perfect saint. A sharif should be—should be—"

"Generous!" they cried.

His hand was full of silver. He cast it into the air. It fell like rain. "Tomorrow," he said. "Tomorrow, no more. No more rain. No more silver. No more anything."

They were sad with him. They wept with him. They drank the wine he bought for them to make them sadder still. Weeping, groaning dirges, they wove out into the night. More wine; they needed more wine. They looked at Hasan. His hand delved into his purse. It came up empty. "No more," he said. "All gone." He giggled through his tears. "*All* gone."

All. Silver, wine, friends. All gone. He stood alone under a shopkeeper's torch and laughed and wept. His feet carried him somewhere. Not home. There was no more home. His head floated among the stars. He sang in his voice that had broken into sweetness. *"O my gazelle, O my fawn . . ."*

No gazelles in the street tonight. No fawns with painted eyes. They were all gone away. But shadows there were in plenty. He smiled at them. "Come," he sang to them. "Come into my embrace."

They smiled back. They came. They circled. They closed.

2

It was most uncomfortable, this bed. Hard. Cold. Fetid. Foul, for a surety. Hasan shifted, gasped. White agony pierced him. His arm. His right arm. His face. His eyes—his—

He whimpered. It bubbled. He choked. Blood. His mouth was full of blood.

His mind was bitterly, mercilessly clear. The wine had abandoned it. It remembered little, but it could guess. He had been taken, stripped of all that his foolishness had left him, and beaten for that it was so little. Beaten badly. His arm was broken, perhaps. His face felt like nothing he knew. He could not see.

Allah! he wailed in the prison of his self. *Take anything, take anything You please, but O Allah, I beg of You, leave me my eyes!*

He could stand, though he keened with the pain of it. He could walk, after a fashion. Hobbling, staggering, clinging to walls. A grey light grew. He wept for joy. God had heard him. He could see.

He did not know where he was. He could not speak, to ask. Passers fled him. Beggars spat and kicked him, driving him away from them. Gates would not open to his feeble hammering. Sometimes he fell. He did something to his foot. He could not get up. He began to crawl. Forward. Into the waxing dawn. How strange: there was darkness in the heart of it. It opened to embrace him.

"Come," a voice said. A warm voice, a beautiful voice, sweet as honey. "Come, poor child. Drink."

He opened his eyes on paradise. Light supernal, heavenly sweetness, a houri's face. A dark-eyed maiden, beautiful as the moon: angelic, perfect. She smiled. He died anew for love of her. "Drink," she bade him.

The cup was silver. It brimmed with milk of paradise. He smiled, lost in bliss, and drank, and went down joyfully into the night.

"Come." This voice was deep. It was, he supposed, not unbeautiful. It was nothing like an angel's. "Drink," it commanded him.

He heard; he obeyed. He gagged and choked and plummeted into wakefulness.

A man bent over him, a very human man. His beard was long and shot with grey; his face was thin, keen-nosed, with eyes both dark and deep; his turban was the green turban of a holy man, a Hajji, a pilgrim to Mecca. He met Hasan's outraged stare with great serenity and said, "Ah, sir, my apologies. My medicines are not always as sweet to the taste as I could wish. Drink, I pray you, and be comforted. The bitterness bears healing in it."

This was not the sort of man whom one disobeyed. Hasan drank, grimacing at the taste. The Hajji smiled. "Peace be upon you," he said.

"Peace," Hasan responded without thinking. It hurt, but he could speak. He was one great bruise. His arm was bound and aching fiercely. He was all too painfully alive. "Where—" he tried to say. "What—"

"You are in my house," the Hajji said, "and you are not as sorely wounded as perhaps you fear. Your arm is badly bruised but not broken; the rest is but an ache or ten."

Hasan's hand went to his face. He did not want to ask for a mirror. The Hajji did not offer one.

"Bruises," the old man said. "Your beauty is marred for a little while, but it will recover."

Hasan sighed and closed his eyes. After a moment they opened again. The Hajji had not moved. "I owe you much," said Hasan. "My—father—" He stumbled and stopped. He struggled to sit up. "How long have I been here?"

"Not long," said the Hajji. "A day and a night have passed since Allah's mercy brought you to our door."

Hasan struggled harder, tangling in the bedclothes. The Hajji caught him with startling strength. He found himself flat again, motionless, well wrapped in blankets. "I shall send him word," the Hajji said.

Hasan stilled in more than body. "No." He had spoken before he thought. He said it again, with his mind behind it. "No. My thanks, but no. I dreamed—I had forgotten. I have no father." The tears came of their own accord. "I have nothing. I am alone."

Perhaps the Hajji would have spoken. Hasan turned his face away, squeezed his eyes shut. The man left him to weep in solitude.

He did not weep long. With no one to watch, there was no profit in it. Perhaps this was best. Let his father think that he had run away. He could linger here, mend, and when he was mended, take his leave. Join a caravan. Wander far away. Redeem his sins, make a man of himself with no help from any bandit of a Bedouin; and come back at last, wealthy and strong, and show his father what in truth he was made of.

He slept fitfully. Once, when he woke, there was food beside him. He ate it.

He dreamed again of his houri. She was even more beautiful than before. She moved about him, tending him. Her hands were soft and light and very real. Her scent was musk and sandalwood.

Slowly it came to him. No houri, she. She was a living woman, but beautiful as any spirit of heaven. She was deft with him; she had no shyness. Drugged, half dreaming, he let her do as she would. Which was to tend his most intimate needs, and bathe him from head to foot, and change his bandages. She clothed him in a fresh bedgown; she drew up the coverlet. He smiled drowsily. She returned the smile. He caught her hand. That startled her, but she eased quickly. "Stay," he beseeched her. "Until I sleep."

She stayed. She let him hold her hand, though it was cool in his own, neither responding nor resisting. He held it to his cheek. So comforted, he slept.

This, he knew, was morning. His body sang with it. His hurts were fading with miraculous swiftness. His head was clear. He sat up, and he was briefly dizzy, but he was strong. He stretched his good arm, arched his back. He yawned until his jaw cracked.

Somewhat gingerly he edged from the sleeping mat to the cool stone of the floor, gathered himself, rose. He reeled, steadied. He essayed a step; then another, growing stronger as he moved.

He circled the small room. He relieved himself in the basin that lay discreetly covered in a niche near the mat; he washed with water from the basin beside it. He counted bruises. They were hideous to see, greening as they healed, but the worst of the pain had passed.

He lay down again, light-headed with all he had done, and closed his eyes. When he opened them again, she was there.

She was veiled now. A very thin veil, hardly more than a token. It aroused him as no bare face, however beautiful, could have begun to do. She smiled through it, murmured a greeting, an exquisite courtesy. He echoed them with a dreamer's languor, or a lover's.

She had food for him. He let her feed him. His eyes feasted on her, but discreetly, through his long lashes. She was lightly clad: a chemise of fine linen, and under it thin drawers, and her drift of veil. None of it hid anything that mattered. She was a perfect beauty, deep-breasted, great-hipped, but slender between; her thighs were richly rounded, her calves a flawless curve, her feet slender and touched lightly with henna.

His blood was rising. Her eyes were bold, level as a man's; they did not lower when he met them. He smiled. She blushed a little, charmingly, but she smiled in return. He drew a breath that caught. He was in love. He choked on a mouthful of gruel; she rose swiftly, bending. She was in his arms.

It was a torrent in him. It bore him all unresisting; it swept her with him. She struggled, startled: a gazelle, a fawn. She was no match for his lion's strength. He laughed and set his lips on hers. She bit. He bit harder. Her hands clawed, raked. He snatched at her drawers. She twisted. Wondrous passionate, this slave of the Hajji. He took high delight in proving himself her master.

He paused only once. Astonished. He was the first ever to pass her gate. He broke it in exultation and cast it down. He made a woman of her.

He dropped from her at last, exhausted. She lay beside him. There was no fire left in her. He stroked her. She quivered. He smiled. "My beauty," he said tenderly. "My beloved."

White pain seared his cheek. He surged up in shock. She was out of his reach, pausing once in her swift flight, turning. Her eyes struck him more terribly than any slash of her nails. Black, burning, relentless hatred. But worse than that: contempt. She spat in his face.

He was up when the Hajji came, pacing, brooding on the incomprehensibility of women. Had he not offered her the greatest gift which he could offer? Had she not begged him in all but words to take her and be her lord? And what had she given him in return? Hate. Scorn. Bitter ingratitude.

"Allah be thanked," he said, "that I was not born a woman."

"It is a pity that you were not."

Hasan spun. He bowed as low as his hurts would allow, but his mind was not on it. His heart had shrunk and chilled. The Hajji's face was ice and stone. "I regret," said Hasan. "Honored master, I regret my error. I thought she loved me."

"You thought nothing but that you lusted after her."

"She is so beautiful," Hasan said. "How could I help it?" The Hajji's eyes were as coldly contemptuous as the woman's had been. Hasan cried out in anger and in hurt. "Why do you look at me so? She's only a slave!"

"She is not," said the Hajji, harsh and cold. "She is my daughter."

Hasan was struck dumb.

"Your name is known to me, Hasan al-Fahl. Hasan the Stallion, Hasan to whom all the laws of God and man are as nothing, whose only law is his own desire. You care not whom you destroy, if only you are sated."

"She tempted me! She was alone with me. She touched me. She laid hands on my naked body."

"We trusted you. Even you," said the Hajji. "We thought that you were a man."

"I am a man," said Hasan. "Not a child or a eunuch or a stone."

"A man rules his lusts. Only a beast would do as you have done: rise up in the mere presence of a female, and seize her, and rape her."

"I am a man," Hasan insisted. "A *man*."

"A beast," the Hajji said, immovable. "But a beast in human form, who knows the laws of hospitality, who breaks them with utter disregard for the consequences."

"I thought she was a slave."

"A man will touch nothing that is another's, without its master's leave. A man will ask at least a woman's name before he forces himself upon her." The Hajji's mouth twisted in his beard, as if he choked on bile. "Why do I speak to you of humanity? You have none. I would destroy you like the dog you are, but you have eaten my bread and salt; and I, at the least, am a man. I cannot take the life of a guest. But you must pay for what you have done."

Hasan humbled himself utterly: he bowed at the Hajji's feet. He said, "I will serve you for as long as you ask it. I will take your daughter as my wife; I will labor to atone for my fault."

"Indeed you shall labor, but never so lightly as you may hope. As for your wedding my daughter..." The Hajji laughed. Hasan shuddered at the sound of it. There was no mirth in it, and no mercy. "Even if I would bestow my sole beloved jewel upon such a creature as you are, she will not have it. Unless," he said, "she has you as her slave."

"But a Muslim may not—"

"And a man entire most certainly may not." The Hajji smiled at Hasan's horrified comprehension. "No, young stallion; I think you do not wish to give yourself to my daughter."

"Then—you will not—you will not—" Hasan was almost weeping with relief.

"I will not," said the Hajji, "precisely." He drew from his robe a thing almost terrifying in its ordinariness: a string of beads such as the pious prayed on, ninety-nine amber droplets for the ninety-nine Names of God, and for the hundredth, the hidden Name, a bead of jade carved with the Seal of Suleiman.

The string fell upon Hasan's shoulders. It was light, as amber always was: startling to one accustomed to the weight of simpler stones. And yet it held him as with chains. His eyes could move, but no more. They looked upon a face transformed. Humble no longer, nor simple, nor ever serene.

Oh, he had erred; erred beyond hope or help. This was no mere holy pilgrim, no poor saint scraping his austere living in the City of Victories. This was a great lord of the hidden arts. A sorcerer. A magus. A master of power.

He rose up in the mantle of it, august, suddenly terrible. He spoke names not meant for mortal ears to hear. He summoned beings whose very presence was madness. He wielded powers such as Hasan had never dared to dream of. He raised a tower of light above Hasan's shrinking soul, and he called a mighty tribunal to judge this one who had sinned so grievously against him. Hasan's eyelids were no defense. Faces out of dream and out of blackest nightmare branded themselves upon his brain. They were above even scorn. They were justice wholly, untempered with human weakness. They judged, they deliberated, they pronounced sentence.

"What your soul is," the Hajji said, "what your deeds have made you, be." He laid his hand on Hasan's head. Light as air, weighty as worlds. "But lest you find contentment in the shape which is your soul, let this geas lie upon you. As all your life women have submitted to you, now shall you be fated to submit your inmost self to the will of a woman. Mute you must be, as a beast is mute, but once and only once, in true and potent need, may you speak in the voice of a man; and you shall die before you live again in that form in which you were born. In the Name of Allah, in the name of Muhammad who is His Prophet, in the name of Suleiman who ruled the races of men and Jinn, by all the power that has been granted me, so let it be. *Inshallah!*"

3

Every teller of tales in the bazaar told of magics such as this. None had ever warned that there was pain. He was torn asunder down to the very soul and made anew, and every bone that was reforged, he traced in lines of fire. He burned, he itched, he throbbed like one drawn on a rack. And he could not even scream. He had no mouth. His voice was air and agony.

Light smote him. He reeled, slipping, staggering. His feet clattered on tiles. He struggled to rise. His head struck stone. He toppled, crying out in fear that touched the edge of madness. No human voice smote his ears, but the scream of a stallion.

He lay gasping. The world was dim, distorted. Twilight sight: flat, indistinct, shaded in greys and blacks. But ears and nose took in wonders. He could hear the very rush of blood in his veins; drink scents for which there was no human name. The stone of the floor breathed an air of . . . red, with brown, a little gold. The wall was silvered gold, with earth and lead and something dusty-sweet. The carpet . . .

Again he staggered. He was erect, but not erect. His hand

stretched. A hoof pawed the carpet. His eyes peered down a long nose, a stream of white in dark-but-not-black. Red. Its scent was red. Like cedarwood, but not cedarwood: the color that was half of its essence. His head swung as no man's could ever swing. Long mane, long body, red, all red. *Horse,* said the scent of it. *Stallion. Stark and screaming terror.* He fled. It followed, stumbling, tangling slender legs, skidding on stone, crashing into the wall. He leaned against it and trembled.

The man was sound and scent far more than sight. Soft tread, the whisper of a robe, the acrid catch in the throat that was humanity. To the eye he was a shadow filled with light, shimmering with magery.

Rage boiled. Hasan lunged.

He struck a wall of light. Bonds of light fell upon him. A hand settled burning between his eyes. "Peace," said the Hajji in a voice as soft as wind in grass. Hasan's wrath sank down. His body bowed to the will of the magus. To halter and lead that bade him follow; to magic that granted him grace to walk as a stallion should walk, and not to stumble like a newborn foal.

Enchanted, he could only accept. He could not marvel; no more could he rebel. The Hajji led him through the streets of his own city, and he found in them nothing that he knew. Something brushed his haunches; he had lashed out before he thought. The magus' touch deepened the spell upon him. He drifted all but witless through a world of shadow and of sudden light.

His nostrils flared. Horses. A fragrance as of paradise: mares. Far below thought where no spell could reach, he began to be afraid. This place at least he knew. The long lines of tethered horses; the awnings spread to shelter the elect of men and beasts. The horse-market of Cairo.

Meek, placid, harmless, he stood in a dealer's circle, while men who stank of commerce ran hard hands over his body, thrust fingers in his mouth, peered at his feet.

"He is young," the Hajji said, "and he has been ill trained. His master made a pet of him; he has never known bit or saddle."

"That's easy enough to remedy," said the rankest of the men. "And his breeding?"

"Princely," replied the Hajji. "But not, alas, pure. His dam is of Circassian stock."

"Unfortunate," the horsedealer said.

"And yet he has beauty, and he can perhaps be sold to one who has more care for the beast himself than for his breeding."

"There are such," the horsedealer conceded. "Franks, maybe. They like our beauties for their ladies; they seldom know enough to mark a cull."

"He is hardly that," said the Hajji.

They chaffered long over him. The Hajji was more than magus and saint; he was a merchant of no little cunning. He drove a hard bargain. And yet at last he struck it. The dealer feigned mighty howls of rage and loss, but his scent was most content. "He must, of course, be gelded," he said as he parted from the Hajji. "Since he is not *kehailan,* of the pure blood, and since a stallion is no fit mount for a lady . . . you understand."

"I understand," said the Hajji, without a glance at the one whom he had thus betrayed.

They tethered Hasan in a place of little enough honor, well apart from the mares, hobbling him front and rear and binding his head. He was given fodder, which he would not touch, and water, which he barely tasted. He could neither struggle nor escape, but he could will himself to death. Surely Allah would understand.

The hours stretched. No gelder came. The sun beat down upon him. He let it. Flies beset him. He did not heed them. He was a thing, a possession. He had will for nothing, except to die.

With infinite slowness a new truth dawned. The spell was fading. His senses were coming clear again.

All the worse for him when the knife began to cut: that he would feel the pain.

Night fell, passed. He slept. In dreams he was a man again, doing what a man could do. Small things. Counting on his fingers. Putting on his drawers after he had bathed. Bowing in prayer.

He woke, and waking was the dream. His bonds and his bondage. His rough beast-shape.

The muezzin's cry called all good Muslims to the prayer of

the dawn. He could not purify himself. He could not bow toward Mecca. He could scarcely move at all. And yet his heart, child of habit that it was, intoned the prayers.

His body scented mares, dawn, urgency. A man strode toward him. No knife was in his hand, and yet Hasan recoiled from him in blind revulsion. He loosed the hobbles, caught the lead, wrenching brutally at Hasan's head. Astonished, taken aback, Hasan was conquered before he knew it, trotting at the man's side.

The horse-fair was in an uproar. A caravan gathered in the square. Hasan found himself part of it, tethered to the saddle of a haughty and flatulent camel. There were other stallions, ridden and led; more geldings than he cared to contemplate; a herd of mares guarded like queens.

Words came in snatches through the tumult. They were meant for Damascus, most of these horses, all of these laden mules and camels. Time was pressing. This caravan like many others skirted the edge of law, taking the shorter way through Frankish lands; but bribes and threats and promises lived little longer than water in the desert. To pass in safety, they must pass swiftly or not at all.

To him, for this little while, this alone mattered: no knife would touch him while his master had need of speed.

No. He had no master. He had only captors.

The caravan began to move. Perforce he moved with it. He found that he could pace just short of the lead's farthest extent, and breathe air that was almost clean, and raise his head a little above the dust of the caravan's passing.

He found himself dancing, because it was easier than walking. His belly was hollow. He regretted now that he had not drunk more deeply of the water which had been so plentiful for his taking.

Foolishness. He wanted to die.

His body had a mind of its own. It wanted to live. It wanted to live and be whole.

With every ounce of will he had, he made himself plod like the gentlest nag in the caravan. No one took overmuch notice of him. He was tethered and he was docile. The mares had all the guards to themselves: some, barely more than foals, were given to straying.

The whole long line of them wound out of the horse-

market up the broad expanse of the Palace Way to the Gate of
the North that looked upon Arabia. They passed beneath its
echoing arch, out under the blue vault of the sky. Away
westward glittered the Nile, broad as a sea, and beyond it the
white splendor of those works of Jinn and giants, the Pyra-
mids of ancient Giza.

Desert besieged all that country, but here the river was
lord. The earth was black and rich beneath Hasan's feet, Nile
earth, bursting with fruitfulness. A myriad of green scents en-
tranced his nostrils. Grass grew near the road, tantalizing for
that he could not reach it. Fellahin toiled in the fields that ran
down to the river; water birds cried in the rushes there, and
somewhere far away roared a bull of the Nile.

The gate was well behind them, the dry land shimmering
ahead. Hasan had skittered round to the Nileward side of his
camel, pretending to shy at a shadow.

He sensed no eye upon him. He had found, in skittering,
the limit of his tether. He reared suddenly, plunging, twisting.

For an eternal moment he knew that he had failed. The
tether snapped. He stumbled, tangling his feet, half falling.

He stopped, amazed. He was free.

Someone shouted. His body mastered his sluggish mind. It
wheeled, gathered itself, sprang into flight.

The man, rousing, mastered the beast, guided it toward the
river and the green thickets. The beast was pure joy, pure
speed. The earth had no power to bind it. The wind was
singing in its ears. He laughed: a shrill neigh of delight.

Horses had left the caravan. He heard them behind him.
They were swift, those tamed creatures, but they were bur-
dened with the weight of men and weapons; and they did not
run of their own free will. He was free, winged, scorning
their bondage.

They divided, circling. Meaning to cut him off. He swerved,
darted, skidded. The hunt was closer. So too, by a degree,
the river. His mind was emptying of aught but flight. To reach
the water. The water, the green, the birds calling.

Hoofs. Ahead. Many. Too many. Despair smote deep.
Defiance slew it. He screamed his challenge. He plunged
through green into a full company of horsemen, rearing,
striking, slashing. They scattered. He laughed. Men cried
out. One snatched at the trailing remnant of his tether. Hasan

swept him from the saddle, storming over him, rolling him screaming underfoot.

This was war. It was sweet. Sweeter even than freedom.

But sweeter still was the mare who stood alone. Poor lonely beauty, she cried in her abandonment. She yearned for ease of the pain that was on her: the blessed torment of her season. He left the battle and the hunt to give her solace.

Nets fell about him, bound him. Struggle only bound him the tighter. The strength of many hands cast him down.

He lay and gasped and knew that now, if he must, he could die.

Men stood over him. They spoke of him. They would not forget him easily, nor forgive. One of them was dead.

How true a prophet his father had been. Rape, and now murder. Only apostasy had not yet stained him; but there was time yet. Iblis would have him. He was all lost, all utterly damned.

A stallion could not weep. A man could, in his heart, in deep and honest sorrow. For what he had lost. For what he had never known he had.

"What will you do with him?"

A young voice, that, and imperious. His own had been like it once.

He could see the man who shrugged. The horsedealer himself, with dust and sweat on him and anger snarling in him. "Shoot him, if I had any sense, young lord. But I paid high for him. I'll geld him here and take him with me. If he dies, so be it: Allah has willed it."

"That is summary justice," said the princely boy.

"Well now, young sultan," the horsedealer said, "there's justice and there's justice. I'm a man of business; I've no place in my caravan for a rogue, and no time to waste in coddling him."

"What if I offer for him? Will you sell him?"

The horsedealer was honestly amazed. The men round about were dismayed. One even ventured to remonstrate: a eunuch's voice, sweet and sexless. "*Sell* him? Have you forsaken all good sense?"

The boy ignored him. "I will take the beast off your hands. He is, as you say, no good to you, and he owes me a debt of blood."

"He's not *kehailan*," the dealer said.

The boy laughed like water running. "Why, sir, you are an honest man! For that I'll pay an honest price. Less," he added, "the value of an apprentice fowler who knew no better than to seize the rein of a charging stallion."

"Master," the eunuch said. "Master, you will not."

"Old nurse," the boy said. "Old nurse, I will."

As indeed he did. Hasan could admire his spirit, if not his sense. The horsedealer left with gold in his purse and peace in his heart. Hasan's new lord remained with a slain servant and the beast who had slain him. Hasan would not have taken amiss a spear in the heart.

At the boy's command, the men with the nets let them go. Hasan did not move. Gingerly, sparking acrid with fear, they unbound him. They gave him no occasion to burst free. They flung ropes over him, tightened them.

"No!" the boy cried.

They stopped, staring.

"Let him up," their master said.

With dragging reluctance they obeyed. Hasan drew his feet beneath him. Men tensed. Steel glittered in a hand or three. Hasan snorted his contempt, heaving his body erect, shaking himself from nose to tail.

For the first time he saw the one who had bought him. Not a prepossessing figure. Thin and dark, not overly blessed with height, but pleasant enough to the nose, for a man. No fear in this one, though Hasan laid back his ears and stamped. The boy laughed his sweet laugh, bowing low. "Peace be with you, O my sultan." Hasan curled his lip. The boy clapped his hands. "See! A wit as well as a warrior. Come, sirs; I think he'll follow us. We've mares enough among us."

That was not why he followed. He hardly knew the truth of it. Weariness, yes, and thirst unto desperation, and blood guilt. And curiosity. To see what this mad boy would do next; to watch the servants watch their master, and to taste their respect for him. No one had ever respected Hasan when he walked as a man. Loved him, obeyed him, even feared him when his mood was dark. But respected him, never.

Once more Hasan trod the streets of his own city. The way back from the river had sapped the last of his strength. What little he had left, he hoarded, walking as slowly as his captors

would let him. They were vigilant; when once he tugged at
the rein, yearning toward a fruitseller's stall, a hard hand
dragged him back.

Hungry, thirsty, nigh fordone, he did not know the house to
which he was led, until the gate had clanged shut behind him.
He stood upon the raked sand of the stableyard, guarded by a
wary groom, and tried to deny it. Allah would not allow it.
That he should have come here. That he, a Muslim, a
descendant of the Prophet, should be owned at all; and by the
one whose name this house proclaimed. One lordly house
was very like another. There were many lordly houses in this
quarter. Surely it was not the one it seemed to be.

There above the stable door was set a carved stone like no
other in his memory. It had come out of old Egypt; it had
found a resting place upon that lintel. A man in a chariot,
bow drawn, his horses stretching to their full and glorious
speed, skimming through rushes, startling a flight of birds.
He had told himself tales when he was young, of that pagan
charioteer and his horses and his hunt. He had mounted his
first gentle nag in this yard, dwelt in this house, known every
curve and corner of it.

Until the Turks came out of Syria. Aid, they called it:
defense of Egypt against the warring Franks. Invasion was the
truth of it. They drove out the infidels. They slew the caliph's
vizier; they cast down Cairo's princes; they hounded the
caliph to his death. There would be no other: not of the true
line, the holy line, the line of Fatima that had stood so long
against the lying sons of Abbas in their lair in Baghdad. The
Turks had seen to that. Fatima's white banners were all fallen;
Abbas' black battle standards darkened the towers of the city.

The caliph's kin lived yet, to be sure, but they lived in
prison. No man of them might ever see a woman; no woman
might ever see a man. There would be no children born to
any child of the royal house.

Ali Mousa had escaped that cruel mercy. His blood was
holy but not royal; he was suffered to keep his women and his
son and his freedom. But he had been a loyal servant of his
caliph, and for that, he had paid. The house of his fathers was
taken from him to be a lair of Turkish dogs.

Of one dog above all. One hound of a Turk: Yakhuz
al-Zaman. They had fought together against the Franks, he

and Ali Mousa. In one bitter battle, a son of al-Zaman had
fallen to his own stupidity. He charged a Frankish knight
head-on, he in his light mail on his light swift desert pony, the
knight a tower of steel with a lance twice as long as a man,
mounted on a giant among horses. Ali Mousa had striven to
beat the boy aside; had only fired the young fool's temper.
The knight had spitted him for his pains.

His brother saw him die. No marvel of intellect himself,
wild with grief, he cried down curses upon Ali Mousa's head;
and there in the battle, with Franks in their hundreds to sate
his lust for blood, he sprang howling upon the sharif. Ali
Mousa raised his sword in swift defense. But the young fool's
mare swerved, shying from a Frankish mace; the sweep of Ali
Mousa's blade, checked too late, cut him down.

Al-Zaman took his revenge. Not Ali Mousa's life. That, he
could not have: his lord had forbidden it. But Ali Mousa's
house, lands, wealth—those he could take. And did. And
kept them in undying enmity.

Enmity that waxed for that Ali Mousa had prospered in his
despite. The young Kurdish emir Yusuf, to whom almost by
chance the rule of Egypt had fallen, had taken a fancy to the
sharif. He would not return what al-Zaman had taken, but he
could and would recompense Ali Mousa in full for all that he
had lost.

Hasan had learned to curse two names only of all that
were. The name of Iblis, and the name of Yakhuz al-Zaman.

Now he stood in the house that should have been his own,
in the hands of al-Zaman's servants. Owned, it would seem,
by al-Zaman's own son.

But al-Zaman had none. They were all dead in that one
battle. His wives had borne him none thereafter; no slave had
done as Ali Mousa's Circassian had been blessed to do, and
given him the manchild who set her free and won her the
name and honor of a wife.

The young hunter dismounted, eyes upon Hasan, approaching
him. He tried to seem meek, but his body had its own will in
the matter. His ears flattened. He sidled. His heels itched to
shed Zamani blood. For surely it was that: nephew, cousin,
adopted son. A Turk to his thin brown fingertips, however
well he aped good Arab manners.

The black eunuch loomed over his charge. "No," he said,

laying hands on the narrow shoulders. "No, mistress. See
how he looks at you. He is a demon, that beast, a red
Shaitan. He hungers for your blood."

A most percipient eunuch. Hasan lunged. The groom went
down. Hasan hurtled upon the Zamani whelp.

Checked, bucked, veered.

Mistress.

It was. His nose had been telling him so, incessantly. This
hunter in turban and boots, riding like a man, this thin young
person with the face and bearing of a boy, was quite as female
as the mare with which she had trapped him. He stood and
stared at her and knew the face of his geas.

Men swarmed upon him. She snapped a word; they fell
back. She came, stepping slowly.

No. His whole body refused. To serve a woman; and this of
all women. Al-Zaman's get. The devil's own.

He backed away, ears flat, skin twitching. One blow and he
would have her, and revenge, and freedom; even if that
freedom was death. But he had never knowingly struck a
woman. He could not make himself begin.

She stopped. He stopped, hating her, powerless to strike
her down. She smiled slightly. Her hand stretched. He snapped
at it. She slapped him. Not hard, but his nose was tender; it
stung. His head snaked out, teeth bared.

It caught. Someone had crept up, snared his lead. He
turned on the skulker. The man clung like a leech; an army
sprang to his aid. Hasan waged red war against them all.

It was thirst that conquered him. Even hate needed water to
live; and the sun was merciless. He let himself be herded at
last into cool dimness, the scent of water, the bliss of its
caress upon his burning throat.

Bolts slid. His head flew up. He was trapped. Imprisoned.
Walled in.

The walls did not yield for his climbing of them. The
manger, the water basin, chipped and shattered under the
battering of his hoofs. He flung himself from end to end of
his prison. He wielded his weight against its door. He
screamed with all the power of his lungs.

The door vanished. He fell into light. Blessed open air. A
passage. Beyond, freedom. He bolted for it.

Again, bolts slid. He wheeled. Sand scattered underfoot. The passage was gone.

These walls were wider, paddock-wide, and sky stretched over them. His wits were coming back. He paced the limits of the space. It was more courtyard than paddock, bounded in walls. One end was a portico, roofed and pillared. He found a deep bed of sand in the shade there, and basin and manger, and no door to trap him.

He shed his halter. It was difficult without hands. The wall helped him, and his own rubbing and twisting, and a hind foot wielded with care after he half stunned himself with an ill-aimed stroke. The damnable binding loosened, slipped. A toss of his head sent it flying wide. He pursued it, trampled it, danced a wardance on it. Buy him, would they? Bind him, would they? Now let them see what they had bargained for. He raised his head and trumpeted defiance.

4

The slave's voice was sweet and plaintive, bewailing lost love to the ladies of the harem. Zamaniyah barely listened. Jaffar labored over her with skillful fingers, kneading away the knots of a morning's worth of mounted exercises, working sweet oil into her newly bathed skin. She sighed and rubbed her cheek against her arm. Her hair slid, heavy with damp. She sighed again, this time for what she was.

Jaffar muttered as he labored, taking the count of all Zamaniyah's bruises. "And so many only today," he said.

"My mind wasn't on it," she admitted. She winced as his fingers found the worst of her remembrances.

She knew what he would say before he said it. "Yes, and if your mind should wander in a battle, you'll have worse than an aching back to contend with." His hands had gentled a little, as if some of his disapproval had drained from them into his voice. "I know where your thoughts were, little idiot. On that useless murdering creature you paid so much for yesterday."

Zamaniyah sat up so abruptly that she gasped. "He is *not* useless!"

"You might," Jaffar conceded sweetly, "sell him to your worst enemy."

"Al'zan says he can be trained. When has Al'zan ever been wrong about a horse?"

"Sikandar is a Greek. All Greeks are liars."

She hissed at him. His narrow black face was bland, unoffended. She scowled as fiercely as she could when she was torn between rage and laughter. "Have you no respect?"

He prostrated himself at her feet. "This worthless lump of clay, O great lady, is the slave of your soul. Your every wish is his strictest command."

Laughter won. Jaffar leaped up with the grace of a cheetah and towered over her. He was barely smiling, but his eyes glinted. She reached up and took his hand. "You wish I could be a proper woman, don't you? Like all the rest of them."

He glanced past her through the thinly curtained doorway, across the wide scented courtyard to the knot of languid women and the slave with the lute. The light had left his eyes. "It is too late for that, little mistress. Years too late."

"For you as for me." Softly as she said it, she knew he heard. His fingers tightened on her own.

He shrugged, sighed, smiled the smile he wore over pain. "God does as God wills; and your father is as he is. But that limb of Shaitan that rages in your stable—stay away from him, mistress. Your death is riding on his back."

Zamaniyah shivered slightly. She told herself that it was only the room's coolness, and she bare to the waist. Allah knew, she had little enough to cover. She drew on silken shirt, coat and belt, low boots: boy's clothing. Her father had commanded it.

He had caught her once before a mirror, playing with a veil. He had not thrashed her. That was not his way. He had struck her once, hard, for remembrance. Then he had burned the veil and locked all the women's garments in a single room and given the key into the care of the eldest of the eunuchs, with strict instructions that Zamaniyah was not to pass that door.

The women had forgiven al-Zaman, who after all was their lord and master. They had never ceased to resent his daughter, quiet though Zamaniyah tried to be, meek and mute and obedient. She could not hide her absences, nor conceal what she brought back from them: the scars, the bruises, the sun-stains of a warrior's training.

"If your mother had lived . . ." mused Jaffar.

"Or more to the point," she said, "my brothers."

Jaffar plaited her hair, which was her one beauty; which at least her father had let her keep, because a good Turk might do so, although he himself shaved his head as the Arabs did, for coolness and for cleanliness. She considered her face in the silver mirror that had been her mother's. Thin, brown, pointed. All eyes and angles. Her brothers had been handsome like their father. She was nothing more than passable.

Perhaps it was as well. Men would not want her even as a boy.

Jaffar's long hand patted her cheek. "Little fawn," he said. His voice was gentle.

She threw her arms about him and clasped him tight. He held her in silence until she pulled away. She had put on a smile. "Go, take an hour for yourself. I'll be with Al'zan."

Jaffar scowled, but he let her go. She looked back once. He was watching her, dark-eyed, expressionless. She turned away from him.

His name in Arabic was Sikandar, but no one ever dared to call him that to his face. He was Alexander Hippias: to Zamaniyah, who alone was so privileged, Al'zan as she had called him when her tongue was too young to shape the whole of it. As she grew older, he seemed to be growing younger. He had been ancient when she was very small, august and wise. Now he was a vigorous man in late middle age, his beard more black still than grey, his hair lightly silvered under his Greek cap.

He had been a slave, taken in the fall of Rum. Although he had never embraced Islam, al-Zaman had set him free; he had chosen not to return to his own country. "My family is gone," he had said when she asked, "and my children are here." His arms stretched to take in her father's stable. "I'm ruined now for lesser creatures; I wouldn't know what to do with them."

He was a sorcerer, people said. He had a magic with

horses; he spoke their language. They would do for him what they would do for no other man.

He was preoccupied when Zamaniyah found him. The *saqla* mare, true to her name, had kicked one of her sisters who was in foal. The kicker had received chastisement; she was sullen but contrite. Her quarry stood quiet under the master's hands, before the interested eyes of several mares and a stable-lad or two. He was talking to her, in Arabic as he always did when he handled his beauties, because they were daughters of Arabia; but in training he spoke Greek, which was the language of instruction. "So, my love; did she wound you? You've taken no harm, my hands tell me. Your little one prospers within you. It's only your dignity that suffers."

Even that seemed much assuaged by his attentions. Zamaniyah greeted one or two of her friends among the mares, wandered from the paddock to the stable to the stallions' court. The stall which her latest purchase had destroyed was still as he had left it. She touched the splintered door, the shattered manger. She left them to climb the narrow stair, to emerge upon a balcony above the inmost courtyard.

At first she did not see him. The sand was pocked with hoofmarks, spotted with droppings: the scatterings of a stallion's agitation. Her eyes sought shade after the sun's glare; and he was there, under the portico. His head was low. His coat was matted with sweat and sand and foam; his mane was a great knot. The beauty that had caught her eye, the brilliance that had held it, were gone utterly. He was only a smallish horse, a common chestnut, somewhat narrow in the chest, somewhat weak behind. He was not even *kehailan*.

Feet sounded on the stair. She greeted Al'zan with a faint smile, which he returned. He folded his arms on the rail beside her. "Did I err badly?" she asked him.

He pondered for a little while before he answered. "No," he said at last. "I think not. He's angry now, and he hates, but there's intelligence in him. He may learn to see sense."

He heard them. His head came up. His nostrils flared. His eyes went wide and bright and wild. He burst into the sunlight, a creature all of fire and swiftness, defying them with every line of his body.

"See," said Al'zan's soft dry voice in the Greek of

training. "He has both lightness and brilliance. And temper—
of that, altogether too much. We shall teach him to master
it."

"Will he let us?"

"With time and patience. And love; that, too."

"Love in return for hate?"

"It's most unMuslim," he granted her. He was amused.

They watched the stallion dance his hatred. Rearing, wheeling,
slashing air with hoofs and teeth; striving to spring upon
them, high though they stood, and railed in stone.

"He is like a wind of fire," Al'zan murmured.

"A *khamsin*," said Zamaniyah. "The wind out of the
desert, that burns as it blows, and scours flesh from bone."
The horse sprang into flight, lashing with his heels, slaughtering
armies of air. "Khamsin," she said, naming him. "Khamsin."

He stood still below them. His sides heaved, but his head
was high, his tail a banner over his back.

"You are Khamsin," she said to him, "and I am Zamaniyah.
We shall be friends yet, you and I."

He turned his back on her and voided on the sand.

Her laughter was wry. "Well and concisely spoken. But I
shall teach you to respect me."

His departure was eloquent in its contempt.

"Intelligence," said Zamaniyah. "Indeed."

"Indeed," said Al'zan, stroking his beard, frowning down
at the empty court.

Zamaniyah dried her damp palms on her trousers. She had
Al'zan's leave for this, and his presence out of sight, and a
pair of days to gather her courage. Time and solitude had
tamed Khamsin, a little. Already he was letting the master
feed him, cleanse his enclosure, linger unmolested in his
presence.

She drew a deep breath, tightened her grip on the bag she
carried. Al'zan held the door for her. She stepped through it.

Even in the portico's shade the sun was blinding. She
blinked hard against it, willing her eyes to clear.

He was in the far corner, hipshot, tail flicking at flies. As
she filled his manger, his head turned. His ears pricked. He
trotted toward her.

She drew back a little. Her palms were cold again. She

willed her heart to slow. Feed him only, Al'zan had commanded her. Linger as close as he would allow. Let him become accustomed to her nearness.

It was hard to stand unmoving. Harder yet to look at him, even sidelong and carefully nonchalant as one should always look at a horse one means to seduce. He was filthy. She wanted to scrub him smooth; to coax his mane out of its appalling knot. He itched: his skin quivered; he snapped where no flies came.

"It's a pity," she said softly to the air just aft of his ear, "that you will let no one touch you."

His head came up, jaws working. He did not shy away from her.

She kept talking. "I know you hate us. But Allah has given you to us; and you have done nothing for your beauty in defying us. Won't you let me touch you at least? Scratch you where you itch? Comb out your tangles?"

His ears went back. One flicked forward. He snorted, scattering grains of barley.

"Suppose," she said, "that I take a twist of straw, so. Will you let me make you comfortable with it? Your poor coat; it was so beautiful when I saw it first. Now it's as drab as a servant's gown."

As she spoke, she edged toward him. He did not edge away. He was not wild, Al'zan had said; he had known human hands. He was merely rebellious.

Lightly, calmly, as if it were the most natural thing in the world, she touched him. He quivered; his eye rolled. But he did not snap or strike. Slowly, crooning she cared not what, she began to curry him. She was gentle: his skin was thin, high-bred, tender. Little by little he eased. He leaned into the rubbing where the itch must have been strongest. "Yes," she said. "Yes, my beauty, my splendor, my Khamsin. How sleek you are still; how strong. And your coat—so soft. Like silk, like red copper. How beautiful you are!"

He was royal indeed, that one. He basked in flattery.

When his coat was brushed into brilliance, his mane and tail combed into silk, she stood back to admire him. He posed for her, arching his neck, preening. Her eye met his. Almost he seemed to smile.

His head snaked toward her, teeth bared. It met her fist. He shied, wheeling, escaping into the sun of the courtyard.

"Well done," Al'zan said dryly.

She whipped about. He gave her no time to excuse herself. "Is that guilt I see? Surely by now you should know how to judge your time with a horse."

"Even with that one?"

"You bought him."

"Allah knows why."

"Trust Him, then," said Al'zan. "And train your stallion as seems best to you. What else have I trained you for, but for this?"

She stared at him. He had just given her the world and all its kingdoms. And she . . . "I'm not ready," she protested. "I don't know anything."

"Of course not. You've never trained a horse from the beginning."

Her heart was bursting with pride and with terror. "But what if I fail?"

"There is no such word in our philosophy," said Alexander Hippias.

Zamaniyah had ample cause to remember that. She reckoned the days in battles. Battles to catch the beast; battles to touch him. Battles to set a halter on him, to lead him, simply to stand by him unbitten and untrampled and unkicked. He gave no quarter. Even when, outflanked, he yielded, he yielded without submission. That warmth which she had known for a brief moment, he did not grant again. Either he suffered her or he hated her. There was nothing of acceptance in him.

"But he will yield to me," she said to Jaffar as she settled to sleep. "He can't fight if I refuse to."

His eyes were eloquent, reckoning her scars. Khamsin had bitten her once, badly. The wound was healing slowly, though by Allah's mercy and Al'zan's skillful doctoring it had not festered.

"He hasn't bitten me since," she pointed out.

"Yet," said Jaffar. "There's a devil in him, mistress."

She could not deny it. "But there's good there, too, though he's buried it deep. I'm going to find it, Jaffar. I'll bring it to the light."

The eunuch smoothed her hair and settled the coverlet over her. "You never take kindly to resistance, little falcon."

She smiled. "No more do you, old nurse."

He, who was not old at all, laughed unwillingly and kissed her forehead. "Sleep well," he said.

"Allah bless," she answered, drowsy already, sliding into sleep.

She slept deeply as she always did. She had a gift: to set troubles aside where they could not vex her peace.

Jaffar had no such fortune. And he had dreams, which was a curse upon him. For wanting them. For hunting them.

He lay on his mat across her door, set the dagger beneath the fold of linen that was his pillow. His body settled easily enough, but his eyes stared sleeplessly into the dimness. *Forget,* others of his kind had told him when he was young enough to listen to them. *Forget what you were. What you are, you are. There is nothing left for you but that.*

They had told him that he was fortunate. The slaver who had taken him had wanted him for himself. Had taken only what was necessary to keep him forever a boy; had kept him, cherished him, called him beautiful. And had died of a fever, casting him still no more than a child into the hideousness of the slave market. Five masters in a year, because he would not forsake his pride; scars innumerable, both without and within. The Seljuk emir's slavemaster had bought him for the harem, because he was as black as mother night and therefore far too ugly to tempt a noble lady, and because he could be fed and trained and rendered fit for the warding of women. His seller had not seen fit to confess that he was dangerous, a rebel, a wicked hand with knife or spear. That he still had either hand, or the life that went with them, he could ascribe only to the fortune that had kept him from turning steel against one of his masters.

His shoulder flexed where the worst of the old scars tended to tighten. It was not easy to see beyond the barrier of pain, the wall of the knife and the gelder's chair. But some madness drove him always to remember. He had been whole once, and young, and a fool. He had seen the awe accorded his grandmother who was a dreamer of power, his uncle who was a great worker of magic. He had coveted what they had.

With a child's arrogance, a young male's impetuousness, he made great sacrifice. He commanded the gods to give him power.

They gave him power. They gave him war, the fall of his city, the slaughter of its elders and its fighting men, the taking of slaves. They took his family and his freedom and his manhood. And of all of it they granted him foreseeing, but clouded, veiled in incomprehension. To know, and not to know. To understand without knowing what he understood.

Vision skulked behind his eyelids. Out of knotted green, a burst of blood and fire. A stallion who was no stallion, who wore the face of a man.

No use to flee the power when it was on him. The sooner faced, the sooner over. He studied the creature which it cast up before him. All a man now, whitely and plumply naked, nothing like his own ebon slenderness. And yet, strangely, kin to him. Young, arrogant, blind to aught but his own perfection: the perfect image of a fool.

He addressed the dream softly in his own tongue, honey-sweet after the harsh rattle of Arabic. "You mean no ill. No more did I. But the gods have no care for what is meant. Only for what is demanded of them."

The white boy could not understand. Jaffar would not give him the slavers' Arabic. Let him learn true human speech if he would converse in dreams.

Jaffar laughed soundlessly, lying there. And what did he call himself? The slave's name, the eunuch's name. Jaffar. The knife had taken his child-name. He had not presumed to give himself another.

The dream-youth melted into the red stallion. Khamsin, she called him. Burning destroyer. She was wise, this mistress of theirs, but no more than any earthly creature could she see through the shadows to herself.

"Nor can I," said Jaffar. "I was given to her to be her thing; to serve her, to be owned by her. But never, I vowed to myself, to let her touch my soul. Nothing left living could do that. Until, all unwitting, she did." He showed the stallion his white sharp teeth. "Be wary, wind of the desert, lest she win you as she won me."

Never, the beast's eyes vowed. *Never.*

5

There was no Hasan. There was only Khamsin. Beast-mind and beast-will. Eater, runner, fighter. Taker of the simplest path. Which was, sometimes, obedience; and sometimes battle. Thought had no part in it. He simply was.

Habits: barley and cut fodder at dawn, cut fodder when the sun was high, barley and cut fodder at sunset. Sleep in the dark, wake to the wail of human voice: words and significance lost with Hasan, only sound left to touch him. And once every day between the barley and the fodder, human presence that lingered, touched, taught. Made him wear the halter, walk on the lead; then trot as she ran with him, slow stilted awkward human creature. He danced his mockery of her. She laughed and applauded him, and then he danced for joy of it.

He had no dreams. He refused them. He was all mindless beast.

Sometimes a man was with the she-human, his hand upon the lead, more potent by far than hers, and more ruthless. That hand tricked steel between Khamsin's teeth, fruit's sweetness soured with cold raw metal. It bound his tongue; it bruised his tender jaws. He flung itself away from it, tossing his head, battling pain, shock, confinement. Vain. It was part of him, and the man with it, strong on the rein, relentless.

He stopped. His sides heaved. His mouth was pure ache.

The man drew near to him, speaking softly. The pain eased. He recoiled.

Again the man approached. Pain lessened anew to discomfort, to the unwontedness of the bit in his mouth. Soft words grated in his ears. Soothing. Praising.

He lunged. Won agony.

The beast was wise. It submitted. It let itself be taught.

Bit, bridle. Band about his belly. Reins. The lead lengthened. He walked now free, yet bound, circling his human center. Yielding to human will. Because it was simpler. Because else he had no peace.

But even the beast set limits on its patience. Fought. Reared against bit, reins, line. Cried defiance upon puny humanity.

Which knew no better than to persist. To come back. To ask again and again, until he answered as, and only as, in its infinite idiocy it desired.

Why? he wanted to rail at it.

But that was a human wanting, and he was not human. He could never be human. He was Khamsin.

Khamsin had a companion. A cat that hunted in the rich fields of the stable had decided that the lone red horse was fit to bear it company. It slept in the hollow of his bed. It stalked flies and the odd lizard in his shadow. It kittened, one long night, in his manger, and was most fierce when the lad came with Khamsin's barley.

Khamsin was fierce in the cat's defense. By sunset he had a second manger and the cat a roof over her own.

"One would think that you were their father," Zamaniyah said into the twitching red ear. He was meeker in his harnessing than he had been, but little the easier for that: his whole body was intent on the small mewling creatures in the manger. She smoothed the mane on his neck, smiling at his fascination, which had not waned in all the days of it. The cat would even let him breathe gently on her children, although Zamaniyah bore scars of her own attempt to touch them.

"Are you lonely?" she asked him. Foolishly enough. Stallions always lived alone. They fought with one another. They were perilous among the mares; and this one more than most. Bad enough that she had bought him and persisted in keeping him. She did not need a stableful of halfblood foals.

She ran the reins from bit to bellyband, bound the long line to the band about his muzzle. Greek sorcery, her father called this. Useless mummery. A bit like a broken bar, no force in it, worse than none at all; a tangle of bands and lines and harnesses, and no Frankish cart to hitch behind. And she would stand all unprotected at a mere spearlength's remove, trusting to one thin line and a wand of a whip to subdue this spawn of Iblis.

"It works," she said, balancing whip and line. "Come, sir. The cats will wait for you."

He moved willingly enough, upon persuasion. "There may be hope for you," she told him, "after all." He cocked an ear at her. It was more by far than he was wont to give her. "What, my lord! Am I to be granted the honor of your attention? So, then. Smartly, if you please."

He fought her but once, and that for but a moment. He came when she bade him, accepted praise, stroking, a handful of fruit. "O splendid," she sang to him. "O beauty. Do you see how simple it is to learn to dance? Can you feel the joy that is in it?"

His eye rolled toward her. Warmth? At last? His head lowered. His breath was warm in her hand. She cupped the velvet of his muzzle.

The earth rose up in revolt.

It was the cat. Jealous, perhaps, or weary of her duties, or simply adventurous. She lofted herself lightly to his back. He started. She wailed as he shifted; dug in claws. Khamsin remembered his name.

He surged to his full height, flinging Zamaniyah from her feet. For a terrible moment she flew. Earth's weight claimed her with redoubled force. He plunged down. Hoofs flailed. Teeth seized cloth, tore, snapped at flesh. Dark whirled close: too close even for fear. She clenched into a knot and prayed.

Stillness.

Shouts, cries, tumult enough, but the madness of hoofs and teeth had passed.

With infinite care she uncoiled.

Froze.

Four legs like the corners of a cage. Round barrel over her. Stallion scent about her, more sweet than rank, but horrible in its closeness.

Beyond her prison, men hovered, helpless for all their armor of whips and rods. And one, foremost and furious, with a drawn sword.

"Father." It was the barest whisper.

She set her life in Allah's hands. She finished her uncoiling. She rolled to hands and knees. She crawled from beneath the stallion.

He did not move. He could not. Khamsin had burned himself away. Hasan woke at last and saw the face of murder.

Small, thin, thick with dust. Her hair was snarled from its plait, her coat and shirt half torn from her body. She was nothing to delight a young man of taste, but she was certainly not a boy.

He had almost killed her.

With a hand that shook only a little, Zamaniyah gripped his bridle. Instinct flung up his head; will checked it. Slowly, gently, she stroked his cheek and his ear and his neck. "I know," she said. "It was the cat. I know you never meant to hurt me."

"Did he not?" Al-Zaman's rage was heavy in the air, acrid, like naphtha burning.

"He was frightened," said Zamaniyah.

"He is a rogue and a killer. I saw his eye. I saw the blood in it."

"Fear," she insisted. "He was working well, Father. He was beginning to be obedient."

"Viciousness," said al-Zaman. "A Greek sorcerer I may not be, but I know a bad bargain when it tramples my only child. Go now; I'll deal with him."

"No," said Zamaniyah.

Al-Zaman's hand was blurringly swift. The blow rang in Khamsin's ears. Zamaniyah rocked against him.

Blind hate, red rage; but human hate and human rage. He lunged.

Al-Zaman scrambled back, stumbling, dropping his sword. Khamsin laughed at the fallen jaw, the hand flung up in feeble defense, the stink of fear. Such a strong brave man. What thought he now of striking children?

His foot turned; he toppled. Khamsin bestrode him, snapped teeth in his face. He cowered.

A hand tugged at his halter, pulling his head about. Zamaniyah wanted to be angry: it was in her voice. But her scent was half fear, half perilous mirth. "No, Khamsin. *No.*"

He tossed his head, but gently, forbearing to break her grip. She pulled harder. "Come, my sultan."

He did not want to, but her hand was firm and her fear was swelling. Not of him. For him. He had turned on the lord of the house. For that, he could expect no mercy.

She was crying, and trying not to. "Please, Father. Don't kill him. He was defending me."

Al-Zaman rose stiffly. His face even to horse-sight was terrible. "Dogs defend their masters."

Khamsin snorted at the insult. Steel flashed before his eyes; he stilled. The Turk had his sword again.

The beast wanted to crouch and tremble. The man gathered himself to die as befit his lineage.

Zamaniyah stood between her stallion and her father. She trembled, but she was immovable. "Very well, Father. Kill him. But if you do, mind this well. I will play no longer this game you force upon me. I will seclude myself in the harem, in another man's if need be, and be all utterly a woman."

That gave him pause. But he said, "You will not. I forbid it."

"I will do it."

She would. Al-Zaman, it seemed, had the wits to know it. And wisdom learned at Khamsin's hoofs, not to beat her into submission. "This beast will kill you."

"He won't. You'll see. He'll be the wonder of Cairo."

"Zamaniyah, little pearl, it's for your life's sake that I do this. Leave him to me; I'll dispose of him quietly. I won't kill him, since you treasure his life so much. I'll sell him. I'll buy you the best horse in Egypt, a royal horse, a horse fit for a sultan."

He was crafty, but she was adamant. She shook her head. "I want no horse but Khamsin."

The Turk's mask cracked; he all but shouted at her. "Then

have no horse but Khamsin! He and he alone is yours. None other may you have. Not one. Do you understand me?''

She bowed, understanding, accepting.

He trembled, fists knotted, grinding his teeth. ''What under Allah do you see in him?''

''Splendor,'' she answered. She wound fingers in Khamsin's mane. ''I heard a Bedouin say once that the will of God grants every man three perfect gifts: a horse, a friend, and an enemy. This is my horse. When the world was made, we were matched, he and I.''

''He is more than your perfect horse. He is your perfect enemy.''

''Inshallah,'' said Zamaniyah.

They went away, as humans did. Khamsin was alone. The cat, who bore him no rancor for her brief wild ride, purred in her nest.

He wearied his body in plunging about his prison. His mind was not so simply vanquished. It had slept too long; it had come too terribly awake.

Night came. He ate to quiet hunger, drank for his body's sake. He lay in the bed which his body remembered.

To these eyes, darkness was but a dimmer day. He stared into it, and faced what he must face.

He had tried to kill Zamaniyah. True, and appalling. But the truth ran deeper than that. She was his enemy, the daughter of his enemy. She, who was all that and woman too, had dared to set her will upon him. He was geas-bound to serve her.

And he could not hate her for it. He did not want to be her slave, but he wanted still less to be her slayer. She could not help what she was. She tried, in her own way, to show him respect. She was worthy at least of his patience.

He would not lose himself again. That was a vow, and solemn. He swore it as best he could, standing in the courtyard, head lifted to the moon.

Its light was pure and cold. Its scent was wondrous. He cried his oath to it; his tongue sang in astonished delight. He could taste it. Finer than the finest sherbet, cool and heady and icy-sweet. It was better than any wine he had ever known.

He drank great draughts of it. He danced, to honor his oath, to honor the vintage.

The sky was full of stars. They sang; and the wind sang with them, and the night, and the creatures of the night.

The moon's wine reft him of fear. He saw the dance of Jinn above the earth: winged like great shining birds but shaped like men, with faces too bright to meet. They were too high to take notice of one enchanted boy, but they suffered him to stare. He yearned for wings, to dance with them. He made what shift he could with what he had. Perhaps, for a moment, he found a shadow of their grace.

He bore it in his memory, with his oath and all that had come before it. Zamaniyah was pleased with him. She told him so. The Greek came, and watched, and though they spoke in that tongue which he did not know, he understood approval.

"Al'zan is a very great master of horses," Zamaniyah said when the Greek had gone. She had fallen into the habit of talking to Khamsin, who listened hungrily, craving human speech. He was even learning a little Greek, from when Al-zan was there to teach him. "There are only a few like him in the world. They don't cry themselves in the market, you see. They have an ancient art which they pass from father to son and from master to pupil. Someone wrote a bit of it down long ago. Xenophon, his name was." She spoke the name with care, with no little pride in her mastery of it. "But he wrote only a little, and that in the barest necessities. The truth goes deeper by far. It's a magic, almost. A high art."

Khamsin's cheek itched. Her shoulder was convenient; he rubbed against it.

"You'll see," she said. "We've barely begun, we two. You're still more than half a wild thing. But I'm not going to tame you. Nothing so simple. I'm going to show you what a horse can be."

He was more than horse enough now. He nipped her, to silence her. She slapped him. He shied. She pulled him back and held him, and he found himself disposed to allow it. With a sound that was not quite laughter, she let him go.

6

The center of Cairo was twofold: the two palaces of the false caliphs, the east that was greater and the west that was lesser, and the great court that divided them. Their riches, Zamaniyah had heard, were beyond belief. She did not know. The last feeble fool who called himself caliph was dead; his dwelling places were fallen into the hands of Yusuf who was the servant of the true Commander of the Faithful. One of the palaces, in piety, he had given over to the care of the sick. The other housed his brothers and his kinsmen, who camped like Bedouin in the splendid halls and warmed themselves at pyres of its furnishings. The royal city itself was royal no longer. Common folk out of Old Cairo, which lay in charred ruin beyond the walls of the Fortress of Victories, had raised their hovels against the very walls of the palaces.

She was a good Turk and a good Muslim, but she was sorry, a little, that victory had come at such a price. She would have liked to see the wonders which lingered yet in all the tales.

Salah al-Din Yusuf, cleanser of the Faith in Egypt, was a

young man still, and modest. He had taken no palace for himself but a house hardly higher than al-Zaman's own, that dwelling near the palaces which had been the old vizier's. It was very plain within, with no glitter of gold save here and there in the hilt of a captain's sword; the livery of the guards was black, mark and blazon of the true Faith and the true caliph, brightened only by the yellow baldric which was the sultan's own.

Zamaniyah found in it the mate of her mood. Her father had bound her to his will. She stood with him in the sultan's diwan, his time of audience.

She had been in public before. She had even, greatly daring, prayed in the mosque among the men. But never in front of the sultan. Never beside her father, for people to stare at, wonder at, speculate on. They thought her a boy. She was, after all, turbaned, and she wore a sword, and no veil concealed her face.

Her back was naked without Jaffar to guard it. Al-Zaman had forbidden his presence. They were all strangers about her; all men. No eunuchs, and never a woman.

She looked at al-Zaman and saw no comfort there. He was handsome, robust for a man of his age, his beard unmingled with grey; his face was smooth and full, his lips curved by nature into a faint and perpetual smile. But that was nature's image only. Yakhuz al-Zaman was not an amiable man. What once he set his will upon, he had. He had never known the meaning of submission.

His hand rested on her shoulder, light and ineluctable. Part of it was honest affection, like the glance he turned toward her, but none of it was gentleness. *Here,* it said. *This is mine. I claim it. Let no man presume to take it from me.*

One man in particular was there to be told, and thereby tormented. He was a subtle rebel: he wore no black. His coat was deep green, the Prophet's color, and his trousers were white. So too his turban and his long beautiful beard. His face was an Arab face, narrow, high-boned, haughty. He never deigned to lower his gaze from the heaven of his lineage to the offspring of a mere and earthly Turk.

She hated him. She had been raised to it. But seeing him in the flesh, she could not help but pity him. Beneath the arrogance of his bones he looked worn and sorrowful. His only child was gone. Vanished, she had heard; dead. And good riddance, people said. The boy had been worse than useless, a wastrel and a fool, a worthless layabout: a blight upon the Prophet's tree. But a father could love a son, even such a one as that, and mourn his death.

Their eyes met, sudden enough to shock. Zamaniyah recoiled, staring with all her force at the toes of her boots. But memory lingered. She had seen grief in those deep eyes; she had seen implacability to match her father's. But not, in that instant, hate.

The labor of lawgiving went on about her. In the diwan, as custom had it, any citizen might approach his lord and call for justice. She had seen her father hold audience for his own people. This was greater by far, and more complex: the settling of a whole realm.

Its focus sat cross-legged on a low dais. The carpet under him was good but worn. He affected no richness of dress nor any ornament; even his belt was of plain leather much softened with use, the sword across his knees plain-scabbarded, plain-hilted, without gold or jewel to mar its simplicity.

It was not, thought Zamaniyah, an affectation. He was comfortable, sitting there. He rested his chin on his hand, stroking his close-clipped beard, listening with every appearance of interest to the petitioner before him. She had heard that he was diffident. Quiet, rather. Young to be what he was, and mindful of it. Feeling his way through this wilderness which was the governance of Egypt.

People were murmuring of his troubles. Frankish armies in the north; rebels in the south; the caliph in Baghdad and the sultan in Syria contesting his sovereignty. None of it seemed to torment him as he heard the tale of a cloth merchant seeking redress for an injury done him by his neighbor the seller of spices.

Zamaniyah shifted from foot to aching foot. There was a dull pain in her middle; her head wanted to throb, but she would not let it. She stifled a sigh. Nothing here had anything to do with her. She wanted the comfort of her own place: the practice ground, Khamsin's courtyard, even her corner of the harem.

A voice spoke close to her, startling her. It was her father.

Calling for the sultan's ear. Receiving it. His hand was on her shoulder again, gripping hard.

He drew her with him from among the emirs, in a murmur that swelled and sank. She was not thinking, not daring to think. She followed him down in obeisance; she rose with him, but kept her eyes lowered. Chance fixed them on the sultan's shoe. Its sole had been mended.

"My lord," her father was saying, "O Malik al-Nasir, O king who is strong in salvation, defender of the purity of Islam, Lord Commander of Egypt, Light of the Faith, servant of God, Salah al-Din . . ."

Zamaniyah glanced up under her brows. The sultan heard his titles as he had heard the cloth merchant, with patient attention. He spared her a glance, a glimmer that might have been a smile; it made him look very young, and very human.

But she was growing afraid. She was here, and she was a lie. And her father . . .

Her father said, "O commander of my loyalty, I seek a favor of you."

"It is granted," said the sultan, "O best of servants." His voice was pleasant, more deep than light, with an odd accent: half of his Kurdish kin, half of his youth in Damascus.

"Unheard, my lord?" asked al-Zaman.

"Unheard," the sultan conceded, "but not unguessed. This youngling with you: he would, perhaps, be your heir?"

"My heir indeed," said al-Zaman. "But not—"

A smooth voice cut him off. "Glad tidings, my good friend! A nephew, is it? A cousin? Even—can it be so?—a grandson?"

The man who spoke stood close by the dais. He was young, though older than the sultan; in face they were very alike, but his was rounder, softer, more self-indulgent. His garb was richer than the sultan's, and his belt was of gold. He smiled at al-Zaman; his joy seemed honest.

Al-Zaman mustered a smile in return, and a tone of respect which struck Zamaniyah even in the midst of her shock. "My thanks, my lord Turan-Shah."

The young man waved them away. "No lord to you, my friend, whatever my brother here may be. Here, lad, stand up straight; show us a little of your mettle."

Zamaniyah raised her head. Her mind whirled, trapped,

beating against its walls. Her shoulder throbbed as her father's fingers tightened.

"This is my heir," he said. "This is the one who will inherit all that is mine. I declare it before you all; I bid my sultan be my witness."

"It is witnessed," the sultan said. His eyes had sharpened. As if—her heart leaped, stumbled. As if he suspected something.

He disappointed her. He said, "But that cannot be the favor which you ask for. Are you offering me a page for my household?"

"In all gratitude," said al-Zaman, "I am not."

That startled the sultan. His brother leaped into the breach. "What, then, old friend? A man may dispose of his property as he wishes; he need not proclaim himself before the diwan. Is there some impediment?"

"No impediment," replied al-Zaman, "but perhaps a misunderstanding." His voice rose a little. "This, O Egypt, is my heir and my successor, the child of my body. My lords, my friends, my sultan whose favor is so freely given, I bid you acknowledge this my heir, my daughter, Zamaniyah."

The silence was more mighty than any roar of outrage. Turan-Shah's mouth was agape.

His brother moved slowly, straightening. Astonishing them all. Bowing his head. Smiling. Saying, "Lady."

"Your pardon," said al-Zaman with great gentleness, "but I think, my lord, that even yet you fail to understand. This is my heir. Entirely. My daughter in the body which Allah in His wisdom has given her. My son in all else. That is the favor which you have granted me. To accept my daughter as my son. To accord her the rights and privileges of a man. To regard her in all respects as you would regard a young nobleman of her age and training."

Someone laughed, hurting-sharp. "Training!" said a voice without a face. "In what? The lute?"

Within Zamaniyah, something snapped. She spun. "The sword!" she shot back. "The bow, the lance, the arts of the hunt, of horse and hound and falcon." Her voice sweetened dangerously. "And, yes, the lute and the cittern; the poets; the law and the sciences. And first and most blessed of all, the heart of all learning, the wonder of Islam, the holy Koran."

They stared at her, too shocked even to laugh. Struggling

to see a woman under the turban, behind the pride and the temper and the high fierce words. She watched the scandal grow. *Appalling*, they whispered. *Intolerable. Unnatural.*

"But not," she pointed out, sweetly still, "unprecedented. Yaquta the daughter of the Caliph al-Mahdi—upon them both be peace—wore the turban even as do I, and rode out with her father, armed and clad as a man. And if she does not suffice, what of those who fought with the Prophet, the blessing and peace of Allah be upon him: Umm Umarah who lost a hand in battle for the Faith, Safiyah who at threescore years and ten struck down an infidel in the siege of Medina—"

Men's voices drowned her out. Drums rolled over them; and the sultan's voice, pitched as for the battlefield. He was on his feet, and his sword was drawn, glittering over Zamaniyah's head. She flung herself flat.

He spoke over her. "My favor is granted. My word is given. The heir of al-Zaman lies under my protection. Who threatens her, answers to me."

She was proud of herself. Having broken once, and then into a fine fire of defiance, she did not break again. Not before her father, or before the clamor of the court, or before the staring eyes of the city as she rode home to haven. Not even in front of Jaffar, who blessed her with silence. She was—yes, she was taking it like a man.

She went in the proper hour to her training of Khamsin. When she had done it, she remembered none of it. The sun dazzled her eyes. She blinked fiercely. He nudged her hand. She started. She had forgotten. She fed him his bit of dried apple.

His mane was cool, his neck warm beneath, silken against her cheek. He was patient: he did not pull away.

She did not cry long. She never did. She stood still, breathing warm damp horse-scent.

He shifted, stamping lightly, startling a fly. She drew back. Her hand smoothed his wetted neck; she played with his mane. "My father is mad," she told him calmly. "He always has been. But since my brothers died . . . He's clever, Khamsin. He knows how to keep people from knowing that he doesn't see the world as anyone else sees it. Today, he showed them. He named me both his daughter and his son.

He made the sultan himself a witness to what he did; and more than a witness: a sharer in it. Oh, I wish—I wish—''

Her voice faded. She hardly knew what she wished. That he were dead? Mad, blind, unsparing of mercy, still he was her father; and she loved him. Which was a madness of its own.

That she were a man? She stiffened, contemplating it. Touching her cheek, her breast. As if the thought could make it so.

"No," she said. "I want to be Zamaniyah. But what Zamaniyah is . . ."

There was always flight: the veil, the harem. Life forever within walls, with a lattice between herself and the sky, and no will in anything but her master's bidding.

She laughed bitterly. "What will have I ever had? My father has always been strange. He had me raised almost as my brothers were. I learned to read, write—even to ride and shoot, because I showed a liking for it, and it amused him to see what I could do. Then they all rode away, he and my brothers, to drive the Franks from Egypt; and my brothers never came back. My father sent for me, all the way from Syria, and when I came, though I was staggering from days of riding at courier's pace, thick with dust, reeking of the road, he had me brought to him. He looked at me as if I were a mare he had a mind to buy. I remember his eyes, how strange they were, how keen and yet how blind. He looked, and after a while he nodded, and then he laughed. 'God has robbed me of sons,' he said, 'but one child still He has left me. That one shall do for all the rest.'" She pulled off cap and turban, stared at them, flung them spinning across the sand. "He gave his orders then, and saw that they were obeyed. No veil for me; no womanly arts. I was to learn what a boy learns. Not only what I had been pleased to learn. All of it. But set apart. Not hidden, not secluded, but not made a public spectacle. He let people decide for themselves who I was, and what I was, and what I signified.

"I let him rule me. How could I do otherwise? He was my father. I thought, somehow, he knew what he was doing." Her face twisted. "Oh, he knew! He was wielding me like a weapon. Using me to mock all his enemies. Even—even to cast his defiance in the face of God."

She stopped. Khamsin had not moved even yet. He watched her, ears pricked. As if he could understand.

She rubbed a stiffened patch where the sweat of his labors had dried, smoothing it, centering herself on it. "I love him, Khamsin. And I hate him. His will has set me between the worlds. Now they all know it; and where am I? Twisting in the emptiness. Neither man nor woman; neither flesh nor fowl." Her teeth ground together. Temper gusted, hot and swift. "What will he make me do next? What will I have to face? How can he *do* this to me?"

Pain stabbed. He had nipped her. His glance was as clear as words. *That*, it said, *is pure self-pity*.

She hit him. But feebly, on the strong muscle of the shoulder, with flattened hand. It could have been a rough caress. It became one, as tears sprang again, lived out their season, passed.

She was hardly aware of them. "I never thought he'd do it. I really never thought . . . It was a whim of his, no more. It eased his grief. It gave me a freer world than I'd ever dared to hope for. If he did try to claim me in public, he'd claim me as a son. I was braced for that. I could have stopped him. But when he told the truth, all unexpected—" She drew a quivering breath. It was almost laughter. "You should have seen their faces! All those fallen jaws. All those wagging beards. They looked like a herd of startled goats."

Khamsin snorted. His eye was bright. Laughing.

Why not? She grinned at him. It was not too deadly difficult. "And there was I, tender little she-kid, telling them all what I thought of them. With the sultan looking on and thinking Allah alone knows what. He placed me under his protection." She paused, struck. Her breathing quickened. She had had a thought. A thought of utmost wickedness. "He bound himself to accept me. And I—I think I'll play this game to its end. I'll show my father what he's done. I'll be exactly what he says he wants me to be."

The horse regarded her with great misgivings.

"You'll see," she promised him. She retrieved her cap and the tangled knot of her turban, tossed them in the air, caught them lightly. Lightly then she left him.

* * *

She was a very strange woman, this mistress of his. Khamsin rolled long and deliciously and settled in the shade. In a little while he had an entourage of cats. A small dust-devil amused itself in the trampled circle of his training. He watched it, interested. How odd that he had ever thought a horse's sight less than a man's. It was less garish-glittering, but it was deeper. It saw worlds within the mortal world.

It could not see into a woman's heart, nor ever understand it. Her words when she left had been bright and bold. Her scent had been both angry and frightened. But determined. And strong.

A woman?

He fled the prospect. The devil snaked long dusty fingers into his mane, clambered onto his back. He bucked it hooting into the air.

7

"Jaffar?"

He started up from his mat, knife leaping into hand. Zamaniyah stood over him in her thin white nightrobe, her hair tumbling down her back, trembling with much more than the lamp's flicker. She said his name again. Her voice was thin and high, like a child's, not like her own at all. "Jaffar, I think—I'm afraid—"

Her eyes were strange, almost as if she dreamed; but wide and fixed on his face. Little as she could have seen of it there in the gloom, with him rising over her, gathering her in.

She was stiff and shaking. She let him hold her, but she contracted in the circle of his arms, shrinking from his touch.

He had never seen her so. It frightened him. He veiled it in soothing murmurs, in strokings that only knotted her tighter.

Fear had a way with him. It made his mind clearer. Carefully he unfolded his arms, stood back. She stared at him still. Her hands were fists. Her face was white.

"What is it?" he asked her with utmost gentleness. "A dream?"

She blinked. She shook her head, broadly, as a child will. Her lips were tight.

"A memory?" he asked. "A spirit of the night?"

She shivered, stumbling with the force of it. "I can't—I don't know—I woke, and I felt—and there was—"

His eyes swept the room. Nothing, not even the shadow of a dream. A long stride brought him to her bed. A glance, and he knew.

And she—by all the gods that were, she did not.

"I'm afraid," she said in that soft strange voice. "I don't want to die. Not like this."

"Who ever told you—" It had escaped him before he thought. He bit his tongue.

"Is it Allah, do you think? Because Father—"

Because her father, indeed. There were curses fit for him. And for the women who had never told her that one, simple, inescapable fact. And for Jaffar himself and most of all, because he had not thought to tell her. He had thought she knew. All women knew.

Jaffar found the laughter that had kindled when he began to understand. He mingled it with love and set it in his voice. "Little bird," he said. "Little fool. You're not going to die."

"My mother did!" The air rang with the force of it.

He stilled the echoes, softly, calmly. "You are not your mother. But a woman, you most certainly are. Now your body knows it. It's telling you in the surest way it can."

Her hand reached, tore at the sheet. "It's *blood*."

"It is life. And womanhood. And pride."

Her head was shaking. "My mother bled. She bled and she bled, and she screamed, and they all said there was no hope for her. I watched. She screamed for a day and a night. Then she had no strength left to scream. And then she died. And they cut her, and something was alive inside her, but it died. And it was all blood. All—all—"

He seized her. He shook her until her head rattled on her neck. *"Zamaniyah!"*

She stared. He glared back. "Listen to me," he commanded her, setting in it all the force of his will. "There is something that happens to every woman. It happens with every turning of the moon. It means no more than that she is a woman. That *you* are a woman, little idiot; but I am a worse idiot by far, for thinking that you knew. Of course you didn't. Your mother dead before you were eight years old, you raised half-wild with no one to look after you, and then your father's spate of madness . . . how could you?''

He stopped. She was shaking. Laughing, weeping. He set his teeth and let her fight the battle for herself.

At last she stilled. Her face was streaming; she hiccoughed and nearly went off again. He had to hold her up. She clung and trembled and wept, and said, ''But can't you *see?* The very day my father unmasks me in front of the whole world—that very night—''

''The gods speak as they will,'' he said.

He could not have said it so to anyone but her. She accepted it for what it was: truth, and trust. ''I knew there was something,'' she said. ''I didn't know what it was. I thought it was growing breasts. Or finding hair in odd places, or needing more time in the baths.''

''That, too,'' he said steadily.

Her eyes narrowed; she paled a little, for all her bravery. ''There is more?''

He shaped a careful smile. ''Little more, O my mistress,'' he said, ''but enough. Your eyes will change. They'll see differently in some respects. Particularly when they come to rest on a man.''

Her hand flew to her face, flew away. Her cheeks were scarlet. ''Do you mean like a—a mare in heat? I *won't!*''

''So they always say,'' he said, ''in the beginning.''

She opened her mouth, closed it with a snap. Her glare was as fierce as a falcon's.

He refused to see it, though it comforted him. ''You,'' he said, ''will bathe, and put on a clean gown, and look after yourself as I tell you. Then you will go back to sleep.''

She was obedient. Suspiciously so. He watched her warily, but she was quiet, bathing, changing her robe, doing as he bade her. When she lay clean and fresh-scented in her clean bed, she looked up into Jaffar's face. He bent to kiss her as he always did; she caught his cheeks between her palms and held him. ''You're beautiful,'' she said.

He straightened with dignity. ''Woman's sight,'' he said, ''takes time to grow.''

Her fingers knotted in the bedclothes, but her face was

calm. Her voice was calmer still. "I never asked for it. I
don't want it. I don't want any of it."

He looked at her who was entirely a woman: he who would
never be a man. He considered wisdom and gentleness. He
said, "*You* have a choice."

She gasped. He throttled guilt, the lash of sudden pain. Her
eyes were huge, like bruises. The tears that filled them
refused stubbornly to fall.

He wanted to touch her, to comfort her. He clenched his
fists at his sides.

"Go away," she said.

He did not move.

Her voice rose. "Go away!" And when he would not: "*Go
away!*" She flung herself at him. He caught her, let her strike
him, reckless, furious, but skilled enough, and strong. He set
his teeth and suffered it.

Her weight, struggling, overbalanced him. He twisted as he
fell. The bed caught most of him; his body caught all of her.

Abruptly she was still. She breathed hard, sobbing. Very
gently he began to stroke her hair.

For a long while she made no move. Then her arms crept
about him. She shifted, coiling childlike, burying her face in
his torn shirt. He rocked her, murmuring what came to him.
A cradle song. His mother's voice had crooned it long ago.

Long after, when she was deep asleep, he wondered that
his cheeks were wet. He remembered nothing of tears.

Khamsin had forgotten how wide the world was. His courtyard had begun to suffice for all of it; and he had not even
thought to care, until Zamaniyah led him out of it. Briefly in
the beginning, testing. He danced at first for startlement and
then for the exhilaration of a different air. He filled his lungs
with it. He called to every horse he saw and heard and
scented. Many called back. It was not words, precisely, and
yet it was speech. A mare's loneliness. A stallion's challenge.
A weanling's piteous plaint.

Zamaniyah's hand was small and warm on his neck, on his
cheek, on his nose. Her scent had changed of late. Deepened,
sweetened. It was almost like a mare's: the same splendor, for
all its tang of humanity. For it, and for her, he suffered the
ignominy of halter and lead. When he danced, he danced

within a finger's breadth of the utmost end. She always grinned then, boyish-wide, understanding.

He would never have been as lenient with a horse as she was. He would have scorned her, had he been Hasan still. He would have hated her.

She led him everywhere a horse could go, though never beyond the walls of her father's house. In the pool of its garden he saw for the first time what he had become.

Imperfect. Narrow before, weak behind. His tail lacked that perfect arch which marked the best stock of Arabia. He would have discarded himself as unworthy of his notice.

Alone in his prison, he brooded. Beautiful, but imperfect. Fiery, but imperfect. Beloved, but imperfect.

Hasan had had no flaw. Hasan had been unmatched in his beauty. His hair, thick and richly curling, red as cedarwood. His eyes, great and dark beneath the arches of his brows. His lips full, his teeth white and even, his chin cleft just so, his neck, his shoulders, his breast . . .

He pawed the sand, tossing his head. His mane swung, heavy, tangling on his neck. The Hajji had done this. Made him worse than beast. Made him unbeautiful.

Made him mute; reft him even of tears.

An itch pricked his side. His teeth tore viciously at it. He spun, cursing. His stallion-voice was shrill and hideous.

Abruptly he stopped. He could not weep; no more could he laugh. So much to suffer, for a few moments' folly. He could not even remember her face. Her body, remembered, woke nothing of desire.

The boy came with water, barley, fodder. Khamsin ate because he could see no profit in hunger. His mood, he knew with perfect clarity, was vile. He did not care.

An oddity of the air, a whisper of scent, led him from the manger to the wall. The door was always barred. He butted it, aimlessly, for simple ill-temper.

And started, snorting. It yielded; it swung ajar. He thrust his nose against it. It opened, rebounded from the wall.

He froze.

No sound of feet; no cry of alarm.

Slowly, as softly as a hoofed creature could, he ventured into the passage. No one came to stop him. He sensed no humanity at all, anywhere within reach.

The stable was quiet. Its dwellers drowsed in their stalls. Now and then one would stamp, snort, shake off a fly. Jaws ground languidly, pondering the sweetness of fodder, the last hoarded grains of barley.

The stallions dwelt apart with their noise and their tempers. These were all mares, one or two with late foals beside them. His nostrils flared and quivered, drinking in so much beauty all at once, so rich and so varied. A deep rumble swelled in his throat.

They paid no heed to him. He was only a male, and they were not in season. He was beneath their queenly notice.

His neck ached, but pleasurably. It raised all of itself, arched, swelled. His tail lifted over his back. He trod lightly, proudly, drunk on mare-scent. He had forgotten that he was flawed. He was all male, and all beautiful.

One royal lady deigned to see him: a red queen with a star on her brow, breathing the perfumes of paradise. Her time was on her, and he was her heart's desire. She summoned him with aching tenderness.

The stallion would have battered down her door. The man knew greater subtlety. The latch was simplicity itself, even to a horse's lips and questing teeth. Disdainfully he flicked the door aside.

Her ears flattened, warning; but her scent yearned for him. He bowed before her. She snorted lightly, pawing. He ventured to caress the silk of her cheek. Her ear flicked, exquisite. Very gently he nibbled her nape. She squealed, swung. Her hindleg threatened; her tail arched, welcoming.

He hesitated. His blood thundered; his loins throbbed. But his brain held him motionless. Man—he was a man. And this—

Hasten! all her body cried. *Oh, hasten!*

He mounted her.

It was mighty. It was passionate. It was eternal; and it was but a moment. He dropped down, spent. She sighed deeply; enchanted him with the lightest of love-bites; let fly with her heels.

Most eloquent, that lady, and most wise. Voices sounded without. He remembered to shut the door, to latch it. He was very proud of himself for that.

The voices swelled, faded. Safety was yonder, tailward: his

courtyard, his bed, his entourage of cats. His nostrils drew in the scent of freedom.

His skin quivered. The mare nibbled the edge of her manger, sated, yet fretting. Almost—almost—he went back to her. His eyes rolled. This was a prison. All this. Doors and bars. Bit, bridle, no will in anything but to do as he was bidden.

He was Hasan. He was Ali Mousa's son, Safiyah's child. He was a prince: exiled, enchanted, but royal still. His blood was holy. He was no one's chattel.

His feet bore him away from the mare who had forgotten his existence, from the path that was safety. Allah or Iblis, whoever guided him, he found a door through a narrow passage, a silent court, a door open upon the green solitude of the garden. It was not the garden it had been. The pomegranate tree was gone. Someone had broken the marble nymph who had stood in the heart of the fountain: most unorthodox, she had always been, but his mother had loved her. Only her feet remained, hacked and beaten amid the falling water.

His hoofs tore the grass, trampled the flowers. He circled toward the wall and the gate which he remembered.

It was a very wide garden, this; Cairo's pride, it had been once, ill-kempt now and overgrown. It had been a world within a world, a web of secret places, and most secret of all the place where the women and the slaves would never go, because it was a haunt of spirits of the air. It was the sort of place they loved: walled in tangled greenery but open within, a long oval of sand and sparse grass, and at the edge of it a remnant that might have been a temple or a tomb.

He had never been afraid in daylight, and his eyes found nothing there. He picked his way through the thicket, mind on the gate that lay beyond the ruin, that had never been locked when he was small, that had never needed to be. Everyone knew of the gathering place of the Afarit.

Everyone had known, once. The bar was new and firm and would not yield to aught but hands. He snapped vainly at it. His teeth could find no purchase.

Desperation swelled. He spun, gathering strength, arming his heels.

Beyond the ruin a shadow moved. He stilled utterly. The shadow sped, silent, elongated, inhuman. It grew an arm:

enormously long, enormously thin, tipped with steel. The shadow flowed to a halt, reared, cast.

The spear bit earth at Hasan's feet, quivering with fury. He started back.

Man. He was a man. He cherished rage. He tore the thing free, tasting wood, salt, man-scent; tossed it clattering aside.

The spearman faced him. He snorted in anger, in startlement, in bitter mirth. Zamaniyah's eunuch leaned on a second spear and regarded him with eyes that were most insolent, and most unfrightened.

"Salaam," said the eunuch, "O prince."

Hasan's teeth, slashing, jarred on the spearshaft. He recoiled, astonished. Strong, this one, for a gelding. He did not even sway against the blow.

The eunuch smiled, white in the dusk of his face. His eyes were on the gate. "Ah," he said. "Wise, O prince. Most wise. If my prince will permit?"

He was behind Hasan, recking nothing of the heels that might have hammered him down. Hasan scrambled about. His ears were flat. They knew when he was hated.

The bolt slid. The eunuch paused. His scent was dark with irony and with something very like triumph. He bowed, beckoned.

Hasan eyed the spear. The eunuch saw; he laughed. Hasan lunged upon that laughter. The eunuch danced back undismayed, offering mockery with the prick of steel. Hasan spurned them all for the open gate.

A man alone at dusk was prey, but no prodigy. A horse alone, unbridled, was both. Hasan made himself as nondescript as he might. He kept to shadows. He tried to remember what he knew of hunting, and of cats. He astonished himself with patience.

The sunset prayer found him deep within the city's mazes. He prayed with something like defiance, bowing as best he might, making what obeisance he could in a body never made for it.

He started, clattering. The shadows had bred people. Beggars, urchins, children of Egypt's earth, reeking of it. They stared at the marvel: a horse who prayed like a Muslim.

He essayed a step. They drew back. None of them had

spoken. Their eyes were wide. Ancient eyes, even in the babe on its mother's back. Eyes that had seen ten thousand years.

They knew him, knew magic. As—he froze—the eunuch had known. And had let him go. Knowing. Seeing what he was. Hating him for it.

He broke into a trot. These ways he knew, dark though they were, labyrinthine. People scattered. Some shouted. None could catch him. He stretched his stride.

He had hastened to it, but it came too soon. Roses and citron. Walls that had been home. No gate opened there for him. It was all barred. Before, behind, all about, barred.

And what had he looked for?

He stood before that first implacable gate and cried aloud. He climbed it. He smote it with ringing hoofs.

It gave way. He all but fell into the passage. People fled: shadows, all of them. He passed the court of welcomes, the court of the white fountain, the hall of honor, all full of shadows. Some had voices. They shrieked or shouted.

The chamber of the blue tiles was empty and cold. Winter had come, and he had not known it. But spring was waking in the garden, where men thought that they had trapped him, pursuing him with cries and halters, circling him, besieging him beneath the lemon tree. He broke their circle with ease that made him laugh, even through his pain.

And there before him, seeking the source of the tumult, stood Ali Mousa. Hasan plunged to a halt. Ali Mousa's beard was as white as his robe; he was gaunt beneath it, leaning on the shoulder of his slave Mahaut, as if he were weary, or worn with age. He stood in the light of lamps and hasty torches, and stared as they all stared, at Hasan who bowed low at his feet.

Words struggled in the alien throat. Revelation. Confession. Profoundest humility. *Father. O Father. See how I pay, how I am paid. Father, help me. Make me a man again!*

He raised his head. Ali Mousa looked down. What the beggars of the street could see, he could not. Nor hear, nor know.

Hasan heaved himself up, graceless in this as in anything that a man could do. His father retreated a step, for prudence. It stung like a lash.

No, Hasan tried to say. *No more.* It was a snort, a strangled gasp. He tried to touch his father. His hoof was a weapon; his head was armed, and so they all saw, perceiving threat in what was only longing. Mahaut set himself between the beast and his master. The others closed in.

Hasan cried his despair. His father had drawn back from him, letting himself be defended, letting them say words that cut to the bone. "Rogue," they decreed. "Demon-ridden." Snare him, bind him, shut him in walls; for he was deadly, a beast gone mad, menacing their master whom they loved.

Whom he loved.

He had never known it. He had never thought of loving anything but Hasan.

The halter waited. The stable that at least was his own stable, in his own house, among his own people. Even if they never knew. They would handle him gently enough. No Alexander Hippias, his father's horsemaster, but no fool either; and no Zamaniyah to vex his peace.

Ali Mousa was speaking. Commanding. "Set him among the stallions, in the barred stall. And in the morning, search. This is no stray: there is breeding in him. His master may be glad to have him back again."

It was the tone of it that felled him. Gentle as always, calm, coolly wise. Disposing of an oddity, an inconvenience, an interruption of his rest.

When the hands fell on him, he chose. He flung them away. Once more he broke their feeble circle. Ali Mousa blurred past, wide eyes, astonished face, all a stranger.

As he was all a fool, for coming back, for dreaming that he could ever be Hasan again. Had not the magus said it? This shape he was bound to, till death should take him. Hasan al-Fahl ibn Ali Mousa was dead, had died for his sins. Most utterly, and most justly.

Khamsin plodded through a city of shadows. He did not care who saw him; but no one pursued him. Ali Mousa's servants had surrendered almost before they began. They were well rid of him, and they knew it.

It was not despair that slowed his pace. That had burned away in the light of his father's face. Mahaut had said it often enough: Mahaut who had looked at him and seen only a maddened beast. A wise man knew himself before he acted.

A sensible man knew himself as he acted. But for a fool, it was always and endlessly too late.

So very much, he had had, and he had never known it. He had taken it as no more than his due; he who had never done more to earn it, than to be born.

If this was sense, it was appallingly like pain. He did not flatter himself that it was wisdom. He was not wise. He was merely a fool who had, through Allah's infinite and implacable mercy, been suffered to see the truth.

The house of al-Zaman rose before him. All of its gates were barred. He laid his weary body beneath the garden wall and waited for the dawn.

8

They never learned how Khamsin had vanished from his
courtyard and appeared outside a locked gate. One unbarred
door, for which the culprit paid the due price, hardly sufficed
to explain the rest of it. It was a mystery, like the mind of
Allah.

To be sure, Zamaniyah reflected, Khamsin's behavior had
been exemplary since. He seemed almost chastened: as if
freedom had taught him the value of obedience. His temper
was no sweeter, but he heeded her more perfectly; he fought
more seldom. Even when she set the saddle on his back.
Even when, at last, with beating heart, she bade him carry
her.

Mincing, hunching, ears now flat and now flicking ner-
vously, he learned to bear her weight. It was little enough; but
what it signified, she knew well. As, she suspected, did he.
Obedience; acceptance. The slow fading of rebellion.

And his door was always, meticulously, double-barred.

She could envy him that. Her father's command and her own
defiance had cast her in the world's eye; she held herself

there by sheer force of will. An emir could not in courtesy refuse to dine at al-Zaman's table if, having sat to it, he found himself compelled to share it with al-Zaman's heir. No more could a man of standing turn away the sultan's favored prince for that that prince had his daughter at his side. She was, at least, quiet, and modest under the outrageousness of the turban. Sometimes, for a novelty, they even spoke to her, and smiled when she answered, as one smiles at a clever beast.

The sultan's smile was sudden, and warm, and not condescending at all. Zamaniyah, summoned before him on a bare hour's notice, brought in growing dread to what could only be a private chamber, was barely comforted. Even though Jaffar was with her. Even though the eunuch who had brought her took station at his lord's back. Even though there were half a dozen men about, and eunuchs, and slaves both male and female: protection enough, surely, and defense against impropriety. As if the Rectifier of the Faith could be improper.

And what was she?

He accepted her obeisance, but he would not let her stand or kneel. He offered cushions. A silent slave brought sweets, sherbet, a bowl of honeyed nuts.

She sat stiffly on a cushion, pretended to sip from the cup. The men murmured together, a little apart. She caught a word or two. At least one of them was a secretary, scribbling busily as a companion read from what looked like a sheaf of dispatches. None of them seemed to see her. They would not, she suspected, unless the sultan gave them leave.

He, however, saw her very well indeed. He studied her—shamelessly, she would have said, if he had not been who he was.

"You are under my protection," he said. "You may regard me as your kinsman."

That startled her, brought her eyes to his face. He smiled as if he had intended exactly that. "Do I frighten you so much?" he asked her.

"You are the sultan," she answered. Her voice was faint but steady.

"Do you know why that is?"

He wanted an answer. She swallowed. She could say what was wise. Or she could tell the truth.

"Because you were the youngest," she said. "The one they thought weakest."

No blade swept down to take her life. No one even gasped in horror. The sultan grinned like a boy. "Just so! And still you fear me?"

"What they thought you is not what they made you."

"You understand," he said. It was not a question.

She blinked. Because she did understand; and because he did. A man was not supposed to understand. Least of all the sultan.

He beckoned her closer. She was shocked enough to come. He spoke softly, almost in her ear. "We have a secret, you and I. We know what we are."

"I am a woman," she said. "Half a man is worth all of me."

"Therefore we are equals: for half a man is what my rivals reckoned me."

"Foolishly."

"Just so," said the sultan.

He had made her smile. She tried to look away, but they were too close. She had not been thinking of him as a handsome man, or as a man at all. He was not handsome, she decided. Pleasing, rather. Good to look at, slender and quick, like a fine hunting hound.

He sat back, oblivious as it seemed to her flaming cheeks. Of all the times there ever were, to wake to woman's sight . . .

"You will attend me on occasion," he said. The words were formal, his voice raised slightly, but the tone was warm still. "By my given word, we are kin, and you have my favor."

He offered his hand. She had the wits to take it. "Allah go with you," he said.

"Now that's wise," said Jaffar: "to grant you favor, to name you friend, but not to keep you by him."

"Wise for whom?" she asked. "For him or for me?"

"For both of you. You have his full protection, but not so much that people can whisper."

"People always whisper."

She was unwontedly sharp tonight. He busied himself

about her chamber, knowing that she scowled at him, not needing to wonder why. He knew. He wondered if the sultan did. Perhaps not. These Muslims were like their own stallions: they could not see past a woman's rump. The sultan would no doubt have decided that Zamaniyah was a sort of exotic boy; and he was not, by all accounts, a lover of boys.

Jaffar sighed gently. When the red stallion came back, he had had all he could do not to slit the beast's throat; and his mood had been black in the days since. This lightened it a little. No harm to Zamaniyah if she cast eyes on her sultan who could not see; less likelihood then of her falling afoul of a man of less honor and more perception.

She could not know that she was fortunate. She was new enough still to womanhood, and somewhat late come to it; she knew only that she did not want it. They seldom did, at first. Later, they learned to take both pride and pleasure in it.

He grimaced at his own wisdom, smoothed his face, turned to her. She glared. "Why do you hover like that?"

"Your father is waiting," he reminded her gently.

"Let him wait."

Her mouth snapped shut. She had alarmed herself. She snatched the coat he held for her, flung it on. But she let him belt it, standing stiffly erect, trembling with the effort of holding still.

He settled on his heels and inspected her. "You'll do," he said.

Her fists clenched, unclenched. "I'm not pretty," she said abruptly. "Am I?"

"Do you want to be?"

She drew a sharp breath.

"It's simple enough," he said. "Paint, kohl, a touch of scent. If you want it."

"But I'm not—"

"Prettiness is an art."

She shook her head hard enough to send her cap flying. He caught it, restored it. Without a word she turned on her heel and left him.

"But beauty," he finished, "is deeper." The air was silent. She had gone before she could hear.

* * *

The *saqla* mare was in foal. Al'zan was beside himself; the
stable was in uproar. She, whether sinner or sinned against,
bore all of it with royal calm. "Who has done it?" Al'zan
cried to her. *"Who?"*

The stable lads were all babbling at once. No one could
have done it. The stallions were locked away where they
could not possibly have reached her. She herself had been
guarded like a queen.

"Like a queen!" Their master tore at his beard. "Like
Messalina! O sweet Mother of God, when I find him I shall
dine on his jewels."

Zamaniyah crept out of the storm. He had started on the
boys; they cowered at his feet. She pitied the one who would
inevitably bear the brunt of it.

"Perhaps," someone ventured, "the east wind—"

Al'zan's roar shook the rafters.

Khamsin was waiting under his portico. He eyed the saddle
askance as always, and sidled as she tightened the girth. She
stroked the satin softness behind his ear, gathering herself to
cajole the bit between his teeth. Al'zan's voice echoed through
the half-open door, flaying some hapless fool alive.

Zamaniyah's eye slid. Door. Khamsin. His own eye rolled
back. He looked—

"Oh, no," she said. "You didn't. You couldn't have."

He snorted with perfect equine vulgarity, and yawned. She
clapped the bit into his open mouth, settled the headstall. He
was very properly startled.

"Do you know what he'll *do* to you?"

He shied. Probably it was her vehemence.

"If he remembers," she muttered. "If he even stops to
think—"

And she had to lead Khamsin past him to the practice
ground. Khamsin whose door opened on the passage to the
mares' stable. Khamsin who was not *kehailan*. Khamsin who
lived already under threat of gelding or death.

If a horse could be said to creep, he crept beside her, head
low, looking as meek as an Arab stallion could. He did not
even call to the mares. He seemed to be trying to hide in her
shadow.

He carried her with something approaching grace. He

hardly bucked at all, and he only tangled his feet once. She slid from the saddle and embraced him. He nibbled her hair.

"If it was you," she said, "if we have to—if it comes to that—"

He pulled back, rearing. His forelegs smote her with shattering force. She reeled, clutched blindly, caught mane. He stood trembling; his eye rolled white. She pressed her hand to her side, to the pain that swelled, black-red, all-encompassing. She drew a very careful breath. It caught. She thrust words through it. Faint, breathless, but clear. "She was there and it was her time, and you're no man, to care that she was never meant for you."

His head drooped. When she took the bridle, he plodded beside her, tail low, dejected. Al'zan never noticed. Even rage has its limits, and he was master of more than one erring mare. The air rumbled with thunder still, and the lads' eyes rolled like their charges', but the storm had passed, for a while.

Zamaniyah's ribs were cracked. She strapped them tight and swore Jaffar to secrecy: a command which he did not suffer easily. No more could she ever persuade him to suffer Khamsin.

That noon in the mosque, bowing beside her father, she prayed that the stallion's secret might remain so. She knew her prayer was heard; she did not know that it was granted.

Her head ached nearly as fiercely as her side. The barbed glances of the men about her, usual though they were, stung. She knew that the imams had protested her presence. She knew equally well that the sultan had overruled them. He held the foremost rank of prayer; he had mounted the pulpit, striking each step ceremonially with his scabbarded sword, to declaim a sermon which she had barely heard.

When the Prophet forbade women to pray with the men, he had plainly been thinking of the latter. But she, aching, fretting for her idiot of a horse, could still notice a fine profile, a well-cut waist, a handsome rump adorning the line in front of her.

She shut her eyes. It helped a little, but then she could not see to bow. She had lost the thread of the prayer.

In the murmur and mingle of the aftermath, she made

herself her father's shadow, and fixed her eyes grimly on her feet. One was not supposed to think about one's aches, but it was better than thinking about one's treacherous eyes. Woman's eyes. They were worse than blind. They saw beauty in every face that was young and male and not too badly made.

Someone spoke her name. She had looked up before she thought, before her mind had named the voice. The sultan smiled and inclined his head to her. "When the day cools," he said, "we ride to the hunt, my brothers and I. Your presence would honor us."

She set her teeth behind a smile, and bowed as low as she could without gasping. "The honor is mine, my lord."

"And mine," he answered, bowing in his turn, letting his followers herd him away.

Her father was delighted. He even lent her his own horse, since by her oath she had none but Khamsin: the bay mare who was swiftest in the chase. Her gaits, at least, were smooth, and Al'zan had trained her; there was no silliness in her.

The same, as Jaffar had made eminently clear, was not true of her rider. He rode a great rawboned mule at her back, with disapproval in every line of his body. He carried her arrows and her bow; he would, if possible, have carried her.

She would, if possible, have let him do it. Maybe men were born to ignore pain. She was a woman, and she hurt. And she would be triply damned if she betrayed herself to any of these gawping males. They gawped at her bow. They gawped when she strung it. They gawped when she brought down a brace of birds in a brace of shots. Easy shots, both. Any of them could have done the same, if any of them had had his mind on his own bow and not on hers.

"You shoot well," said the sultan as his huntsmen retrieved her kill.

A flush crawled up her cheeks. "I have been taught well," she said, clear and miraculously steady.

"By your father?"

She glanced at Jaffar, who was very carefully not listening. "By my father's command, sire."

He nodded. "A very unusual man, your father."

"Very unusual," she agreed, "sire."

He grinned, startling her. "Was it he who taught you to be so careful?"

She looked down in confusion, but then, up. "My father is not a careful man. He does as his heart moves him, and as his loyalty commands. I have his heart. You, sire, have his loyalty. Of that, you may be certain."

"I never doubted it," said the sultan.

They had paused on a hill, a low rise above the river. "Not so very long," said one of those about the sultan, "until all this lies under the Nile."

"Allah willing," said someone else.

Zamaniyah shivered a little in spite of the sun. She knew what great blessings were in the river's rising, in the great sea of it that swallowed the land and cast it up again with its strength renewed. But she had been born in a country that kept much the same face between summer and summer. This river was too strong; it ruled too absolutely.

She turned her back on it, her face to the city. From here she could see the whole of it, the ruin of the Old City, the huddle of the royal city with the new walls rising to guard it, the gardens stretching wide and green between.

"See," said the sultan beside her. "There." Her eyes followed the stretch of his arm, up beyond the city to the steep dun crag and the spur of its peak. A mosque stood there all alone: the Dome of the Air where the falcons wheeled. "There I shall set my citadel, in the high places where no enemy can fall upon it."

"You mean to endure," said Zamaniyah.

"I mean to matter." His arm swept round. "I never chose this country. It chose me. It can break me; or I can break it to my will."

"Do you hate it so much?"

The hiss of breath about her was louder than the wind. There were things one did not say.

There were things one did not do. If one were a woman, one did not ride, one did not hunt, one did not speak to one's sultan as if one were his equal.

She was never careful when she had only herself to think of. She watched him ponder his answer, frowning, but not with temper. At length he said, "When I first saw it, I hated it. I hated anything that was not Syria. Then I hated it because it took my uncle, because it bade fair to take me. Now...I have no liking for it. I don't know that I love it. Does the wood love the fire that consumes it? Does the camel love the burden that she bears?''

Zamaniyah was silent.

Suddenly he laughed. "How grim I sound! This is the portion which God has allotted me. I accept it. And it has beauty. Look! Have you ever seen a sky so wide?''

Wide beyond conceiving; and even the horizon had no end to it. One could almost believe what the old people whispered, that the gods dwelt beyond the shifting edges of this world.

"Allahu akbar," murmured Zamaniyah. "God is greater than they.''

He sent a flock of geese wheeling and crying over them. Her hands flew, bracing, nocking, loosing. The arrow flew true. The quarry fell like a stone, plummeting to earth at the sultan's feet.

"Allah's gift," said Zamaniyah, "to the lord of Egypt.''

But her eyes had shifted to the luminous line that was the horizon, and her mind, feckless creature, had dared—for an instant—to wonder.

9

"I think he likes to talk to me," said Zamaniyah.

Khamsin had not seen her in too long. He had betrayed it: he had run to her when she came, demanding with every line of his body where she had been, why she had not come, what had mattered so much that she could so heartlessly have forsaken him; and Al'zan coming all too often to set him on the long line, and he dreading endlessly, helplessly, that the man would take a knife to him for his transgression with the *saqla* mare. But he had recalled himself, and put on an air of nonchalance, which she was ignoring. Her scent had an ache in it; she moved more slowly than usual, and somewhat more stiffly.

"He's had me with him every day," she said. "Riding. Talking. Keeping him company. Yesterday it was polo. He has a passion for it."

She, plainly, did not. She set to work unraveling the knot which always bedemoned his mane. "Jaffar is livid. I was starting to mend, and then I took that ridiculous fall, trying a shot I knew I couldn't make."

His head swung up, round. Mend? What in Allah's name had she been doing?

"At least now no one can blame you. I cracked my ribs playing polo with the sultan. They all admired my fortitude. I didn't tell them I'd been riding in bandages ever since you knocked me down."

A horse could gasp. He could also yearn with all that was in him for the power to answer her. To cry apology. To upbraid her for her stupidity. She was acting—damn her, she was acting like a man.

"I'm not supposed to ride you today," she said. "I'm supposed to be in bed, with the sultan's doctor clucking over me. He won't look at me directly, since he's not a eunuch. He makes Jaffar look, and Jaffar doesn't like him, which is fortunate for me and for you. He's gone to tell his master that I'll live, but I'll need a few days' peace. It's wise, that. I shouldn't be with my lord too much. People are deciding that I'm not really a woman; I'm a sort of peculiar boy, like a eunuch, but braver." She laughed, little more than a snort. "Brave. I. So much they know. I don't want people to remember what I really am; and I don't want to remind them."

Khamsin never needed to be reminded. He had wounded her again in his heedlessness; she had forgiven him again, as she breathed, because she could do no other. He could have hated her for that.

She rubbed the tender place beneath his jaw, leaning lightly against his neck. "Do you know what I think? I think I'm carrying it off."

He did not know why she should be surprised. She was like no one else he had ever heard of.

She walked with him from stable to practice ground to garden, idling in the heavy heat. He was bred to it, horse and man. She had no love for it. Her hair clung damply to her forehead; even in light loose clothing she suffered.

They paused by the pool. Khamsin had schooled himself to endure what he saw there; if not, yet, to accept it. He drank, ruffling the image. Zamaniyah sat on the pool's edge and trailed her hand in the water. She bent her head, laved her face. Khamsin nibbled grass beside her foot.

She stood suddenly, startling him. She knotted his lead

about his neck; and as he watched, astonished, she dropped her every garment. Shock held him rooted. Had she no modesty at all?

She slid into the cool water. She was as supple as the bright fish that fled before her, and no more shamefast, never knowing what manner of creature stood and stared and forgot the grass cloying upon his tongue.

It hurt, that she did not know. Even though, if she had, she would never in all the world have done as she did now, lain on her back in the water's embrace, offering herself to the sky. He would have given kingdoms for a hand to touch her, there, where bruises marred the fine brown skin, and there, where bandages bound her poor wounded ribs; for a human tongue, to tell her—

To tell her what? That he was her bitter enemy? That he had been the scourge of the women of Cairo? He might have sired a child, or two, or three. He could not remember. He had never cared enough to care.

She rose, streaming water, enfolding him in a cool wet embrace. Her breasts burned against his neck. Her laughter rippled in his ear. "Oh, you marvel! You never moved."

He had had no power to.

She wrung out her hair, drew on her garments one by one, reluctant, sighing. But no more reluctant than he. He wanted to count her bruises. To trace the thin lines of scars—such as he had never had, who had evaded all but the barest inescapable beginnings of the arts of war. He had set himself to master other arts. Drinking. Roistering. Whoring.

Zamaniyah led him back to the place he had won for himself. She went away as she always did, free in her humanity. "Tomorrow," she promised as she left him. She did not ask him if he were content with it. The world was not so ordered, that a woman need respect the wishes of a beast.

The messenger was waiting when Zamaniyah came to the harem: a eunuch, old and august and redolent of ambergris, with a pair of languid pages. Even in the sultan's livery they had a look of the caliph's palace. They bore a gift for her, which they spread before her widening eyes: shimmering beauty, silk the color of a peacock's fan, sewn into a robe for a queen.

"My lord the sultan, Salah al-Din who is mighty in salvation, bids you accept this small token of his goodwill," said the eunuch in a voice as high and fluting as a bird's.

The pages were on her before she could stop them, setting the robe over her worn and rumpled shirt, bowing at her feet.

She stammered something. It must have sufficed: they bowed again, all three, and took their leave in a cloud of ambergris.

She sneezed. The robe slipped. She caught it, stared at it. "It's too beautiful for me," she said.

"Nonsense," said Jaffar. He swept it out of her hands. "Now," he said, "for once you obey me."

He kept to the letter of her father's law. He clothed her in nothing that was not her own; he adorned her with neither scent nor paint. But he freed her hair and combed it until it rippled free and silken down her back. He set her jeweled cap upon her head and her jeweled slippers on her feet; all between he covered in white, with the splendid robe cast over it. Then at last he led her to the mirror which she had always, and studiously, avoided. It was nigh as tall as she: a Frankish shield beaten flat and sheathed in silver. It hung in a room of its own, much frequented by the women, and heavy with their scents and their presence.

Her coming chilled and silenced them. She was used to that, but it hurt still, as old scars can. She held herself straighter and lifted her chin.

Jaffar led her to meet a stranger, a slender creature with great eyes like a gazelle's, and beautiful hair. Even her face was pleasing to see, its sharpness softened by the alchemy of freed hair and shimmering robe. She raised a hand to it: fingers less thin now than slender, their brownness more than comely against the splendor that was blue and green and gold and silver all together.

She stroked the silk as if it had been a living thing. For no reason in the world, she wanted to weep. Therefore she smiled valiantly at all the staring faces, and pirouetted. "Do you like my robe?" she asked them.

They startled her. They nodded. Some even smiled. One actually spoke. "I like it very much," said the newest one, the Frank who was all that Zamaniyah was not: a pure and alien beauty, skin as white as milk, hair the color of wheat in the sun, eyes as blue as the Middle Sea. Her Arabic was laughable, but Zamaniyah was not minded to laugh. "Was it the king who sent it to you?"

"The sultan," said Zamaniyah.

The Frankish woman drew close. She had learned, by force, to be clean; her fingers were light on the silk, her eyes wide with wonder. "You are honored," she said. "He likes you, no? He lets you ride with him."

She sounded wistful. Frankish women were scandalous, Zamaniyah had heard. They were not kept in honorable seclusion. They knew nothing of proper Muslim modesty.

"Do you like to ride?" she heard herself ask.

The woman—Nahar, she was called, for her strange beauty—drew a breath that said all she ever needed to say. Her hands had clenched into fists. "Yes," she whispered. *"Yes!"*

A demon had possessed Zamaniyah's wits. She leaned close and lowered her voice. "There is a way. Are you brave?"

The blue eyes flashed up. "My father died at Damietta. I was with him. I killed an infidel."

A Muslim, she meant. Zamaniyah stared at those white hands, soft as they were, clenched at the silken sides. That was hate that burned in the beautiful eyes, that hardened the lovely flower-face.

"You are brave," said Zamaniyah. The others were closing in, alert to conspiracy. Her whisper lowered, quickened. "Talk to me tonight. Late. After the lamps are out."

Her name, she insisted, was Wiborada. Zamaniyah struggled to say it. It helped that she knew Greek: her tongue knew what it was to shape outlandish names. Wiborada was not, precisely, amicable. She had not accepted Islam; she had not surrendered to the will of Allah. She was a wild thing in chains of silk.

"You understand," Zamaniyah said. "This is not a road to escape. You belong to my father; I don't intend to alter that. If you mean to betray me, be warned: I can do worse than shoot you down. I can give you over to your master."

Wiborada did not flinch where Zamaniyah could see. She lay back in Zamaniyah's bed, sleek as a golden cat, and laughed a rich alien laugh. Abruptly she straightened, coiled, leaned forward. Her eyes were level. "I understand. I see no escape from here. Too many people. Too many infidels. I make a pact. You give me air to breathe, and sky. I give you honor. No escape while I ride with you."

"Fair enough," said Zamaniyah.

She had done it. It was the sultan's robe, and the pain of her twice-cracked ribs, and the shock of knowing that she had, after all, some small claim to comeliness. Her father's Frankish concubine had always shunned her—or was it she who had shunned them all? Bound by al-Zaman's command, caught up in her loneliness, finding rejection because she expected to find it.

Never trust a Frank, people said.

Between women, perhaps, it could be different. Zamaniyah had never been one, to know. Jaffar would not presume to judge, which meant that he did not approve. It was not his office to approve.

"Sometimes," she said to him, "you are too dutiful for words. Unless they be curses."

He came perilously close to a smile, for which she came perilously close to hitting him.

It was simple enough to manage. Wiborada was tall and, for all her cultivated softness, robust. She made a passable mamluk, from a distance, with her headcloth drawn across her face to guard it from the sun; and she could sit a horse well, for a Frank. Al'zan, whom Zamaniyah did not even try to deceive, honored her. He held his tongue, and he mounted her on the gelding which he had been training for himself.

Zamaniyah made sure that her companion would not be questioned: she provided a diversion. She began to ride Khamsin beyond the walls of the house.

Wiborada was enchanted with him. If he had been a man, Zamaniyah would have said that he was enraptured with her. He made himself beautiful for her: arched his neck, flared his great nostrils, danced until she clapped her hands in delight.

Zamaniyah realized, startled, that she was jealous. Wiborada had the grace at least not to ask if she could ride him; perhaps his bright wild eye deterred her, or the saddle. Al'zan had had it made for training, on a Persian model, but altered out of recognition: light and almost flat, without ornament, nor ever with the height before and behind that secured a Frank on the back of his charger.

"But what keeps you there?" Wiborada asked.

"Balance," replied Zamaniyah, "and milord's assent."

Wiborada had seen how milord flinched from the touch of hand on his back, and edged away from the saddle itself; and bucked when Zamaniyah was settled there, not to dislodge her, simply to remind her that he was Khamsin. The Frankish woman was well and visibly content with the bay gelding, whose spirit was tempered with plain good sense.

She was an excellent companion. She rode quietly, without chatter. She kept her mount out of the way of Khamsin's restless heels, but she rode close enough to hold off the press of people on the road to the south gate.

Zamaniyah stopped watching her and centered herself on Khamsin. He was remarkably calm, but he was very far from quiet. He danced with excitement; he snorted at every shadow. Once she shifted too abruptly and nearly lost her seat altogether.

"Red horses," said Wiborada, "are for fire, no?"

"And for war." Zamaniyah was surprised. "How did you know that?"

"I listen," Wiborada said. Her eyes were bright between headcloth and veil, taking in all that there was to see: Cairo's rising walls, and the splendid new gate, and the roar and seethe of the city.

It was louder than Zamaniyah remembered, and wilder. Khamsin altered it by being so new to it; and Wiborada whose presence would enrage al-Zaman if he learned of it. She was being twice a fool, and knowing it, and refusing to give way to the knowing.

Jaffar's mule drew level with her, ignoring Khamsin's flattened ears. "Best we turn back," the eunuch said.

Anger sparked, heated with guilt. "What for? We've hardly started."

They both had almost to shout to be heard. Jaffar's mouth opened. Zamaniyah clapped heels to Khamsin's sides. He shot forward, bucking in outrage. A flood of people swirled between. They were moving together, shouting. Something flew: a stone.

Her body knew before her mind. Riot. She snatched the
reins. Too late. Khamsin had the bit in his teeth. She armed
all her strength to haul his head about. He tossed it; the reins
burned through her fingers. The flood caught him, carried
him.

Grimly she set herself to guide him. Not thinking, not
daring to think, who he was and what he was, and how little
she dared to trust him. He heeded her command, or seemed
to: breasted the current, angled slightly away from it, slanting
with painful slowness toward its edge.

She was not the only rider within sight. She was the only
one on a horse and not a mule or a camel. The others likewise
struggled to escape the press. Their faces twisted as they
cursed; they flogged their beasts, which brayed and balked.
One tall mule swerved broadside, kicking.

Above the featureless roar, a new sound went up: a sound
hideously like a snarl. It had words in it. *Turk! Filthy Turk!*

Zamaniyah watched. She could not do otherwise. She was
trapped. She saw the mule go down; saw hands stretch,
clawed, tearing.

Khamsin squealed and snapped. Faces blurred, stretched
out of all humanity, howling, hating. Bodies buffeted them
both. Fingers tore at her coat, her belt. She snatched her
swordhilt; but her hand froze there. *Never,* Jaffar had taught
her. *Never draw steel in a mob. Better to taunt the buffalo. He
kills quickly.*

Helpless, helpless. Something plucked at one of the plaits
that hung below her turban. A voice shrilled. "Turk! *Turk!*"

Khamsin went mad. She clung blindly to mane, saddle,
sides. A small cold creature sat behind her terror and smiled.
This, it decreed, *is a warhorse.*

Shame smote her to the bone. Her fingers twitched, tightened.
The whip which she carried looped to her wrist, stung her
thigh. She seized the haft of it, swung. Aiming for eyes,
heeding nothing but that, and staying astride, and escaping
from the mob.

A black face loomed over her own. She caught her blow at
the utmost instant. Jaffar pulled her down into the blessed,
numbing quiet of an alleyway. Wiborada was with him.
Zamaniyah clung to him and strove with all her strength not
to burst into tears.

She thrust away. There was no safety here: it was a cul-de-sac, scarcely deeper than it was wide. The course of the mob had slowed and begun to eddy. The shopkeepers who had been slow to bar their doors were suffering for it now.

"Greed will hold them," Jaffar said in her ear, "for a while."

She nodded. She was still shaking, nor could she stop it, but she took no notice of it. She had lost her turban somewhere: she had not known it until Jaffar set his own cap on her head.

Close together, leading their mounts, they ventured out into the street. Khamsin blocked Zamaniyah's view of what passed there, mincing half ahead of her, eyes white-rimmed. She tried to pull him back, but Jaffar slapped his rump and drove him forward again.

At first she had dared to hope that they could do it. On foot, with Jaffar's cunning in the hunt to aid them, perhaps they might have. But the horses were conspicuous; and Zamaniyah would not abandon them. Not Al'zan's beloved bay, and not ever her Khamsin. His neck foamed with the sweat of his terror, and yet he went on steadily, lashing out at bodies that stumbled or fell against him. She had gripped his bridle tightly; she loosed it, freeing his head for the swift slash of teeth.

He was valiant, but he was a rich man's chattel, and the fellahin knew it. Like jackals in the wake of a kill, they began to close in.

This time she would draw her sword. A charge, a spray of blood, a blaze of battle rage—they might rend her limb from limb, but they might fall back.

Jaffar saw the baring of steel. His hand was strong. She fought it. She won, snatched mane, pommel. And Khamsin flung her staggering back into the eunuch's arms. For an improbable moment she thought that their eyes met; that Jaffar said, "You know this city, prince. Save us from it." And that, most improbable of all, Khamsin nodded with human understanding.

Jaffar had the horse's bridle. She found herself with the mule's, and Wiborada between them with the bay, silent, steady, admirable.

Zamaniyah's sword was still in her hand. She did not

sheathe it. She had lost her bearings. It was all a black dream of tumult, jostling, violence. It was like war; but war was a planned thing. This was raw chaos. More than once she stumbled, or her foot caught on softness, or crushed what had been living flesh. One at least was still alive: he screamed. She could not stop. Something mad, that might have been human, sprang at her. She beat it away.

Instinct drove her to seize Wiborada's belt; Wiborada, wiser or swifter-witted, had caught Jaffar's already. In a straggling, stumbling, much-buffeted line, they made their way along walls and under awnings. They were perfect fools. They should have stayed in their sanctuary.

And been trapped there, and even killed.

What would happen to them here?

Jaffar must have been leading. It looked as if Khamsin was; and as if the eunuch insisted on it. Did they confer? She could not hear.

The mule screamed like a woman and fell, dragging her with it. Howling demons fell on it. Wiborada hauled at Zamaniyah, kicked her, cursed her in guttural Frankish. The woman vaulted to the bay's back. Jaffar flung Zamaniyah upon Khamsin. He had drawn his long knife. Wiborada had a dagger. She seemed to know how to use it. "Now!" cried Jaffar. "Run!"

The bay's rein cut into Zamaniyah's knee. It was tied to her saddle. Khamsin plunged, kicking, across the mass of struggling, smiting, looting human beasts.

He had aimed himself like an arrow to a target: another alleyway, but longer, crowded with huddling people, animals, a waterseller doing trade with remarkable aplomb. Beyond it opened a new face of the mob.

Khamsin checked, half rearing. His sides heaved. He gathered himself, plunged again, dragging the gelding and the woman, and Jaffar clinging to a stirrup.

Zamaniyah knotted her fingers in Khamsin's mane, shifted her grip on the hilt of her sword. Her mind had darkened. She knew the way at last. They were half the width of the city from home and safety. They could not go on as they went now. Khamsin would burst his heart; Jaffar would fall.

The stallion swerved. A wall loomed, a gate. It could not but be barred. He turned his back on it and kicked it down.

They tumbled together into a passage. It was black after the glare of daylight. Zamaniyah's skin knew the presence of men, weapons.

Jaffar's voice rose. "In the name of Allah! We mean no harm. We seek sanctuary."

Khamsin stamped, echoing in the vaulted space. She could see his ears against light. He trumpeted, deafening, dragging them all into the sun.

It was a house like their own, gracious, with a wide green-rimmed court. Servants crowded there, armed, and at their head, of all things, a Frankish man-at-arms.

His garb was of Cairo, and of Cairo's Arab lords at that; and he spoke Arabic, rapidly, easily despite a heavy accent. "Down blades!" And truncheons and staves and what looked suspiciously like a pruning hook. He squinted at the invaders. What he thought, she could not read. His great sword lowered to the tiles; his body eased a fraction. His eyes scanned, pondered, settled on Zamaniyah. He bowed as Franks did, the head only, an inclination like a king's. "I grant you sanctuary," he said, "in my master's name." Servants, barked at, ran to salvage the gate. None too soon, from the sound of it.

Zamaniyah slid from Khamsin's back. Her knees buckled; she stiffened them fiercely, shaking off hands. "My horse. See to my horse!"

One of the servants exclaimed. "These are women!"

She was far enough gone to want to laugh, so swiftly did the guard change. Women flocked, and eunuchs. Only the Frank did not go. It was all she could do not to scream at him. "My horse. We are alive because of him. I pray you by Allah, by your own Christ, see to him."

The blue eyes blinked once. Contemptuous? Amused? They ran over Khamsin. His hands followed, gentler by far than she would have expected. Khamsin shuddered under them, eye rolling. "Good horse," said the Frank. He called; servants came. The gelding went docilely. Khamsin dug in his heels and shook his head and struck with his forefeet.

Zamaniyah wanted to lie down and howl. Khamsin had been a wonder and a marvel, a hero, a champion. Now of course he must be plain mad Khamsin again.

Jaffar had gone mad himself. He seized the bridle, held the rebellious head: he who had no skill with horses, and no love at all for this one. To the Frank he said, "I shall tend him here, if I have the wherewithal. See to my ladies."

They needed seeing to. Wiborada was hurt: a great blackening bruise on her shoulder. Zamaniyah bled. She had not even noticed the knife that slashed her arm, though once she was aware of it, it hurt appallingly. Soft-handed women washed her, bound her wound, clad her as one of them. She could not muster voice to protest. They brought food, drink. She ate a little for courtesy, sharing with Wiborada who, unveiled, was paler than even a Frank should be.

But steady, and not at all like to faint. "You know this house?" she asked.

"Not at all." Zamaniyah worked at being undismayed.

"Your horse seemed to," said Wiborada.

"My horse has a mind of his own. As," she added, "does my eunuch."

"He is a good servant," Wiborada said. And after a moment: "I never saw a eunuch before I came here."

"What, none? Who guards the women?"

"Men."

Zamaniyah was shocked.

"We have no harems," said Wiborada. "Nothing so separate that it needs the guarding of geldings."

Zamaniyah rose, wounds forgotten. "Never call Jaffar that. *Never.*"

The lady saved them both. A very beautiful lady, with a queenly carriage: a Circassian with skin as white as Wiborada's and hair the precise, burnished chestnut of Khamsin's coat. She greeted them with soft words and perfect courtesy, and gave them her name: Safiyah.

"Nahar," said Wiborada, both wise and circumspect.

"Zamaniyah," said Zamaniyah, bowing as deeply as her hurts would allow. "We owe you our utmost gratitude. It was deadly, what we fled from."

The lady waved it gracefully away. "You are safe with us for as long as there is need."

"Not overlong, with all due respect," Zamaniyah said. "My father will be distraught."

Wiborada's eye caught hers in profound agreement, and profound unease. Safiyah saw, and seemed to comprehend.

"I think, perhaps, a message . . . a boy alone may pass where you could not. To whom shall I send him?"

"I shall go, madam," said Jaffar, entering, bowing low. "If you will permit."

"I do not!" snapped Zamaniyah.

His glance stopped her short. It was wild. It was trying to tell her something.

"You can't go," she said. "You'll die."

He prostrated himself at her feet. "Mistress, I beg." And under his breath in rapid, if abominable, Greek: "Stop it, little fool. Would you have them learn who you are?"

Her astonishment was complete. She had never known that he knew Greek. "But—" she began.

"This is your enemy. Her husband killed your brothers."

She went cold. Her eyes darted before she could stop them. Wiborada was speaking to Safiyah—to Ali Mousa's wife. Gracious, beautiful, hated; and hating, if she discovered what she harbored. What had not merely accepted her hospitality but demanded it, eaten her bread, drunk her sherbet, become her guests before the eyes of God and man.

Zamaniyah's chin set. "Pardon, madam. My eunuch stays with me. If your boy will go, he need only say that I have found sanctuary in the house of a friend."

"And your father?"

Jaffar's eyes burned. Zamaniyah stared them down. "Yakhuz al-Zaman."

There was a brief but impenetrable silence. The lady broke it with a slow sigh, the merest shadow of a shrug. She bowed her head. "It shall be done," she said.

Her courtesy abated not at all. Wiborada, who knew nothing, still had the wits not to include herself in the message. Her own tale was long since spun: an excursion to the baths, with maids well and, Zamaniyah could hope, thoroughly bribed.

It would have been pleasant here, had it not been the house of an enemy. Safiyah was a great lady; she seemed kind. There was a sadness on her as there had been on her husband in the sultan's diwan. It deepened, perhaps, as she perceived who her younger guest was. A daughter; an heir. Zamaniyah found no blame in her, no hatred, though another might have laid on her husband's great enemy the blame for her son's loss. It would have been a just revenge.

This forbearance was, perhaps, worse. It took all of Zamaniyah's strength to sit still, to maintain a quiet face, to listen as Wiborada told the tale of their riding. The Frank told the truth, of which she had no shame; Safiyah was not visibly shocked to hear it, although she was appalled that they had done it through a mob.

"The horse led us," said Wiborada. "He brought us here."

"Truly?" Safiyah was exquisitely polite. "A wise beast."

Not so wise, if he had led them here of all houses in Cairo.

"He is most unusual," Wiborada said. "Mad, people at home will tell you. He will accept no stall. He lives in a courtyard with an entourage of cats; he lets no one touch him but the young mistress."

"He sounds like a tale in the bazaar," said one of the women about Safiyah. "Like an enchanted prince."

Zamaniyah glanced at Jaffar. His expression was utterly strange. Then it shifted; it was his own again, blankly placid.

The women were smiling. None but Safiyah seemed to have heard the name of al-Zaman. One said, "We know of enchantments. One night a Jinni broke down our gate and roared through the house; we held him at bay in the garden. Then our master came and blessed him, and he ran away."

"Truly?" asked Wiborada.

"Most truly," said another of the women.

"What did he look like?" Zamaniyah asked, to spin out the tale, to free her mind from its circling about the name and house and sins of Ali Mousa.

"Why, lady, he looked like a horse. A horse made of shadows, with a thunderbolt on his brow. But surely he was a Jinni. He opened our gate; he let no one touch him till the master came. He knew our master. He yielded to the blood of the Prophet, on whom are blessing and peace."

"Blessing," they all murmured devoutly, "and peace."

Jaffar was fixed like a hound at gaze. Zamaniyah could not see why. It was only a story, even if Safiyah seemed inclined to indulge it. "My horse is quite mortal," she said, "if somewhat odd. He had no training till I bought him, and he was no colt then. He does," she conceded, "have a great deal of intelligence. Too much, I sometimes think, for his own good.''

''One might say the same of children,'' Safiyah said, sighing.

''Do you have many?'' Wiborada asked, too swiftly to be stopped.

''I had,'' answered Safiyah, ''one.''

Zamaniyah leaped before Wiborada could worsen it. ''Maybe the streets will have cleared a little. We should go, truly we should. My father—''

''Please,'' Safiyah said. ''Linger yet a while. I would not wish you to be lost, when you could have been safe here.''

Trained hate drew taut the skin between Zamaniyah's shoulderblades, cried *Treachery!* behind her burning eyes. But her heart regarded this woman and knew no ill of her but her name and her husband. It was a great pity, Zamaniyah's deeper self observed, that Safiyah had had none but the single worthless fool of a son. Her beauty and her dignity deserved better.

''A woman does not of necessity choose her husband.''

''Nor need she choose to be the enemy of his enemies,'' Safiyah said.

Zamaniyah started, blushed. She had not known that she spoke aloud. Safiyah's smile was gentle. ''We are women,'' she said, as if that explained everything.

It was hard to hate a woman for what her man had done, when she was so perfectly, royally kind. Having given hospitality before she knew her guests' names, she did not stint it after. Her conversation was much less dull than Zamaniyah might have feared. She was educated. She knew the poets; she knew music, and philosophy.

She was also tactful. She did not mention her husband's name. No more did she speak of al-Zaman.

And yet the servant's coming was a rescue. ''Lady,'' he said. ''The horse—''

Zamaniyah barely paused to excuse herself. In silks and slippers and forbidden veil, she bolted in the eunuch's wake.

Khamsin had done nothing visibly perilous. He had simply eluded confinement to take station in the courtyard. His head flew up when she came; he trotted to her, sniffed her arm, lipped it with utmost gentleness. He had wounds himself.

Cuts, cleaned and tended; the swellings of bruises. She
cupped his muzzle in her hand. He sighed. "Did you fret for
me?" she asked him.

People had followed her. They were staring. Safiyah came
through them.

Khamsin saw her. He whickered softly, softly. He had
never whickered for Zamaniyah. Very gently he stepped
toward Safiyah, setting each foot down with meticulous care,
as if he feared to frighten her. His ears were erect, quivering.

She was not, it was apparent, a woman for horses. She
lacked the touch; yet she lacked also the fear that so often
went with inexperience. When he laid his head against her
breast, she neither shrieked nor fled, but stroked it, smiling a
smile of remarkable beauty. "What a lovely creature this is!"
she said. "Is he your strange one?"

"Isn't it clear to see?" asked Zamaniyah. She should have
been pleased and proud. She was unendurably jealous. She
had to fight hard to keep it out of her voice.

Safiyah did not hear it. "He is beautiful. So long a mane,
and so thick; so silken a coat. And so docile."

"He likes you," Zamaniyah said. "Very much."

He looked fair to swoon at the lady's feet. She, for all her
queenliness, was doting on him. Had she spoiled her son with
such blind tenderness? Small wonder then that he had come
to a bad end.

As would Zamaniyah, if her father discovered where she
had waited out the city's storm. With perseverance and the
armor of a servant's foray into a much quieted street, she won
her proper clothing and her host's leave to go. She offered
due, and deep, respect, and thanks that were heartfelt. She
was not at all sorry to see the last of that house and its
inhabitants.

10

Khamsin was almost at peace. He had sought his father's house of his own will, for the sanctuary he knew he would find there, and despite the pain that had gone with the finding. He had seen his mother; he had felt her hands on him. She had not known him, and he had endured it. He was stronger than he had ever known he could be.

But before Allah, he would not, could not, do it again.

Zamaniyah did not let that first terrible riding deter her from taking him into the city, even beyond it. They had ample escort: a troop of her father's mamluks, armed and watchful. Sometimes one of them was a little smaller than the rest, riding a bay gelding and exchanging no speech with the others. Nor did they try to speak to her. Khamsin knew an understanding when he scented it; it interested him. He wondered how long either woman thought she could hide this trickery from al-Zaman.

The city was quiet again. The sultan's men had quelled the uprising swiftly and ruthlessly, but once it was quelled, they had withdrawn to simple vigilance. It was well done, people opined in Khamsin's hearing. Egypt had never lain content

under Islam; the exchange of Turk for Arab had reminded its
people of all their grievances. But the sultan was not minded
to crush them. He had lowered their taxes. He had been
forceful with the Christians and the Jews, but that sat well
with Muslims of all sides. He was showing signs of great
canniness and no little subtlety.

"That's his father," a mamluk said as they rode beyond
the walls. "Ayyub is a king of foxes, and his son has the wits
to listen to him. Do you know, he's the only emir who has the
right to sit in the presence of the sultan of Syria?"

Zamaniyah, in Khamsin's mind, was much too tolerant of
loose tongues among her slaves. She not only forbore to
reprimand this one; she circled Khamsin round to fall in
beside him. His mare was distractingly lovely. For all of that,
Khamsin heard his mistress say, "That right has been re-
voked, I think. Nur al-Din is hardly pleased to find his young
servant made sultan of Egypt, and avoiding a return to him
with constant and convenient excuses, and never quite sending him the tribute he asks for. My lord lost his fiefs in Syria
when he won Egypt; his family fares no better there, though
more than well enough here."

"That's economy," said the mamluk. Like all of al-
Zaman's soldier-slaves, he treated Zamaniyah as if she had
been a boy; free as his tongue was, it managed, somehow, to
be respectful. "They're carving a kingdom, those Kurdish
foxes. What will you wager that Yusuf stretches out his hand
for Syria?"

"I won't wager anything," she said, but not as if he had
angered her. "My lord loves his lord in Syria. He tries to live
as Nur al-Din lives, because he finds it admirable. It's
only... Egypt is his now. He has to rule it as best he
can."

"And if Syria sets out to drain Egypt dry—what then?"

"Then," answered Zamaniyah, "my lord does as he must."

Khamsin did not know why he listened. He had too much
else to fret him. The mare; and the woman in mamluk's
clothing, riding just ahead. The stallion in him snorted and
preened before the great-eyed grey. The man remembered
beauty unveiled, a mouth like a flower, skin like milk and
roses.

He was beginning to suspect that something in his enchantment was subtly, cruelly awry. All that was native to this body, he had. Hasan would have scorned the barley which he ate with such relish, which was given only to beggars and to beasts. Hasan would have recoiled in horror from the thought of taking pleasure with a mare. And yet this creature that he was, could gaze with longing at both the mare and the woman, and yearn equally for both.

His mistress gave him something blessedly, cursedly new to divert his mind. He hated new lessons: they were difficult, and sometimes he could not understand, and always he raged that he could not learn them perfectly, absolutely, all at once.

Hasan had been nothing short of lazy, body and mind. Khamsin, in body, was anything but that. But his temper had not changed at all, his utter impatience with anything that did not bend at once to his will.

Cajoled and often frankly seduced into doing as Zamaniyah commanded, he gave obedience, but he made her pay for it. Her patience was not infinite. Yet it stretched beyond belief, and it almost never broke. She could even laugh when he fought her, light upon his back as he bucked and plunged, clinging it seemed by sheer will.

This time he did not fight. They had come to a wide level plain between the river and the hills, empty even of birds though it was early yet, the heavy heat of day in Cairo's spring barely begun. The mamluks unburdened their horses of odd bundles which Khamsin had barely noticed, and raised them: targets. He shied more from what they meant than from what they were.

Zamaniyah rode him round and about them, gentling him, explaining considerably more than he wanted to know. "Everything you do," she said as he snorted and sidled, and she stroked his neck and urged him relentlessly on, "is to make you, in the end, a warhorse." She was speaking Greek. He cursed himself for understanding it. "You have a gift, though your temper mars it; you have fire, and you have intelligence."

He bucked, angry. He did *not*. A dim-witted beauty he had been born, and a dim-witted beauty he would quite happily die. And he most emphatically did not want to carry her while she shot at targets. Targets, it was true, could not shoot back. Men could.

She would not go to war. Even al-Zaman was not that perfect a madman.

He had calmed in spite of himself. He trotted, then cantered, through the staggered circle of targets. He was almost disappointed when she did no more than that. Why did she drag it out? Could she not smite him with it all at once?

That was not the way of this Greek mummery. Slowly, slowly: Al'zan lived by that wisdom. It was the wisdom of seduction. Gentle degrees, lulling him into peace; and then, all at once, he was won. It humiliated him. He was a man, not a beast; and he had done his own fair share of seducing. He should have known what was being done to him.

Perhaps he did know. Perhaps he wanted it.

They went back to the plain. Not every day. Some days Zamaniyah did not come at all. Often there were exercises on the familiar practice ground, exercises ever more like a dance of horse and rider, precise, cadenced, captivating. At first they came close to hurting. They were hard, and Zamaniyah relentless, pressing him always to his utmost.

Then the truth struck. She never pressed him harder than he could bear, whatever he might have thought before he did it. And it grew easier. He was lighter. He was stronger. He was wonderfully, joyfully supple. He who had always only watched the dancers, he was one of them, one with them, on his four feet with music beating in his brain. His own music, but not his alone. She shared it. She as much as he set its cadence. She was part of him. One mind, one will, one dawning delight.

Ramadan passed in fasting and prayer. He fasted, he prayed as best he could. The river flooded amid rejoicing; the land shifted as it had since days began, and begot anew the riches of Egypt.

In the lessening heat of autumn, Zamaniyah rode her stallion among the targets. Her bow was strung, her quiver full. He was eager, dancing and snorting.

Her hand on his neck quieted him a little. He felt her gather herself, heard her draw a breath. She drew up the reins in her right hand. Her escort watched, her father's concubine among them, more interested than perhaps she knew. Some of the mamluks had wagers riding on her marksmanship.

His duty was to run as smoothly, dart as swiftly, obey as perfectly as he could. When he was minded to oblige, she shot very well indeed. She could bend a stronger bow than her slightness might have hinted at; her eye was straight, her judgment sound. Her mamluks, who did not bestow praise easily, called her an archer.

Her heels touched his sides. He bunched, resisting because it was his habit to resist. "Now," she said. He sprang forward.

She spoke to him: a subtle speech of leg, hand, shifting weight. She called the steps of the swift complex dance. Arrows sang from the string, over his head, his neck, his croup; to right, to left, as he wheeled, as he swerved, as he galloped headlong from target to target.

It was sweeter than wine, headier than the smoke of hashish. She commanded, he obeyed; he the body, she the brain. His feet spurned the earth. His lungs drank the wind.

It ended too soon. He protested her hand that halted him. She flung her arms about his neck. "O marvelous! O splendid! You have it now—you have it!"

"He does indeed."

Caught up in the joy of the dance, she had never seen the swelling of her escort, nor felt the doubled and trebled weight of watching eyes. She started like a deer. The sultan leaned on his pommel and gave her his best grin, somewhat to the shock of his companions. Who were many. Who were princely.

He swept a bow before she could gather wits to move. "A fine morning, cousin, and a fine horse to do it honor."

"My lord," she said stupidly. "You were riding in the wars."

"I was," he said. "Now Cairo has me again." He urged his mare closer. Khamsin was duly fascinated: he arched his neck and rumbled in his throat. Zamaniyah smiled in spite of herself. The sultan smiled back. "Once or twice, while we raided, we paused to hunt. We would have welcomed your archery."

Her face was on fire. She mumbled something. He had not been away so very long, but it had been quite long enough. She was heart-glad to see him again; she wished that he had never come back. It had been quiet without him. Peaceful. She had let herself sink into her old solitude.

Now he would end it. He was beckoning, wanting her with him, admiring her stallion. By that art of his which was princely, he won from her the whole tale, even to her father's unbending disapproval. "And now," her tongue babbled on its own, "it's a year exactly since I bought Khamsin, and you see what a warrior he is already; but Father only remembers that once, when he was frightened, he nearly trampled me. Fathers are unreasonable."

"They are," agreed the sultan. "It's their nature. As it is the nature of children to try the limits of everything, and most particularly of their fathers' love."

Khamsin jibbed, tossing his head. She soothed him.

The sultan smiled. "You see? He understands."

She ran her hand down Khamsin's neck. "Khamsin understands much too much."

"They do, these servants of ours." The sultan watched Zamaniyah's mamluks retrieve the targets. His eyes had sparked. She wondered what had come into his head so suddenly, that made him look so youthfully eager.

He turned to her as if she had spoken aloud. "Games," he said. "A contest. Races, contests of arms, polo. Archery, of course, mounted and afoot. You and your red warrior . . ."

She shrank inside herself. "No, my lord. Oh, no. I couldn't."

He had not heard her. "A holiday. A celebration of our return. And for you, proof to your father that you chose wisely in this your stallion."

"But I am—I am not—" She could not say it. Too many ears strained; too many eyes glittered, daring her to speak the truth. She was a woman. She had no part in anything that befit a man.

Her head bowed, lest she fling it up in sudden temper. The sultan was full of his new game. He had drawn the others in; it would happen for all that she could do. She could not even slip away. She was trapped beside him, her silence unheeded in the flurry of plans set in motion, orders given, suggestions taken, servants sent at a gallop to begin what must be begun.

The day of the new moon, they chose. Time enough to call in champions and to ready the field. No time at all to prepare the green novice who was Khamsin; or the greener novice who was Zamaniyah.

"I shall go," said Wiborada.

Her Arabic was better now that she had Zamaniyah to talk to. Her manners were subtly worse. She wanted to ride out far too often for safety, and she was, Zamaniyah feared, growing careless in concealing what she did. Sight of the sultan seemed to have robbed her of the last vestiges of good sense.

She shrugged off Zamaniyah's telling her so. "I want to see the fighting."

"There won't be any—"

"Games, then." She lay as usual in Zamaniyah's bed, more lovely than ever in her insanity. "I'll be your mamluk. No one will even notice me." And as Zamaniyah opened her mouth: "No one noticed me on the field. I stayed away from your sultan. Is it true that he has sworn to drive the Franks from the face of the earth?"

Zamaniyah was not to be distracted. "You cannot go. It's too public. My father will be there."

That old fear, it seemed, had lost its power over Wiborada. "How will he know me? I'll be disguised."

"He will know," said Zamaniyah.

Wiborada made a soft derisive sound. "He's a man. I'm his slave. He'll never see me outside of my proper place."

Zamaniyah struck her. She swayed, astonished, making no effort to strike back. But her eyes had changed. Zamaniyah shivered. For an instant she saw hatred, raw as a wound; and something that was like madness. The madness of the trapped beast.

"He is my father," Zamaniyah said. Explaining. To a Christian, a slave. "I know him. If he sees you, he will kill you."

"But not you. You, he cherishes as his own soul."

One blow was enough. Zamaniyah's fist clenched into pain.

"You have nothing to fear," said Wiborada. "I would rather die than live in a cage."

"You lived well enough before I let you out of it."

"Did I?" Wiborada held out her arms. There on the white

skin were long thin scars, visible only if one looked for them.
"I tried. More than once. I kept failing. I was let live
because—and they told me this, little Saracen—because I was
beautiful, and therefore valuable. If I had been ugly I would
have been killed with my father. Beauty is property, O
daughter of my master."

"You did nothing to mar your own."

She had struck home. Wiborada rose, graceful even in
rage. "I don't like you, Saracen. I don't like you at all."

"What does liking have to do with needing me?"

The Frank stopped short.

"You use me," said Zamaniyah. "I allow it, because it
suits me. This I do not allow. You will not taunt my father
with your freedom."

"But I do," whispered Wiborada. "Every night when he
comes to me, uses me, sleeps like a trusting fool beside me, I
laugh. If he only knew, I tell him. If he only guessed."

"You are mad."

"Yes," said Wiborada. She smiled. "You had better do
your best shooting for the sultan. I'll have wagers riding on
it."

"You will *not*—"

She was gone. Back among the rustling, whispering wom-
en, where she knew Zamaniyah would never follow.

11

The *maidan* stood beyond the walls of the city. Al'zan called it the hippodrome, the field of races, but of games also, the play that honed men for war. Zamaniyah had ridden there at polo with the sultan; had seen races, even contests of archery, emir against emir or champion against champion. These games were greater than those, but not so very much greater.

In none of them had she been called on to distinguish herself. And none had been meant for Khamsin's proving.

"It's too soon," she said. "He's not ready."

Al'zan was calm. Easy enough for him. It was not *his* father who sat among the emirs, ignorant as yet of his daughter's part in this. It would be her gift to him, this proving before the princes. With so many witnesses, and taken by surprise besides, surely he could not refuse it.

If Khamsin did not shatter it all with unreadiness.

"He won't," said Al'zan, maddeningly serene. He inspected the girth, brushed a fleck of dust from the saddle. Khamsin stood rigid, head up, tail high, trying to take in everything at once. He thrummed like a bowstring under her hand.

"Nor," Al'zan continued, "will you."

He had found the root of her fear. No more than Khamsin had Zamaniyah ever made display of her prowess. Only her mamluks and her teachers—and, once, the sultan—had ever seen what she could do.

She looked at the broad stretch of the *maidan* and knew that she would forget everything she knew. So many men. So many horses. So many watchers under the pitiless sky.

Her mamluks made themselves a wall about her. One, smaller than most, met her glance. Blue eyes smiled. Wiborada had no shame, and no fear at all. Her grin shone even through the headcloth wrapped about her face. "Fifty dinars if you finish in the money," she said. "A hundred if you win. Make me rich, little Saracen."

"I'd rather make you sane," muttered Zamaniyah. But there was comfort, however crooked, in that pagan recklessness. She wished a little of it on herself.

Al'zan beckoned. Her heart stopped. So soon? The lancers were still wheeling on the sand, shrilling battle cries.

Slaves waited, bearing targets.

She vaulted astride. Khamsin started forward; she snatched rein.

Al'zan had him. "Ride him lightly," the Greek said. "Be at ease. If you have no fear, he can have none."

She nodded. Words were beyond her. Jaffar passed up her bow in its case, her quiver, her rings: the ring of silver that her father had given her, that guarded her fingers against the chafing of the string; the ring of leather through which ran the reins when she wielded the bow. Jaffar saw them all settled; he touched her knee to wish her well. She was glad that he did not smile.

Khamsin tossed his head. His forelock swung, braided with blue beads against ill fortune. He snorted, stamped. *Get on with it,* his body said. *Show the world how splendid I am.*

"Allahu akbar," she said. Entrusting it to the One who knew best of all how to give them, if not victory, at least the strength to finish the course.

The lancers hurtled together, wheeled, charged the sultan. A bare lance-length from his smiling face, they plunged to a halt and swept down their spears in salute. He bowed; they spun and galloped, shrilling, from the field.

Now it lay open for the archers. Zamaniyah wove with Khamsin among the rest of those who would try the mounted contest, grown men and boys, steady to a man, on seasoned horses. They kept together, men with men and boys with boys. None approached her. Most of the boys were mamluks, some as fair as Wiborada. She edged toward their corner of the waiting-ground.

A herald in the sultan's black and gold divided them. She was not to go with the raw boys; she was set among young men. She knew none of them. All of them seemed to know her. None spoke or smiled. She was younger than they, and female. They would not have been human if they had not resented her.

The herald explained to them all what they all knew. They would ride the course of targets one by one. Each must ride it swiftly, and shoot swiftly, and conquer by surety of aim.

Khamsin sidled, ears flat. He had taken a dislike to one of the stallions. She slapped his neck. He threw up his head, rebellious. It was all too much for him. He would never heed her, with all there was to see and hear and shy at.

He had to. She shortened rein and set to work distracting him: riding the figures of the Greek art. He resisted, but the training was strong. It mastered him. It calmed him, a little.

The boys rode their simple course, awaited the tallies, hailed a champion. The young men inspected their horses, saw to bows and arrows and strings. Perhaps they were not as calm as she had thought. There was remarkably little of the boisterousness that young men were given to.

One by one they answered the drum and the calling of their names. Zamaniyah did not watch them. Khamsin objected to standing still while another leaped into a gallop before him, nor did it mollify him to trot sedate circles. He was growing angry, slipping what control she had.

The drum beat, none too soon. The herald called her name. Her eyes flashed to the sultan under his canopy; to the emirs about him. The sun was too bright. She could not see her father's face. Whether he was startled, or angry, or oblivious. Whether he was there at all.

There was, there must be, only the field. Her hands flew of

themselves, stringing the bow. Her lips moved in brief and
silent prayer. Khamsin gathered himself. She settled deeper in
the saddle, firmed her grip on the bow, slid the reins a little
farther along the ring that circled the longest finger of her
right hand. When she drew bow, they would follow, not so
tight as to check her horse's gallop, not so loose as to
abandon him altogether.

The herald signaled. Her heels touched the quivering sides.
Khamsin sprang into flight.

It was all one. Sun, sky, field. Targets in their course,
blurred with the gallop's speed: Franks mounted, afoot,
kneeling on the ground, leering like devils. Khamsin singing
with tension, wavering subtly, yielding to the touch of leg and
rein. Arrow to string, arrow to string. Aim, nock, loose. Let
it fly, spare it no glance, aim, loose. Khamsin stumbled,
bucked—one lost, no time, no time—recovering, aiming, in
the name of Allah, a hit? A hit. Three more, two more,
one—out.

Wind roared in her ears. No; not wind. Voices. A clamor
of—cheering?

Khamsin carried her before the sultan. She bowed; and the
stallion, serene as any Muslim for all the foam that spattered
his neck, bent his knee and did obeisance. Applause burst
forth. She wheeled her improbable courtier about and trotted
back to her place.

Her face bore a smile, fixed as if carved there. Nowhere
about the sultan had she seen her father. If he had left—if for
anger he had withdrawn, or for shame—

Her teeth set. A new rider ran the course, his mount steady,
no flashes of temper to cast his aim awry. She relieved
Khamsin of her weight, loosened the girth, led him slowly
about.

Perhaps al-Zaman had never come at all. She had been
caught up in her secret, and in her fears; she had never
thought to ask him if he would go.

She almost laughed. So much fretting, and for nothing.
Whether she won or she lost, her father would not see.

It did not matter. She had ridden for herself, and for
Khamsin, and for the sultan. And for Al'zan who came to
take the bridle; for Jaffar, for Wiborada, for her mamluks in

their loyal circle. Their pride in her was sweet, though it made her blush.

"You rode well," said Al'zan: his highest praise.

"You shot well," said Jaffar, higher praise yet.

Khamsin snorted. "And you," she said to him, "ran very well indeed."

She had not been heeding the rankings. Her father was not there, that she could care whether she had finished last or second from the last. When they called her name, she did not hear it. Jaffar was tugging at her; people were making a great deal of noise.

"Last?" she asked. "But why—"

"Not last!" Wiborada shouted in her ear. *"First!"*

Wiborada's Arabic was worse than she knew.

Jaffar was saying the same. Dragging Zamaniyah. Flinging her bodily into the saddle.

The tumult was protest. A woman had won the robe of honor. What man could endure it?

Any man fairly defeated, cried a faction of surprising size. There were the targets, there her arrows, there the tallies taken and sworn to. For the one she had not even touched, six were slain with arrows in heart or brain, five sore wounded in the body. No other had shot so skillfully.

The horse, then. The horse had won it for her.

His scream rang over the clamor of voices. He bolted through her mamluks, past men and horses, bit clamped in teeth, Zamaniyah borne unresisting, unable to resist. On the open field he bounded to a halt. He released the bit. Slowly, too subtly at first even for her understanding, he began to dance.

Training was strong. She found her seat. Her hands found their place, the reins light in them, but firm. Her will remembered itself.

She rode the figures, serene as if she were alone, absorbed. They bore her closer, closer, to the targets that awaited the approach of the champions. She was not that, not yet, perhaps not ever, but an archer, she was. No idiot male could take that from her. Khamsin was supple beneath her, pure joyful obedience. She freed her bow from its case, strung it at the canter—a feat, and they both knew it, and were most proud of it. Two arrows yet remained in her quiver. Two shots.

For the champions they had raised beyond the targets a more difficult target still: the single tall mast of the Turkish art, and atop it, glittering, a golden cup; and fluttering on a string, now on the cup, now in the air, a dove. One rode past the mast at full gallop—if one were a champion, one all but brushed it in passing—and aimed upward, and shot the cup from its mooring; and if one were a master, one slew the dove with a single clean shot; and if one were more than master, one caught cup and dove together and brought them down.

Zamaniyah had trained at the mast. Everyone did. But always on seasoned horses. Never on Khamsin. One false step, one stumble, and the horse could strike the mast, slay himself, slay his rider.

A clear voice rang out behind her. "A pretty dance. Fit for a lady, if lady she were. To be so brazen—to ride against men—to *win*—"

Anger was white and pure, cold in the heart of its fire, clear. She stroked Khamsin's neck. It sweated, but he was strong beneath. One run still, no more. "Will you?" she asked him. "Can you?"

He slowed, smoothing his gaits. His head rose, as if he measured the mast, the cup, the dove. He snorted at them.

No one moved to stop her. Many had forgotten her in their outrage at what she had done, or in the headiness of a battle brewing. Soldiers and heralds moved to quell them. The sultan had risen and drawn his sword.

She filled her lungs until surely they must burst. *"Allah!"* she cried. That Name drew eyes. She deepened her voice as much as she might, made it as strong as one small woman's could be. "In the Name of Allah, listen to me! I ride here at my sultan's command. I wield my bow in his name. See if I may call myself an archer—strike a wager with me. If my arrows take both cup and dove, the robe and the title are mine to keep. If I take neither, or one alone, I surrender all to the man who would have had them but for me. That is my oath. May Allah be its witness!"

She gave them no time to gainsay her. Khamsin was ready. More than ready. He threw up his head and neighed. She flung him into a gallop.

Aim. Nock. Cup, first: simpler, steadier. Loose.

Metal rocked, rang. The arrow bounded wide. Groans chorused at her back.

Two together now: possible. If Allah willed. If her skill sufficed. The mast at arm's stretch, blurring to sight, knee burning with the closeness of it, passing, losing all: pride, honor, prize fairly won. But gaining—gaining—

Nothing.

Her body twisted in the light flat heretical saddle. Her eye locked on the mast's summit. The cup, glittering. The dove sensing death, casting itself upward. The cord stretched taut between them: thin black line, frail as a hair.

Loose.

The arrow flew straight and clean and true. The dove hurtled astonished into the sun. The cup swayed, wobbled, stilled. Between them was empty air.

Khamsin slowed, wheeling. His head was high, his eyes on the vanishing fleck that was the dove. He halted, staring.

She slid from the saddle. Her anger was gone. Her mind was empty of aught but light and air and something remarkably like gladness.

Her knees bent to Allah who had willed it. She staggered up. Khamsin's body steamed; his sides heaved; but he was proud, proud, proud. He knew what they had done, he and she. He understood. She flung her arms about his neck.

The crowd roared. It sounded dim and far away. Someone was tugging at her. Come, she must come. Someone else was trying to take Khamsin. Al'zan, quietly persistent, until she knew him, let him tend her marvel of a horse.

The sultan was waiting for her. He would not let her bow to him. He refused her homage. He bowed—shockingly—to her. "To your victory," he said.

Her nape knew the stab of eyes, her ears the mutter of voices. Where she could not see but could sense as utterly as sight, the man who would call himself victor stood in his robe of honor. "I have won nothing," she said, "O my sultan."

"Nothing," he said, "and everything." His voice lowered. "Every man with eyes knows who won the course. Everyone with wits admits it. A few can even comprehend what you did after."

"I missed the shot."

"Did you?"

"I lost my wager."

"That," he granted her, "you did."

Her cheeks were burning. "My lord, I didn't—"

"Of course you didn't plan it. Shots like that are God's gift. People will remember, cousin: that you let a man have his petty rags of honor. He is content. The rest of us know which of you has won the victory."

There was iron in that. As in the embrace with which he favored her, and the honor he accorded her in bidding her to feast with him when the games were ended. Then at last, for a little while, he had mercy. He let her go.

They were together on the field's edge, her mamluks, her eunuch, her master of horses with her stallion. And before them, one regally alone, a man not tall but broad and strong, with a full and handsome face and a faint, perpetual smile.

Her servants greeted her with words she barely heard. Her knees shook; but she bowed, child to father. He did not touch her, nor bid her rise.

"I suppose," said al-Zaman, "that you know how suicidally reckless you were."

"Father," she said. "Shooting at targets is not—"

"Shooting at the mast with an untrained horse very certainly is."

She snapped erect. "How do you know he isn't—"

"I told him," Al'zan said.

She stood utterly still. Al'zan was pale. They were all pale, all her conspirators. They had known what she did. Because she could not rule her temper. Because anger was the truth, and all her meekness no more than a mask.

Her father's hand rose. She steeled herself for the blow which she had earned, and richly. None came. He tilted her chin up, compelling her to meet his stare. "Little fool," he said. "Little madwoman. Little champion. Don't you know that there's no need to prove anything to me?"

"Except Khamsin," she said, daring even yet to rouse his rage.

It did not even stir. "He proved himself the day he suffered you on his back."

He had robbed her of speech.

"If he had not," he said, "you may be most certain, I

would have sold him well before he brought you to this. If he had harmed a hair of your head, I would have had him killed.''

Her hand quivered, wanting to seek ribs from which the ache had long since passed. Al-Zaman did not see. He embraced her, which was a ceremony before so many eyes. ''You honor our house,'' he said, clear to be heard. And softer: ''Honor indeed; enough for a good long while. When next you do this, young hothead, you will ask my leave.''

Her head bowed. It was easy, now that her anger had passed. ''When next I do this, O my father, I will do it for you and not for the sultan.''

''On a horse which knows the way of it.''

''He will,'' she said. ''I promise.''

12

" 'Take her bow,' he said." Wiborada danced with glee.
" 'Fetch her arrows,' he said. 'Boy,' he said. He never knew
me. Never once!"

Zamaniyah did not want to listen. She was clean, stroked,
oiled, and pampered. She did not need this barbarian to keep
her from her sleep. Sleep she had earned, after the day she
had had: not merely winning in all but the forfeited name,
but having to rejoice in it, seated by the sultan, souring the
stomachs of the men who feasted with him.

The Frank dipped and whirled, singing in her uncouth
tongue. It was barely musical. It gloated shamelessly.

Zamaniyah reached, snatched, overbalanced her into a
mound of cushions. She struggled out of it, grinning
most unlike a lady. "Your manners are appalling," said
Zamaniyah.

"Yours are excruciating. Bow and grovel, grovel and bow.
O my lord and *O my master* and *O my sultan*. God wills it;
God always wills it; and everyone's wish is your command.
How do you do it?"

"I'm civilized."

Wiborada made a very uncivilized sound. "My uncle was a priest. He always said that your people were heathen savages."

"You don't want to know what pious Muslims say of yours."

"I've heard it. It's all lies.

"Or mostly," she said, folding her hands under her chin. Her brows had drawn together. "He warned me against capture. I'd be destroyed, he said. I'd be borne away to a fate worse than death. He would never tell me what that meant. I think . . . it means this."

"Is it worse than death?"

She pondered, sighed. Her eyes met Zamaniyah's; she smiled fleetingly. "A priest would think so. I'm a slave. I'm exiled from my church and my people. My body belongs to a turbaned infidel."

"And you? What do you think?"

The blue eyes glittered. "I think it could be worse. Infinitely worse."

"But also infinitely better."

"I could wish," mused Wiborada, "that he were a Christian. Handsome, I don't ask for. Or young, or even faithful. Men are men wherever they are, whatever the priests would like them to be.

"Are you betrothed?" she asked abruptly.

Zamaniyah, startled, could only shake her head.

"I was. He was old. Thirty at least. He was good enough to look at, for an old man: he had most of his hair, and more of his teeth than not. He was always kind to me. He used to pet me as if I were one of his hounds, and give me pretty things, and say that I was prettier than they. He would have made me a baroness."

"Was he in Damietta?"

"He was in Jerusalem, guarding it for the king. He'd never have me now. I'm worse than dead. I'm a Saracen's plaything."

"You hate us," said Zamaniyah, not surprised, not even frightened.

"No," said Wiborada. "I should. Often I want to—oh, how I want to! But hate is too hot. It burns itself away. It becomes weariness. Then, before one knows it, it has become acceptance."

Zamaniyah regarded her sidelong. One should never trust a

Frank. But it was hard, with this one. Cool distance had become familiarity; a bargain born of pity had shaped itself, somehow, into full-fledged complicity. It struck her that this was not the first time they had lain together in the evening and talked, nor the second, nor the tenth.

She blinked. Could this be friendship?

Odd and uncomfortable, if friendship it was. But there was trust in it, and truth. She could ask, barely blushing, "Have you ever loved anyone? The way people love in stories?"

Wiborada wound a lock of hair about her finger, let it spring free. Her eyes were dark. "How do people love in stories?"

"Beautifully. Tragically, sometimes. Perfectly and eternally."

"I thought I loved someone once. He was young and beautiful; all the women adored him. He never had eyes for us. All his love was given to a dark-curled jongleur from Languedoc."

"That's sad."

"It's silly. I was fifteen," said Wiborada, as if that explained everything.

Zamaniyah bit her lip. "I'm fifteen," she said.

Her father's concubine had the grace to be surprised. "So young?"

"So young," said Zamaniyah, a little sourly.

"Are you in love with someone?"

Zamaniyah blushed furiously. "No! I only . . . I'm fifteen."

"Ah," said Wiborada. "You know what I should say to that. Your father might be wise to find you a husband."

"I don't want one."

"Of course you don't. A husband would lock you away. You need a lover."

This was getting out of hand.

"Men have them," Wiborada said. "Boys younger than you are given slaves to slake their passions."

"They are men," said Zamaniyah.

"Aren't we women? Don't we have bodies? Don't we have desires?"

"We're weak. We have to learn to rule ourselves."

"Nonsense. Look at you! You ride and shoot better than any boy; you're brave, you have a high heart, you can be captivating when you try. But when a man opens his mouth, what do you do? You crouch and cower like an obedient slave.''

"Not always," said Zamaniyah.

Wiborada clapped her hands. "Indeed not! And you sound *ashamed* of it. You should be proud. Sometimes you have a mind of your own. Sometimes you see what fools these men can be. They're no stronger than we are, and certainly no wiser."

"Maybe. But Allah has set them over us. They can kill us if we stray."

"Not if we're careful."

Zamaniyah's eyes narrowed. "Are you proposing—"

She was glad to see shock in Wiborada's face. "Of course not!" But then the madwoman said, "I haven't seen anyone worth the price."

"And if you did?"

"I'd give him to you." Wiborada laughed at her expression. "Did you think I'd keep him? I'm not as mad as that. Besides," she said, and her voice softened, perhaps in spite of itself, "what I have is enough. I'll give myself to no other Muslim."

There was a silence. Wiborada rose in it. Zamaniyah did not try to stop her. She went to her Muslim; and Zamaniyah lay alone, discomfited, and distressingly wide awake.

"Should I take a lover?" she asked Jaffar as he went about his nightly duties.

He was not shocked, or even much surprised. "Do you want one?"

"No," she said quickly. "I don't think so. I don't know."

He nodded, as if that were an answer.

"If I were a boy I could ask for a concubine. My father says I'm to be treated as his son. Should I ask him?"

"Is it a woman you're wanting?"

She could have hit him. "Is that all it is to you? Something to laugh at?"

His face was as sober as a *qadi*'s. "Am I laughing?"

"You think I'm being ridiculous."

"Now you are."

Her fists clenched. She said it all at once, before she could get her temper back, and thereby lose her courage. "Tell me what it is that I'm wanting. Tell me what a man does with a woman." And in his silence, with the passion of shame: "No, I don't know!"

He looked down. He was too dark; she could not see if he blushed. Briefly, piercingly, she regretted that she had asked him.

He answered levelly, as if it had been a question like any other. "You've seen the stallions with the mares."

Her insides flinched. "Like *that?*" Great teeth closing in one's nape, great loins thrusting in one's tenderest center, screams that were like rage . . .

She must have been bloodless. Her hands were icy. Jaffar seized them, seized her. "Not all like that! Men aren't animals. It can be gentle. It can be the sweetest pleasure in the world."

Her teeth set. Her head shook of itself. How could she want that? How could her knees melt for thinking of it?

"I know," said Jaffar. His voice was rougher than it was used to be, more like a man's; though it was never precisely like a woman's. "You frighten yourself. It comes hard, sometimes. And you're where you can see men, and talk to them, and be free with them."

"That's why women are secluded," she said. She had heard it more often than she could remember. She had never known what it meant. "To keep them from doing what I want to do. It doesn't stop them, does it? It never stops them from wanting it."

"I've never noticed that it did," he said dryly. "Frankish women tramp about like men, and never veil their faces. I've counted no more virgins among the slaves your people have taken, and no less, than among your own. When the will is strong enough, it finds a way."

"And gets a child. I know that much." She drew a shuddering breath. "It's hard, Jaffar. It's starting to—it's *pleasant,* this pain."

"Is it anyone in particular?"

Her mind saw the sultan's face. She shook her head. "No one. Just . . . No one."

Perhaps he believed her. He did not cry falsehood. He did not even smile. She embraced him suddenly, loving him for it. He was warm, familiar, gentle as he held her, his strength not a woman's but not yet a man's. She breathed his faint sweet scent, a little like new bread, a little like spices, and listened to the beating of his heart. Her eyelids drooped. "I wish," she murmured. Already it was eluding her. "I wish—"

I wish you were my mother.
I wish you were my brother.
I wish . . .

The foal without a father came early, as far as anyone could judge; but it seemed sturdy enough. The first to know of it was the lad who, entering the stall to feed the mare, met a whirl of hoofs and teeth. From the safety of the passage, he and his master, and Zamaniyah come early to her training of Khamsin, could discern the small tottering shape beside the large watchful one. It was red, as its dam was: no revelation there. It turned its head.

It had a bright eye, even so young. It had a fine profile. It had a most distinctive marking. A star, it began to be. It slipped, slid downward in a narrow stream, broadened to pour over the half of a nostril, trickled to a halt upon the lip. It was unusual. It was not, alas, unique in the world.

"A filly," said Al'zan, entering the stall with serene confidence. The mare laid back her ears but suffered him. His hands ran over the newborn body. "A little narrow before," he said. "A little weak behind. But fire enough, and strength. She'll be a beauty."

Zamaniyah swallowed hard.

The master addressed the mare, whose pride was conquering her temper. "She's her father's daughter, I think. Though how you did it, you two . . ."

"He couldn't have!" Zamaniyah burst out. "It wasn't long enough ago."

"Did I ask you?" he inquired mildly.

"He's my horse."

"Ah! You have a question about your stallion?"

She was beginning to understand. But she could not leave it so. "What will you do with her? You won't sell her?"

"That is for your father to say."

"I want her," said Zamaniyah.

She had not thought about it before she said it, but she did not try to take it back.

"Your father may intend otherwise," Al'zan said.

"She won't be sold. Promise me, Alexander Hippias."

"You know I can't."

She stamped her foot, which she had not done in a very long while. It was, she knew when she had done it, an error. He was smiling as one does at a petulant child.

"A foal," he said, light, almost idle, "needs its mother for a substantial while. Then it requires weaning, and that can be difficult. If in that time it proves itself worth keeping—if truly it is its mother's child, and its father's . . ."

Her breath caught, choking her. She was furious. He was being—damn him, he was being Byzantine.

"You, of course," he went on at his maddening leisure, "can't own her. You've sworn to have no horse but Khamsin."

"This is Khamsin's get!"

"Is it? Can it be proven? Was it you who brought him to this mare just as she came into her season, when she was meant for al-Ghazal the prince of racers, to found a new line for your father's pride? Do you want your stallion, after all, to pay the price of his trespass?"

"But if she has no father at all—"

"She seems none the worse for it. Once she's proven her quality, if she has any to prove, who knows? Lineage alone has never won a race. Or a battle. Or," he added, "a contest of archery."

Her head wanted to bow to superior wit. Yet she was still angry, more at herself than at Al'zan. She kept her chin up. "I may, at least, assist you with her. There are so many foals to look after this year, after all, and so many still unborn, and a stable full of horses needing your care. Surely, one less filly, if she proves as difficult as her parentage portends . . ."

At last she saw the gleam of his approval, subtle as it was, masked in the semblance of reflection. When he had stretched it out quite long enough, he said, "Help is always welcome. Provided, of course, that you don't neglect Khamsin."

She was no subtle Byzantine. She grinned, embraced him quickly, spared mother and daughter a last long glance, and went rather more than dutifully to train her stallion.

Zamaniyah's scent proclaimed excitement, and eagerness, and joy that was more than half fear. It infected Khamsin. He was hard put to heed her teaching. His body wanted to dance and snort and battle the bit. She did not rebuke him. It was not patience; it was impatience with the exactions of art.

She babbled somewhat, telling him of a mare she called *al-Saqla,* the Kicker. An inauspicious name for a mare. The lady had, it seemed, committed an indiscretion; its consequence had fulfilled itself. A filly foal, a little beauty, the very image of her sire.

Khamsin stopped short, very nearly losing his rider.

He had not forgotten. Never. But he had put it out of his mind. He had not paid for his transgression with the red queen—kicker, was she? She had been most gentle with him. He had hoped with waxing confidence that he would never need to pay.

He moved forward at the touch of the whip, bucking his displeasure. His mind was less than half on it.

A daughter. He had a daughter.

A man would have preferred a son. A stallion could beget nothing more precious than a daughter. Colts were a nuisance. Fillies grew into mares, swift in the race, peerless in battle, mothers of champions.

He had never known how joyful it was possible to be, and still be trapped in this enchantment.

Or how very desperate he could be, to speak, to voice his gladness, to demand to see her.

His throat filled with words. They burst forth. A rumbling whinny mocked his ears. It bore no faintest resemblance to a human voice, or to the pure Arabic of which, once, he had been so proud.

Trapped, mute, helpless, he let himself be ridden, cooled, left alone. Zamaniyah barred the door behind her. The rattle of bolts was eloquent, and inescapable.

He gathered to kick down the damnable thing.

Paused.

Plodded slowly to the farthest shaded corner of his prison. Turned his back on temptation. Schooled himself, painfully, to patience.

Speechlessness had never been as bitter as it was now. He had fancied that he was resigned to it. Fancy indeed. He had never needed to speak.

Zamaniyah doled out tales in tantalizing fragments. How the little one took to the halter, how she ran among the foals, how she was proving headstrong yet amenable to reason. None of it was enough.

Of course he could not see her. What did a stallion care for his progeny? She was never in sight when he passed through the stable. Sometimes he thought he scented her: a hint of newness, the sweetness of milk, mingled with the remembered scent of her mother. Remembered more keenly as al-Saqla drew closer to her foal-heat.

She was guarded unceasingly. Zamaniyah told Khamsin so. This time they were not to be thwarted. The mare of royal lineage would go to none but the royal stallion.

Even she could say it, arrogant as every human was, recking nothing of what it did to him. *His* mare. *His* consort. And some brute beast would have her, some mindless animal, fit only for begetting animals.

And what could he do? If he escaped again, took her again, they would cure him of his trespassing.

When he was calmest, he could see irony in it. The horsedealer could have lied. Could have given him a proper lineage and spared him this humiliation. Any other would have done just that. The Hajji had been most careful, and most merciless: he had sold his victim to the only honest horsedealer in the world.

But Allah, unlike the Hajji, had mercy. Khamsin, who had doubted it, was given time to rebuke himself for a blasphemous fool.

He was on the practice ground. He had just completed a round of exercises, and been praised for excellence. Zamaniyah was trusting him: he stood unbound, reins on his neck, while she freed him of the itching bonds of the saddle. His mouth had readied itself for the sweetness of the fruit she always gave him once the saddle was disposed of.

The gate was open. It always was; he never tried to escape. Where could he go?

Swift hoofbeats startled him. Zamaniyah did not seem to hear them. They were very light. Their maker was very small, trotting through the gate, dancing, curvetting: red wickedness in infancy, escaped from her mother and cocky with it.

His presence astonished her. She sprang into the air and came down stiff-legged, poised, staring with her whole body.

He knew her. She was part of himself.

His neck arched. He uttered the softest of sounds, a bare flutter of the nostrils.

She raised her head, whickered back.

Her bravery must be of her mother; Allah knew, he had none. She came to him, bold, fascinated. Surely she had never scented anything like him before.

Zamaniyah snatched the bridle. He spun free. His daughter followed. Ah, her body said, delighted: this large one was a marvel. He liked to play.

She was lighter, but he was surer of his feet. She danced in circles about him. She ventured an impudence: a flashing nip, a flick of heels. He laughed as he eluded them.

A scream spun them both about; and a clamor beyond it, human noise, meaningless.

The mare saw horror. Her daughter escaped, lost, abducted; and a stallion. Hoofed death barring her way to her child. She hurtled upon him.

He retreated rapidly. The little one, baffled, bleated a question. The mare examined her from nose to tail. Sighed. Glared at Khamsin. Paused.

His skin quivered. Her scent was that most wondrous of all scents. Sweeter now, more enchanting, for that it was of the foal-heat: the foal he had begotten.

Her daughter was patently unharmed, safe at her side, nuzzling a nipple. She was aware, all at once, of what a stallion was good for.

She remembered him. He saw it in her eyes. She knew her lover who had come to her in the night, who had taken her maidenhood.

She did not soften as a woman might. She was al-Saqla, the swift one, the fierce one, the one who endured no taming. But she ceased to glare. She tilted an ear. She bade him court her.

Humans circled, baying. She showed them her heels. They crowded back. "Allah," someone was praying, or cursing. "Ya Allah!"

Khamsin courted as she commanded, arming all his beauty, laying it at her feet.

"Khamsin!" A new voice, clear and desperate. *"Khamsin!"*

The bit in his mouth, the rein on his neck, the will that dreamed that it mastered his own.

They meant her for a stranger. His mare. His consort. His body's beloved.

He shared the sweetness of her breath, tasted the sweet sharpness of teeth. Her threat was all love.

"He's still bridled."

"Pull them apart."

"Ropes—a whip—"

"Catch the foal!"

"Aiee!"

The mare's heels had caught that one. She was no human's chattel. She was Khamsin's. She turned, offering. Demanding.

One did not refuse one's queen.

A stallion screamed. Khamsin wheeled. Rage flared, red as blood.

A human wielded the enemy, the rival, the interloper. Great grey stormcloud of a beast, no mind in him, no wits, no will but lust and hate and battle.

Khamsin would give him battle. Free as he was not, wise as he would never be, drinking death with the wind and the sun and the hot sweetness of desire. *My* mare! Khamsin shrilled. *Mine!*

Mine! bellowed the grey.

Take her, human wisdom cried. Take her now, before any of them moved to end it.

Any of them.

His body lunged, hating. His mind stood still, small and cold and passionless. Seeing a mare, a pair of stallions closing in war, humans milling, shouting, tangling in confusion.

He could conquer the grey. He knew it with perfect certainty. He was smaller, but he was quicker, fiercer, wiser in battle. He could kill if he must. He could even elude the nets that waited for him. Fool, did they take him for, to be trapped twice alike?

And then?

The mare.

And then?

Implacable, this mind of his.

And then, the price. He would have his mare; and they would geld him for it.

He could not even bargain. Surrender the mare, if only he might keep his daughter.

That was not a stallion's bargain.

He was not a stallion. He was Khamsin.

He scrambled to a halt. The grey lunged against his bonds, mad with fury. The mare watched, coolly interested, awaiting the victor. The humans babbled like geese in a den of foxes.

Every grain of blood and bone cried battle. His head snaked about, seeking. His mistress stood alone and silent in the tumult, clenched fists, set face, wide wounded eyes. His mare watched, guarding his daughter.

His enemy screamed a challenge.

He screamed back, mocking them all. He leaped, curvetted, flourished his heels. His daughter mirrored him; he laughed though only he could hear, with tenderness, with pride in what he had wrought. He sneered at the stallion. His body drew him toward the mare, helplessly, inescapably.

He tore it away, shouting with the pain of it. Trotted, cantered, charged the knotted men. They scattered. Only one did not move. Only one mattered. He bowed his head before Zamaniyah, and nudged her, not too gently. Not as if he yielded to anything but will and—of all things—wisdom.

For a deadly moment, he knew that she would fail him. The will was strong, but the body had not seen the end of it: a mare in heat, a stallion in rage, and battle beckoning.

She freed him from it. She took his bridle, stroked his neck, filled his nostrils with scent that was nigh as sweet as any mare's. Wisely, wordlessly, with wonder in her every move, wonder that was alarmingly like awe, she led him away.

13

The old fox was dead.

The sultan's father had never had anything to do with Zamaniyah. His dignity was too great to trouble itself with a mere woman, particularly a woman who conducted herself as a man. Nor had she ever tried to win his notice. She had never had any skill in currying favor.

But Ayyub had mattered.

"I was more of my uncle's making," the sultan said. "He taught me what I know of war; he set me where I would become what I am. But my father was my father."

Zamaniyah did not know what to say. People were about, as they always were, but he had rejected them. One of his kinsmen grieved quietly by himself: the youngest brother, handsome al-Adil who acted now and then as if he knew that she was not a boy. She sat mute in all that grief, and listened because she could think of nothing else to do. She could not mourn a man whom she had hardly known. But she could share the sorrow, a little.

The sultan seemed hardly to know that he wept. His coat was ragged where he had torn it in ritual grief. His beard, of which he had always been so fastidious, was frayed and torn. He looked as if he had forgotten sleep.

Yet he smiled at her, sudden and warm. "You didn't come here to hear me chant dirges. Did you bring your Khamsin?"

"Always, my lord," she said. And her eunuch, and her handful of mamluks, and one who was not a mamluk at all.

"Ride with me," said the sultan.

He did not ask more of her than her company, and perhaps a tale of that oddity who was her stallion. She had told him of the day when Khamsin chose her over a mare and a rival; it had become one of his favorite tales. She had even heard him tell it to a gathering of emirs. They had been most polite, and most politely incredulous.

"Ah well," he always said. "We know truth when we tell it."

Now he was quiet. Sad, a little, but less than he had been. She made no effort to trouble his peace. This was her own peace, to ride her stallion, to be at the side of her sultan, with small attendance, and no walls to bind them. She watched his face ease, the farther they rode from Cairo. She won a shout of laughter in a swift mad gallop, a pounding halt, a flash of Khamsin-temper.

They sat their snorting mounts and grinned at one another. They did not speak. There was no need.

The rider met them on the far side of the Old City. He came at a great pace, swaying astride a racing camel, flailing with the goad. Ill news, Zamaniyah knew, her lightness fading and dying. The sultan waited. He did not move to meet the messenger: dreading it, surely, as much as she. There was death in that urgency. But whose, if not Ayyub's?

"Nur al-Din," the man gasped as his camel lurched roaring to a halt. "Syria—sultan—" He drew a deep gulping breath. "Nur al-Din is dead."

The sultan stiffened as if he had taken a blow in the vitals.

"Nur al-Din," said the messenger, hammering at him. "Dead in Syria of a sickness. His son claims the sultanate; or his regents claim it for him."

The sultan swayed. "Dead?" he asked, barely above a

whisper. "The Light of the Faith? The one who was my overlord? Dead? But he was never going to die."

"No more was your father."

Zamaniyah had said that. Her brain had nothing to do with it.

The messenger looked from one to the other, uncomprehending. The sultan's voice snapped him about. "How did he die?"

The man's relief was palpable. This, he could answer. "There was a festival in Damascus, O my sultan, a great occasion: the circumcision of the lord's only son, the Prince Ismail. On the day after it, the lord rode at polo as he was fond of doing. He rode as well as ever, until he missed a stroke. That cast him, my lord, into such a rage as none had ever seen in a lord so clement and so pious. He roared like a lion; he shattered his mallet; he fell down foaming on the ground.

"His people were frozen in shock, until one or two dared to calm him, to help him up, to coax him from the field. His fury passed as inexplicably as it had come; but it left him weak and ill. The doctors would have bled him to release the evil humors; he would not let them. A man of threescore years, he decreed, is not to be bled. Even in his sickness he awed them. They yielded: to their lasting sorrow. He lingered for two hands of days, sinking ever more swiftly. Then at last he died, commending his soul to Allah and his son to his loyal princes."

"May the peace of God be upon him." The sultan was white under the weathering of cheek and brow. His hands clenched and unclenched upon the reins; his eyes burned, as if even tears were too little for his grief. "My uncle, my father, my sultan. All gone. All dead. And I..." His breath caught. A sob, perhaps. Or a gasp of laughter.

Again he startled the messenger. "Who rules in Syria?"

"No one, my lord. Or everyone. Ismail is a child. The nephews of the sultan are caught in disarray: Zangi makes no move, nor has he the power to make one. Saif al-Din mourns his uncle's passing in a flood of wine and a fever of conquest; but he conquers in the east, and pays no heed to Syria. The emirs array themselves as they will, with one or another, or with none at all. The Franks, it is said, are closing in for the kill.''

''Indeed they would,'' said the sultan.

''The lady,'' said the messenger, ''the sultana, some call her—she tries to act on behalf of her son. But she is a woman; she lacks the force of a man.''

Perhaps the sultan glanced at Zamaniyah. He did not smile as he sometimes did when people spoke of woman-weakness in her presence. She could not read his face at all.

She heard his sigh even over the wind. ''Back,'' he said. ''Back to Cairo.''

He would not let her go. Her mamluks, yes, not all of them willingly. Jaffar was escort enough: better than any man knew.

She was not needed for anything that had to do with governing. There were men and to spare for that; and they flocked to grief like vultures to carrion. Nor did he want a servant. He had slaves in plenty, and wellborn pages, and the mamluks of his guard in their sun-colored coats. It seemed that he simply wanted her there, sitting in a corner, saying nothing, watching everything. Her father came with the rest of the emirs, greeted her with affection if with some little surprise, gave her the gift of forgetting her. The others were slower; but what brought them here was both new and mighty. Her presence dwindled to nothing beside it.

Sometimes, in the long hours, the sultan wept. ''I loved him,'' he said more than once. ''I admired him more than any man I ever knew. He was all that was admirable. A true Muslim, a true king: strong, and just, and merciful; obedient to the laws of the Prophet, whom God has blessed and granted peace, and to the will of God. All that I strive to be, he was.''

But then he would harden. His eyes would glitter. He would say through gritted teeth, ''He was my lord and my curse. He bade me rule, and then he forbade me; he acknowl-edged me his equal, and demanded that I pay him tribute. From his palaces in Syria he dreamed that he knew how best to rule in Egypt: he who had never set foot in Cairo. He pricked me with needles; he cut me with knives. He tormented me beyond endurance.

"And if he had not died by the mercy of Allah—if he had lived—he would have come to cast me down. His armies were gathered. His war was readied. First the lord of Egypt, then the King of Jerusalem: so did he intend to conquer all, and be emperor in truth.

"And yet," he said, as if the words were torn from him, "I loved him."

Love, Zamaniyah thought as she listened, and enmity. Both together; both the lot of kings.

This king mourned his master, and yet he was glad. At last, all in a stroke, he was free.

Free for what?

"Wait," said his counselors. "See. The jackals in Syria will quarrel over the lion's leavings, and wear themselves down in doing it; and perhaps some of them will die."

"Egypt is enough," others said, "and safe at last from the greed of Syria. When they come again, if they come, let them find a barred gate and an impregnable wall."

"They will come!" a third party shot back. "Unless Egypt moves first. Even now the Lord Turan-Shah seizes the wealth of the Yemen and gathers to advance upon Arabia. Why waste his victories? Crown them. Take Syria swiftly, before another Nur al-Din can rise and grow strong and set us under his heel."

"There is another Nur al-Din," one of the emirs pointed out. "He named his son his heir."

Lips curled; heads shook. "A child. Eleven summers old, subject still to the care of eunuchs and women. He counts for nothing."

"Who holds him, holds the right to rule in his father's stead."

Eyes narrowed. Men murmured, speculating.

"And what of Egypt?" a sudden clear voice demanded. Zamaniyah heard it with a small shiver. Her father's enemy stood as far from her father as his own will and the sultan's stewards could set him; that they shared these walls at all, measured the magnitude of the council.

Ali Mousa repeated his question. "What of Egypt? The prince plays at soldiers in Arabia; and well for us that he does, for his extravagances have drained the treasury dry. Byzantine hounds sniff even yet at our gates in the north; Nubians snarl in the south. In Egypt itself the people are barely reconciled to the rule of the Turk. Are your memories so short? Have you forgotten the conspiracy so lately broken, the rebels who would restore the old rule of the caliph? The ravens have barely picked the bones of those who dared it. Would you abandon all for yet another realm in turmoil?''

"A fine sermon," drawled a voice she knew as well as her own, al-Zaman settled at his ease among the emirs. "Preached most knowledgeably, and most loyally. Are you frightened, revered sharif? Do you dread the uncovering of a new conspiracy?''

Ali Mousa's response was silent: a thinning of the nostrils, a narrowing of the eyes. "O my sultan," he said with exquisite dignity, "perhaps Allah has willed that you rule in Syria as in Egypt. If that is so, then that is well. Yet now is not the time to move. Syria will settle itself, or it will shatter. Whichever befalls, you are here, with Egypt's strength behind you, strength which can only grow as you wait upon events. When their passage is clear to you, then may you strike, whether to fell a new and feeble sultan or to proclaim yourself lord of a lordless country.''

"Why go at all?" asked a small man in a very large turban, a scholar with ambitions toward government. "You are safe, and free of your overlord. You can rule in peace.''

"For how long? The Franks—''

"Snapping at Syria, as we should be. If by the malice of Iblis they seize it and turn upon us . . .''

"Allah forbid!''

"Egypt—''

"Syria—''

Zamaniyah's head ached. She rested it on drawn-up knees and sighed. How men could talk so much, to so little purpose, she would never know. And they accused women, scornfully, of precisely that. Could they never hear themselves?

If she peered sidewise, she could see the sultan. He had said nothing for a long while. His head was in his hand; perhaps he was not even listening.

The currents of debate had swirled away from him. Fac-

tions eddied, babbling. None seemed to notice that he was
not part of it. He was alone, forgotten.

Softly she settled at his feet. For a while he did not see her.
She was content. He needed presence, and silence; not
endless chatter.

When he spoke, she started. She had begun, all unwitting,
to drowse. "Are you tired?" he asked her.

She shrugged a little. "There will be time enough to
sleep."

"I should never have kept you. This is ill entertainment for
a young creature."

"Learning is like that," she said.

He raised his brows. "Have you learned anything here?"

"Oh, yes, my lord," she answered truthfully. "Much."

"What would you do if you were I?"

It was the sort of question he would ask. She swallowed a
sigh. "I don't know, my lord. There are too many choices; I
know too little. What do you want? To hold what you have?
To bow to a new overlord? To take the lordship for yourself?"

He frowned. She was cold, suddenly. It was hard to
remember what he was. He had always been gentle when she
saw him, more man than king. But he was not known for his
gentleness. He had killed the caliph's vizier—with his own
hands, people said. He had ordered the captivity of every
royal seed, male apart from female, female apart forever from
male. He had crucified the conspirators against him.

He was, when it came to the crux, sultan. And it was
dangerous to tell the truth to kings.

He did not order her flogged. He did not even rebuke her.
He rose; he smote his hands together. Even before silence had
the wits to fall, he said, "We thank you for your counsel. We
shall ponder it with all due care." He bowed to them, abrupt,
courteous, oblivious to protests. His guards hastened to attend
him. Without a word he strode from the council.

He pondered most duly and most deliberately. He sent messengers to the child prince, offering condolences, implying
loyalty. He gathered his army, wielded it in defense of his
domain. He made no move to set foot in Syria.

Allah rewarded him, people said. The Frankish king died
ignominiously after all his feats in battle, of a sudden sick-

ness; his son was a child and, more grievous yet for his people, a leper. The north and the sea were safe by force of arms; the south had yielded to the sultan's captains; the Yemen lay in the hands of his brother. Syria was weak and weakening.

"Ripe," said al-Zaman. "Ripe for the plucking."

Zamaniyah watched him partake hungrily of his first dinner in his own house since he left to ride with the sultan. He had taken a small wound or two, nothing for any but wives and servants to fret over; he was lean, bronzed, honed with fighting and hard riding. He always looked younger when he came back from the wars, even when they had gone less than well; as these, by Allah's mercy, had not. They were his greatest pleasure. Muslim wine, he called them.

He had brought gifts for them all. Hers was a coat of silk from Byzantium, and a sword, balanced for a smaller hand and a shorter arm than most, with a silver hilt. The blade came, he told her, from India, but the hilt had been wrought in Damascus.

"We'll be seeing its gardens again," he said, smiling at her. "I'm not here for long. The sultan is staying in camp with the army; he'll march again soon."

"To Syria?"

"To Syria." He grinned, showing his white teeth. He was a handsome man, she thought, taking pleasure in the sight of him; though it was pleasure alloyed with pain, and fear for him, that he must ride again to war.

He pulled her to him and set a kiss between her eyes. His own were glinting as they always did when he cherished a secret. "Now there, catling. Do you miss me so much?"

She nodded mutely. Her eyes, being woman's eyes, wanted to run over. Her mind would not let them; dried them, somewhat, with a flash of temper.

He kissed her again and held her tightly, smiling down at her, sparking mischief. "Do you know why we're going to Syria at last? It's happened—what all of us prayed for. Damascus has sent to the sultan of Egypt. In Allah's name, for the sake of the love that was between his lordship and the sultan of Syria, let him come to the aid of the realm. And so," said al-Zaman, "he shall."

"And you with him."

"Of course. Where else would I be?"

Here, she almost said. *Safe. With us.* She did not say it. Peace had never been his element.

His smile broadened once more into a grin. "Would you like to come with me?"

Her heart stopped. He had not said that. Oh, surely he had not said it. That he would take her to war.

"It's time," he said, "that you learned what all your training is for."

She swallowed, coughed. Her mouth was dry. "Will the army allow it?"

The light of mischief left him. He was cold again, hard again: the man the world knew and was justly afraid of. "The army will allow it."

She contemplated all the facets of a single word. *No.* She knew what he would do. Be angry. Strike her. Call her a coward. But, in the end, yield. Because at last he had gone too far; and she was his child. She could be as implacable as he.

"The sultan has given leave," he said.

"Willingly?"

"Honorably."

She sat motionless within the circle of his arm. Feeling her body. It was all a woman's now, more than she had ever thought it would be. Even her face was changing. Smoothing. Softening. A man would have to be very blind, or very obstinate, to take her for a boy.

I am a woman, she said in her mind, framing it with care, because he must hear it when she spoke it; he must understand. *I have been obedient. I have bowed to your will, as a woman must. But in this I cannot obey. A woman does not ride to war.*

Did she not?

Her mind uttered madness in Wiborada's voice. Zamaniyah was never the child her father could have wished for. But Wiborada—she would have reveled in this. And she was trammeled in the harem, and Zamaniyah was trammeled in the world, and never a hope of altering it.

Was there?

Would she fulfill her ancient threat, take refuge in the harem: even the harem of a husband? Could she?

She closed her eyes. Truth, now. She wanted what she had. Freedom. This was its price.

Was it so high? Men loved it, yearned for it. She was trained as well as any. She thought that she might have courage.

She had never prepared herself for this. She had never thought that her father would ask it. No man, even a madman, would trust in battle to a female.

And why not?

Wiborada's voice again, joyously heretical. All this time, and Zamaniyah had fancied that she was civilizing the barbarian; and the barbarian had been corrupting her. Making her think—by Allah, making her think as her father thought.

Maybe he was not mad at all. Maybe his nature was simply, and utterly, a barbarian's.

She laughed suddenly, startling him. "When do we go?"

Khamsin was appalled.

"I didn't want to," Zamaniyah said, "until I stopped to think. Why shouldn't I go to the war? I'm trained for it. I'm not afraid to die, I don't think."

He was. And he was terrified of pain. War hurt. It wounded; it left scars. It killed.

"I have Jaffar to take care of me. And my bow, and my new sword. And you. Now you can show them all what a warhorse you are."

He would show them all what a coward he was.

"Two years, now, since we began. Can you believe it? You've done splendidly. You have a gift, Al'zan says. You'll make us proud."

He bit her. She yelped, slapped. "*Ai!* Keep it for our enemies, idiot."

He shook his head and stamped. She refused to understand. She soothed what seemed to be his restlessness, and babbled of battles. She was going to cast her life away, and his own with it.

If he threw her, wounded her a little, enough to keep her from riding with the army . . .

He could not.

Wound himself?

Mar his precious skin?

Let another horse carry her? Entrust her life to some witless animal? Some beast who would never care whether she was safe in its saddle or fallen on the ground, nor set her life above its worthless own. He would die first.

As, indeed, he very likely would.

14

Drums beat. Banners whipped in the wind. Horses stamped, danced, cried aloud. In a roaring of laden camels and a clatter of weapons, the chosen of the sultan's army mustered for war. Seven hundred mounted men and one lone woman in her father's shadow, stiff in new armor, calming herself with her restive mount.

A small number for an army of Islam, but a brave one, and proud. Vanguard and rearguard shone in the yellow gold of the sultan's guard, mingled with the black and scarlet and sacred green of picked emirs, each under his own standard, and over all the black banners of Abbas. The rearguard was al-Zaman's to command. He ruled it easily, unblinded by the honor; his emirs and his soldiers minded him as well out of the sultan's sight as in it.

They prayed in their long lines, those who would go and those who would linger in the camp of the sultan's wars. The drums were, for this while, silent. The wind sang the louder above their bowed heads.

They rose in a wave of armed exultation. The drums rattled forth anew. *Mount*, they commanded. *Mount and ride*.

Khamsin's saddle was warm from the sun. Zamaniyah settled as deep in it as she could, taking her time about it, because she wanted to clap heels to his sides and bolt, toward Syria, toward Cairo, it did not matter.

The sultan faced his brother al-Adil who would rule Egypt in his name. They parted with dignity, with ceremony that betrayed nothing of sorrow. It was the lot of kinsmen who were princes, to meet most often only to part.

Zamaniyah had known it all her life, but she had never hardened to it. Jaffar was here, her best-beloved shadow; and the mamluks who seemed to have decided that they were hers; and Khamsin. But Al'zan was leagues away in Cairo, with all the servants who had startled her with weeping when she left them, and Wiborada veiled and grimly silent in the harem. Even the women had seemed dismayed that she was going, as if, after all, she had been more to them than resentment and unending scandal. All of them had shaped the greater portion of her world; and she might never see them again.

Hard to think of; but hard to dwell on, here in the sun, in the beating of the drums, in the singing of war songs and the chanting of the name of Allah. Her heart had leaped in spite of itself. Oh, they were a fine brave army; wonderful in the arrogance of their smallness. They would be enough, they and their sultan. All of Syria would fall before them.

'Allah!'' they shrilled. *'Allah-il-allah!''*

The drums quickened. The vanguard shifted, formed, began to move. Rank by rank, the army followed.

Heat. That was war. Dust; flies. Thirst slaked in grudging sips. Riding endlessly, relentlessly, from dawn to blazing noon to dusk. In this army there were no stragglers. They were the chosen of the sultan's chosen. If Syria would be theirs, it must be theirs swiftly, wholly, incontrovertibly.

"Eleven days from Bilbais to Busra." The men about al-Zaman's fire looked at one another and shook their heads. "I'd never believe it if we hadn't done it."

"The horses believe it," said one of the emirs.

"My backside believes it." The man who had spoken shifted and groaned most piteously. They all laughed.

One instructed him, in detail, in what to do with his backside. "We're here, aren't we? Busra's emir has an army waiting for us; and every Turk and Kurd and Bedu on this side of Syria is coming to back us. This war is ours. God is with us. Didn't we ride through the very kingdom of the Franks, in broad daylight, and camp in their demesnes, and never a one moved to stop us? Syria will fall like a ripe apple. We'll only have to open our hands."

"Allah willing," said al-Zaman, mindful of the honor of his position, and therefore of his piety. He took great care not to see the flask that went round, filled with what purported to be rosewater. It never went past Zamaniyah. His hand always managed, as if by sheerest chance, to direct it elsewhere.

She had never been overly fond of rosewater.

She clenched her teeth against a yawn. Her backside had reckoned every stride from Bilbais to Busra. She could count each separate muscle and bone. Her mind echoed with the question she would never fall so low as to ask. *Why? Why this of all the wars I might have been dragged to?*

Because, her father would have been sure to answer. It was time. It was always time when he decided that it was.

His men were paying her their highest compliment. They had forgotten that she was there. Strangers who came to share their fire were not enlightened as to the sex of the slender young person beside the emir.

Al-Zaman leaned toward her, touched her arm. "Go to bed," he said.

She never argued with eminent good sense. She returned his kiss, found a smile to answer his, made her protesting bones carry her to her tent.

For that much she was granted of her father's charity: she had a tent of her own, small but ample, pitched beside his and guarded by her mamluks. Once on the march, a soldier—drunk on forbidden wine, or led to folly by a wager—had tried to creep inside. He had greeted the dawn pegged to the ground outside the camp, his bowels spread temptingly to lure the vultures. No one since had dared to trouble her sleep.

Jaffar had water for her, and a basin unearthed from Allah knew where: the blessed luxury of a bath. He looked baleful, which meant that he was pleased with himself. "You are a wonder and a marvel," she told him solemnly, "and you are going to take your turn in it."

"After you," he said. And when she was blissfully clean and robed in clean linen and laid in bed, he folded his slender length into the basin and made excellent use of it.

She was tired beyond thought and somewhat beyond sleep. She watched. He knew, but he did not seem discomfited. He was not a Muslim, to trouble himself with modesty, though for her sake he had always been careful to remember it.

She yawned and settled her aches in something like comfort. If she closed her eyes, the ground beneath her pallet seemed to sway, as if she rode still astride Khamsin or one of her father's remounts.

At the thought, a smile hovered. Khamsin was a jealous companion. He hated it when she left him for another, though she did it solely for his sake, to spare his strength.

Jaffar finished his bathing. Lamplight caught the glitter of water in his tight-curled hair. The two soldier-slaves who guarded her came, eyes politely averted, and carried the basin away. She yawned again. Her eyelids were growing heavy.

She felt more than saw Jaffar slip out of the tent, as he did every night, to see that all was well about it. In a little while he would come back and lie in front of the flap, guarding her as he had ever since she could remember.

A quiet clamor rocked her on the edge of sleep. Voices hissing; a scuffle of feet. Before her eyes had well opened, she sat up, tensed, remembering against her will the stranger in her tent, locked in silent deadly struggle with Jaffar, wrapped in the stink of wine and man-sweat.

The flap burst open. She leaped for her dagger. A shape fell rolling at her feet. Armor, helmet, turban half unraveled; and Jaffar a shadow of wrath behind. He wound his hand in a coat that was the livery of her father's mamluks, hauled the culprit up, struck helmet and turban from a head as bright as gold.

Even in grim captivity, Wiborada could grin at Zamaniyah's expression. "Salaam," she said in her broad Frankish accent.

Jaffar let her go. She dropped to the carpet, flushed, breathing quickly, and completely unrepentant.

"This," said Jaffar with deadly quiet, "was standing guard in front of your father's tent."

Wiborada tossed her head with its crown of yellow braids, now somewhat disarrayed. "And so I should be still! You could at least have given me time to call in another."

"So," he said. "They all know. Dare I ask what sweetened it for them?"

"You do not!" She was whitely and beautifully angry. "If anyone answers for this, it will be I alone. I conceived it; I executed it. One man, or perhaps two, or three, abetted me in it, under duress."

"Indeed," said Jaffar.

"I am faithful to my master. I guard him!"

Zamaniyah caught her before she could fly at him. She was larger and heavier, but not yet blind with fury; she yielded, slowly, glaring terribly at Jaffar's immovable calm.

Zamaniyah stood over her and thought of screaming. Not overlong. There was no profit in it. "Why?" she asked at last, when she could trust her voice.

The damnable woman shrugged, smiled. "Cairo was a prison without escape. War, I have no fear of. And it was possible, and I wanted to, and maybe I can be useful. I know how to fight."

"Father will flay you alive."

"You won't tell him."

"I have to," said Zamaniyah. Her voice was as tired as she felt. "At home, at judicious intervals, that was one thing. This is war."

"I know that," Wiborada snapped. "Better than you."

"Do you?"

"I was with my father when your kind killed him."

"So," said Zamaniyah. "You have reason to betray us. You defy nature and the will of God that made you woman and slave; you deny Islam. And now you set yourself among armed men, standing armed over my father while he sleeps."

"Guarding him," Wiborada said, still angry, still defiant; but her eyes had widened. Perhaps she was beginning to understand what she had done.

Zamaniyah pulled on her coat, her trousers, her boots. She twisted her hair into the hasty semblance of a plait.

Jaffar gripped Wiborada's arm. She struggled, but he was stronger. She flung up her head. "Let me go! I'll go with you. I give my word."

The eunuch took no notice of her. "Let her go," said Zamaniyah. "But watch her."

That, he would obey. It angered Wiborada.

It was no more than she deserved. Zamaniyah waited until the Frank had retrieved the fallen helmet and covered her braids with it. Then she led them both into the night.

Al-Zaman had retired to his tent. He was awake still, unattended; puzzled to see his daughter, and disturbed at her disobedience. He greeted her with a frown.

She abased herself before him. That was unwonted. It startled the sharp words into flight and left him silent, scowling at her, seeming not to see the eunuch and the mamluk.

Which was precisely what she had prayed for. "Father," she said from the carpet at his feet. "Father, I have a confession."

She dared a glance. His scowl had turned to bafflement. "Are you ill?" he asked her. He turned on Jaffar. "What is this? What has happened?"

Zamaniyah answered before Jaffar could begin. "No, Father, I'm not ill. I'm only troubled. I've done something I shouldn't have done."

His eyes were full on her again. There was no anger in them, not yet. He waited for her to speak.

Her throat closed. He had not thought the worst of her. He trusted her.

She could spin a tale, tarry a little, escape. He would never know.

Damn her conscience. It held her there; it made her say, "I've never had a friend, Father. A man was not possible nor proper. A woman could never understand this that I am. I've been alone, and lonelier than I knew." He was listening. He did not try to silence her. She swallowed. Her heart was beating painfully hard. "But there was one . . . your Frankish concubine. Nahar."

"I had known that," he said, less rough than gentle. "I allowed it. I saw no harm in it."

"But you didn't know!" With an effort she muted her voice. "There was more to it, Father, than an evening or two of gossip in the harem. Whenever she won leave to go out—whenever she could elude her duennas—she used to ride with me. Dressed as I was, with her face covered. She was taken for one of my—for one of my mamluks.''

She stopped. She ventured to raise her head. He sat utterly still. His face was frightening: there was no wrath in it. There was nothing at all.

''How long?'' he asked at last, calm and cold.

''A year,'' she answered. She was shaking.

''And you never told me?''

''I didn't dare.''

He nodded once. ''Why do you tell me now?''

She drew a breath. Metal clattered behind her; a fierce and fearless voice rang in the heavy air. ''Because the concubine has gone too far.''

Wiborada stood uncovered, brightly defiant, even as she dropped down in obeisance. ''My lord, you must not punish your daughter. I made her take me riding with her. She never knew until now, that I have been riding with the army. That is my sin, and mine alone. She is not part of it.''

They had shocked him quite as much as Zamaniyah had feared. His face went livid; then it paled. His fists clenched and unclenched. He rose, as if the force of his wrath could not suffer stillness. He bulked above his daughter and his concubine.

The Frank had never learned humility, nor ever prudence. She rose to face him. She was as tall as he. ''My lord, I have done nothing dishonorable, save that I never asked your leave. You may beat me for that; I've earned it. But no more.''

His hand flew up. She braced herself.

The blow never fell. They both stared. Zamaniyah clung grimly to her father's arm. ''No,'' she said. ''I began it. I offered her what I had. I had no right.''

''You had every right!'' flared Wiborada.

Zamaniyah spun upon her. ''I had none! You were never mine to set free. And I did it. Keeping the secret. Because—''

''Because?'' said al-Zaman when she did not finish.

''Because she wanted it with all that was in her, and I who had it . . . I accepted it because I had no choice.''

The silence sang on a strange high note. Zamaniyah had never told the truth: never where her father could hear.

"She is what you wanted me to be; and you commanded that she be a woman as all the rest are women. She is bright and strong. The free air is her element. She should have been your heir; never I."

"Is it such a burden?"

His voice was rough. Zamaniyah shut her eyes. Her head shook. "I am what you command me to be. If it pleases you, I school myself to accept it."

She could feel Wiborada's contempt. She did not care. He accepted her submission. It was fit and proper; it calmed him.

But not wholly. He turned a deadly eye on Wiborada. She was his possession, and she had sinned. She had left the place ordained for her. She had mocked his pride.

She did not even know what she had done. Zamaniyah should have hated her, or at the least despised her. Her head was high, her back unbending. Whatever she had learned of pleasing her master, she had forgotten. She was all Frank, all insolence.

He could flog her, sell her, even kill her. She, most surely, would spit in his face. She was gathering herself for it. Zamaniyah could tell. She looked as Zamaniyah all too often felt.

Zamaniyah caught her father's hand, pulled him about. "No, Father. I beg you. She doesn't know. She was born barbarian; and she was raised as her father's son." That brought him up short. Zamaniyah prayed Allah to forgive the half that was a lie, and kissed the hand that made no effort to escape. "May I have her, Father? She's like me. And she's loyal. Didn't we ride through the Franks' land? None of us knew that she was there, and she stayed with us. She never tried to escape."

His face did not soften. "She has dishonored our house."

"How, Father?" Zamaniyah asked, pressing not too hard, holding his hand to her cheek. "She's been doing no more than I do; and more modestly. She's always veiled her face." She raised her eyes to him. "Please, Father. What better companion for me? She'll guard my honor as she guards my body."

At long last Wiborada perceived the game. She seized his free hand, dropped to her knees. "Truly, my lord, I will. I will guard her with my life." And when he said nothing:

"Am I so appalling? Your daughter is as she is, by your command. May not your concubine be like her?"

They had trapped him neatly. His eyes glittered upon them both; his hands tightened to pain. Zamaniyah steeled herself to bear it. Wiborada had paled, but she was silent.

Abruptly he let go. Neither would stoop to cradle her throbbing fingers. A smile's very distant kin touched his mouth; he shook his head. "Wise men warned me when I began this dance. Let me loose one woman on the world, and all of them would clamor to follow."

"No one else had the wits or the will," muttered Zamaniyah.

She bit her wayward tongue. He had not heard, or he chose not to hear. "This one, O my dearest mistake, you may keep. But no more. I will not have my harem turned to a company of cavalry."

She bowed to the carpet.

"Nor," he said, "will she ride with you to battle. You must; honor demands it. She must not."

"She will not," said Zamaniyah.

"See that she does not." He flicked his hand. "Go." But when his daughter rose, he pulled her to him, kissed her. Then he let her go.

Wiborada did not follow. Zamaniyah had not expected that she would. Al-Zaman's anger would die, or it would smolder unregarded; but Wiborada would do her best to soothe it, now that Zamaniyah had allayed the worst of it with words and wickedness.

Words were never a Frank's strength. Zamaniyah laid her weary body down amid the blessed quiet of her bed, and let herself fall into sleep.

Khamsin drowsed uneasily in the horselines. The Bedouin kept their horses by their tents, even within them: wiser by far than this, and more respectful. Here he was roped into a line, beset with stinging flies, and laid bare to any wind that blew. The spirits of the air liked to mock a captive beast, particularly if they scented magic on him.

Allah and Iblis were not finished with him. An emir had charge of the beasts and the baggage. It was a great charge, for without them the army could not live, still less come to battle. The sultan would never give it to any but a man of both wisdom and experience. Both of which, Ali Mousa had in plenty.

He liked to walk the lines of an evening, to see that all was well, horses and camels fed and watered, hobbles and leads secure, guards at their posts. Tonight the destiny of God had stopped him by Khamsin, hearing a guard's whine of complaint. And having resolved it, with little enough gratitude from its maker, he had lingered yet a while, as if in thought.

He looked thin and drawn, and much older than two years might account for. A scent of old sadness lay upon him.

Khamsin strained against halter and lead, stretching them to the borders of pain; but he could touch his father's arm, rest his head lightly against it. It was all the comfort he could give.

Ali Mousa accepted it. He even smiled and fondled Khamsin's head, saying nothing, letting presence suffice. In a little while he went away. And Khamsin, whose every fiber ached for sleep, could barely pass the borders of it.

Past Busra the pace slowed almost to an amble. The army had swelled; it was a proper army now, wide enough to fill narrow valleys, long enough to seem immeasurable from the midst of it.

It was neither long nor wide enough to sunder devoted enemies.

A small thing began it. One of the baggage camels was given to straying; she had a way of shedding her burden and bolting for freedom. Her handlers knew her: they kept her on a lead, but she was clever in slipping it. A day out of Busra she broke it altogether. Because escape was clear from the line of the army full across the west of Syria, she veered eastward, tangling the baggage in confusion, and plunged squealing into the heart of the rearguard.

They lost a good half day of marching, and a horse that, evading the camel, caught its foot in her trailing lead and went down; and its rider was much bruised and battered, and most outraged.

The commander of the baggage train and the commander of the rearguard faced one another that night across the sultan's fire. They were exquisitely, poisonously courteous.

"The very least," purred al-Zaman, "which my lord emir

might deign to bestow, would be the life of a worthless camel in return for the life of a queen of coursers, a mother of champions, the light of her master's eye.''

Ali Mousa's head was high, his eyes dark and haughty. ''My lord Turk may be pardoned his ignorance in demanding the execution of a royal beast, a swift runner, a bearer of mighty burdens, a beauty and a thoroughbred: and for a cull of a lesser stable, who was suffering sorely from the strain of the march. Yet the rider has suffered; he shall be consoled from my own purse and from my own mounts.''

That was a noble recompense. Al-Zaman bowed to it. But he said, ''My lord emir is most generous, but most unwise. He suffers the sinner to live unharmed. He offers her no punishment. Tomorrow, perhaps, she will essay a new escape. What then if no beast dies, but a man? Can my lord offer a man in place of a man?''

''If needs be,'' replied Ali Mousa, ''yes.''

Al-Zaman smiled with purest pleasure. ''For a camel, lord emir? For a camel you will threaten the lives of our men? Is it an Arab doctrine, sir? Or is it a Shiite heresy?''

''I am quite as orthodox as you,'' replied Ali Mousa.

Breaths caught. Al-Zaman's smile never wavered. ''Ah then, lord emir. Perhaps it is merely your way. A man's life is little enough to pay for a good beast; if he be a Turk, so much the better. So much the fewer of us to vex your sacred peace.''

''Peace is to be desired, if it be peace from enmity that has no end and no foundation.''

''Before I saw your face,'' said al-Zaman, soft almost to silence, ''I had sons.''

''I am not answerable for the folly of children.''

''Nor, I presume, for the folly of camels. I understand, my lord emir. You answer for nothing, to no man; perhaps not even to God. Are you not of the lineage of the Prophet, may Allah shed blessing and peace upon him? Are you not above the angels?''

''Certainly,'' said Ali Mousa, ''I am neither a fool nor mad.''

Steel rang. Al-Zaman's sword was out. Ali Mousa's leaped to meet it.

* * *

Zamaniyah looked from face to face round the circle. They were like men at a cockfight: eyes glittering, eager, reckoning stroke and stroke, casting wagers on the victor. The sultan made no move to stop it. He was not there. Need had called him away; and his deputies were as greedy as the rest for a taste of blood.

She set her teeth. She slid between two burly emirs, under the arm of a third. They barely noticed. The enemies stood face to face, nearly body to body, locked in a perfection of hate.

She thrust herself between them, braving steel, braving the white heat of rage. They moved in the concord of hatred, lowering blades, flinging up empty hands to cast her aside. She braced her feet; their hands met, locked, recoiled. They stood still. The reek of their anger was like hot iron.

She bowed as well as she could, with as much respect as she could muster. "My lords, have you forgotten? The army rides to war. Its commander needs you both. Would you have him lose his war so that you may win yours?"

They did not want to hear it, and never from her. She made them hear it. "If the sultan were here, he would never allow this. Will you give him cause to despise you both?"

She cast her dice. She bowed again, backed away. "Your pardon, my lords. I overstep myself. If you will draw blood, I pray you draw it quickly, before the sultan comes to stop you."

She turned her back on them and walked away. She prayed that no one could see how she trembled.

There was silence behind her. The emirs let her pass. She yearned to look back, but she must not. That would be a surrender.

Only when she was out of the light could she turn. The space about the fire was empty. The voices that began to speak were none of them the enemies', and none of them edged with rancor.

Her knees nearly gave way. An arm about her shoulders held her up. She looked into her father's face. It was grim, but it was not suffused with rage. He said nothing. She did not try to make him speak. Mutely, side by side, they walked back to their tents.

15

Zamaniyah had kept the feud from turning anew to blood. Barely. It abated not at all. Certain of the emirs, whether at the sultan's command or of their own will, kept the enemies well apart.

Little good it did. Al-Zaman had begun to brood again, blackly, as he had not since his sons were killed. Wiborada slept in his tent still, but it was only that. "He doesn't want me," she said, sharp with anger and hurt. "All he wants to do is pace and snarl and curse the Egyptian."

It was all he did when he was not riding or being emir. Zamaniyah could divert him, sometimes, for a little while. Less as they rode deeper into Syria, and met no enemy, and gained both numbers and strength. Damascus fell to the show of arms and to the sultan's largesse: the queen of the cities of Syria with its orchards and its sweet waters, and no man in it bold enough to withstand the upstart out of Egypt.

Victory so easily won only fed the rivals' rancor. "We need an honest fight," said Wiborada.

In Damascus she had not seen fit to take back women's dress; and al-Zaman cared too little to compel her. She was not concealing her face any more than she must. Here in the stable of the house which the emir had claimed, she bared even her head, her hair in plaits like Zamaniyah's, her eyes interested as Zamaniyah fretted over one of Khamsin's shoes. "Is it loose?" she asked.

"It wants to be." Zamaniyah let it go. Khamsin was restive, shifting from foot to foot, trying to chew on the posts of his stall. He calmed infinitesimally under her hand. "Maybe we'll get a fight," she said as she combed his mane. "The Syrian sultan's heir is in Aleppo, walled in defenders and defying our lord. We'll be marching there in a day or two."

"Will Saladin"—she always mangled his name so—"will your sultan bow to the prince and rescue him from his wicked viziers, or will he stop pretending and take the kingdom?"

"Salah al-Din Yusuf," said Zamaniyah with precision, "believes that a land requires a man of experience to rule it; that a child under regents of little competence can only weaken, and perhaps destroy it."

"Saladin wants Syria," Wiborada translated, incorrigible. "Syria seems to want him. God knows, he's paid them enough. My father used to say that generosity was all very well, but it were best begun at home."

"You people are barbaric," said Zamaniyah.

Wiborada was not at all insulted. "Some of us know when to stop."

Zamaniyah leaned on Khamsin's neck. Suddenly she was very tired. "I wish my father did."

"Battle will distract him," said Wiborada. "Honest war and an honest enemy: give him those, and he'll forget his old ranklings."

"I hope so," said Zamaniyah.

The Frankish woman was wise enough, Khamsin supposed. If it were wisdom that he waited in sweating terror, with Zamaniyah on his back trying her utmost not to tremble; and al-Zaman beside them on his nerveless grey stallion, awaiting the signal to attack. If he brooded now, he brooded upon the enemy: a walled town, a broken gate, a bristle of defenders.

Their own line had no order to it that Khamsin could see. That it had two flanks and a center, he knew: he had heard people speak of it. He saw only a mass of men and beasts, a glitter of weapons and helmets, a restless eddy and swirl about no common center.

A clear voice rose up to heaven. "God is great! God is great! There is no god but God, the Muhammad is the Prophet of God! Come to prayer, O ye Muslims! Come to prayer!"

Drums beat, sudden and swift and fierce. Men's voices shrilled above the muezzin's wail. *"Allah-il-allah! Allahu akbar!"* Swords flashed out, up. Arrows flew. The tide of Egypt swept upon this small islet of Syria.

There were no limits to terror. It mounted and mounted and mounted. It swelled from pain into sheerest, starkest exhilaration. He cried aloud. Zamaniyah's voice echoed him, thin and high. Her arrows sang above his head. His feet bore them both where her will, his madness guided. Forward, spurning earth. Forward into death's maw.

This was the mightiest prayer of Islam. Holy war. War that is holy, just war, war in the name of one's God and one's Faith and one's sultan.

Charge met charge with the clangor of steel on steel. Horses screamed in rage and in agony. The air throbbed with the iron sweetness of blood.

Zamaniyah thrust her bow into its saddle-sheath. It slapped Khamsin's side; he bucked lightly, offended. Her sword rang from its scabbard. They waded in a sea of steel. He leaped, struck, slashed with teeth and heels. Bodies shrieked and reeled and fell.

It was nothing, this battle. A mob, armed. A city, hostile. Had he not seen it in Cairo? and he all but alone then, unarmed, unready; but walled now in army, a flood of shrieking, slashing, steel-toothed champions. They were splendid. They were God's own. They were victorious.

Jaffar had thought that he had borne all that a human creature need bear, and somewhat over. He had been a perfect innocent. He had never sent his mistress off to battle. He had never stayed behind in his proper place, the servant's place, on guard over her tent; and known through every instant that she could be dying, now, while he kept useless watch over trifles.

Nor could he suffer in merciful solitude. Ah, no. The

master's tame Frank had to plague him with her presence. Her substantial, stone-still, ostentatiously sullen presence.

"You look like a panther," she growled, "prowling. Can't you ever sit still?"

"No!"

She gratified him, slightly. Her eyes widened at his vehemence. His mind took the measure of her. Bleached corpse, stone-eyes, straw-hair, hideous. White, gold, eyes the deep pure blue of lapis, face carved in ivory, rare and unflawed beauty. Even in mamluk livery. Even scowling.

He, as beautiful among his own kind as was she among hers, as hideous here as she would have been to his slender ebony people, met scowl with furious scowl. "How can I sit still? She could be dead."

"I could be fighting beside her."

His head tossed, contemptuous. "What use would you be? You'd never be thinking of her."

"And you would?"

"Always."

Her scowl smoothed to a broad mime of astonishment. "By the saints! How you love her!"

"She is my mistress."

The Frank laughed, loud and mocking, barbarian. "Oh, certainly she is." Her eyes narrowed. "You couldn't really? Could you?"

He could have killed her. It would have been simple. She fancied herself a warrior. He was one. And no one knew; no one but Zamaniyah.

He sat by the tent's flap and smiled his sweetest smile. "Would you truly like to know?"

She had no shame, and precious little fear. "People tell stories. They say your kind aren't all alike. Some of you have enough for the purpose."

His smile widened to a panther-grin. "If I did, would I tell you?"

"Of course not," she said. She clasped her knees and rocked. Movement. At last. He almost laughed. "What would her father do if he knew?"

Jaffar did laugh then. "What makes you think he doesn't?"

"But—" she said. "But he—you—she—"

"I was bought for her. Because I am what I am. Because a

fat capon could never guard her as she of all women must be guarded. Our kind are valued, O innocent. Some of us rise high. The one who wards the little prince of Syria, who rules the kingdom in the child's name—he's one of us. Didn't you know?"

Even ignorance could not shame her. "You want no more than Zamaniyah."

"Should I want more?"

"There's power," she said. "Riches. Freedom to revel in them."

He spread his hands. "What are they? Will they give me back what is gone? Will they free me from death?"

"Death is better than life."

"Is that why you evade it so cleverly?"

She hissed at him. "I would be free."

"Would you? You could have been. You need only have walked out of camp in the Franks' country."

At long last she flushed. Her eyes darted. "Where would I have gone? My father is dead. Others would long since have taken our lands. What could I expect but beggary and scorn?"

"What," he asked, "indeed?" She glared at her knotted fingers. He contemplated his own. "I think you did want to go. I think you pondered it, long and cruelly hard, and chose what you have. There are flaws enough in it, and Islam is never the Faith for you, and your man is hardly a tender young lover; but he is, as much as any man can be, yours. So is my mistress mine.

"We do choose," he said, "in the end. Even when we hardly know what we have chosen."

"No more do they know. We're slaves. Bought fidelity. We're nothing to them, unless we vex their peace."

"And then they forbid us to die with them."

"Yes," she said. "Yes!"

Zamaniyah did, after all, come back. Alive; whole, as far as he could see; mastering her demon of a horse. There was blood on her armor, on her sword. She was greenish pale, although she smiled, dismounted with her wonted grace, accepted willingly Jaffar's entirely unwilled embrace. He clutched her blindly, babbling nonsense, shaking her and railing at her and clutching her again. "Never," he said. "Never leave me behind again. Never!"

No matter that he had chosen it, because it was his duty. He was beyond reason.

Briefly enough. He let her go, cheeks burning. "Mistress. I didn't—"

"I missed you, too," she said. No one else could have heard how her voice shook. She held out her hands, stiffly, as if they did not belong to her. "I'm all blood. I'm supposed to be clean. I have to go back. Father—the sultan—"

"Did they command you?"

Her eyes flickered. "There's so much still to do. Khamsin—"

"I have Khamsin," said Wiborada, who knew him well enough to ignore his flattened ears and shaking head. She led him protesting away.

Jaffar led his mistress protesting to bath, bedgown, bed. He had almost to sit on her to keep her there. But her body had more sense than she; it conquered her before she knew what it had done.

She kept him by her, holding his hand in her small cold one. In the tent's dimness, lamplit, her face was thin and pinched. "Have you ever killed anyone?" she asked.

He nodded.

"Does it get easier? The more you do it?"

"Some say it does."

She shivered and clutched his hand. "I don't want it to. I want to remember what it is, and how it is, and what it does to souls. I never want to forget."

It would have been easy to turn his hand. To fill it with the new and startling fullness of her breast. To know what it was that a man could have.

He sighed invisibly. Even a eunuch, it seemed, could be a fool for love.

She did not know. His fingers were limp under hers, oblivious to the lure of her, to the beauty that was growing in her, slowly, surely, wondrously. Pain was shaping it, fining it.

Let no one know, he prayed to any god who could hear. Let no man see, and rouse to lust, and take her away.

"You should remember," he said. "But not too much. Not beyond bearing."

"It should be unbearable. It has to be." Her fingers had

warmed upon his, fever-hot. "War is not holy, Jaffar. War is horror."

He bowed his head to wisdom.

"It's a madness," she said. "Blood is beautiful: so red, so bright. It leaps in fountains. It enriches the earth. But death . . . death is blood when it has dried. Death is hideous."

She was beautiful, living, drifting on the borders of sleep. She was slow to cross them. Dreading, surely, what waited there. Dreams; horrors.

It was bitter to see, in her who had had the art of dreamless sleep. He stroked her hair with gentle fingers, and murmured words in his own tongue. His mother had spoken them over him when he was small: a spell, very old, very strong; a ward against ill. Inch by reluctant inch she yielded to exhaustion. He watched nightlong, guarding her body as his words guarded the gates of her dreams.

The dead wandered the field of their slaying, dim shapes, bewildered, bewildering. Why did they linger? Could not an angel have been spared to snatch them to Paradise? They were not supposed to wander thus, lost, drifting shadow-frail across the world of the living.

They seemed not to see one another, or the men who labored in the aftermath of battle. Perhaps they could see Khamsin. They moved aside as he passed, although they made no move to evade the woman who led him. She walked through one shadow warrior: terrible to see, her ripe humanity filling for a moment the shape of a ghost. Then they flowed apart, the dead questing for he knew not what, the living for something other than the horselines. Those were well behind.

She was not like Zamaniyah. She did not waste speech on beasts. Her hand was hard on his bridle, not cruel but not gentle; simply unfeeling. She was wiser than to try to ride him, though there might have been purpose in that. A mamluk leading a horse was a common enough sight after a battle. Horses lost their riders, ran free, were captured and taken to the captors' masters for counting and claiming.

He could have wished that she had thought to rid him of the saddle. It itched abominably where he had sweated; he thought there might be a gall beginning. Zamaniyah would have the woman's hide if she knew.

He was thinking of it. But first he wanted to see what she was up to. He had suspicions; as yet they were no more than that.

They passed the fallen gates of the town. Guards called out a challenge. Wiborada answered in her huskiest voice. "The Emir al-Zaman. Have you seen him?"

Her livery was her passport. They peered at it, nodded, pointed. "Yonder," they said.

It was simple, once one knew. The sultan must have been on his way to the citadel to treat with its garrison, which had refused to fall with the fall of the town. In the heart of the market, empty now, its stall shuttered or swept away altogether, he had paused. Two of his emirs confronted one another, both mounted, both armed, both bristling. Men of the sultan's guard gripped their bridles firmly, despite fierce resistance. A crowd of soldiers milled and muttered. Their mood was venomous.

Khamsin could have groaned aloud. His father was in a white rage. His mistress' father was in a red one. "This man," grated al-Zaman, "interferes with the execution of my duty."

"My duty," said Ali Mousa, "is to gather what I may of provisions for the army, and to pay a fair price as you, my lord, have commanded. This man has attempted to seize and sequester a large portion thereof for his own use."

"I take my proper share for myself and my command. Else," said al-Zaman, "for your malice, we would have none."

"I gather and divide as my sultan ordains," the sharif said stiffly.

"Oh, aye! And a little over for everyone, but for what is mine, a bare sufficiency—and that of soiled goods, weeviled flour, meat run to maggots."

"You receive no more and no less than any other emir. But always you strive to seize more, to take the best and leave the worst for the others; and you feign that you have done nothing. And that, sir, is common thievery."

"Thievery!" al-Zaman cried. "And what is it that you do, you son of a Frankish dog?"

The sultan had been trying in vain to break in upon their battle. They wrenched at reins, spurring toward one another with swords drawn. He snatched a spear from one of his guards and hurled it. Their mounts shied. The spear buried itself to the haft in the ground before the dancing hoofs.

The sultan followed it. His anger was rare, and all the more deadly for that. He beat back their swords. He shouted at them. *"Enough!"* They gave way, snarling still, but shocked into the beginnings of sense. "Are you my emirs or my enemies? What word of God or Prophet sets you free to wage your war in the midst of mine?"

"This offspring of a Turkish camel—" Ali Mousa began.

"This child of an Egyptian ass—" snarled al-Zaman.

The sultan roared them into silence. "I will not have it! You will fight for me or for yourselves. One or the other. Choose!"

They glared at one another. Their men shifted, restless. The sultan wheeled his horse about. "There shall be but one war in Syria. Mine. If you would pursue your own, you shall pursue it elsewhere. Serve me or leave me. *Choose!*"

The air rang. The enemies were rigid, quivering just visibly, hating. Their eyes burned upon the sultan; upon the town which they had helped to take; upon each other.

Slowly they blinked. Slowly, slowly, they sheathed their swords.

The sultan was not satisfied. "While this war endures, you will not indulge your enmity; or you depart in dishonor. Will you swear?"

They swore. Low and hard, but clear enough for that.

The sultan nodded once, brief and sharp. The anger was taut still in his face. He saw them go, each to his separate duties, each to his separate forces. Then at last he continued his march to the citadel.

Khamsin braced himself to break free. But the Frank had seen enough. She did not try to impose herself upon her master; she turned back, her hand no gentler on his rein for that he came willingly.

He would have run if there had been any wisdom in it. He wanted his peace, his handful of barley sweetened with mutton fat, his brushing and his freedom from bridle and saddle. He did not want to be Hasan whose loyalties were all torn anew. He wanted to be plain witless Khamsin.

He checked, jibbed as the woman wrenched him forward. It was Hasan who had been the witless one; whose fidelity had never been to any but himself. Khamsin was the one who suffered agonies.

It was not supposed to be like that. He was an animal. He was simplicity made substance.

He tucked in his head, speeded his pace a fraction. The woman, surprised, shifted her grip. In the instant of almost-freedom, he snatched the bit and bolted. Her cries diminished behind him.

Let her rage. He knew his place, as she had chosen not to. Once free of her, he settled to a trot, making his way toward the lines and the grooms and the pampering which he had richly earned.

16

Damascus was the door to Syria, the lesser cities the posts of
its lintel; but Aleppo was the key. Here had been the capital
of Nur al-Din's kingdom. Here his son had made his stand;
here gathered the princes who had vowed never to serve
Yusuf. He had offered them clemency. They responded with
naked steel.

The land about the city seemed wan and old, a plain of
dust and of bitter wind. Low dun hills rose up in it; a little
river watered it, the merest trickle beside the great ocean of
the Nile. The city lay between, a circle of walls under the
lowering sky, and looming out of them like a mountain out of
the sea, the sheer and sudden crag of its citadel.

Towns, Khamsin was learning, were only the nut. Citadels
were the meat. The battle before Homs, of which even yet he
did not know whether to be proud or ashamed, had won no
more than the town; its fortress had fallen only to a month's
determined siege.

He was seasoned now, he supposed. He was losing count
of his battles. They were all alike. Stark terror; running,
fighting, yelling; swelling exhilaration; and numb exhaustion

after. Whether by some twist of the Hajji's magic or by
the will of Allah, neither he nor his rider ever took a
wound.

She kept calling him valiant. He had no way to tell her that
it was not courage, it was panic. And being the idiot that he
was, he did not know enough to run away from his terror; he
ran full upon it.

He looked at the citadel of Aleppo and knew, quite calmly
and quite clearly, that he was mortal; that he could die. The
knowing did not frighten him. War was fearful. Fate was
fated.

Jaffar was not a Muslim. He had never learned to submit to
the will of Allah. When he slept, he dreamed death. When he
woke, he looked about him and saw death.

He tried to hide it from Zamaniyah. He told her, when she
pressed him, that his thinness and his grey pallor were his
body's hatred of the bitter Syrian winter: cold that no fire
could warm, rain that no tent could keep out. Perhaps she
believed him. She made him eat far more than he wanted.
She fetched him sweet things, dainties found the gods knew
where, bits of fruit and meat; even wine, because he was not
forbidden it, and it was strong, warmed with spices. She
hovered and fretted until he would happily have driven her
out. Or told her, flatly and most cruelly, the truth. *I dream
your death. I cannot stop dreaming it. It drives me mad.*

He did not say it. He followed her everywhere. If she
protested, she protested for his sake. He heard her out in
silence, and went on being her shadow, though thinner and
paler with each day that passed.

The sultan sat his horse before the gates of Aleppo. Robes,
turban, banner, all were black. His mail and his helmet were
gold. His mare was of that color called *al-ashab al-marshoush*,
the flecked grey, the color most favored of kings.

Zamaniyah, in black and grey steel, on Khamsin who was
the red of battle, sat not far from him. She had begun beside
her father, but Khamsin's restlessness or the mare's allure had
brought him, and his rider with him, among the sultan's
bodyguard. They, who knew her, made no move to prevent
her. One even smiled.

On the gates above them, weapons bristled. None moved to attack. This was a parley, and for the moment, if not amicable, at least not violent.

Of those on the gate who professed authority, only two mattered: the magisterially fat Turk who was the regent, Gumushtekin; and the small figure of the prince. The child spoke for himself. Well instructed, no doubt, but also well schooled. His voice was thin but clear. "Have you come to accept me as your overlord?"

"I have come to free you from ill counsel," the sultan answered, giving him no title as he had given the sultan none.

The boy's head turned from side to side, taking in his emirs, his elders, his impassive eunuch. He looked down again upon the sultan. "Is it ill counsel that bids me claim what is rightfully mine?"

"The claim and the counsel have brought no peace to Syria. Therefore the wisest of its princes sent to me, beseeching me to come to the kingdom's aid. Most of its people have welcomed me, and most without bloodshed. Why do you resist me, when I would do you naught but good?"

"If you meant me well, you would not stand here in arms."

"The arms are Syria's," said the sultan. "We would wield them in your name, if you would allow it."

All along the wall, men hissed and spat. The sultan did not waver. No more did the prince. "You want the kingdom for yourself," he said. "Go back. Go back where you came from." He raised a hand. A rain of arrows blackened the sky.

"Sharp," said the sultan, "and to the point."

He was not visibly discomfited, although an arrow had presumed to pierce his cloak as he retreated. He sat in the shelter of his tent while wind rocked the walls and a true rain beat upon the roof. His servants warmed him and his emirs with kaffé. Many of them were warm enough with anger or with outrage; one, lightly wounded, swore vengeance over and over as the surgeon dressed his hurt.

Zamaniyah sipped the sweet, scalding kaffé and tried not to shiver. She was wetter than she liked to be, and colder; until she thought of Khamsin roofless in the rain. Then her teeth chattered on his behalf.

"What will you do?" someone asked the sultan.

"Take Aleppo," he answered swiftly. "However long it takes me, however long the city holds against me, in the end it will fall."

"And the young pup?"

"He makes war on me. So be it. Allah knows which of us is better fit to rule."

He said it calmly, and unshakably. Some of the emirs seemed surprised. Either they were fools, or they were feigning it. She would not have liked to have a wager riding on either.

She was not a good soldier. She kept thinking of the wrong things. The Syrian prince could have been wise. He could have accepted Yusuf's regency; let it make peace in Syria, at little enough cost to himself; learned from it; and at last, when he was grown and strong and well able to rule a kingdom, claimed it for his own. Had not Yusuf himself done much the same?

He and his counselors had chosen war. No one seemed dismayed. Most of them were delighted. War was the strong choice, the man's choice.

Certainly steel was simpler than speech. If, all too often, no quicker, nor any more absolute.

Khamsin welcomed winter's passing, even knowing that, slowly as the siege went, he would have to face the furnace-heat of Syrian summer. Now, at the gates of spring, it was pleasant to sleep under the stars, or to idle under the sun while men labored over the siege engines, or on occasion to partake in a swift sortie. Sometimes Zamaniyah hunted for the pot, trying his speed against the gazelle or her archery against the birds of the air. Every day that she could, she took an hour to remind him of his training: the gentler art, the Greek mystery that took his body's own dances of joy and challenge and fear, smoothed and fined them, taught them cadence, transmuted them into art.

He was becoming a dancer. On a day of sun and wind she told him so, dancing a little herself for joy of it. He took joy to match, but in her presence, in the touch of her hand, in the scent of her hair as he nibbled it.

She went away. Reluctantly, he liked to think. But she was

wanted. In camp it was the custom that everyone who was not on guard should dine together, sultan and slave alike. They ate from the same pot, drank from the same jar, in the equality of war.

It was clever, he had heard someone say. A poisoner might hesitate if he lacked the certainty of dainties prepared expressly for the sultan.

Khamsin idled hipshot in his place, content for once to stand still, resigned to halter and lead. They had stopped trying to hobble him. He fought the damnable bonds; he found ways out of them; he turned on grooms who dared to try again. They were not fools, the horseboys of the army. They haltered him, pegged him in place, let him be. He tried not to envy the others who could wander at will. Some were very clever at outwitting their hobbles and straying far in search of grazing.

He thought more than once of being clever himself: pulling up his peg, finding a place that suited him—by the river, maybe, where the grass was sweet and water plentiful—and pegging himself down again. He had never quite dared to do it. There was always someone watching, or someone passing, or something to quell his courage.

It was quiet now, the wind a little gentler, a cloud or two circling coyly about the sun. Here at the army's back, away from the city, the guards spread wide. For every one who stood visibly at his post, a handful scattered among hills and hollows, alert for any scent of ambush.

Khamsin's nose had found and marked each one, for diversion, and because he could do it. They were eating: bread, mutton, a hint of oil.

His nose twitched. The wind had shifted a fraction. Something new drifted upon it. Something odd.

Human. But strange. Clean, as men went, clothed in clean—linen? Cotton? The strangeness overlaid it, part of it. Sweet yet pungent. Faint, but strong.

He snorted, sneezed. He knew that scent. Its name eluded him.

Magic?

Not—quite. Not wholly.

Out of one of the hollows where no guards were, men came. They were quiet, yet they advanced without stealth. He had never seen or scented them before. They all wore white, white headcloths drawn over their faces, swords and daggers white-sheathed and white-hilted.

He blinked. It was far from hot enough to draw a shimmer from the air, and yet these men seemed to flicker and blur. Out of the corner of his eye he could see them clearly. A straight stare turned them to a dizzy dance.

Instinct deeper than thought eased him from his taut and prick-eared tension, lowered his head, sent him ambling in search of one last unnibbled bit of fodder. The strangers paused just beyond his trampled circle. There were twelve of them and one. They were calm, unhasty, as if they belonged there; as if they had no fear.

He started, turned it to a stamp, a snap at a fly. There was an enchantment on them. None of the horses who were near seemed even to have scented them. No guard challenged them. A groom dozed in the tent of his cloak, oblivious, though when a stallion sidled toward a mare he was up at once and catching the stallion's halter.

His back was to the strangers. Their eyes measured him. Dark eyes, strange, as if they walked in a dream; but keenly, vividly awake. A fire seemed to burn behind them.

One of them, who seemed to lead them, nodded. Softly, swiftly, silent as cats, they glided toward the camp.

Khamsin's head snapped up. Their scent. Magic; and hashish.

And death.

The groom was caught up still in the stallion's resistance. Khamsin blessed him, and the wind, and Allah who had ordained it all. Quickly and as quietly as he could, he caught the peg in his teeth and tugged. It held. He dug in his feet and pulled. It yielded, twisted, leaped free. He rocked back on his haunches. He looked, he knew with the clarity of the hopelessly vain, absurd. He scrambled up the lead as best he might— swift, swift, no time to break it, none at all to cast it off. With the coil of it in his teeth, he bolted on the strangers' track.

They were all at dinner, all the army, gathered in and about the center and the sultan's tent. Khamsin stopped, dismayed. A man could have done what he had to do. A horse alone, unattended . . .

Already they had seen him. Fingers pointed. Someone shouted.

Thirteen white-clad figures moved among the ranks. They had divided. Like servants they carried jars, platters, mounds of flat bread. Their progress, always, was inward. To the center.

Khamsin drew the deepest breath he could with a mouthful of rope, gathered himself, and took the straight way.

Men rolled out of his path. Men staggered into it. He hurdled them. They snatched. He flung them off. Tumult surged before and behind him.

His eye fixed on one face out of all the gaping, yelling faces. One narrow, brown, big-eyed face; one that knew him and called his name. He plunged toward it.

Zamaniyah heard it first: an uproar on the fringes of the army. Then she saw him. Red horse, wandering blaze, tail flagged stiff and high as only Khamsin's tail could be. He had something in his mouth. Rope, coiled. Peg swinging, striking hands that stretched to halt him.

The men about the sultan had turned to stare. She was on her feet. Maybe she called the horse's name. She could only think that her father would be furious.

Khamsin swept his head about. The peg smote a white-clad servant in the face. Blood spattered. The man screamed, reeling, falling.

"No," she said.

People ran. Soldiers. Emirs. Servants. Did all the servants wear white? Did they all cover their faces? Did they all have such eyes?

Red ruin fell upon another.

Daggers gleamed.

Zamaniyah fought her way through knotted men. Khamsin was coming toward the sultan. Unless she stopped him. Unless . . .

One of the emirs swept out his sword. A Syrian. New come to them; newly sworn to the sultan's war.

Treachery?

"Hashishayun!" he bellowed. "Assassins!"

A servant leaped. Away from the mad stallion. Upon the

emir with his sword and his hate-mad face. Dagger out,
stabbing. Blood dyed white robes scarlet.

"Assassins!"

Khamsin reared over Zamaniyah. Her fingers snatched
mane. Briefly she flew. Spun. Dropped bruisingly to his back;
clamped legs to sweat-slick sides. He wheeled. The sultan's
face blurred past. Her sword was in her hand. White gleamed.
A dagger stabbed from it, the sultan full in its path, sword too
far to reach, raising the frail shield of a hand. She swung, the
stallion spun. Her sword caught, bit, wrenched free.

Her world stopped. The army roared and seethed. Twelve
Assassins and one, known and named for what they were,
died; died gladly, died crying the name of Allah. Two had died
by a stallion's doing. One lay dead at the sultan's feet,
headless, stretching even in death to take the life which he
had been sent to take.

She had done that. She, and Khamsin. Her arm alone could
never have struck that head from its neck.

"You knew," she said to the twitching red ear. "You *knew*."

Did he nod?

She looked at her notched and dripping sword, and up, at
the sultan. His face was stark white. She saluted him, bowing
over Khamsin's neck. "Your life," she said, "O my sultan."

17

Aleppo had done it. Bought Assassins; bargained for the sultan's death. Through a stallion's madness and an emir's swift warning, they had failed.

"Assassins do not fail," said the sultan. "There is no word for it in their dialect."

Zamaniyah would not have called him frightened. Wary, rather. Roused to prudence. Aware, at last, of what his title meant: the freedom, and the unending confinement. The power, and its price.

A doubled guard was the least of it. Even in sleep he wore mail.

"They have arts," he said. "They can come upon a man in his own castle, take his life without a sound, and depart invisible. Or they take the shapes of his most trusted servants, and surround him, and while he rests complacent, destroy him."

"Is it magic?" she asked.

"Some of it." He paced his tent. Eyes glittered in its corners: men of proven constancy, armed to the teeth. And one unarmed, an old man, long-bearded, in the green turban of the Hajj. A physician, perhaps, or a scribe, though he wrote nothing, only sat in silence, reading from a book. She had glanced at it, bowed in reverence. The holy Koran.

The sultan turned to face Zamaniyah. "Much of it is absolute trust in Allah. He defends them, they believe beyond all doubting. They perfect their faith with prayer and with the waking dreams of hashish, and with utter fidelity to their master. He has taught them that they may know Paradise in this world, while they live this life, if only they do their lord's bidding: betray whom he bids them betray, slay whom he bids them slay. And when they die, as is their deepest desire, they dwell there forever under the eye of God."

"Then there's no way to stop them?"

"I intend to. When Aleppo is mine. The heart of the madness dwells in Persia; but these were servants of the Syrian sect, of the stronghold of Masyaf, whose lord is called the Old Man of the Mountain. His heresy is Shiite, and the Shiites are strong in Aleppo; his own power is greater in this kingdom than any king should endure." His fist rose, hammered down. "I will stop him. I will set my foot upon his neck."

"Perhaps, my lord, you should rest content with your life and your kingdom."

It was the old man who had spoken, with respect but without servility. The sultan rounded upon him. "What is his secret? A little sorcery. An excess of fear. I refuse it. I will not be cowed by a nest of heretics."

"Then," said the old man, "you had best beware. Asleep or awake, in camp or on the march, by day or by night, you must look for his servants, and guard against them; or in the end they will have you."

"Do you prophesy, sir?"

The old man smiled. "Have I need? I know your enemy. Of the arts of which I am called master, he is reckoned a novice of great promise. And Aleppo will have paid him splendidly. A sultan's ransom; and more, perhaps. Are your emirs looking to themselves? Have you warned even your regent in Egypt?"

"All of them," said the sultan. "And, now, this my savior."

She flushed. She wished he would not call her that. The old man regarded her gravely, as if he measured her. She stiffened, but less with outrage than with puzzlement. People never looked at her like that. Not as if she were an oddity, or a perversion, or a thing he had to school himself to accept. As if she were simply human, and he judged her so.

He nodded slowly. "You are stronger than you think," he said.

She frowned, puzzled. "Are you an oracle?"

He rose and bowed. "Ah no, young warrior. Merely a servant of God, and sometimes, in some small fashion, of the hidden arts."

"A magus?"

"You may call me that."

She had heard of his like. She had never seen one. "You look..." She pondered. He had sat down again. His eyes glinted, wicked as a boy's. She could not help it: she glinted back. "You look like a magus," she decided. "Though I never knew that magi could laugh."

"We are quite human," he said. "It is nothing remarkably uncanny. Only learning and hard labor."

"And wisdom."

"That comes as it wills, and not to all of us."

"To you, I think, it has."

"Perhaps. Sometimes I fail."

"Ah," she said. "The word is in your dialect."

He laughed, which startled her a little. "I think that I would call you wise, young warrior."

"I can't be a mage," she said a shade quickly.

"Why not?"

"A mage can't be a woman."

"Why not?"

Her brows knit. She was growing, unwisely, annoyed. "A woman can't be anything."

"You are a warrior."

"My father is mad."

"Then so, perhaps, am I."

"You have a daughter?"

"Yes." He paused. His face darkened as if with sadness. He sighed. "She will be greater in the Art than I. If..."

"If?" she asked when he did not go on.

The darkness deepened. "If she remembers her strength. If she can master herself. It is a bitter battle, and long, and perhaps she cannot win it. Perhaps the wound is too deep ever to heal."

"She's hurt?" Zamaniyah dropped beside him, taking his hand, not needing to think. "Was she in a battle?"

"Of sorts." His hand was thin and cold. His eyes were black. "An old battle in an ancient war. A guest forgot his place. He seized her, though she fought. He had his will of her."

Her throat closed. Not that he said it; that he said it so, with such deadly calm. She choked out words. "That is a man's right. So they say." Her eyes met his. "Death would have been too gentle for him."

"Indeed," said the Hajji. "He serves a woman now, utterly, with body and soul. And so, when he has paid in full, shall he die."

"But your daughter can't forget."

"I pray that she may. She dwells among women who are masters of the Art; she rises high and swift. But she will not suffer the presence of a man."

"Even you?"

His head bowed, rose. "I am part of it. I taught her magic, but I had not taught her enough. When it came to the crux, she could muster no defense. She was no mage then. She was only a woman, and weak, and free for any man's taking."

Zamaniyah held his hand tighter. "Maybe," she said. "Maybe in time. Maybe she can learn to forgive herself. Maybe she can even forgive him." Anger gusted. "How could a man, a guest—how could he?"

"He knew no better." She stared, astonished; for he was almost gentle, almost compassionate. "He paid, and pays. So do we all. There are always prices. The wise know, and accept them, and pay as they must. Fools dream that they need never pay."

"Do fools grow wise?"

"Sometimes. Sometimes too late."

She nodded. "I've heard that." She stood. "I'll pray for your daughter."

"Allah will surely hear you," he said.

"Allah always hears. Sometimes," she said, "He's slow to

answer." She hesitated. Then she said it. "If you'd like . . . you could share me. Father won't mind. He's only mad about making me his heir; and he's very generous." She was starting to babble. She swallowed. "I know I'm nothing to a great mage. But I'm here and I'm willing, and I'm not afraid of you."

His laughter was sweet and deep. "Indeed you are not! And indeed I would share you. With your father's leave, and your sultan's permission; and my gratitude. Will you call me Uncle?"

"Uncle," she said.

He smiled, kissed her hands. "May Allah bless and keep you. May His angels watch over you. May the spirits of the air guard your coming; may the spirits of the earth look upon your going. Go in the Name of God."

"That was magic," said Zamaniyah, bemused.

Jaffar had forgotten what it was to be glad. Strange. Light. Wonderful. He danced about her, singing. He swept away her garments one by one. He bowed with a flourish. "Your bath, O wonder of the age."

She stepped into it, puzzled but pleased. "You're happy tonight."

"Happy!" He laughed for plain joy. "O wise! O splendid! Who but you would have known exactly how to win the heart of the greatest mage in Egypt?"

"Is he really?"

"And Syria, too. As truly as I live."

"Ah," she said. She frowned. "I didn't do anything. He was just so sad, and so kind, in spite of what he is. I wanted to comfort him a little."

"And so you did. And he laid his blessing on you. That's mighty, mistress. There are princes who would kill to have even a fraction of what he gave you all unasked."

"The sultan didn't seem to mind."

"How could he?"

She smiled and shook her head. "You're not logical, Jaffar."

"I don't have to be." He scrubbed her as she liked, hard but not too hard, raising a cloud of rose-scented foam. She purred like a cat. He kissed her suddenly, too quick to catch. "I don't have to be anything but glad."

For his valor Khamsin had won a great prize: a groom to himself, one of the sultan's own, and freedom from lead or hobble. He was circumspect in it. He slept by his mistress' tent, with his groom snoring gently within his reach. He grazed as close to the camp as he might, and as far from the mares. Though it was spring and they were in season, and he was sorely tempted.

It was astonishing how much strength of will a stallion could have. More than a man. More by far than Hasan al-Fahl.

Zamaniyah smelled of roses this morning. He closed his eyes and breathed it in.

She wielded the brush with good will and no little insouciance. The groom had just learned his lesson. The mistress cleaned her horse herself. He sat on his haunches in the tent's shade, narrow-eyed, critical. She ignored him with conspicuous care.

Khamsin could not decide whether to be amused or displeased. She could have been kinder. It was not the boy's fault that he was here; and he was a good servant. Better than that haughty eunuch of hers, who carried himself as if he were the King of Nubia.

Ah well, thought Khamsin. He had the wits to love Zamaniyah.

"I met a magus yesterday," she said. In Greek, which was rude. It would be no more than she deserved, if the boy proved fluent in it.

A magus?

Khamsin's back hunched; his ears flattened. He pawed the ground, tossing his head, as if he could fling off a word as one flings off a stinging fly.

She slapped his shoulder to stop his pawing, seeing no reason in it, taking no great notice of it. "He's come to help defend the sultan against the Assassins. He's very wise and very learned and very sad."

Khamsin did not want to hear. His mind darted, hunting escape. But where could he go? If a mage wanted to find him, a mage would, for anything that he could do.

He was being an idiot. The magus had come to aid the sultan, she had said it herself. One smallish horse, even a horse who had been born a man, could not possibly matter to him.

"I like him," said his blissful innocent of a mistress.

His head snapped about, incredulous.

She scratched the hollow under his jaw. "Poor man, he's suffered horribly. His daughter has gone away and won't let him visit her; she's sworn enmity against all men, even her own father. Because once they had one as a guest—they found him in the street, Khamsin, all beaten and battered, and healed him and fed him and showed him every courtesy; and do you know how he paid them?"

Allah, Allah, he knew, why must she know, why could he not move? Her hands woke dim bodily pleasure. Her words flayed him to the bone.

"He raped her," she said, hating the very word, spitting it. "That's what he gave them in return for his life. Can you believe it? Can you imagine it?"

He tried to shrink down. A horse was not made for it. He could only drop his head, clamp his tail to his flanks.

She pulled it up again, attacking it with the comb. "I hope," she said, words coming out in spasms between sharp angry strokes, "I hope he learns—learns perfectly—exactly what he did. He didn't know, the magus says. He just wanted. He didn't care what he did to anyone. He wanted and he took." The comb caught on a tangle. She worried it free. Paused. "God help anyone who tries to take anything from me."

Oh, that he could melt into the earth. Or die. Or be anyone but Khamsin who had been Hasan.

She left his tail, started on his feet. "It makes me angry, Khamsin. It scares me. That a man can do a thing like that. They do it in war, I know, though the sultan tries to stop them. They do it in the streets of any city there is. But in one's own house, from one's own guest . . . it goes beyond unspeakable. It makes a mockery of God and law and plain humanity. If a man can do that, what can he not do?"

Escape unscathed.

Innocently, mercilessly, she twisted the knife. "But you, you're not a man. You don't know about hosts and guests and courtesies. You just know sense. You won't take what a mare won't give.''

He, no. Never. Never again.

She linked her arms about his neck. "I'm glad you're not a man,'' she said. "I'm glad you're Khamsin.''

Such comfort, that was. Cold and raw; unendingly cruel.

She noticed something when she rode him. He was obedient out of the habit of it. There was no spark in it. No joy. It was all slain.

She decided that he was tired. She cut it short; and that too was cruel. Everything she did was cruel. Because of what she knew, and of what she did not know. Which, surely, surely, the magus would tell her. Then she would hate Khamsin as she hated Hasan; and his punishment would be complete.

18

"Enough," said the sultan. "Enough of this."

He stalked in front of his tent, hands knotted behind him, glaring at motionless, impervious Aleppo. His engines had nicked a tower or two. His army had quelled a sortie or three. The city was no more his now than it had been when his siege began.

He could, Zamaniyah knew, wear it down and starve it out. But that might take a year; and his army could not live on grass, even if it fasted throughout as now it fasted in Ramadan. No more would it linger if he ceased to pay it.

They needed a battle, and plunder. Something solid and swift.

"Mosul," said one of the emirs, "is moving at last. Saif al-Din will gain little enough profit from conquest of the east, if you wield his uncle's realm behind him. If he allies with Zangi his brother..."

"Not if we can help it," the sultan said. There was a smile or two, quickly quelled. Zangi needed no encouragement to thwart his brother, whom he despised most cordially; he had welcomed the aid of a company of the sultan's troops. With

Zangi's malice to engage it, Mosul could not strike Syria with
its full force.

But even that could catch the sultan between its hammer
and Aleppo's anvil.

Their voices contested, now mingling, now distinct.

"We cannot give up this siege."

"Why not? We hold the south. We can withdraw, replenish
our strength, firm our grip on what we have; then strike again
in a better hour."

"There will be none better. Aleppo and Mosul between
them can hammer us to dust."

"And have you forgotten the Franks? Aleppo would as
easily ally with them as fight them."

"They? Their king is a child."

"Just so is Aleppo's; and have we won it yet?"

"The king is not the only lord in Frankland. Some are
stronger than he. One of them in arms, summoned by our
enemies, or simply seeing our disarray—"

As often while his emirs shouted at one another—council
of war, they called it, though it was more war than council—
the sultan kept his distance, saying nothing. He would speak
when he judged it time to speak. He would do what he,
himself, chose to do. The emirs never seemed to notice how
little account he took of all their warring counsel.

"See," cried an emir, brandishing the letter that had
brought them together. "See what insolence Mosul compels
us to endure! 'Yusuf,' the whelp informs the world, 'has
scorned the laws of humankind. He has forgotten what he is
and whence he came; for all that the father did for him, he
recompenses the son with rebellion and with treason. Therefore I, kinsman and loyal servant, lord by my lord's bestowal
of Mosul—' "

They shouted him down. "Mosul is a yapping dog! Has it
moved? Has it done aught but smite us with words? The
Franks, now—"

"The Franks have moved." That, at last, was the sultan,
soft and level. A messenger knelt at his feet; a letter
was in his hand. Both had come quietly, unheeded in the
uproar.

The sultan rose in spreading silence. "The Franks have
moved," he said again. He seemed calm, but there was a

spark in his eye. It was not, Zamaniyah perceived, fear. "The Count of Tripoli has crossed our borders; he has passed by Homs and moves upon Hama. Aleppo," he said above a rising roar, "Aleppo and Mosul have sworn alliance with him. Do we endure this, my lords? Do we sit like ladies in a harem, while the infidel ravages the lands we have so newly won?"

He had them. Not as quickly as that, and not as simply, but the tide was against resistance. They could see as well as he, that the siege had accomplished nothing.

But to chance open battle, in Ramadan—

"We have no choice!" He was roused, quiet no longer, diffident no longer. "We march at dawn. We stay for no man. The infidel has set his foot in Syria."

The sultan was not a hasty man, nor a rash one. But when he determined to move, he moved. At dawn as he had commanded, hard upon the first prayer, the army departed from Aleppo. They left nothing behind but scouts and spies and the hacked and useless remnants of siege engines.

They rode like the wrath of Allah. They stopped for nothing and no one. The weak and the stragglers dropped away. The strong clung grimly to their saddles or ran stoically at the stirrups of the horsemen. They had perforce to remember an art of necessity: changing mounts at speed, and resting as seldom as men and beasts could bear.

Zamaniyah tricked Khamsin thus once, but only once. The second time he would not allow it, though she cursed him. He was acting like a man. Flaunting his hardihood; killing himself. "You idiot!" she shouted at him. "We have to fight when we get there. Do you want someone else to carry me then?"

He checked, snorted, veered. Her knee brushed the side of the remount. She snatched the saddle and swung over before Khamsin could know what he had done.

Unless he had intended it. His eye was bright as he fell in beside her.

"Damn you," she said. "You understand Arabic."

He nipped her boot and skittered to the very end of his rein, and there stayed, matching the soft-gaited bay pace for pace.

She watched him out of the corner of her eye. Sometimes he worried her. No, she admitted to herself. Sometimes he frightened her. He was not like any horse she had ever seen, even the horses of Arabia, who could be half Jinn and half fire. None of them had ever come quite so close to human wit and wickedness.

She shifted her aching body in the saddle. The bay barely noticed. Khamsin was intent on keeping his footing in the rutted and trampled road. He looked like any horse in that long undulating line, smaller than some, handsomer than most. Somehow, while she was not looking, his chest had deepened, his haunches rounded and grown strong: narrow no longer, weak no longer, yet elegant still. She reached, brushed his neck with the tips of her fingers. He bent an ear in acknowledgment. Perhaps it was an apology. Perhaps he accepted it.

It was twenty-five leagues in the hawk's flight from Aleppo to Hama, across a plain from which the splendor of spring was already retreating, giving way to dust and sere grass and pitiless sky. Yet Hama was no city of open spaces. It was a secret place, a place of green shadows and windless stillness, set in the deep furrow which the river Orontes had carved in the earth. Other cities stretched high up to heaven. Hama nestled within the circle of its cliffs, girdled with gardens, embracing its river.

It wore now a crown of steel. From far away they could see one another, the Franks in their mailed lines, the army of the sultan pressing grimly onward. Word had flown back through the ranks. They would halt only to fight.

Zamaniyah straightened her aching body. At the mention of battle, the infantryman who clung to her stirrup had raised his head; a light had come into his face. He grinned up at her, a white gleam amid the dust.

She managed a thin smile. Her heart had quickened, but not with pleasure. She was barely sure of herself against Muslims. How could she face the towers of steel that were Franks?

They had slowed, to gather strength, but still they moved much too swiftly for her peace. Through dust and massed men she could see nothing of either city or enemy.

The drums beat, thudding in the center of her. *Halt; form ranks.* Some idiot was singing. A Bedu love song, of all improbable things in this hateful place.

Khamsin was waiting for her, with his groom smirking beside him. The whelp had mocked her with a miracle: spotless horse, impeccable caparisons. They might have come fresh from the stable.

She had not, and she felt it in every bone. Jaffar had her weapons, her bow, her quiver. For the boy's sake she sprang lightly into the saddle; the eunuch passed up her arms.

This was war, and holy. Therefore they were allowed to break the fast. She took her share of water, eyed the bread and the cold mutton with little favor. Because Jaffar was there, glaring horribly, she choked down a bite or two.

The drums beat again. *In ranks. Battle order.*

They spread across the rolling level: left, right, center. Baggage behind, guarded. The sultan on a rise with his standard, overseeing the field. Voices shrilled high, exultant, weariness forgotten.

Khamsin had raised his own deafening paean. Now at last his rider could see the enemy. Against the milling hordes of Islam, the Franks stood up in clear and ordered lines. Their knights were tall and terrible. Their banners were barbaric: beasts, birds, creatures both and neither, ramping on gaudy fields, defying the simplicity of holy words sewn and painted on the black and gold and green of the sultan's standards.

Zamaniyah slid her bow from its casing, drew out the coiled string.

Someone shouted near her, deep and sudden. Khamsin started. She snatched rein.

The Franks were moving, milling.

She thrust the bow between thigh and saddle, snapped straight the string.

Stopped.

The ranks of steel had blurred, wavered, shrunk.

A roar went up. They were retreating. Fleeing. Ordered, deliberate, imposing even in their cowardice.

Drums and cymbals loosed a wing of whooping pursuers. Shouts and laughter sped them on their way. An arrow or two flew, mocking.

Zamaniyah sat her startled stallion and loosed a slow

breath. She wanted to be relieved. She was—though she
hated herself—disappointed. So much fear and so much
fretting, and a ride like a storm rising, and all for nothing.
The terrible Frank had turned craven and slunk away.

One did not need a great battle to win a great victory. The
sultan camped outside of Hama; and as the sun went down,
his army's joy went up.

They had a prisoner or three for their amusement: Franks
whose horses had failed them, or whose ire had held them
when all their fellows fled. Some had even tried to fight.

The sultan had forbidden cruelty. These were guests, he
decreed; honored prisoners. Some knew decent manners, and
Arabic or Turkish with them. Others, scowling savages out of
darkest Francia, seemed set on proving every scurrilous tale
that anyone had ever told of them.

Even in her tent Zamaniyah could hear the voices about her
father's fire. One of the Syrian emirs had come with a
handful of rowdy young men, all of them gagging in unison.
"Ahmad has himself a Frank," the emir explained. His voice
was young, and rippling with mirth. "Eee, the stink! I swear
by the Prophet's beard, the man hasn't seen a washing since
the midwife pulled him yelling from the womb."

"That's Franks for you," said another, older but no less
merry. "Do you know, they sew themselves into their shirts at
summer's end, and cut themselves out when summer begins
again?"

"What do they do between?"

"Go naked, of course!"

Laughter ran round the circle.

"Ah now," said the young emir, "it's not as bad as that.
The ones who've been here a while, they pick up a bit of
civilization here and there."

"A bit," the older man agreed. "But sometimes, barely
enough. My cousin's a rich man: he owns a fair number of
bathhouses in one of the towns near Antioch. He tells of a
Frank who used to come to one of them—Franks will tell you
that bathing is a deathly danger to a man's health, but they'll
make exceptions for our kind of baths. This Frank I'm
speaking of was almost as regular in his bathing as a Muslim,

but being a Frank, he knew nothing of modesty; he never covered his loins while he bathed.

"One day he grew curious, or maybe he thought it a fine jest to mock a Muslim's decency. He snatched the attendant's loincloth and tossed it clean out the door.

"Salim the bathman kept his dignity. The Frank, I'm told, goggled like an idiot. 'What's this?' he said. 'What's this you have?'

"Salim, who had no more or less than any man has, took a moment to find an answer. It was obvious enough, of course, upon reflection. He explained, with what composure he could muster, what use we Muslims make of razor and stripping-paste.

"The Frank was astonished. 'Splendid!' he cried. 'Magnificent! Will you do the same for me?'

"Salim obliged him. He had, my cousin says, a veritable beard between his legs. When it was gone he felt how smooth it was, and laughed. 'We shave our faces,' he said. 'You shave below. I think you have the better of the two.' Then he leaped up with his jewels still in his hand and went laughing out.

"A little later he came back. He had a woman with him, a brazen unveiled Frank. He brought her right into the baths, in that hour when no woman was permitted; and she staring about with no shame at all. He led her to poor Salim, laid her naked on the table, and said, 'What you did for me, do for my lady.'"

"And did he?" the young emir asked when the laughter had died down.

"Certainly," the older man answered. "And was paid handsomely for it, too. It was a good day's work, my cousin said."

Zamaniyah pulled the blanket over her head. It muffled the voices, a little. It did nothing for her blushes.

The flow of talk had shifted, ebbed. They were rising one by one, saying farewells, straggling to their beds.

She knew when her father sought his tent. He had companions: the young emir and the older man who had told the tale of the Frank. Some quality of the air or of her weary ears brought their voices clearly to her. She caught the emir's name: Abd al-Rahim. He held a fief close by Damascus; he was, the older man indicated with delicacy surprising after what she had heard of him by the fire, of an old family, well connected, with excellent prospects.

The emir had remarkably little to say for himself. The other man was saying it all.

Zamaniyah found herself well outside of her blanket, and wide awake. Abd al-Rahim was shaping into a paragon of virtue, beauty, and piety. Al-Zaman was allowing it with, it seemed, perfect patience. Was the boy so highly placed, then? But if that were so, why did he need to curry al-Zaman's favor?

She crept from her mat and pressed her ear to the wall.

"Why do you come to me tonight?" al-Zaman was asking, quite amiably still, but in a tone that bade them cease their circling and come to the point.

"Opportunity," the spokesman answered, "and long desire that comes at last to the end of its diffidence; and the stars are auspicious for us all."

"Indeed," said al-Zaman.

There was a pause. Perhaps the emir whispered to the other. At length the man said, "My lord is modest, lord commander, and not given to presumption; but the desire of his heart drives him beyond his wonted bounds. Therefore he comes to you. He begs the honor of your regard. He cries your pardon if he taxes your patience."

"He does not," said al-Zaman. "Yet."

Someone swallowed audibly. Perhaps it was Abd al-Rahim. The other said as steadily as ever, "Lord commander, my lord asks your indulgence. He is scarcely himself. His eyes are dazzled; his heart is smitten. He is, in a word, in love."

"Indeed," purred al-Zaman.

"My lord." That was the emir himself, swift and breathless and somewhat muffled, as if he had flung himself to the carpet. "My lord, I love her with all my heart. My dreams are full of her. My waking is alight with her. My lord, if I might have your leave—even to think of aspiring to her—of taking your daughter as my wife—"

Zamaniyah fell backward. Her hands were clapped over her mouth. Her heart was like to leap out of her breast.

She could still hear him through the drumbeat of her pulse. "My lord, today I saw her in the line of battle, all bright and splendid; and I knew, I knew surely, that I must speak to you. You may strike me. You may cast me out. I will not stop you. I know I am not worthy of her; but surely, my lord, surely I may dream?''

"You may dream," said al-Zaman.

"Oh, my lord!" The young man's voice was trembling. "My lord, you have shown me the face of joy."

"You may dream," al-Zaman repeated. "I promise you nothing."

"It is enough," said Abd al-Rahim.

"Mistress?"

She looked into the shadow that was Jaffar's face. "He's not talking about me. Is he? He thinks I'm someone else."

"I doubt that, mistress," he said.

She let him put her to bed again. It was easier than fighting. "He doesn't want me," she said. "He wants my dowry, or my father's power, or my favor with the sultan. Real people don't swoon for love the way they do in stories. And even if they did, how could anyone swoon for me?"

"It's not as hard as you might think," said Jaffar.

She gaped at him. Then, shakily, she laughed. "It is a good joke, isn't it? Who'd ever have thought this would happen?"

Jaffar said nothing.

She curled on her side and yawned. Her eyes were pricking. She refused, fiercely, to weep. "I wonder," she said. "I wonder what he looks like."

Jaffar knelt by her until she slept. He had seen the tears she refused to shed. He had said none of the things he could have said. And some he should, if he had been as good a servant as he pretended.

He had seen the hopeful suitor. A comely young man, well spoken of both in war and in council, well versed in manners and in courtesy. Altogether a perfect nobleman, and no hypocrite. Jaffar had watched him watch Zamaniyah. If his passion was pretense, it was surpassingly well played.

It tore at Jaffar. The man's perfect suitability, which al-Zaman could not but see. The lady's conviction that it was all a seeming, or a cruel jest. And Jaffar was glad that she felt so. Glad that she held herself so low, that she could see in honest desire only the merchant's calculation: that she had no innocence, nor any hope. It racked her with pain, and he rejoiced, because he need not lose her to any man.

And why not? he demanded of himself. Any man who took her would insist that she be a woman. Would veil her, seclude her, set his will and his seal upon her. And she would allow it; and it would kill her. She thought herself a sparrow forced to fly as a falcon. She did not know that she was an eagle.

She must not yield. This trouble of hers was youth, womanhood waking and waxing insistent. It would ease. He—

He knotted about his middle. He could ease her. He who loved her. He who would never give her the pain of a child.

Painfully he drew himself erect. "No," he whispered. That way was madness. She loved him; she had the eyes to see that he was beautiful. She would accept what he had to give, would believe sincerely that she was glad of it. But it would not be enough. She would want more; and suffer for the wanting; and end in desolation.

Better that she go on as she had begun. Through the inspired madness of her father, she had what no woman should dare to hope for. She was accepted as a man. She commanded loyalty; she had the sultan's goodwill. She could be a great power, herself, untrammeled by any will but her own.

In this world?

Why not? Already she had wrought the impossible: won a place in the army of Islam, simply by being present and doing her duty and asking no man's indulgence. They had accepted her before they knew it. Whatever she did hereafter, the way was laid. She had only to set her foot upon it.

Jaffar lay by her. She stirred uneasily, dreaming. He stroked her hair. She sighed, stilled. He closed his eyes.

19

The Franks had drawn back well beyond their own borders, shut themselves in their mighty fortress of Krak and there defied their pursuers. Empty defiance. They had accomplished nothing in all their riding but empty shame.

The sultan had won more than an easy victory. The army of Mosul had come to Aleppo. He was free of that trap; free to choose the ground of battle, if battle there must be.

Zamaniyah noticed. It was impossible not to. But her mind could not center upon it. There was Abd al-Rahim. And there was Wiborada.

The Frank was gone. It came on slowly, that fact. That first night before Hama, she had gone, she said, to al-Zaman's tent. That none of the men in their conference had spoken of her, Zamaniyah at first had not stopped to wonder at. A woman in a warrior's tent was invisible, like the bed and the carpets.

Had she ever been there at all? Al-Zaman had not come looking for her. In the morning she had not been among Zamaniyah's mamluks. Zamaniyah had forborne to fret. Her mind was otherwise occupied; and Wiborada hardly conducted herself like a loyal slave. She liked to wander.

Anxiety grew slowly. A Frankish prisoner brought it to bloom. He was doing nothing, simply sitting in front of a tent, sneering at men who passed, looking filthy and lice-ridden and most appallingly seared by the sun. He was simply there, a Frank, with eyes nigh as blue as Wiborada's.

And Zamaniyah knew.

She refused it. She hunted in all the places a mamluk could be, and a few in which one should not. Her own soldier-slaves had nothing to tell her. They did not know where the lioness was: that was what they called her, though the boy who let it slip went scarlet and would say nothing thereafter. None of them had seen her since the night of the victory.

Wiborada had kept her belongings in a box in Zamaniyah's tent. The bow was there; it seemed untouched. It held her armor, her sword, changes of linen and clothing, even, wrapped carefully and laid beneath the rest, the silken garments of a concubine.

She could not have gone naked. She must have gone unarmed, unless she had taken a dagger. She was no archer, to have owned a bow, or stolen one. She had vanished like a Jinniyah in a story.

Zamaniyah lowered the lid; rose; strode toward the flap.

Jaffar barred her way. She scowled at him. He could not stand even in the tent's peaked center; here at its side he stooped low over her, motionless, expressionless. "No," he said.

"No, what?" she snapped.

"No. Don't go after her. She's made her choice."

"She'll get herself killed!"

"Are you certain?" he asked. "Those are her own people. She's noble born; her father was a high lord among them. She can win them with her face and hold them with the pathos of her story."

Zamaniyah's head shook. She could see it, and yet she could not. "She'll be casting her wager on it. Maybe if she can find her way into a lord's protection; and their priests give sanctuary, don't they? But what if she can't? Those are savages out there, eating our bread and cursing their captivity. What would they do to a woman alone, unarmed, dressed as one of us? And a man of us at that, if I know Wiborada. I have to find her. I have to get her back.''

"She's been gone at least a day and a night. Whatever they would have done to her, they'll have done long since.''

"At least I can bring back her body!''

"How?'' he demanded. "Do you think the Franks will let you come and go as you please?''

She barely hesitated. "I'll trust to Allah to keep me safe.''

"And what then? What then, little idiot? If she's dead, maybe she prefers a burial among her own kind. If she's alive, accepted, welcomed, what makes you think she'll even want to acknowledge your existence, let alone come back with you?''

"If she is alive, if she hasn't been accepted, how am I to live with myself if I don't come to help her?''

"How can you help? Be a slave with her? Let them rape you while she watches?''

She struck him. She had never done it so, hard, flat-handed, ringing in the small closed space.

There was a long silence. Slowly he backed away, into the blinding sunlight. More slowly still, she followed.

She could not have hurt him badly. Not in the flesh. But the stiffness of his back, the glitter of his eyes, made her want to cry aloud.

She would not. Could not. "Whatever she may have reckoned me, I reckon her my friend. I can't abandon her to cold prudence.''

He set his lips together. She knew that look of his. It boded most ill.

He said nothing. But Khamsin was not there to be saddled; her saddle was nowhere visible; when she strode grimly toward the horselines, her father's mamluks stood in her path. They did not speak. They would not let her pass. When she would have broken away and seized any beast she might, they hemmed her in. "Jaffar,'' she said with vicious softness. "Jaffar!''

Better and more useful to curse the wind. With one ill-considered blow she had lost all claim to his indulgence.

They guarded her like a prisoner, her eunuch and her mamluks. She could go wherever she pleased. After the first day she could even ride: but guarded always, surrounded always, and never an opening that stayed for her.

Jaffar was as immovable as stone. He did not even threaten to tell her father. He did not need to. His vigilance was more than enough.

Hours stretched into days. With each that passed, hope retreated further. Wiborada was lost now, lost utterly, whatever had become of her.

On the third day Jaffar gave her a gift. He won her father's leave for her—guarded as always—to enter Hama.

She was not given to sulking in her tent. There was too little profit in it. She offered no gratitude, nor felt she owed any; but she took the gift. Knowing what he meant by it. Refusing to be taken in.

Grief and rage huddled on the edge of her mind. But it was hard to center on them in the cool sweetness of Hama's gardens, or in the manifold splendors of its market. In spite of herself she began to soften, even to take pleasure in her wandering. She found cloth for a new coat, and a belt for her sword, and a saddlecloth and a tasseled neckband for Khamsin. He preened in them. She found herself smiling, though not, and never, in Jaffar's direction.

Others of the army were abroad in the city, notable for their arms and their armor and their proud carriage. Some she knew; some greeted her, freely, as one of them.

She paused by a sweetseller's stall. While Jaffar chaffered with the merchant, she wandered from among her mamluks. Khamsin was much interested in a fruitseller's wares. She bought him a handful of dried apples, but though his nostrils quivered, he turned his head away. She shook her head and sighed. "What, do you keep Ramadan too?"

He showed no sign of understanding. She sighed again. Sometimes there was no pleasing him.

She knew what her damnable eunuch would have said to that. She tucked the apples away and wandered back toward her jailers.

Another small company seemed to have conceived a desire to spice their nightmeal with sweetness. The chief of them was young, though still rather older than herself, and most pleasant to look at. He carried himself lightly, with remarkable grace; his face was very fine, less a Turkish face than a Persian, with brows that met above his kohl-dark eyes. They caught hers. She looked quickly away. Her cheeks were hot.

Like her, he had a servant to do his bargaining for him. Unlike her, he left his mount to a groom: a stallion as handsome as himself, of the Barbary breed that was broader and thicker-bodied than the strain of Arabia. It suited him. He was no slender reed of a youth; he had a fine breadth of shoulder in his scaled and gilded corselet.

A thought struck her. She shook it off, though it clung, tenacious. That would be too mighty a coincidence.

Unless he had followed her.

He was too splendid. He could not be Abd al-Rahim.

She glanced sidewise. He was doing the same. A smile betrayed them both. She bit hard on hers. This was ridiculous. Worse: scandalous.

She busied herself assiduously with a tassel of Khamsin's bridle. It had, most conveniently, begun to unravel.

The young emir was in the corner of her eye again. He seemed to have discovered a stain on his sleeve. A tall jar of water stood near her, loosely covered, set there for defense against fire. The emir approached it with every appearance of casualness, lifted the lid. It slipped.

She caught it. They were face to face, just close enough to touch. He was blushing under the down of his beard.

That shocked her out of her own silliness. He was only a boy. Bold enough to set a trap for her, too shy to close it about her.

This time she did not try to swallow her smile. "Have we met?" she asked him.

His face was as scarlet as his coat. He shook his head; bit his lip; looked so furious and so nonplussed that she could not help herself. She touched him. Only his arm, meaning to speak, to give him comfort.

Khamsin, forgotten, sank his teeth into her shoulder. It was armored, but his jaws were strong. She reeled back. The emir leaped, sword drawn. She flung her arms about her stallion's neck. "No!"

Khamsin's ears were flat, his teeth snapping in the emir's face. She hauled him back, winced at what it did to her shoulder.

They glared at one another, man and beast. The sword, at least, was sheathed.

"Mistress," said Jaffar, cool and sweet and oblivious. "Come, choose. Will you have halwah or sugared almonds?"

Neither! she wanted to cry.

Khamsin pawed, snorting. He had taken an appalling dislike to the emir.

She tried to apologize with her eyes as she dragged him off. The emir did not follow. His anger was fading: that much mercy he gave her. With an effort that wrenched at her center, she turned away from him.

Zamaniyah's shoulder bore a shocking bruise. More shocking still was Jaffar's response to it. He barely even frowned. He laid cool cloths on it and bade her rest, and never said a word against her stallion.

That hurt worse than any wound. He had stopped caring what happened to her. She had made him hate her.

She cried out in rage and pain. "*Damn* you, Jaffar! Don't you turn against me, too."

He had been withdrawing to his corner. He paused. His face bore no expression at all. "I, mistress? Have I ever given aught but loyal service?"

"Too loyal," she shot back, "and not loyal enough."

He bowed at her feet. "I am your servant, mistress."

Her hand flew up. She caught the blow before it began, seized him instead, pulled him up to face her. "Why do you hate me so much? Because I hit you? I repent it with all that is in me. I swear to you, I'll never do it again."

His head shook. He looked surprised; even a little dismayed. She throttled a stab of satisfaction. She was not calculating this. Not altogether. "Mistress," he said. "I could never hate you."

"You despise me, then. You torment me with cold courtesy. You make me pay and pay and pay for that one moment's folly."

"You make yourself pay. I have done no more than keep you from folly greater still."

Her lips tightened; she tossed her head. "Stop it, Jaffar. I can't bear it. That the only friend—the only friend I have in the world—"

She appalled herself. She clutched at him. "Don't you go, too. Promise me, Jaffar. Promise!"

She was too close to see his face. His voice was quiet. "I promise," he said. "Never, in life or in death. I will never leave you."

A small wind traced her spine, waking a shiver. She pulled back. Her shoulder throbbed; she did not heed it. His eyes burned upon her. "Never," he repeated with all the force of a vow.

Khamsin paced a restless circle about his mistress' tent. His mood was black. Part of it, to be sure, was hunger. This body could not fast as a man's did. He was harming it, his groom had told him. He had to eat or he would sicken. He ate, but not, if he could help it, when the sun was high. The boy was resigned to his feeding at night and in the dawn.

This close to sunset, he was all one great yearning for sustenance. But that, he could bear, if not happily. Something else made him snap and strike at unresisting air.

That man—that popinjay—that mincing Turk with his Persian face. How dared he cast his eye upon Zamaniyah? How dared he dream of touching her?

She was her own woman. She was no rutting man's.

He stopped, stamped. He would not have it. He would—

What? Challenge the man? Order him off? Claim her for his hoofed and speechless self?

He raised his head and cried his helpless rage.

She came out to him. He noticed little more than that she was there; that she bridled him, saddled him. Her eunuch watched as if he would object, but said nothing. Nor did she. Even when he attached himself to her stirrup and would not let go.

She did not ride far or fast. She did not even leave the camp. By the sultan's tent, among the guards and the princes and the petitioners, men with untiring voices chanted the Koran. She stopped to listen.

It mattered little what words they were. They were holy. They comforted.

" 'There is not an animal in the earth,' " sang the clearest of the voices, " 'nor a flying creature flying on two wings, but they are peoples like unto you. We have neglected

nothing in the book of Our decrees. Then unto their Lord they
will be gathered. . . . ' ' '

Even what was neither man nor beast? he wanted to ask
them. Even what had lost its wits for a silly chit of a girl?

Because he had. For all that he was and had been, he was
worse than geas-bound. He had never even known that he
was falling, until he woke and found himself cast upon his
face.

This was worse than lust. Lust could die. This was immortal.
He was hers beyond even wanting to be free.

And by Allah, that popinjay would not have her.

It was late when Zamaniyah came back to her tent. Jaffar had
led Khamsin there long since; she had broken the day's fast
with the sultan, at his insistence. She had had stomach for
very little of what he offered her.

Her father had been there. She had not been able to speak
to him, lest he ask for his concubine; lest she break, there
where everyone could see, and shame them both.

Her tent was warm with lamplight, her pallet spread, her
eunuch waiting patiently in his corner. She barely acknowl-
edged him. She wanted to crawl into her blankets and hide
from all her follies.

There was someone there, in the shadows, watching. She
whipped about. Jaffar had not moved. His eyes were glittering.
She would have said that they were angry; but that was over.
She had given him no new cause that she knew of.

She turned again, more slowly. The shadow had eyes. Blue
eyes, reddened now, black-shadowed.

Zamaniyah leaped. Caught solidity. Pulled Wiborada into
the light. She was dusty, draggled, her coat torn, her face
bruised and scratched. Zamaniyah clutched her close; thrust
her away, holding her at arms' stretch, shaking her, glaring
through a fog of tears. "Why, Wiborada? *Why?*"

Wiborada's head shook. Her Arabic had deserted her. She
swayed when Zamaniyah loosened her grip.

"Jaffar." Zamaniyah's voice was passionate in its stillness,
in all that it was willing itself not to say.

He spoke without fear; without emotion altogether. "She
won't let me touch her."

Zamaniyah eased her down. She went as if she had no will for resistance.

Zamaniyah fought a brief battle with modesty. Damned it. Uncovered her. There was no great wound on her, but bruises in hideous profusion; and her feet won a gasp from Zamaniyah, and a sharp breath from Jaffar who had crept up unheeded. He retreated rapidly.

In a little while he was back with water, cloths, his box of medicines. Some of the water, cool in a jar, was for Wiborada to drink. Zamaniyah cajoled it into her.

Jaffar gave a name to each hurt as he tended it. Perhaps it was his own peculiar kind of atonement. "Walking far in boots meant for riding. Falling on stones. Thorns, stinging flies, the sun's fire." He hesitated, said it too levelly. "Men's hands. A fight."

Wiborada shuddered. Her head tossed. Her hair was matted and dulled with dust. Slowly, gently, reining in every flicker of grief or of anger, Zamaniyah began to comb it out.

Wiborada's hands clamped shut about her wrists. The blue eyes were wide and staring. She spat out a stream of Frankish.

Zamaniyah sat still through the flood. It stopped abruptly. Wiborada's face twisted. Her mouth worked. She spoke again, laboriously, in Arabic. "They were not fighting. They wanted—they tried—"

It was hard to comfort her with both hands going numb in her grip. Zamaniyah tried. Her words were feeble, forgotten as she uttered them. Wiborada never heard them. "I left," she said. "I saw the banners before Hama, and I knew. I was of them. I had no place here. I waited for night. I lied to you. I put on my plainest clothes, I stole a horse from your father's enemy, I rode away. It was simple to perfection. No one even saw me."

Zamaniyah tried to speak. Wiborada rode over her, relentless. Tearing Zamaniyah's soul with the telling, with the proof of all Zamaniyah's forebodings; gaining from it, perhaps, some surcease from the pain. "It was a good horse I stole. By dawn it had carried me to the Franks' lines. They were trying to rest, with infidels harrying them: letting them settle, then raising a clamor out of hell, clashing spears on shields, shrieking war cries, shooting the odd arrow over their heads, but melting away when they tried to strike back.

"I went in in a bit of quiet, when the infidels had stopped to eat before the dawn prayer. Once a stallion called, but my mare had manners. She didn't call back.

"I walked up to the sentries without trying to conceal myself. It was light enough by their fire; they could see that I wasn't armed. It should have been obvious that I wasn't an infidel.

"They seized me," she said, "which I had expected. I asked to be taken to a priest. I said that I had been a prisoner; I asked for sanctuary." She laughed, too high, too breathless. "Sanctuary! They gave me sanctuary. They called me spy and infidel. Do I look like an infidel, I ask you? They thought I was a man until they decided I was a eunuch; and then one of them had a stroke of genius. He stripped the cloth from my head. He tried to strip the rest of me.

"I told them who I was. I shouted at them. I demanded a priest, a lord, anyone of authority. I threatened them with dire vengeance. I prayed them to remember honor, faith, charity. I invoked every saint I knew, and every devil I could think of. They laughed and fell on me. I was nothing. I was less than nothing. I was female, and there, and they had a bitter defeat to forget. What better way to remember one's manhood than to thrust it upon a woman?"

Her eyes narrowed. She was not seeing the tent, or Zamaniyah's horror, or anything but memory. "I let them think they had me. I lay and cowered and made certain that they saw a great deal of me. I was very shakily defiant. 'Yes,' I cried. 'I am a spy! Come, what will it be? One at a time? All at once? All the better for my masters, to lead their army past you.'

"I would have laughed if I had been able. Their eyes rolled like animals'. They smelled like animals. They were nothing that I could ever have called kin. And oh, they were terrified of the cruel Saracen! 'Saladin is here,' I told them. 'Saladin will roast your ballocks for his dinner.'

"They drew lots. Some went off, snarling, to watch for the terrible sultan. Some stayed. I tried to soften them. 'Please,' I begged. 'In God's name. A priest will know me for what I am. Or if not a priest, a Templar, or a Hospitaller. He can give me justice.'

"One or two weakened. 'She looks like one of us,' they said.

"But others knew no mercy. 'She belongs to the infidel.'

"'Then,' said the gentle ones, 'the fighting monks can judge her.'

"'But first,' their comrades said, 'we take a little for ourselves.'

"They were clever," she said, "those soldiers of the Lord. All the while they decided my fate, they never stopped to think that I was free. No one even stood by to watch me. I slid by anguished inches from the middle of them. Every instant I knew that they would stop me. They never did. They were determining who was entitled to have me first.

"The shadows had me. I slipped, I crept, I bolted.

"I didn't care where I went," said Wiborada, "if only it was away. From men. From Franks and Saracens. From everyone. Even from life, if God willed it so." Her eyes blinked, shifted. She turned her head slowly about. She giggled. "See where I came! I walked and I walked, and no one stopped me, and sometimes—I think—I drank, or I ate. I came back to my chains. My sweet golden chains. *My* chains. I'm a Saracen now. Tell me I'm not a Frank. Tell me I'm not an honorless barbarian."

"You are my sister," said Zamaniyah.

Wiborada tilted her head, frowning. "We don't look alike," she said.

Zamaniyah bit her lip until it bled. Her arms were free at last. She clasped Wiborada in them.

"I tried to come," she said. "Before God, Wiborada, I tried."

She met Jaffar's eyes over the matted head. He faced her steadily. He grieved; he shared Wiborada's pain; he would bear lifelong the knowledge that he had done nothing to prevent it. But he had done his duty. His mistress had not run headlong and heedless into that same horror. He had no shame of what he had done, and no repentance.

Wiborada had stiffened at Zamaniyah's touch; yet slowly, by infinite degrees, she eased. Her head dropped to Zamaniyah's shoulder. She sighed. It was a long moment before Zamaniyah realized that she was weeping.

She wept silently at first, then more noisily, great racking sobs that swayed them both. Her fists came up and closed in Zamaniyah's coat; she clung there with all her strength.

There were words in it. "Don't tell your father. Please don't tell him."

Zamaniyah promised her. Not thinking, but not needing to think. Some things went beyond duty. Some things were unspeakable.

She was safe. Zamaniyah told her that, over and over. She was home. She was with her own.

Maybe she believed it. Maybe she would learn to. Zamaniyah dared to hope for it. Not in that she had come back to slavery from Frankish cruelty: that could have been mere helpless retreat. But she had stolen the mount of her escape from al-Zaman's great enemy. That was more than expedience, more even than malice borrowed from her master. It was kinship.

20

Wiborada needed little more than food and sleep and the passing of time to restore her to some semblance of herself. She was quieter than she had been. She stayed close to Zamaniyah; if men crowded too near, she shied away.

She tried to lighten it with mockery. "I'm like a beaten dog," she said.

"You let me touch you," said Zamaniyah, putting an arm around her.

"You're not a man." She glared at her clean and mended self. "What if al-Zaman calls for me? What will I do?"

"Face it when it comes."

"I hope it never does." Wiborada covered her face with her hands, briefly, straightening with an audible snap. "No. I'll be brave. That's all we Franks are good for."

"You're very good at it," Zamaniyah said mildly. Wiborada stared at her, patently struggling to decide whether she should be offended.

Zamaniyah gave her no time. She yawned, stretched. "Ramadan is hard. Getting up abominably early to eat before the light comes, and not even water all day."

Wiborada's brows knit. But she had been trained as a courtesan, whether she would or no; and she was not an utter fool. She played the game as Zamaniyah had chosen to play it; perhaps she took some comfort from it. She spoke almost as lightly as Zamaniyah had, and almost as easily. "Can't you take dispensation from fasting? This is war, after all."

"And make it up later? When I've already lost a week to being a woman? No; better now. It's good for my soul."

"That's what Christians say." Zamaniyah bridled. Wiborada smiled. It was her first honest smile since they left Aleppo. "Lent is longer, but we don't have to fast all day; though we can't have meat."

"Is that how you atone for eating pork?"

"Pork is good. There's nothing better."

Zamaniyah shuddered, swallowing bile. "They say it tastes like manflesh."

"Would they know?"

Jaffar, coming with bread and dates and cheese, could not understand why the two of them had so little appetite; or why they laughed at it.

Mosul's armies had left Aleppo, swelled with forces loyal to Prince Ismail. They moved slowly, almost leisurely, as if to mock the pace at which the sultan had taken that same way.

They sent envoys ahead of them. Zamaniyah watched their entry into the camp. They came in princely state, with fine horses ridden and led, and their two commanders haughty under gilded canopies. He of Mosul she did not know, but he of Aleppo was quite high enough to content any defender of the sultan's dignity: the regent himself, Gumushtekin, balancing his bulk upon a great white mule, escorted by a company in Nur al-Din's own colors.

"I at least," the sultan observed, "have the grace not to claim a dead man's livery."

She heard him, but faintly; and she was standing very close to him. To the public eye he was all courtesy. They were not a sham, those gracious manners, but they were not all of him. "Diplomacy," he had told her once, "is the art of lying truthfully.'' And, she could have added, of being lied to with wide-eyed sincerity.

It was very slow. It was, most of the time, excruciatingly polite.

She was there because no one forbade her. Wiborada was there because Zamaniyah was there. Zamaniyah wondered, often, what the ambassadors would have done if they had known the truth of the mamluk and the slender girl-faced nobleman. They won glances enough from their own people.

The young emir was there, standing with those of his elders who spoke for southern Syria. His glances were very different from the rest. They warmed her more by far than the sun's heat could account for.

Maybe, she thought, they were not for her. Wiborada's beauty shone even through a mamluk's livery; and Persians did not care whether their lovers were women or boys.

It was good for her, that reflection, like fasting in Ramadan. Even though he was, after all, Abd al-Rahim: she had browbeaten Jaffar into confessing it. As he had confessed that the emir had followed them that day in Hama, and he had known it, but he had said nothing. It was not at all proper that she knew what she knew.

Sometimes Jaffar was all too well aware of his office.

She tried to keep her eyes modestly lowered. It was hard. Especially when Abd al-Rahim, by design or chance, stood nearly close enough to touch. She liked to look at him. He was much more comely than the lords in their interminable council.

They were bartering away cities. When she made herself listen, to keep her mind from a pair of dark-lashed eyes, she swallowed an exclamation. ''Baalbek,'' the sultan was saying, ''and Homs and Hama. Those, Aleppo may take. Damascus only shall we keep.''

He was giving up everything. He had fought for it; he had won it; he held it firmly in his hand. How could he let it go?

He smiled sweetly at the ambassadors. He looked much younger than he was, and much less kingly. He looked somewhat of a fool.

They were as startled as she; but she saw no suspicion in them. They did not know that glint in his eye.

"Baalbek," mused the emissary of Mosul. "Homs. Hama. That is most of Syria."

The sultan bowed his head. His simplicity of dress, his plain turban and his worn coat and the glint of mail under it, shrank beneath their eyes, dwindled into shabbiness. Even his army—that, surely, would melt away without gold to hold it. Had he not left Aleppo because his coffers were empty? And the Franks had given him no battle, and thus no booty; only a prisoner or two, none worth more than a few dinars in ransom.

Zamaniyah shook herself. He played it wondrous well: with never a word, he had befuddled even her who knew him.

The Mosuli stroked his handsome beard and pondered. The Aleppan, who had no beard to stroke, lowered his heavy lids, and raised them slowly. His eyes were full of lazy malice, like a cat's as it drowses in the sun. "You will not give up Damascus?"

"Damascus is dear to me," said the sultan. "I would keep it to console me."

"Can you hold it?" asked the Mosuli.

"I can try," he answered with the merest quiver of doubt, set clear where they could hear.

"If we accept the cities which you offer," said Gumushtekin, "we should take also what lies beyond and about them. One fief, to take a plain example. One small holding north and east of Aleppo, in which we have discovered your people: al-Rahba that lies on the Euphrates. Since you will hold nothing north of Damascus, surely then al-Rahba should be ours."

The sultan paused. A secretary murmured rapidly in his ear. His eyes flickered. His mouth twitched just visibly, stilled. "Ah," he said. "Ah, sir. Haven't I offered you enough?"

"Al-Rahba," Gumushtekin pointed out with ponderous delicacy, "lies deeper in the north of Syria than Aleppo itself. How can you hold it from Damascus? How can we allow it? So would the commander of a fortress set his enemy on guard at the postern gate."

The sultan seemed most grievously distressed. "Alas, my lord Gumushtekin, of all the fiefs which you might have asked for, al-Rahba is one which I cannot surrender. This my loyal servant, my *qadi*, his excellency Imad al-Din ibn Muhammad, begs me to remember that the lord Nur al-Din, on whom be peace, granted it to my kinsman, my uncle's son, who regrettably is not here to speak for it. I cannot strip it from him without cause, without even a word of warning."

"Cannot or will not?" demanded the Mosuli.

The sultan frowned. "Do you question my good faith?"

The Mosuli stiffened. Gumushtekin sat back at his ease. "If it comes to that," he said, "yes. Your men are holding al-Rahba: that is fact, and proven. Your cousin's right to it is no right at all. When you seized Egypt, O servant of my departed master, that same master relieved you and all who followed you of your holdings in Syria. I do not recall that you objected. Egypt, I was given to understand, held recompense enough."

The sultan rose. His face was thunderous.

"My lords!" It was one of the sultan's Syrians, bold with age and fearful of bloodshed here in council. "My lords, need we quarrel? Three strong cities will pass into Aleppo's hands. Surely one town with its lands is little enough price to pay: far as it is, and weak, and surrounded by Aleppo's allies."

"So is a worm small and weak and hemmed in; but it devours the apple," said Gumushtekin.

"Shall I speak of worms?" the sultan asked with vicious softness. "Shall I speak of your pact with the infidels? You paid them well, did you not? To lure me from Aleppo. To destroy me if they could."

"Thereby sending you direct to Paradise," Gumushtekin pointed out, "as is promised any Muslim who falls in holy war."

"Holy! How holy is treachery? You bargain even yet. You promise them my captives in return for those of yours whom they hold. You sell them back the lands which Muslim blood has won. You give them hostages for my defeat. You are traitors to Islam."

Gumushtekin was on his feet, bulking huge before the slender figure of the sultan. The sultan faced him undismayed. The regent's lip curled. "You were a cringing pup when your master was alive. You are a bold cur, now that he is dead.

Grant us al-Rahba and we suffer you to keep Damascus.
Refuse us and we take all, and your life with it.''

''I refuse you,'' said the sultan.

The broad face stilled, closed. The Mosuli was on his feet.
Gumushtekin turned like a ship under sail. He spoke no
word. His hand rose and flicked. His attendants hastened to
their feet, turning their backs, every one, upon the sultan. It
was sublimest insolence.

Half of the army would have risen to destroy them. But the
sultan would not allow it. He shocked the innocents among
his people: he sent men after the ambassadors, sworn to
courtesy, to beseech them to master their tempers. They did
not even pause in mounting their horses. In a storm of hoofs
and dust and half-furled canopies, they thundered from the
camp.

''He planned it,'' said Zamaniyah.

Al-Zaman paused in breaking the evening's bread. ''Of
course he planned it. So did they.''

''It's all a deadly dance. They've said the words the pattern
bids them say. They've stung each other into fury; they've
remembered their pride. And their men saw it. They'll fight
all the harder for it.''

He nodded. His eyes approved her. He offered her half of
his loaf dipped in the pot between them, watched as she ate
it. ''Did you notice how small the army seems,'' he asked,
''with so much of it spread so wide, warding villages all
about Hama?''

''And more yet holding Homs; but none so far that the
army can't be whole again quickly if he needs it.''

''Just so.'' He smiled. ''You see, then. Our enemies know
that they can win a battle, even without Aleppo's walls to
shield them. Now they know that they cannot lose.''

''Aleppo knows how large our army is.''

''Does it? It's known that the sultan's resources are hardly
infinite. It's whispered abroad that he can barely hold his men
together.''

''That's not true.'' She nibbled a date, pondering. ''Both
sides want to fight. They both try to avert it if they can, to
win by wit and pretense, without the shedding of blood.
Honor, glory, holiness, even a throne—those aren't the heart

of it. The heart of it is gold. Gold to pay one's army in order
to win plunder to pay one's army.''

"What else need war be for?''

He meant it. She stared at him. Sometimes he baffled her.
Logic was logic, but there were shades of it that made sense
only to a man.

"I don't think,'' she said, "that we should need war at
all.''

Now she had baffled him. He had no answer for anything
so improbable, and so contrary to the Prophet's teachings. It
stung him; he frowned, absorbed himself in the remnants of
his dinner.

She bit her tongue. Sometimes she had no sense.

The silence grew. There were only the two of them, with
servants, and Wiborada. Here, in seclusion, the Frank was
bareheaded; her hair, plaited simply down her back, shone
burnished in the lamplight.

Al-Zaman's eyes had turned to it, drawn by its brightness.
Her own eyes flicked up. The meeting was like a crossing of
blades.

Zamaniyah wanted to retreat, and rapidly. But she was
trapped between them.

This was nothing like her own shy fumblings with Abd
al-Rahim. There was fire in this, a white heat. She did not
know what to call it. Love did not seem to fit it. Passion was
too murky. Desire? Too feeble.

Wiborada was stark white. Zamaniyah sensed rather than
saw her trembling.

He held out his hand. Wiborada's fingers clenched and
unclenched. Her jaw set. Under skillful paint, a bruise was a
paling shadow.

Zamaniyah swallowed painfully. He did not know. If he
saw, as he must; if he asked . . .

Wiborada accepted the proffered hand. Her breath was
sharp, her face taut. She tensed as if to recoil; caught herself
with a visible effort. Held fast. Sighed long and slow, and
eased, muscle by taut-strung muscle.

Zamaniyah turned craven. She left them to it.

21

On the second morning after the envoys' departure, the army, swelled with the forces which had been hidden from the enemy, marched out from Hama. The armies of Mosul had advanced perilously close, to Shaizar that was but five leagues up the Orontes. They were ranging themselves for battle. The sultan hastened to prepare the field.

He chose the rolling level that rose into stark dun heights, the hills called the Horns of Hama. There in the open, with no walls to defend him and no city to guard his back, he waited for his enemy. It was not the stretching frustration of a siege, nor yet the breathing space of the days at Hama. This was a mounting tension, a bracing, a firming of will before battle.

"Is it certain?"

Zamaniyah paused in honing her sword. "The sultan has sworn himself to it."

Wiborada was undismayed. She had been spending her nights again with al-Zaman. There was no glow on her that Zamaniyah could put a name to, no intimation that her fear had miraculously melted away; but she was calm, and the haunted look was leaving her eyes. "He's kind," was all she had said. "Much kinder than I deserve."

She set herself to polishing her helmet. Zamaniyah eyed it but said nothing. "I've heard," Wiborada said, rubbing hard, bending her eyes upon it, "that the sultan has given way to expedience. That he has made the same bargain with the Franks as the one for which he castigated Aleppo and Mosul."

"Hardly as sweeping as that," said Zamaniyah. "He's promised to give them back their prisoners if they stay out of this war."

"But he's been thundering anathemas against his enemies for treating with the infidel."

"That's rhetoric," said Zamaniyah. "It's always high and furious before a fight."

"Like dogs snarling."

"Or stallions challenging one another." Zamaniyah sighted along her blade. It was straight, and keen enough to draw blood from the wind.

"You people lie at will, don't you?"

Zamaniyah glanced up sharply. "Only to enemies. And to merchants. And to people we love, to keep them from pain."

"That's everyone."

"Not quite," said Zamaniyah, sliding her sword into its sheath.

Wiborada bent to her polishing. "I know what you want to say. Franks never tell the truth at all."

"Not to infidels."

"What does that do to us?"

"You're family. You get the truth."

"Even if it hurts?"

"It would hurt you worse to suffer a falsehood."

Wiborada hugged her suddenly, without any softening of face or eyes; and let her go just as suddenly, and went back to the scouring of her helmet.

Zamaniyah nodded as if Wiborada had spoken. The silence was hardly comfortable, but the strain in it had use and purpose, like the tautness of a bowstring. It marked the presence of something strong, with truth in it, and a little— but a sufficiency—of joy.

* * *

"Butterflies!" the sultan cried.

His temper frayed easily of late. He was not turning
capricious, as far as Zamaniyah could see, but he was easily
pricked to wrath; and a king enraged is a deadly beast.

She was there because he had summoned her. What he
wanted her for, in the ants' nest that was his tent, she could
not guess. Surely he would not abandon it all to ride with her
in a country full of spies and deadliness.

She had found a place out of the main thoroughfare of men
and messages, a corner where she could sit and watch and
listen and only rarely be fallen over.

The sultan was dictating a letter, with impassioned com-
mentary. "Write," he said sharply, "to my uncle, may God
preserve him from harm: 'Allah knows that we do not swear
truce with the infidels by our own will; that the perfidy of our
enemies has forced us to it; that we strive ever and only on
behalf of the people of the Faith. But those very people,
lighter of mind than butterflies—'" He tossed his head,
remarkably like Khamsin in a temper. "Why can't they see?
I've taken on two armies at a time. I can't leave a third
unbound at my back. If I am to wage holy war, I must—I
must—unite Islam. Half of Islam refuses union without battle. Therefore I give it battle; and requite treachery with
treachery, bargaining with the devil behind, the better to
overcome him when the time comes."

"Shall I write all that, my lord?" his secretary asked,
treading softly in the storm.

"Yes. Write it. Write it all. Then give it to the messenger.
And pray God that the Franks accept my terms before the
battle begins."

One or two people, overly dutiful, did just that, in loud
voices. The sultan snarled at them. "Egypt," he muttered.
"Egypt comes to strengthen us. But slow—all of it, too
slow." He spun. His finger stabbed. A secretary leaped, pen
in hand, to write whatever he should bid. Sweetness this
time, and sugared indirection, and never a word of bargaining
with the devil: a letter to the Commander of all the Faithful,
however feeble in truth his sway may have been, the caliph in
Baghdad.

* * *

"Does it trouble you to see how a king must be?"

Zamaniyah greeted the magus with a smile and, when he would not let her rise, a bow of the head. But her answer was grave. "It's necessary. He doesn't like it, I can see. But he's good at it, and he doesn't let it go to his head."

Anyone else would have smiled to hear such words from her, young as she was, and female besides. The Hajji simply nodded. "He knows his own measure."

They listened to him lament the treachery of Aleppo and Mosul. "He's eloquent," said Zamaniyah. She did not know that it was admiration. She had mooned after him like any silly girl, once. That was gone.

Yes, after all, she admired him still. Liked him very much. Loved him?

She loosed a small sigh. She would follow him anywhere. Even, she realized, without her father to command her. "How odd," she mused. "I didn't want to come to Syria at all. I was deathly afraid."

"And now?"

The Hajji's eyes were bright and dark at once, piercing to the heart of her. She tore her own away. Her palms were cold, for no reason at all, except maybe that she had remembered what he was.

She rubbed them against her thighs, warming them. Her voice was almost as light as it wanted to be. "Now I can't imagine not having come."

"Are you still afraid?"

She started to deny it. Then she shook herself. She was no good at lying. Not to a magus. "Still. Now I know what I'm afraid of."

"Death?"

Again an answer came: the simple answer, the obvious one. Again she changed it. "Pain."

He nodded slowly. "He needs you, you know."

She blinked at the shift, but she understood. Her cheeks warmed a little. "What would a king need from me?"

"Truth," the magus answered. "Loyalty. Respect without servility. And, with it all, a clear eye and a thinking mind, and the wisdom to know when to use them."

"But I hardly—"

"It is what you are."

"What I am—"

He was not there. She had been looking at him, glaring for a fact, and she had not seen him go.

She finished it because she had to. "What I am is neither fish nor fowl."

What you are is yourself.

She had not heard that, that voice like wind in her ear. She had imagined it.

Then the sultan called her, and there was no time to ponder anything.

He wanted to ride, or at least to walk alone and unharried under open sky. Cheated of that, he dismissed everyone he could dismiss. "Go," he said to them. "Rest; take an hour's peace. Come back for the noon prayer."

Some tried to protest. He would not listen. "Imad al-Din" —The chief of his secretaries, who was also his friend, raised cool intelligent eyes and nodded—"will see to anything that needs seeing to.

"Because," he said when there were only guards and her silent eunuch and the two of them, "I need time to breathe."

"Should you have it, my lord, this close to the fight?"

He stopped short in his pacing. She watched his temper rear up, waver, break into laughter. "Of course not! But I shall. I'm the king. My will is law."

She bowed at his feet, and that was true, but so also was the wickedness of her glance as she came up. She sat on her heels. "And what is the king's will for his lowliest servant?"

For a long while he did not answer. He paced, restless as a panther in a cage. She watched. Hunger was a familiar ache, dull, ignorable. Her arms and her hands twinged a little from a full morning's practice in archery. She flexed her fingers, feeling of the calluses, the roughness that was nothing like the soft smoothness expected of a woman.

For once it did not trouble her to think that old and painful thought. The Hajji had done something. Or time had. She was aware, watching that man who was a king, of what she was. Her slenderness that was nothing like his. Her shape under light mail and quilted coat. Even that she had no beauty. It did not matter.

When he stopped, turned, she was ready. He seemed

nervous suddenly, uncertain, as if he had had a purpose and now he did not know if he dared to speak of it.

She could not help him. She could only wait and be quiet and try not to fidget.

"Are you in comfort?" he asked at last.

She nodded.

He shook his head sharply. "Not here. I meant, *here*."

And she had called him eloquent. She bit her lips to keep back the smile, lest he misunderstand it.

"Here," he repeated, annoyed with himself. "In the army."

"Do you ask that of every emir's heir?"

She bit her tongue, much too late. He flushed darkly. "You are not—"

Some things could still hurt. It depended on where they came from. "I see," she said. "I am not a man. Has it taken you so long to notice?"

"That is not," he said with strained patience, "what I meant."

"But I'm *not* a man. It matters, doesn't it? After all. You tried so hard to convince everyone that it didn't. Has someone said something invidious?"

"Invidious," he said, "no." He dropped to the carpet. She admired his ease in managing skirts, scabbard, and temper, all at once. He fixed his eyes on her. Seeing her, perhaps, for the first time as she truly was. "No one else is like you," he said. "And yet you make yourself seem . . . not ordinary; not harmless. But not a monster, nor ever a threat. You are what you are, without pretense. You give no man cause to inveigh against you."

She kept her eyes down, somewhat in confusion and somewhat in embarrassment. Yes, she was like that; she worked at it. Why did people keep thinking that it was something to praise her for?

"You could be a mockery or a scandal," he said. "You manage to be neither. You acquit yourself well in whatever you do, but never so well as to rouse envy or to waken outrage."

"Except once," she muttered.

He had to pause for remembrance. He laughed a little. "You were angry then, and you made up for it after. I've

noticed: when you're angry you forget. You let people see the
fire in you.''

He stopped. The silence lasted long enough that she looked
up, to find him blushing visibly and shockingly, as if he had
said something scandalous.

"Listen to me," he said, sounding angry himself. "*Allah!*
My tongue staggers like a drunken Frank. I only mean to ask
you. To tell you. Whatever befalls, you always have my
protection.''

She frowned without thinking; realized what she did; smoothed
her face. "I know that, my lord. I've always known it. You
gave your word.''

"I give it again. I bid you remember it. No one can force
you to do anything against your will. If anyone—*anyone*—
tries, he will have to deal with me.''

"Are you talking about my father?''

"Anyone," he repeated.

She rose slowly. It was not proper, but her legs were doing
their own thinking. "What are you trying to tell me, my
lord?''

"That your will is free. That I will stand behind it in
whatever it elects to do.''

"My lord," she said. "That is a very great trust.''

"You are worthy of it.''

Her head shook, slightly, of itself. He had answered nothing of what she asked. He would answer nothing. Even
tongue-tied, he was a king.

She must have taken proper leave. No one upbraided her; no
one tried to call her back.

She fetched up against Khamsin, who was grazing by her
tent. "He knows about the emir," she said. "Or . . .''

She could not say it aloud. Or he was telling her that he,
himself, would offer, if she would accept.

She shook herself. That was foolish. The sultan would
have asked for her if he had wanted her. He was no callow
boy, to sigh and blush and languish in her wake. And he
knew as well as she, that the lord of Egypt and Syria could
not take a wife who rode to war like a man; and he had as
much as told her that no one could shut her up in any harem,
not even himself, unless she consented to it.

"Is he telling me I shouldn't accept the emir? Or telling me I should, even if my father forbids?"

Khamsin was no help. Neither was Jaffar. The two of them were exchanging glances of shameless complicity.

She cursed them both and went to drown her sorrows in the midday prayer.

It was easy to watch the sultan make a fool of himself over Zamaniyah. *He* did not know why he did it. Setting her free to be what she had always been for him: his private oddity, his falcon whom he kept for her wild beauty and her sudden fire.

And yet, as the sun sank, Jaffar's spirits sank with it. He had not liked the feel of this place when he came to it. There was blood on it, and the promise of violence. Now the word had gone out. Tomorrow the enemy would have come close enough to fight.

He dreaded sleep and the dreams that would come with it. He thought long on waking the night through; but his mind was made up, his weapons honed in secret, and he could not fight with his every bone longing for sleep. Still less could he trust to wine or a sleeping draught. What if she woke and needed him?

Sleep, then, it must be. He had armor against dreams, but not against what waited for him now, crouched under the very arch of the gate. Even awake he knew its shape. Its claws were the color of blooded blades.

Naming it would take a little of its strength. "Death," he said in his own tongue as he lay on his mat. "I name you Death."

It barely waited for his eyes to close. It seized him at the very edge of sleep and devoured him. It rent him asunder; it trampled his bones. It showed him what must, ineluctably, be. It spat him up on the shores of the dawn.

The camp had been stirring the night long. He lay and listened to it. The dream was with him. Part of it was bitter clarity. Part was clouded; and that was not mercy. The clouds veiled the pitiful little that might have hinted at hope.

She was awake. He felt it under his skin. He went to her.

She was gazing dark-eyed into the shadows. When he came she smiled, a sweet drowsy smile with no fear left to stain it.

He wanted to seize her, clutch her close. He dared not. He must speak calmly, reasonably. "Mistress," he said, "dawn is coming. Will you rise?"

She nodded, sat up. Her hair tumbled over the curve of her breast. She shook it out of her face, yawned, stretched.

While she ate the food he brought, he said it. "Mistress. The sultan set you free to do as you please. Did he not?"

She paused. Her eyes widened slightly. She nodded with care, with waking suspicion.

"I think," he said, "that it might please you to forgo this battle."

At the first word he saw her harden. He pressed on in spite of it. "You don't need to prove your courage. You've done it over and over. If you won't stay in camp, you can set yourself with the sultan. Then if he's endangered you can defend him; but you needn't endanger yourself or your Khamsin on the open field."

Her eyes narrowed, as if she had seen the calculation in Khamsin's name. "You know I can't do that. I have a place near my father."

"The sultan would welcome you."

"Oh, certainly," she said, scornful. Eyes and voice sharpened. "Why are you talking in circles? What are you getting at?"

He was not the sultan. He could say it—almost—straight. "I don't want you to fight today."

"You never want me to fight."

"Today is more than plain not-wanting. Or asking you to hide in your tent."

"No; only under the sultan's skirts, while my father faces the full heat of the battle. Did I misunderstand my lord completely? Is this what he meant?"

"Maybe," said Jaffar. It was not a lie, precisely.

She hissed. He had angered her; and when she was angry, she knew nothing of reason. "I won't be protected like this. I won't!"

"Even though I know that you will die?"

She checked, hard. But she did not know of his dreams. That had always been his secret, alone; his alone to suffer.

Now that it was too late, he tried to tell her. His words raveled and fell uncomprehended.

"You *know* this?" she demanded.

"I know."

Her eyes scanned him slowly, as if he were a stranger, and she did not know if she dared to trust him. "You're a . . . soothsayer?"

He tossed his head in desperation. "I dream dreams. My gods send them to me. They tell truth."

They were tangling his tongue now, clouding her mind, firming her will against him. He watched and he knew, and he could do nothing but make it worse. "My gods," he tried to say again. "My gods—"

"There is no god but Allah."

Blind in her damnable Faith. Blind and deaf.

So would they all be. Even the Frank. None of them would help him. If he bound her, hid her, won her hatred but preserved her life—

Darkness came between them, shattering even that dim hope. It bore a Frankish shape, a glimmer of pale hair. She greeted Zamaniyah shortly enough and sought her belongings, unheeding of the tension that stretched the air to breaking. As she drew out the corselet in its wrappings, he cast the last of his spears. "Very well," he said. "Deny me. And know that I ride at your back."

"You can't," said Zamaniyah.

"I can't what? Ride? Fight? Die with you if you insist on this lunacy?"

"But you have no armor."

He had his own box. He burrowed in it. Under a thin shield of clothing lay weight and solidity: the quilted coat of a Nubian soldier. It was cut for riding.

"You aren't a Nubian."

That was feeble, and they both knew it. Grimly he pulled on the coat, belted it, hung from its belt the helmet that had been wrapped in it.

"You can't," she said, falling back once more upon simplicity. "I can't let you."

"Are you afraid my presence will unman the troops?"

Her breath caught sharply.

"If you go," he said with a shade less cruelty, "I go. If I can defend you I will. If I can't, I don't want to live."

"What if you die and I don't? What then, Jaffar?"

He spoke through cold and rising dark: the dream returning, possessing him. "You know how you can prevent it."

Her head shook, obstinate. "This is my portion. I won't run away from it."

His people said that death's nets were strong and not to be resisted. Hers spoke of fate and of what their God had written. It was all the same.

And she was Zamaniyah, and Zamaniyah never did anything that accorded with prudence. The moment he had spoken of death and danger, he had lost her. He should have kept silent and spirited her away.

Too late. Too late now for anything but what must be.

22

Even before it begins, battle has a taste, like iron that is the core of blood. The air was full of it. Khamsin's fodder reeked of it. It made his skin shiver; it set him dancing.

Most often when his servant murmured and stroked and cajoled him into calmness, he let himself submit, because it was easier than disobedience; and it pleased Ali. Ali, pleased, was pleasant company. He had a sweet voice in singing, but he would never lift it where a human could hear. Most of them thought him mute. It suited him to have them think so; for then they left him alone.

But now Khamsin could not yield to those hands or that subtle voice. Ali pursued him doggedly, brushing him until he shone like polished cedarwood, combing his mane to silk, knotting his tail and weighting it with leaden beads. The beads in his forelock were glass, and blue. His caparisons were green and gold. The familiar weight of them wound him tighter still. He shied away from the mace in its saddle sheath; Ali came as close to cursing as he ever came.

A shadow unfolded itself from Zamaniyah's tent. Khamsin

stopped short and stared. The eunuch was got up, by all that
was holy, like a man of war. The heavy coat lent bulk to his
slenderness. His beardless face would have passed muster
among the clean-shaven Nubians. His weapons had the patina
of much use; and he carried them as one who knew what they
were for. He looked most martial, and most dångerous.

He faced Khamsin. He ignored the silenced horseboy. He
glared without saying a word, until Khamsin stamped and
snorted.

"Patience was never your strength, was it, my prince?"
Khamsin snapped, warning. The eunuch seized his bridle.
He tensed to rear; but the black eyes held him more firmly
than any hand. "I know what you are," said Jaffar, soft as a
tiger's purr. "I know what you must have been."

Khamsin's eye rolled. His head jerked, stilled.

"Protect her," said this terrible creature who was infinitely
more a man than he, and infinitely less. "Or by all gods that
are, I will hound you to the gates of death, and beyond them,
to the world's ending. That is a vow, O my enchanted
prince."

Khamsin damned pain. He tore himself free. The eunuch
did not try to seize him again. He met those eyes as best he
could, and gave them hate, which was for the two of them;
and promise, which was for Zamaniyah.

The eunuch pondered both hate and promise. After a
stretching moment he turned on his heel. His scorn was open,
his doubt perceptible. But he had said what he had come to
say. The rest, said his retreating back, was between God and
Khamsin.

By full daylight the army was up, armed, fed, and entrusted
to Allah. The sultan held the center behind a wall of men and
steel. A page stood by with his charger, but he now sat, now
stood, now paced, in a flurry of messengers.

For a little while Zamaniyah was one, bringing word that her
father's ranks were in their places, and seeking word of the
enemy. Khamsin was even more restive than usual; it took
most of her will and her patience to hold him in.

As she brought her stallion to a bucking halt near the
sultan, she heard him speaking rapidly, dictating to a secretary who struggled to keep pace. "'Uncle, nephews, my

kinsmen, I bid you, fly. If the journey is too much for you, take your ease; but send your men to me. I stand between Mosul and the Franks; Aleppo approaches my lines. Allah, Allah, let not my uncle read this letter unless he has set foot in his stirrup!' ''

From the hilltop and from the promontory of her saddle, Zamaniyah could see far and clear. The hills at the army's back; the river before, carved deep into the plain; and moving on it, a confusion of armies.

Wings flapped over her head. One of the sultan's guards, warden already of a cage of cooing birds, caught this new one: a brown dove, a messenger. He unbound the message from its leg.

The sultan was up, his letter forgotten. "What? What is it?"

The man bowed, presenting the tiny scroll. The sultan read it rapidly. A great light grew in his face. "Allah, *Allahu akbar!* The Franks have agreed. My envoy comes with their terms. Ya Allah! Now it begins to go as I would have it." He spun back to the scribe. "Tell my uncle. Deplore the need for this bargain that our enemies have forced upon us. Beg him to come on wings if he may; or even this small victory will come to nothing."

Zamaniyah shook herself out of her fascination. There were men about, emirs whom she knew vaguely, accepting such messages as her own. She gave it; received the orders which she had been sent for.

As Khamsin began to circle back toward their place in the lines, the sultan's eye found her. Armored, she looked like any young archer in the army; but he knew her horse. She took his smile back with her, a warmth to remember in the cold clenching of battle's beginning.

The ranks of Islam were nothing like ordered Frankish lines. They shifted and flowed about the standards of the captains. The young and the eager tested their weapons, limbered their mounts, simply fretted in and about their places. Seasoned fighters took their ease in what shade they could contrive; some even seemed to sleep.

Messengers galloped back and forth. Men of neighboring companies mingled, companionable. There was a great deal of laughter and song; and Zamaniyah could see a game of dice in progress. The players were wagering their hopes of plunder.

She had dismounted to spare Khamsin. After all his fretting, he seemed to have seen the virtue in quiet. He had an understanding with Jaffar's mule; they were side by side, nose to tail, flicking the flies from one another. Terror or no, she found herself smiling at the sight of them.

Someone was standing near her. He had been standing there for some little time, saying nothing. She turned. Whatever she would have said, she forgot entirely.

Abd al-Rahim bowed like a courtier. "Lady," he said. "Have I your leave to wish you well?"

She was conscious of Jaffar standing as close as her shadow, and of her father caught up in his command. She was sharply, almost painfully conscious of the young man who had risen to meet her eyes. She had no voice to speak. She nodded.

His smile was luminous. He dared mightily, almost unpardonably: he touched her cheek.

His hand leaped back even as it touched, as if it burned him as it had burned her. "Allah protect you," he said.

Jaffar's snort was as eloquent as Khamsin's. She could have hit them both. But Abd al-Rahim was there still, bowing again, leaving her in a faint scent of musk and leather. His place was far down the line, among the Syrians.

She willed her eyes to stop following him. Thunder rumbled all about her. A shout went up. She snapped about. An army was coming at the charge.

Her body never stayed for her sluggard of a brain. She vaulted into the saddle, snatched her bow.

People were raising a deafening clamor. Its sense dawned slowly. Not dismay. Not enmity, or the madness of battle. Joy. "Farrukh-Shah! Shihab al-Din! Taqi al-Din!" The sultan's kinsmen, his uncle, his brother's sons, come at last as he had prayed. "Egypt! Egypt has come!"

In force, with a high heart, singing. Suddenly all the sultan's army was the center, and Egypt spread wide in its wings; and they who had been a small force to be so strong, were a mighty army.

And Aleppo, on the plain, had flowed together with Mosul

and come on with the speed of war: agonizingly slow, appallingly swift.

Zamaniyah did not know how it was for other people. For her everything was both bitterly clear and lost in a haze of terror. She could read every word on every banner of the army that came against her; but she could see nothing of the warriors' faces, only a blur of white, brown, black, and a gleam of eyes, and a glitter of sun on bared steel. That undulating roar was the massed voices of the armies, and the thunder of hoofs and drums, and the shouted commands of the captains.

She had learned, by laborious degrees, to focus. To see only what was directly about; to hear only her own commander. Since he was her father, that was less difficult than it might have been. It gave her an anchor in the sea of milling, shrieking, murderous humanity.

She was aware, as she must be, of who nearby was friend, and who was enemy. The emirs who had been with the sultan throughout this war were together, apart from the Syrians and the half-wild Bedouin. The Egyptians flanked them all, riding and fighting too far away to matter.

As she moved with the mounted archers to begin the charge, her eye's edge marked the nearest banner. At first she did not know it except for *ours*, and then for not there when she had looked before. Recognition struck as she strung her bow; it nearly flew from her slackened hands.

Pray God her father did not see who had come to flank him. Luck, fate, design, some failure of the sultan's vigilance— no matter what it was. Hard upon the right hand of the Zamani cavalry rode the levies of Ali Mousa Sharif.

Everything in battle was an omen. She fumbled with her bowstring, all skill deserting her, all courage reft away.

Khamsin tossed his head and neighed. Her father's voice rose strong and deep and much beloved. The drums quickened to the charge.

Khamsin sprang forward. She lurched; he jibbed, offended; laughter tore itself from her. She found her balance with her strength. An arrow leaped from quiver to hand to string. With a high fierce cry she aimed it into the seething mass that was the enemy, and let it fly.

Bow to lance to sword. That was the way of her people in

war. For the sultan there would be order in it, and shape, and plan. For her there was only battle. Her father's standard was beacon and guide. Her duty was to hold fast beneath it and to cut down any who hindered her. She felt in her skin the eunuch fighting like a tiger behind, and the Frankish woman close by him, mutely defiant, wielding sword with a man's deadly strength. They were an army of their own, an arrow shot into the enemy's heart.

Khamsin lunged at a howling Turkoman, smote him down, trampled him. Her sword bit flesh beyond him. Her back quivered; she flattened. Steel sang over her, clashed on Wiborada's sword.

Her stallion bore her out of it. Nothing leaped to strike. She drew a breath, glanced quickly about, started. Her father's banner was far to the left of her. Close, so close that she might have belonged to it, Ali Mousa's green standard whipped in the wind.

Khamsin squealed, kicked hard. The battle had found them again. Its course bore them steadily rightward.

There—an opening; a path to al-Zaman.

Khamsin bucked and balked. The path closed. The tide bore her toward her father's enemy.

23

Khamsin hardly knew what he was doing until he had done it. Making choices when he thought they were all made. Being drawn to that banner as if he had no will of his own. *God is great,* said the letters upon it, *and inscrutable are the ways of God.*

Green and gold. He could not see or taste them, but he knew. So too his trappings. It was too perfect for irony. It must be fate.

His rider's resistance was sharp, but steel was sharper yet. She wasted no strength in fighting him. There were enemies enough to hand.

Two who belonged to al-Zaman were with them yet. The woman on her tall gelding; the eunuch on his mule that had the spirit of its dam. They fought well. He could notice that, slashing, twisting, standing taut and poised as Zamaniyah crossed swords with a glittering warrior.

He was aware, always, of his father. Ali Mousa was sharif, sayyid, descendant of the Prophet. He could have chosen quiet: the life of the scholar, the saint, or even the prince. But the Prophet had spoken. *War is ordained for you,* he had said.

And Ali Mousa, who hated killing, who abhorred the ugliness of violence, had chosen war.

Yet, having chosen it, he had made it his element. He had the commander's art: he could both defend himself and order his troops. He found weaknesses in the enemy's line. He judged them for traps or for truth. He wielded his men as he wielded his sword, with honed and tireless skill.

If he had marked the three who should not have been there, he betrayed no sign of it. They were driving back his enemies. They were heeding his commands because Khamsin was, and Khamsin carried Zamaniyah, and the others followed her.

After the headlong rush of the charge, their advance had slowed. But not to a standstill. They moved forward step by step. That meant something. Khamsin had no time to remember what.

Battles had eddies and shallows, pauses and sudden flurries. Ali Mousa seemed most often to be in the thick of it. Enemies aimed for the standard, for the glory and the profit of felling an emir. It would be very thick indeed in the center, where a trebled wall of fighters defended the sultan.

Khamsin's advance and his mistress' valor had brought him almost to Ali Mousa's side. She was a little heavier on his back. Tiring, and fighting it. And enemies innumerable before, about, behind.

Even behind.

Khamsin slashed with his heels. Hands clutched his trappings. A sword thrust upward.

With a panther-scream, death fell upon the swordsman. The eunuch's mule half reared, flailing. Fighting.

Falling. Its belly opened, spilling its secrets.

The eunuch flung himself free. He had a spear, scarlet-headed. Even in the air he wielded it. It found flesh. As his flesh found steel: a hedge of blades. Khamsin saw his face with deathly clarity. There was no fear in it; only exaltation. His long hands closed about the yelling throat, circled it. The man hacked at him. He laughed, light and glad and free, though his life's blood bubbled in it; and snapped his slayer's neck. They went down together into the dark.

Khamsin stilled. He had seen death enough to last a

thousand years. But never anyone he knew. Never anyone his mistress loved.

A cry smote his ears. It was low, raw. "Jaffar," cried Zamaniyah. "Jaffar!"

And she shifted. To dismount. Here. In the jaws of battle.

He knew how to shed a rider: oh, perfectly. But never this. How to keep one if she would not stay.

He lunged forward. Instinct ruled her, thrust her down into the saddle, tightened her hands upon the reins. His head snapped up with the sudden pain of it. His teeth clamped upon the bit. She hauled at it, wailing aloud, cursing, pummeling his sides, hacking at anything that came near her. "*Jaffar!*"

He would never hear her now.

No?

Wind in Khamsin's ear. A shadow amid the seething shadows of the battle. And Zamaniyah gone mad, and the Frank vanished, Allah knew where, for Allah knew how long; and Ali Mousa . . .

Alone. Afoot. Ringed in death. His charger lost, his banner fallen, his warriors scattered, and everywhere the madmen of Mosul.

Khamsin forgot his rider. He forgot his shock. He forgot even his bone-deep cowardice. He leaped into the worst of it.

The weight on his back rocked and nearly fell. The wind in his ears keened in helpless rage. The weight steadied. The wind skirled away.

A horse reared, wheeling. The man on its back whirled the black blur of a mace. Khamsin sprang.

He stumbled to his knees. A body rolled underfoot, screaming. The mace swung keening down. Ali Mousa's back opened wide for it, all undefended.

Zamaniyah flung herself out, up. Her sword clove air. Her body caught the mace.

In all the clamor, in all the whirling and plunging and shouting, Khamsin heard that one small sound. A ringing of metal on metal. A soft thick echo afterward: the meeting of mace and flesh and bone. And the thud of body on earth, abrupt and absolute.

Khamsin stood like a true beast, mute and witless. His back was empty. It was not supposed to be empty.

There was a great deal of noise. Men in green; horses. More men running away. They were nothing.

The wind cursed him endlessly and with great eloquence. It almost had a shape, a long dark shadow-shape with eyes like faded moons. He walked through it.

She was all disarrayed. Her helmet was gone. Her hair was a snake, coiling in blood. He touched nose to her shoulder. Blood, and breaking. She was broken.

She could not be. She was his. She could not be broken.

People were there. A mamluk whose scent was a woman's, blood-tainted. A man whom he had known once. Whom he had loved. For whom—he—

He climbed the sky, screaming. He smote earth, battering its blind indifference.

A hand held him. A voice spoke to the will beneath the madness, calming it. Ali Mousa looked down at the one who had fallen, and his shock was black, like ancient blood. "A woman?" he asked, a dry whisper. "A woman in war?"

"A woman, yes!" This voice was patently no less, even raw with grief. "And one you know, if you know anything at all."

He did. He was refusing it. Even Iblis could not mock him so. Destroy him so, by making him the destroyer of all the house of al-Zaman.

The Frank knelt with none of her trained and womanly grace. There were wounds on her. She took no notice of them. She bent her ear to the crushed and bleeding breast, held her hand to the motionless lips. Her eyes opened wide. "She's still alive!"

Khamsin froze. Not so Ali Mousa. He bent. With strength that could startle the man locked deep in the beast's body, he lifted Zamaniyah. He shook off the Frank, who was snatching, shouting, drawing sword.

He came to Khamsin. "Kneel," he said, expecting obedience.

He received it. He bestrode the saddle. At a word, Khamsin rose, balancing the doubled weight. As softly and yet as swiftly as he had ever moved, he bore it away from the roil of battle.

Someday he would remember how it was. The enemy driven in rout, its back broken, its brief flurries of resistance scattered. Such as the one from which he came. The one which had felled Zamaniyah.

Ali Mousa's men were quick enough to flock to their commander, now that he had no need of them. Most he sent away under the chief of his captains, to harry the enemy until the sultan should call them in. Some he kept. Of their spears and their cloaks he made a canopy; he laid Zamaniyah under it.

Wiborada said, heatedly, what Khamsin could not. "Why here? She should go to the camp, to the doctors."

Ali Mousa sent a man to fetch one. Then he spoke to her, not looking directly at her, as a man should do with another man's woman. "She would not survive the journey."

Wiborada dropped beside Zamaniyah. "She won't survive the hour if you leave her here." Even as she spoke, she struggled with coat and corselet. No one would help her. Khamsin could not. His heart ached for hands; for speech; for tears.

The Frankish woman had no shame of stripping Zamaniyah to the skin, baring the great raw wound. Red blood, white bone; side and shoulder shattered, arm dangling broken. She breathed, rattle and catch, rattle and catch. Death had pitched camp in her face. It bubbled in her lungs. It rode her heart to foundering.

Wiborada cursed in Frankish, softly and at length.

That was not what Khamsin wanted to do. He wanted to howl like a dog.

Wiborada tried to bind the worst of it, to stop the blood, to straighten shattered bone. Her hands were deft, although her tears must have blinded her.

A cloak settled billowing over the bared and helpless body. Wiborada regarded it without gratitude. She stroked the sweat-sodden hair, over and over, as if will and hand could mend what iron had broken.

People came, stared. Some spoke to Ali Mousa. Most went away. Khamsin barely noticed. He watched the white linen—Zamaniyah's own shirt, set to this last grim service—turn slowly scarlet. He felt the ebbing of her life. She was fighting, clinging against all hope, but her body was too badly broken. It could not house her.

After an age a doctor came, reluctant, muttering, sparking

with outrage when he saw that she was a woman. "Why did you drag me here? There are men yonder who need me. This is beyond need of anything but a shroud."

"She will not die," said Ali Mousa.

Even that irascible small man could perceive the iron in the sharif's voice. It silenced his muttering. It brought him erect. "She cannot live."

"She must. That wound was meant for me."

"Sir," said the doctor, "it was written that she should take it. It is certain that she will die of it.

"She is only a woman," he pointed out, meaning comfort by it.

Ali Mousa stared him into silence. "She is a warrior, and valiant." His voice rose a very little. "Go. Send me a man who knows some glimmer of healing. Send me a man who is not a fool!"

The doctor drew himself up. "A fool I may be, sir, but I know death. This woman is his. No mortal man can alter it, nor any lord's command."

"No," said Ali Mousa.

The doctor went away. Khamsin would have comforted his father if he could; but there was no comfort in him.

A shadow had taken up residence under the canopy. It had eyes, and those eyes were Jaffar's, implacable as death itself. Khamsin had no fear of him. *Yes, I did this. Yes, I killed her. There is no pain in hell to match this that I will upon myself.*

A new shadow, eyeless, barred the sun. Mare-scent distracted dimly. A boy held her. A man stood staring at them all.

"No," said the sultan.

The world had shrunk to a single word. The sultan bent as they all had, to see what they all could see. He spun upon Ali Mousa. *"What have you done to her?"*

"Nothing." Wiborada's voice was sharp and cold and sane. "There's nothing anyone can do. Except watch her die. Will you tarry with us, O my sultan? Maybe you can say a prayer for her."

He was weeping openly, without shame. "Ah God! This was to be my victory. I wanted to tell her—I wanted to hear her say—"

Zamaniyah was past hearing him. Khamsin whose ears

were bitterly keen could hear how her breathing faltered; how her heart battered itself against the walls of her body, desperate as a moth trapped within a lamp. His nose caught sparks of agony in endless, sour-sweet pain.

Pray God she did not wake and know it. Pray God—pray God she went gently into Paradise.

The sultan had fled. Wise man. Let him try to remember her as she had been. Not as she was now, shrunken, broken, mere crushed clay.

As the sun sank, her life sank with it. Wiborada tried to pour water into her, as if she were a flower that could rouse again for so simple a remedy. Ali Mousa sat and swayed gently and prayed in a soft and ceaseless murmur. He wept stone-faced as he did it. His mamluks hovered, helpless.

All helpless.

Khamsin flung up his head and screamed. They started like deer. Swords leaped into hands. He scorned them with tossing head, snapping teeth. He broke the bridle and cast it at their feet. He wheeled and bolted.

He hunted as the beast of prey hunts, by scent and sound and instinct. He was swifter than any but the swiftest; and his mind was a man's, fixed with human purpose, immovable. No shadow sped beside him. The eunuch's spirit had sworn to haunt him, but before him there had been Zamaniyah. When she died she would find him waiting, faithful as ever he had been.

Perhaps, dead, he could be a man for her. Allah was the Merciful, the Compassionate. Allah would reward such love as he had given her.

Khamsin shook himself even in his running. His own recompense would, and must, be only sorrow.

The camp swirled about him. The sultan's tent was an eddy in it. The sultan was there, newly come, harried by his servants. At sight of Khamsin he forgot them. His cry of grief rose sudden and piercing.

Khamsin snorted at it. He had not come for the sultan. He had come for the one with whom the sultan spoke; to whom the sultan spoke the name of Zamaniyah.

Cold horror congealed in Khamsin's heart. Only for Zamaniyah could he have done this. Only for her.

He barely saw the Hajji. Green turban. Silvered beard. Great roaring flame of power, banked in mortal flesh. He bowed before it.

"Too late," the sultan mourned. "Dear God, for my people I tarried; and for that—"

"Not yet, my lord," said the Hajji. He laid his hand on Khamsin's brow. It burned; it froze him where he knelt. "Take me to her," the Hajji said.

His weight was the weight of worlds. Khamsin bore it as if it had been air. He knew that he had escort, and it ran valiantly, but it struggled far behind. By himself he was swift, as swift as he was beautiful. Beneath the Hajji he outran the wind.

24

Thicker than death beneath the makeshift tent was the reek of
hate. Al-Zaman at last had found his daughter, and his
enemy. They both bore marks of struggle. Their mamluks
were ruffled, baleful. Wiborada stood between them. "Yes,"
she sneered at them. "Kill one another over her. She'll love
you for it, I'm sure. She'll reckon her life well lost."

One of them had struck her: she had a bruise rising.
Khamsin would have wagered on al-Zaman. She was, after
all, his chattel.

Khamsin would happily have trampled the man for daring
it. He, blind and deaf in enmity, spat at Ali Mousa's feet.
"Are you content, O my nemesis? Have you drunk your fill
of my children's blood?"

Ali Mousa met hot hate with hate both cold and haughty.
"How could such a swine have sired such a pearl?"

Al-Zaman lunged, snarling. His dagger glittered in his
hand.

His mamluks were ready for him. And Khamsin. His teeth
closed on the emir's wrist. Gently; but his jaws were strong.

Al-Zaman struggled. Khamsin tightened his grip. If he must gnaw that hand from its mooring, by Allah he would.

The Hajji's hand seared his neck, slackened his jaws. "It is grief," he said, soft and cool. And barely louder: "My lords. May I pass?"

Wise man, to pretend that they could stop him. They fell back before him. The sultan's swift coming absorbed them: they bowed, sundered by his presence, reduced to warring with glances.

The Hajji knelt by Zamaniyah. His hand was gentle on her brow. His face was ineffably sad.

It was Khamsin to whom he spoke. "She is dead," he said.

The words fell like stones, empty of meaning. Of course she was not dead. Khamsin had brought the Hajji to make her whole again. She was supposed to be alive, so that he could mend her. How dared she die before he could begin?

"It is said," said the sultan, "that in Ramadan, when the night has come, the angel of God passes over the earth, and whoever shall see him clearly may ask a boon of him; and if the seeker's heart be pure, it shall be granted. It is also said that if a mage has the strength and the courage, he may command the angel's will, and even raise the dead.

"It is Ramadan," said the sultan with exquisite and royal logic. "Night is coming. You are a mage, and holy. Make this child live again."

The green-turbaned head shook slowly. "Allah has written her death. I am not a black mage, to undo what God has ordained."

"Indeed," said the sultan. "Then they lied who told me of you. They said that you had done just that, to restore to a widow her only son."

"This is his only daughter," said Ali Mousa. Even al-Zaman stared, astonished.

"Would you have me call her back from Paradise?" the Hajji demanded of them.

Khamsin pawed the ground, snorting. Paradise, nothing. Will of Allah, nothing. Allah would allow what it pleased Him to allow; and He had given this player of games the power to conquer death. But he did not want to. Why should he trouble himself? She had never been aught to him.

"No," the magus said, rough with pain. "Oh, no. I loved her."

Then bring her back! Khamsin cried with all his soul.

The Hajji drew himself erect. His deep eyes burned upon them all. "You ask that I work the mightiest of all the arts of magic. That I chance failure, if she will not come, or if Allah does not wish to let her go. And the price of my failure is my death."

"Ah," said the sultan. "You fear what you must conquer."

"Certainly I fear that dread angel. He is strong and he is terrible, and his sword is pain. She knew, the young warrior. Now she knows the savor of his gift: and that is peace."

"Wizards' games," said al-Zaman. "You can do this. End your babble; do it."

"So I would," the Hajji said, "if my babble were to no purpose. I tell you what you ask of her: return to flesh and pain and mortal frailty. Of me you ask all my skill and power, and perhaps even my life. What, my lords, do you ask of yourselves? What price will you pay for this miracle?"

"All that I have," said Ali Mousa. "Even my own life, if so it must be. She died for me."

"I am her father," said al-Zaman, swift and fierce, furious that his enemy should have offered before he could speak. "Whatever you ask of me, that I will pay."

"I was her friend," said the sultan. "Today, in full truth, I am a king. You may have this kingdom that I have won, if you will rule it well, and wage the Holy War as I had intended."

Khamsin had nothing to match what they had: no wealth, no kinship, no kingdom. His body had been the Hajji's since he committed his great sin. All he had left was his life.

He shrank down, head low, trembling. He was not his father, to offer so freely all that was his. Ali Mousa was old; he would die soon enough. It was easier for him. Khamsin was young. His life had barely begun. How could anyone ask him to end it?

He had paid enough. He wore a beast's body. He was mute as a beast is mute. He had been soul's slave to a woman. A small, headstrong, forward-tongued snippet of a woman. She was not even pretty. She strode about like a boy. She had got

herself killed doing what no woman should ever presume to
do.

He did not love her. His soul was stunted. It could not
stretch itself to anything so wide or so high.

Let these great lords pay. They were rich enough.

And they had duties; responsibilities. People who needed
them. Lordships, kingdoms. Women. Kinsfolk; children.

Why was the Frank silent? Had she nothing to offer?

She had offered while he crouched and cowered. Everything. Freely. With all her heart.

The Hajji had choices enough. Perhaps he would take them
all. He would bring Zamaniyah back. Then Khamsin would
have her, and she him; and they would live out their lives in
blessedness.

The Hajji sighed. His head shook more slowly even than
before. "You all love her. And the price is love; but it must
be perfect."

"I am her father!" al-Zaman cried in naked pain.

"So you are," said the Hajji. "But do you love her for
her simple self, or for what your need has made her? Did you
ever consider her wishes when you imposed your decrees
upon her? You set her free; you gave her more than women in
the House of Islam are ever given. Yet you never gave it for
her sake. Only for your own."

Khamsin would have savored the sight of al-Zaman smitten
senseless by the truth. But someone else had come in all
unasked and all unlooked for. Had stared dumbfounded at the
one who lay in the midst of them. Had heard what they said;
had wept and cried, "*I* love her truly. I love her with all that
is in me."

Khamsin's teeth ached to sink into that scented neck. But
the Hajji was there, and his presence was stillness. "Would
you die for her?"

Abd al-Rahim never hesitated, not even for the fraction of
an instant. "Yes," he said. "Yes!"

Khamsin closed his eyes. This puppy's life for hers. How
perfect. He could not have ordained it better himself.

And his heart had twisted, and his mind had whispered,
No. He knew to the last stab of furious jealousy, how
al-Zaman had felt when Ali Mousa offered his life for his

enemy's child. So had this young idiot done; and done it with never a moment's pause.

Never a moment's worth of brain, either. He hung over Zamaniyah and sobbed, and spouted broken bits of poetry.

That, Khamsin's heart knew, was hardly fair. The boy was young; he was passionate; he was in love, and that was honest, and clear-sighted enough for all its extravagance. In among the poetry were bits of sense. He knew what he was grieving for.

She had not returned that passion. There had been no time. But something had been waking in her; something that could have been splendid, or could have died in its due and proper time. Not as now, cut off all untimely.

Her hand lay abandoned by her side. Its warmth was cooling. Her scent was fading, sinking into the dankness of death. He laid his nose in the stiffening palm.

A terrible ache closed jaws in his throat. He flung up his head, gulping air. His gullet spasmed. It was full of stones, and every one jagged, many-edged, grinding flesh to agony.

His heart thudded. Not stones. Words.

But he was mute.

Once. Once only might he speak. That was his geas.

The mage took no notice of him. They were all caught up in the young emir, in his great show of love and loss.

A magus did not need eyes to see or voice to speak. Clear in Khamsin's soul was the truth. He could do this. Or he could not. He had paid in full the price of his transgression. This was free choice.

The words were there, edged in anguish. This body was never made to contort itself in human speech. But it could speak. It could say anything it chose to say.

Reveal his name, his sin, his expiation. Cast himself upon his father's mercy.

Choose one of them for the sacrifice.

Say, "I am not a man. I do not know what love is. But I will die for her."

It was not a human voice. It was the voice which one might expect of a stallion, hoarse and shrill at once, deep in the chest and high in the nose, and thin with the pain of it. Yet it was clear, and it rang in the silence.

His geas had said nothing of laughter, or he would have

laughed at the circle of fallen jaws. They had all thought they knew what magic was. Until they saw it plain; and then it was plainly impossible. A horse speaking. In Arabic. With the accent of a Cairene prince.

The Hajji, who knew magic, spoke softly in the midst of it. "Do you know what you offer?"

Khamsin swallowed. The word-stones rolled, tearing. "I know."

The Hajji's eyes probed deep, searching. Khamsin met them as best he could. He did not try to pretend that he was unafraid, or that he was glad, or that he wanted to die for dying's sake. It was the only thing he could do. She would grieve when she knew, if she woke to know, but she would heal. And no guilt would sear her, ever, that a man had died to give her life. A beast . . . that was fitting. Were not beasts made to serve mankind?

The Hajji sighed. Khamsin's mind roiled. Grief; relief; rage. He could not refuse. He must not.

Mirth flickered, small and mad. All of them felt exactly the same. They all saw the perfection of Khamsin's logic. The mingling of scents made him sneeze.

The thin old hand cupped his muzzle, stroking lightly, tenderly. "O my lord," said the Hajji. "O valiant. You are no less an idiot than you ever were."

"A better grade of idiot," said Khamsin. "Perhaps. O my lord."

"Perhaps," said the Hajji. He smoothed the mane on Khamsin's neck. "I accept your sacrifice."

The words were all gone, every one. He was all lost. Trapped, tricked, cozened; and too much a fool to be sorry that he had done it.

And he could not even tell the man to hasten.

The Hajji dragged it out interminably. First they all had to say the sunset prayer. Then they had to fetch the tools of the Hajji's magic. The sultan left, all unwilling, to be sultan. The lesser lords eyed one another and growled in their throats. They wanted to tie Khamsin. The Hajji, most cruelly kind, prevented them. If he had been tied, he would have had no choice. He would not have had to battle with every ounce of will and strength, the urge to turn and bolt.

None of them lingered near him. He was marked. With uncanniness; with sacrifice.

The magus made his preparations. They were odd, even for magic. He closed the makeshift tent within the circle arcane. He circled that circle with men puzzled and doubtful and frankly hostile: holy men all, skilled chanters of the Koran. They were, when bidden, to perform their office, turn and turn about, continuously, from the magic's beginning through dawn and day and dusk to dawn again.

Then the magus told the emirs what they must help him to do. Bolster the spell with prayer. See him blood the sacrifice. Aid him in flaying it; in burning the body on a pyre of rare and enchanted woods; in wrapping Zamaniyah in the hide, and raising over her a true tent with walls and sealed door, and leaving her there alone in the circle and the chanting, while the magus wielded his power.

"This is mummery!" al-Zaman burst out in anger. "Give me my daughter's body. Let me bury it in dignity. Not in this mockery of magic."

"Very well," said the Hajji with perfect calm. "Take her."

Al-Zaman stared at him, all his rage shrinking, failing, crumbling into shock. "But——"

"It was not I who demanded this. She is at peace. I am content to leave her in it."

"But you promised——"

"I yielded to compulsion."

The emir seized him with bruising force. "Bring her back. *Bring her back!*"

"I think not," said the Hajji.

"The horse is not enough," said Ali Mousa heavily. "After all. What will you have, sir? My life? His? Both?"

"I am not a merchant," the Hajji said.

Abd al-Rahim looked from one to another of them. His eyes were wide, incredulous. "With all due respect, venerable sage, this is absurd."

"Indeed?" asked the Hajji. "To what do you refer? My spell? These gentlemen's assessment of it? The world itself?"

Abd al-Rahim glared terribly at his feet. His jaw clenched and unclenched, as if he did battle against words even more unwise.

The enemies looked at one another. For the first time since

the world began, one thought dawned in both their minds. It shocked them. It repelled them. They fought it with all their great and seasoned strength. Yet it was stronger than they.

The sharif said it. "We regret that we have offended you. In recompense, we offer the one thing that is dearest to our hearts. We give you peace. We forswear our enmity for all the time that is left us. Only deign, we beseech you, to restore this child to life."

The Hajji flicked not an eyelash at that vow, though it rocked the earth on which they stood. "I cannot restore her save as I have prescribed. You must accept it. And," he said, "you must hold by what you have sworn."

Al-Zaman's lip curled. "We'd better take it, old enemy," he said. "Before the price goes up again."

Ali Mousa did not find it easy to speak to him as if he were a man like any other; but it was not too badly feigned, for a beginning. "Indeed, old enemy," he said: "before he bids us couple truce with amity."

"That may come," said the Hajji, appalling them both. He drew the dagger that hung at his belt, turned to Khamsin.

Now at last it had come. Khamsin had been hoping, desperately, that the end would be easy. Or if not that, at least endurable. He had not lived well, when all was said. He wanted to die in something remotely like dignity.

As the blade approached him, his eyes rolled. He trembled and sweated. He shamed himself beyond shame. He voided in the circle.

"But," said the Hajji, "you do not run."

He could not. His knees, like his bowels, had turned to water.

The Hajji's hand settled once more between his eyes. He gasped, swayed. "Peace," said the magus. "Peace be upon you."

He closed his eyes. The air stank of his own terror. It was sweet, sweet. It was life.

It was his gift; his sacrifice.

His head came up. His fear swelled huge: too huge by far to hold. Its heart was quiet. Acceptance. Even, at the end of it all, peace.

The chanting had begun.

Praise be to Allah, Lord of the Worlds,
The Beneficent, the Merciful.
Owner of the Day of Judgment,
Thee alone we worship; Thee alone we ask for help.

Yes, thought Khamsin. Yes, and yes, and yes.

There is no god but God; and Muhammad is the Prophet
of God.

Hands of power raised his head. The moon was full. Its light filled him; its beauty smote him to the heart. He drank it in joy. He poured out his soul.

There was no knife, no fear, no pain. Only light.

25

It had been a very long dream, and very strange. Some of it was terrible. Some was beautiful beyond enduring. Some was simply incomprehensible.

Zamaniyah burrowed into her blankets. People were chanting rather too close for comfort, intoning the Koran.

The Beneficent
Hath made known the Koran.
He hath created man.
He hath taught him utterance.
The sun and the moon are made punctual.
The stars and the trees adore.
And the sky He hath uplifted. . . .

"God is great," she murmured automatically, groping back toward sleep.

She sat bolt upright. She was sleeping through the prayer. "Ya Allah!" she said, appalled. Her eyes were full of sleep. She blinked hard. "Jaffar! Jaffar, how could you let me—"

Her voice died. This was not her tent. It was too large. It

was too empty. There was nothing in it but herself and the heap of blankets and carpets on which she lay, and the lamp that flickered on its stand, and—

And.

She was pressed to the central pole, shaking, goggling like an idiot.

And a man. A very solid, very unconscious, very naked man.

Her memory floundered desperately. Battle. A battle. Jaffar—Jaffar dead. Then—

Nothing. Nothing at all.

Jaffar could not be dead. She must have dreamed it. As surely she dreamed this.

A Frank. Surely. His skin was nigh as fair as Wiborada's. His hair was the color of cedarwood. There was a great deal of it. It tumbled over his shoulders, down his back, across the blankets. His beard was long, curling to his breast; it bore an oddity: a finger's width of white, just right of its center. He was not filthy as Franks were supposed to be, but wherever he bathed, it was not in a Muslim bath. He was entirely, and fascinatingly, as God had made him.

Her body had a will of its own. It knelt beside him. He was not dead as for a moment she had feared: he breathed slowly, but deeply. Under lids as fine as veined marble, his eyes flickered in dream. His lashes were thick and long.

A man grown who shaved his beard, marred the perfection of his beauty. But surely there were limits. Was his face so uncomely that he must mask it in uncut thickets?

Or so comely?

She straightened with a snap. Her hand had almost touched him.

He was beautiful. Everywhere, beautiful. No Frankish face, that, for all its pallor: its bones were eagle's bones, the fine strong bones of Arabia. He had not the Frankish bulk. He would not be tall, standing: just at the middle height, perhaps, or a little more. He was made like a good horse, slender-limbed, lean-flanked, but deep of chest and shoulder, well and smoothly muscled under silken skin.

She snatched back her errant hand. Was she mad? Or had she died and gone to Paradise?

Her soul stilled. She had meant mockery. She had raised a scent of truth.

Battle. Ali Mousa unhorsed. A mace falling. She had flown. Or leaped. Then . . .

She looked at herself. She was in white, fine linen, long and loose. Her hair was free. Her feet were bare.

She peered under the gown. Her body was her own, with scars in all the proper places. And some that were new to her eyes but old in healing, pale: her shoulder, her arm, her side. She was still far short of storied beauty. She was too thin and hard. Her hips were barely wider than a boy's. Her rump was a scant handful. Her breasts were a little better, but they failed of their valor: they had too much to make up for.

She sighed a little. They were, at least, her own.

Her eyes wandered back to the carpets. The Prophet, God bless his name, had only mentioned the women of Paradise, though he had granted equality to every human soul. So, then: women too were given fair companions. Very fair. Very—very—

His eyes were large and dark. No; no Frank, this one. Eyes of Arabia, soft now with sleep; but there was fire in them. It kindled as they met hers.

He moved like an animal, all of a piece, with grace and power that made her think of stallions. He poised on his feet, eyes wide and rolling white; with a soft wordless sound he toppled.

She leaped. They fell together, clutching at all there was to clutch at, which was only one another.

Only, she thought, lying tangled with him, struggling for breath.

Muscle by muscle he contracted, shrinking away from her.

She scrambled up. Bitterness was heavy in her center. Even the spirits of heaven could not bring themselves to want her.

They also, on the evidence of this one, could blush and fling blankets over their nakedness. He stared at what the blanket did not cover. Turned his hands; flexed his fingers. Ran them down his arm. Raked them through his hair, tugging at his beard. "Allah," he said in perfectly good Arabic, with an Egyptian accent. "Ya Allah." His eyes rose to her. Their expression was an astonishing tangle. Joy; grief;

awe and wonder and delight; all leavened with a passion of despair. "I failed," he said. "After all, I failed."

She did not know what he was talking about.

He regarded himself again. His brows drew together. Very elegant brows, finely arched, a shade darker than his hair. He pinched himself hard; winced. "I don't feel dead," he said.

"Nor do I." Her robe was very palpable. So too the bruises she had won in falling with him. "Are you human, then?"

He nodded. Paused; caught his breath. Joy leaped in his eyes, high and bright and splendid, keen enough even at the tent's width to catch in her throat. "I am human. I *am*."

It was something to rejoice in, she supposed. She would be more inclined to exult that she was alive. "But if you're human," she said, "and I'm human, and neither of us is dead, what are we doing here? Alone," she added with a start of wonder, and of something that should have been dismay. It felt remarkably, and scandalously, like delight. "Who in the world would put us here alone—and—"

He could not say it, either. He pulled his blanket higher. His blush had fled. "A magus," he said.

It took her a moment to realize that he had answered her. "A magus?" she echoed stupidly.

"A magus." His voice was sharp, though he smoothed it with admirable swiftness. "A trickster in a green turban. High magic, indeed. Sacrifice—" He snorted. "Oh, your father had the right of it. It was all mummery. Every bit of it. Except . . ."

She spoke very carefully. "Please, sir. Whoever you are. If you know my father, you know me. I fear I don't share the honor. If you would be so kind as to tell me—"

He started as if she had struck him. The last faint glimmer of color drained from his face.

He tried again to stand, forgetting his blanket. He fell again less catastrophically, to hands and knees. With great care he raised himself on the latter. He wobbled, but after a little he steadied. "One forgets," he said as if to himself. "Damn you, Hajji. Couldn't you have added that one small spell?"

He caught himself, flushed. "Please. Lady. I've been— I've forgotten how easy it is to talk."

"It's easy," she agreed. "It's much harder to say anything when one does it."

His head drooped. "I'm sorry, lady."

"Whatever for?" she snapped. "And stop calling me that. My name is Zamaniyah."

"Mine—" He swallowed. He was, inexplicably, shaking. "Mine is K—Kh—Hasan." His eyes closed, opened and met hers. "Hasan ibn Ali Mousa."

Her head inclined itself, gracious. Her mind caught up with it and staggered. "Ibn Ali Mousa? Hasan ibn Ali Mousa?"

His nostrils flared. He looked like a frightened horse. Or, she thought, an angry one. Or both at once. "I may be a worthless layabout, my lady, but I've never been a liar."

"But you're dead."

"So were you."

She sank down slowly. All at once she was very tired. "I don't understand."

She thought he would not answer. He took time enough about it. When he did speak, he spoke softly, clearly, and with studied steadiness. His eyes were on the carpet, as if he read the story there. "You took a great wound in battle, saving my father's life. The wound was mortal. You . . . you died of it.

"But no one wanted you to die. One—one of us went to fetch the magus. He said that he could bring you back. For a price."

She waited. He did not go on. "For a price?" she prodded him.

His breath shuddered as he drew it in. "A price," he said. "Yes. Peace between our houses."

"And?"

His eyes flashed up. "Isn't that enough?"

"It hardly explains this." Her hand took in the tent. Hesitated. Almost touched him.

He pulled at his beard; saw what he was doing; stopped. His fingers had wound themselves in the streak of white. They recoiled.

He looked like a nervous boy. He bit his lip, closed his eyes, scowled terribly. "Damn that man," he said.

"Yes," she agreed, all sweetness.

His head tossed. "O Allah! Yes. *Yes,* there was more.

There had to be a sacrifice. Someone—someone who loved
you more than life.''

"Someone . . .'' Her voice was very far away. It could not
seem to make itself mean anything. "Someone—died for
me?'' She was clutching at him, shaking him. "Who was it?
Who was it?''

"Not who,'' he said. "Strictly speaking. If you think
about it.''

Babble. She cut across it with a voice like a knife's edge.
"*Who?* Not my father. Tell me it's not my father.''

"It's not your father. Nor mine. Nor the sultan. Nor''—his
face soured—"your pretty emir. Though to do him justice, it
very nearly was.''

"Jaffar,'' she whispered. "It was Jaffar. I dreamed—''

"Jaffar died in battle. He went before you.''

The tears ran of their own will. She let them. "Wiborada,
then.''

He shook his head.

Her fists clenched. "*Tell* me, damn you.''

He did, starkly. "Khamsin.''

"Kham—'' A great wail welled up. She swallowed it. It
choked her. To mourn her eunuch with mere silent tears, to
want to howl aloud for her horse—that was not seemly. She
had loved Jaffar as her own kin.

Khamsin had been the other half of her.

He was holding her. This stranger. This enemy. This man
of ill name. This warm and living presence, that let her cling,
that let her cry and never tried to tell her that she was a fool.

She pulled away, raging. "You dogs. You pigs. You bas-
tards! You killed him. Because he was only an animal.
Because it was the simplest way. Because he couldn't stop
you. He couldn't call you traitors. He couldn't—couldn't—''

He shook her until she stopped. His hands were strong. His
face was frightening. "He could. The mage gave him the
power. He offered himself.''

"You're lying.''

He let her go. He drew back, inch by careful inch. His
hands were shaking, clenching and unclenching. Was he, she
wondered in a dim cranny of her rage, doing his utmost to
keep from hitting her? "Zamaniyah.'' She snarled. How

dared he speak her name? He drew a breath, spoke it again. "Zamaniyah, look at me."

Look, no. Glare, yes. In pure and killing hate. "You did. You. You killed him."

"Yes, I killed him!" The force of it rocked her even in her wrath. "I killed myself."

"Obviously," she said with vicious sweetness. "Was it a bargain, as in the market? Two miracles for a single spell?"

He tossed his improbable mane and stamped. "He killed me. For the sacrifice. I was Khamsin. I was your stallion!"

It was horrible. Because it was mad. Because it was impossible. Because he *looked* like Khamsin.

Her head shook, hard. "You can't be," she said.

"I was." He held out his hands. Long, strong, very human hands. "I was, Zamaniyah. Shall I tell you how you bought me? How you trained me? How you rode me to war?"

She closed her eyes against him. His hair that was the precise, cedar red of Khamsin's coat. His beard with its strange blaze that wandered right of center, widening as it spread over his chest. "Anyone in the army could tell me that."

"Can anyone tell you where the *saqla* mare got her foal? It was easy, mistress. The bolt of her door—"

"Don't call me 'mistress'!"

"You bought me," he said. "I belong to you."

"I bought a horse. I wanted a horse. I want him. I want—" She was crying, sobbing like a child. Knowing how blackly shameful it was. Helpless to stop.

He held her again. He kept holding her. She kept letting him.

If he was. If, in truth, he was. The things she had said to him, not knowing that he understood. The secrets she had told him. Opening her heart to him, laying herself bare.

Her hands were knotted in his mane. It was finer than a stallion's. Human. It tangled in the same places, with the same indomitable persistence.

She pried herself free. "How?"

"Magic."

She glared. "Oh, indeed; who'd ever have thought it?" His silence rebuked her. She flushed a little; then more than a little, as anger rallied. "Why?"

"The Hajji's daughter."

"Not who, damn you. I asked you—why—" Her throat closed. Her eyes dimmed. Bile rose to choke her. She backed to the wall. "It was *you?*"

She had seen eyes like his. In men who were dying in great and hopeless pain.

Her jaw set. She measured each word with meticulous care. "Do you know what you did to her?"

His voice was low. "I know." Lower still, barely to be heard: "You told me."

She flinched. "I didn't know—" She bit her tongue.

"I didn't want you to." Tears fell unheeded down his cheeks. "I wish I had never come back. I wish I had died. Or lived as I was. I wish I could be your Khamsin again."

"I wish you had never been born."

He gasped. She snatched. They froze, hand clutching hand, eye to wild eye.

Her free hand reached, touched the streak of white, the brand that had been Khamsin's. "Did you—the mare—"

"*She* was willing."

His voice was bitter beyond enduring. Her hand rose to his cheek. It was rigid, trembling invisibly.

She began to laugh. It was worse than cruel. She could not stop.

Until she saw his eyes. She struggled to speak. "It's not—it's not you. It's . . . He left us here. Knowing what you were; what his magic would do." Laughter gusted again. She throttled it. "He trusted you."

"Allah knows why."

She glared at him. "And you don't? Maybe you've earned it. Maybe he thinks you've grown a little. You died for me, didn't you?"

He blushed. It dawned on her, ages too late, how very young he was, and how very deeply she had hurt him. Her voice softened. "You gave your life for me. And I've given you nothing but hard words and the back of my hand. Can you even begin to forgive me?"

His answer was so faint that she had to strain to hear it. "I could forgive you anything."

Her hand was still on his cheek. She watched it wander down to his shoulder. He shivered slightly, away from it.

It fell. Her cheeks were hot with shame. Her heart was cold. "Please. Pardon me. I keep—you're so beautiful. And I—"

"I look like a wild man."

A smile twitched, fled. "A very comely one," she said. "At first I thought you were a Frank."

He did not smile back. "Please. Don't— I earned the name they gave me."

"Yes; you had an eye for beauty. And a hand, and anything else you could bring to bear. It's lucky, isn't it, that I'm nothing to tempt you."

His eyes opened wide. They were angry.

"Oh, come," she said. "I'm not insulted. I'm used to it."

"You," he said, "are a babbling idiot." And as she choked on that, he stretched out his hand. He tipped up her chin. It came before she knew what it was doing. "Do you know what you look like to me?"

"Thin, brown, and tasteless."

She did not know how he did it, but he looked as if he had laid back his ears. "Tasteless, never. You've a bite to you. And under it," he said, his voice going soft and wondrous deep, "honey sweetness."

Her teeth clenched. "So I'm soft under the thorns. And you're a poet. And I don't need to hear it. I set you free. I forsake all claim to you. Now are you content? Now will you go and leave me in peace?"

"No."

That startled her speechless.

"I don't know," he said, "how it is possible for one human being to be so utterly, maddeningly, exasperatingly obtuse." He drew a sharp breath, spat it out again. "Damn it, woman, can't you see? You're beautiful."

"I am not."

He threw up his hands. "A curse on my name! If I were a prancing Persian you'd believe me."

"Abd al-Rahim is not—" She tottered on the brink of the trap. Damned it, and him. Let it swallow her. "He's in love with me."

"And I'm not?"

She choked on air. "You were a horse."

"That should have made a difference?"

"But you can't— You can't. I can't let you."

"You let him."

Her eyes narrowed. "You're jealous."

"He's not good enough for you."

"And you are?"

"Of course not!"

"You bit me. To keep me away from him." She throttled rising, and perilous, hilarity. "Can you imagine the tale people will tell? Two rivals and their beloved. Beautiful as a brown mouse, she was. And she wore a turban, and one of them wore a bridle, and with his teeth and his heels he won her."

"I haven't."

She blinked.

"I haven't won you. You hate me. I appall you. What I am, what I did, what I was—I'm a monster. You can hardly bear the sight of me."

"I can?" She was losing her wits. "You're wonderfully easy to look at." And to touch. This time he did not try to slide away. He let her trace the line of his shoulder. He raised a trembling hand to her cheek.

"Don't," he said. "Don't let me—"

"I could stop you?"

"With a word."

She believed him. She did not say it. She was rapt in the wonder of him.

Fear was far away, and sense, and prudence. They were out of the world. They had come to the far shores of death.

Words shrank and fell away. So many, they had spoken, and so few of them mattered. He was the other half of her.

Her heart mourned what he had been, what he would never be again. Her swift charger. Her wind of the desert.

"Khamsin," she said in the midst of him. "Khamsin."

26

She named him anew, and it was true naming. He felt it swell in him. The fire; the swiftness. The fierce elation. *She loves me. She loves* me.

He ruled himself with all the will he had. This body, this shape more strange than familiar, was at once more amenable than the stallion's and less. It could not grow drunk on her scent. Not quite. But it could drown in her eyes.

His senses were all strange. His memory was flawed. Some of them, surely, should have been duller than they were. Those that should have been keen were keen almost to pain.

Magic. He cursed it. Though it had given him this. Beyond hope; beyond anything he had ever dared dream of.

Now at last he could bury his face in her hair. Kiss her eyelids, her lips, her throat. Fill his hands with her breasts. She was smaller than he had conceived of her in that other shape, and sweeter. He wanted to savor every inch of her.

Part of him was astonished. Hasan al-Fahl, savor anything? Far more like him to fall upon it and devour it.

Hasan al-Fahl was dead.

Thanks be to Allah.

Her fingers wandered in his beard. That, by the Prophet's own, was going. Soon. When the world broke upon them.

And then?

With tearing reluctance he drew back. His voice came faint and breathless. "Lady. I think . . . Do you hear . . . ?"

She raised her head. "I don't hear anything."

"Yes."

She had worked her slow delightful way to his middle. She was coming, with mighty courage, to what rose tall and proud there. She did not want to know what he was saying.

He sat up. It hurt. He wanted to lie forever, and love and be loved, and forget that they had ever come back from Paradise.

Her hair tumbled silken over his center. He gasped. With the last vestige of his strength, he staggered to his feet.

She came with him, arms about him, protests flooding.

He flinched from the stab of sunlight. From eyes like blue stones, hardened against grief, widening with shock at what was there to see.

Beauty, yes. White and gold. His eyes found it pleasant. His body was cool to it. It was not Zamaniyah.

The Frank fled into the glare. The flap fell slantwise, letting in a spear of light. Her voice rose beyond it.

Khamsin had lost the power to move. He stood still in the sudden flood of light. He watched the tent fill to bursting with men, steel, outrage. Hard hands tore at him, rent him from Zamaniyah.

He fought. He surprised himself with strength. But they were too many, too merciless. They hurled him down. They set steel to what mattered most.

He wanted to laugh aloud. That was always the first thing they thought of.

One of the swordpoints twitched too close. The prick of pain slew his laughter. He lay very still, struggling to breathe softly.

Zamaniyah was crushed in her father's embrace. He held her as if he would never let go; he rocked her; he wept.

But his eyes were on Khamsin, and they were implacable.

At last his arms unlocked. He held his daughter back a little, stroked her hair out of her face. Her cheeks were as wet as his. "Little one," he said, rough with tears. "Little pearl. I thought I'd lost you." He touched her face, her shoulder, her hand. "How warm you are! You were so cold."

She shivered. He drew her to him, more gently now, wrapping her in his robe. He kissed the top of her head.

"And now," he said. His voice had changed. His face had gone terrible. "And now, daughter. What is that?"

His finger pointed to Khamsin. Who knew that he was far from prepossessing, sprawled naked on carpets with a half dozen swords pinning his privates; but surely he had not earned such scathing contempt.

Her cry was soft, but it was deadly fierce. She broke free and leaped, beating back the startled swordsmen, dropping beside Khamsin. She was even more angry than he. Their eyes clashed like blades; she hissed, even though she could see that his captors had not harmed him.

She pulled him up. He let her. But when he stood, with utmost delicacy he eased away.

For all her fire of temper, still she could see what he was doing. She let him go. She smoothed his hair with a hand that spoke more than any flood of words. She spun upon her father. "That, as you put it, is the man who died to give me life."

"He lives," al-Zaman pointed out. "And it was not a man who died for you. It was a stallion."

"It was Khamsin. This is Khamsin."

Tensed for incredulity, Khamsin reeled before belief. Al-Zaman was mad, if most methodically so. He could accept what had his mamluks, even his concubine, rolling their eyes and muttering. "And for that, he was given human form?"

"He was born a man," said Zamaniyah. "He offended a mage. For that, he walked in beast's shape. When he offered his life for me, he redeemed his sin. He won back his humanity."

Khamsin took note of how she said it. And of how her father received it. Al-Zaman's eyes narrowed. "He carried you? He served you?"

"With heart and soul," Khamsin said. He mastered his rearing temper. He bridled it; he won it to his will. He bowed low before his mistress' father. "Your servant, my lord."

The booted foot rose over him. He braced for the blow.

"I would not," said a gentle voice.

Khamsin stilled where he lay.

"Faithful service," continued Ali Mousa, "should receive a just reward."

"I am just," said al-Zaman. "I do not geld him with my own hands. He was alone with my daughter."

"Alone, yes!" she cried. "And too exquisite a gentleman to do more than look at me."

"That is enough," said al-Zaman.

Khamsin rose to his knees. The Turk's sword hissed from its sheath. He tilted back his head, parting his beard, baring his throat. His eyes, he knew, were anything but cowed. He could not make himself fear the steel that glittered so close, so thirsty for his blood. What did it matter? The man had the right of it. Zamaniyah was not for him. Could never be for him. He had had that brief sweet hour with her. It sufficed. He could die for it; he did not care.

Except...

Another face hung over him. Far finer, paler, older than the face of al-Zaman, though not much older in years. Sorrow had aged it; care; weariness.

Slow light was dawning in it. Khamsin's glance flicked. Thin ivory fingers closed about the hand that held the sword. Dark eyes peered, seeking a face beneath the forest of hair. Tensing, lest it not be the one he prayed for; darkening, brightening, as hope ebbed and flowed.

Ali Mousa broke al-Zaman's grip upon the hilt, cast the sword away. Al-Zaman stared uncomprehending at his empty hand, his frail and aged enemy.

The sharif had forgotten him. Khamsin blinked against the blaze of joy. "Hasan?" whispered Ali Mousa.

It was less a nod than a collapse. Ali Mousa was there, holding him, thin and startling-strong, saying his name over and over.

It ended quickly. Ali Mousa had drawn taut. "You were... you were slave to... these?"

"To the woman who died for you."

That struck true, and deep. He looked long into his son's face. "You have changed," he said, very low.

"I'm older," said Khamsin.

"Older," his father said, "and thinner, and harder. And

stronger. So much stronger.'' He took Khamsin's hands in his. They were broader than his own, and smoother, uncalloused; and younger. But the shape was the same, the long fingers, the elegant oval of the palm. He held them to his heart. It beat hard. His eyes were bright with the tears which he was too proud to shed. ''All the while, so close, so very close. And I never knew.'' He spun in sudden, icy rage. ''You! O my enemy. Did it amuse you, this mockery? Did it cost you dear to purchase the spell, to enslave my son to your daughter? And then, at last, to kill him. Knowing that I did not know. Laughing behind your eyes, to see what a fool I was.''

''No.'' Khamsin's voice barely rose above a murmur, but it brought them all about, even his father, even al-Zaman poised to leap for his sword. ''No, Father. It was my doing, every bit of it. They never knew. They never gave me aught but honor.''

''Slave's honor,'' grated his father.

''Servant's honor. And far more than I ever deserved. I took a woman by force, Father. I was her guest; she had healed me; and I destroyed her. I deserved worse than death. I received not only justice but mercy.''

Zamaniyah spoke above his head. ''We didn't know, my lord. We would never have shamed you so.''

Ali Mousa's head bowed. He looked shrunken, tired. ''Was he a good servant?''

''He learned to be.''

The sharif frowned faintly. ''I would hardly have believed it possible.'' His frown darkened. ''If you touched whip to my son's body—''

''Never,'' said Khamsin. ''Not once; though I provoked her richly. It's a Greek way. It is,'' he said, considering it, ''very strange.''

''It works,'' she said.

He looked at her. His heart melted and flowed. His body yearned toward her.

Sternly he mastered himself. ''Father, I earned what I had. Sheikh Uthman would never have spared the lash as this lady did. He would have beaten me to death inside of a month, or sent me back as a worthless dog.'' Khamsin met the outraged eyes. ''You wanted me trained, Father. Do you care how anyone did it?''

"I care who—" Ali Mousa stopped. Suddenly, astonishingly, he laughed. "Ah, Allah! How inscrutable indeed are Your ways."

He had not yielded. He could not look with hatred upon Zamaniyah. But al-Zaman, who had given him nothing but hate, whose sword he had found raised to cleave his son where he lay. . . "A Muslim," he said very gently, "may not enslave a Muslim. Do you contest that, O my enemy?"

Al-Zaman met his subtlety with brutal directness. "It is yours. Take it. My gift to you: I leave it whole. Only let it never again cast eyes upon my daughter."

Ali Mousa bowed with flawless courtesy. "For my oath," he said, "which purchased your daughter's life, I leave you unslain." He beckoned. One of his escort covered Khamsin with his own green cloak. "Come," said Ali Mousa.

Khamsin was trained to obedience; and, O miracle, to prudence. He came. It cost him high to come with eyes that did not turn, did not yearn, did not cling to Zamaniyah. Still more did it cost him to hold back the tears.

It was better thus, to end what could never have been. Without a word. In the cold fire of their fathers' enmity.

27

Zamaniyah watched them go. Her soul was empty. Jaffar was dead. Khamsin was lost. There was too little left of her for speech.

Someone buzzed at her ear. Abd al-Rahim, rapt in righteous anger. Had he been there all the while? "That appalling creature," he said, glaring at the open tentflap, at the light now freed of their shadows. "That he dared—that he dared to lay hands on you . . ."

Her eyes burned, dry as sand. Such daring. Such sweetness. Such perfect cowardice. He could have left her with more than this stretching emptiness. He could have given her what the Hajji's daughter had had. Zamaniyah, at least, had wanted it.

She sucked in a breath. "I died," she said. "I died, and I don't remember. I slept, I dreamed, I woke and he was there. And so much was gone. Is gone. I'll never see him again. Or Jaffar. Or—"

She swallowed the rest of it. Her throat spasmed. She fought it open. "I didn't know that I was happy."

If any of them spoke, Zamaniyah did not hear him. The

silence stretched. For all that she could do, the numbness was passing. She was alive. She felt. She grieved; and yet she breathed, and in breathing was a subtle joy.

The world was a shadow and an exile. But such a shadow. Such an exile: sweetness clothed in pain.

Abd al-Rahim was gazing at her. For a moment she saw his eyes unguarded.

No wonder he always made her blush. His adoration was as naked as—as—

She must not think of that one. He was gone. This was present, and permitted; and yes, fair to see. Very fair. And he loved her to distraction.

Her heart was cold. All the sweet warmth that had roused in her was gone. Death had taken it. Khamsin's death.

"Lady," said Abd al-Rahim. "Oh, lady. To see you alive again . . ."

She let him take her hand. She even let him kiss it, though only once. He held it to his heart. Such joy, he took in it. She was glad that he could be so glad.

Maybe the sweetness would come back. When she had rested. When she had forgotten ivory and cedar, and a narrow Arab face, and dark eyes startling against the pallor of it.

"Lady," Abd al-Rahim said again, more diffident now, though he spoke quickly enough to tumble the words together. "When it seemed that you had died, when we dared to dream that you would live again, I asked—your father said to me—he allowed me— He has given me leave to win your favor. If you would, lady. If you could . . . I would joyfully ally my house with yours."

She stood very still. Oh, indeed. Did her father think that she was a fool or an infant? Could he not have given her even an hour's grace before he loosed on her this eager child?

There was no answer in al-Zaman's face, no anger, no triumph. He had done what he had done. He willed what he willed. And he had seen deadly danger here, and he had moved as swiftly as mortal man could move, to turn it aside.

She spoke almost gently. It was not, after all, Abd al-Rahim's fault that her father had decided to sell her quickly, while anyone was willing to have her. No more was it her father's fault that he wished to preserve the honor of his house. "This is very irregular, my lords."

"It is," said Abd al-Rahim. "But it is permissible; and we do it only and always for your sake."

She stifled the spit of rage that wanted to burst out of her. "For my sake. Yes. My word is not enough, nor my honor sufficient; I am tainted with his simple presence."

Abd al-Rahim's eyes glittered. "That—that—there is no word for him in any human tongue. An animal, a shambling animal. How dared that sorcerer inflict such a horror upon you?"

He did not know, she reminded herself. Again. He was only a boy, and in love, and a stranger to magic. "It's over now," he said, soothing. "Never again. I'll defend you. I'll keep you in joy and in peace. You can forget it all, and know only contentment. My love, my protection; if Allah wills, my sons—"

They were chains, those words: gentle, and loving, and merciless. They bound her. They led her from the tent. Already Abd al-Rahim had claimed her even for her father's eyes to see. It was his arm, and not al-Zaman's, which circled her shoulders; his strength which bore her through the stares and murmurs of the camp; his cloak which slipped as if of its own accord to veil her head.

The war was won. The alliance was broken, Mosul driven back, Aleppo laid low and suing for peace. On the morrow the sultan would begin his march on the city.

He kept no greater state for that he was now a king twice over. He sat in the glittering throng of his emirs, in his accustomed lightless black; but his smile had gained a new brilliance. He saw her passing well beyond the circle, wrapped in the cloak, walled in her lords and masters, and yet he knew her. He stood up in front of everyone, forgetting rank and dignity to abandon his place, to thrust through the emirs, to seize her in a bruising embrace. The force of it spun them both about, left her breathless and dizzy.

He held her at arm's length and drank her in. She was aware, dimly, of Abd al-Rahim hovering, of her father standing close. Then she forgot them. The sultan was drawing her with him. Emirs were retreating, doing their best not to stare.

She kept her eyes down. Or tried. They had a will of their own, to wander upward, to reckon faces. Simply for prudence, she told herself. She should know who was there; who had seen what there was to see.

With every glance her spirits sank lower. At every white turban her heart would jump; at every long white beard her eye would catch. None was both long and red, and branded with white.

Of course they were not there. They were mindful of their promises. They had gone as far from her as they could go.

Her eyes yielded at last to her will. Her hands knotted in Abd al-Rahim's cloak. She fixed her gaze on them.

As if from very far away she heard the sultan dismiss the emirs. Some protested. "Later," he said, sharp and imperious. But to her he was most gentle. "Here, sit, where it's quiet, and out of the sun. Or if you'd rather—my tent—"

"It's better here, my lord," she said. He had set her in his own place, under his canopy, banked in cushions. One of his servants set a cup of sherbet in her hand. She touched her lips to the rim but did not drink. As unobtrusively as she could, she set the cup aside.

The sultan sat by her. She saw her father's face beyond him, caught between obeisance and resistance; and Abd al-Rahim seeming not to know whether to be outraged that he must share his new possession so conspicuously, or transported with joy at so potent a proof of the sultan's favor. Neither could sit until he bade them, and he was intent upon her, simply and purely glad to see her here, alive, solid to his touch.

A flash of green caught her eye. Someone was coming toward them through the ordered tumult of the camp. A Hajji's turban, a magus' face, though blurred with distance. He had companions. An old man and a young.

Her breath came short. The sun was too bright. She could not see them clearly. But the young one—no wild man, that. He looked like any young man of breeding, walking a discreet step behind his lord. His turban was white, and modest. His robe was dark and simple. His beard was short, hardly more than a shadow on his cheeks; its white brand was shrunk to a glimmer. He was all changed, all a prince, with a tang of magic in the swiftness of it.

He moved like an Arab stallion still, light and smooth, with a long, flowing stride.

Al-Zaman could not see them: they were behind him. With all the will she had, she looked away from them.

The sultan was calmer than he had any right to be, with flint and steel coming inexorably together before him. "My lord," she tried to say.

He turned to her, brow raised.

She could not say it. She scowled at the cup beside her foot and waited for the fire.

It was very cleverly done. They did not see one another until the newcomers had reached the shade of the sultan's canopy; and then they could only stop, stiffen, glare.

Khamsin—Hasan Sharif—would not look at her. Even bowed, his head was haughty. The shadows loved the planes of his face.

As he went down in obeisance, she saw the braid beneath the turban. And he no Turk at all, but Arab of the royal Meccan line. Vanity? Or defiance?

She must not think of him. She could think of Abd al-Rahim, who was going to marry her. Or of her father, who was deathly close to forgetting where he was and what he had sworn.

Or of the Hajji, whose design she saw written plain in every turn of this tangle.

She knew when al-Zaman crossed the edge. Her fault: she had let her startlement distract her. She tried to catch him as he started forward, but he was beyond perceiving so light a weight as hers.

She braced herself for a roar of rage. But once he had moved, he seemed to collect himself. He bowed with rigid correctness. "O my sultan," he said, "I am always and faithfully your servant. Yet, now that you have won your victory, I beg your indulgence. Give me leave, my lord. Free me now to take my daughter to her rest. Free us both, my lord, to prepare her wedding."

His audacity was breathtaking. Abd al-Rahim smiled at her, a warm and peaceful smile, the smile of a man who has gained his heart's desire.

Only one of them all had the wits to say the proper words. "I wish her happiness," said Ali Mousa. His bow was for her, and his long grave glance. She could not guess what he was thinking. Whether he wondered at the suddenness of it: he who knew better than any, what his son had been most famed for.

He did not wield that weapon against al-Zaman. She was in his debt for it.

"And this, I presume," he said, "is the fortunate young man."

Abd al-Rahim bowed. "Indeed, my lord, I am the most fortunate of men."

"Allah willing," said al-Zaman.

"And what," asked the sultan, "does the lady say to that?"

He sounded strange. He looked much the same as he always did, neither smiling nor scowling; merely a little worn. He must have been deathly weary.

She swallowed. Her throat was dry. What she could have said in his simple presence swelled to bitter labor before these others. That one other. Who had never, even once, spared her a glance.

"The lady," she said, rough-throated as a boy, "is her father's obedient daughter."

Khamsin's head flew up.

She would not look at him. She had said nothing to be ashamed of. Her words were modest, and they were proper. If they lacked passion, that was only fitting in a maiden of good breeding before a gathering of men.

"Zamaniyah," the sultan said.

She turned at her name. His eyes were very steady. "Do you remember," he asked her, "what you promised me?"

She nodded.

His tension did not ease. "This is your free will?"

"My lord does not approve the match?"

"The match is excellent." He was fighting to keep the harpness from his tone. She wondered if the others could ear it. Not, most likely, her husband-to-be. He was rapt in liss. "I ask if you do this because you want it. Or because ou are weary, and new come from death, and trapped by the wiftness and the cleverness of it; and because you cannot but e obedient to your father's will."

"I—" This was a battle. So many of them, listening. Her

father mute, strangely subdued. As if his will were not unshakable. As if . . .

"Perhaps," said the Hajji, "my lord al-Zaman will explain why he has done what he has done."

Al-Zaman's chin rose with his pride. "Is she not my daughter?"

The Hajji said nothing, did nothing.

Al-Zaman's throat convulsed as he swallowed. His anger could not seem to rise high enough to content him. "Damn you, magus! Without you I would never have done it. You forced it on me. Telling me that she wanted to be a woman. Proving it with that defiler of virgins. All but commanding me to give her the choice: to be woman and wife, or to be as she has always been."

"But she refuses to choose. She buries her will in yours." They all wheeled about. Khamsin faced them. His robe was silk; it shimmered, for he was trembling. "Tell them, O my mistress who was. Tell them why you do it."

The sight and sound of him were purest pain. His beauty; his fire. The scorn which she heard in his words, which smoldered in his eyes.

She said what he defied her to say. "Yes, I am a coward. I always have been. I'm afraid of what I can be when I forget myself."

"And therefore you give yourself up. You bind your body in silk; you submit it to the will of a man. Do you hope that your soul will quench its fire, once you make yourself a slave?"

She forgot that there was anyone else in the world. She screamed at him. "What else is there for me?"

"Everything!" he shouted back.

"Everything but you!"

The silence was thunderous. A slow flush crept up her body. She saw eyes. Everywhere, eyes. And shocked faces And Khamsin.

They were face to face. It was most improper. And he s proper now to look at. A perfect young gentleman. With hi Arab face and his Turkish braid and his eyes that saw nothin but her. Nothing, ever, but her.

She tried to push him away. Her hands knotted in silk They remembered skin that was silk. "We can't," she said

Someone was angry, somewhere. "This is unspeakable!" he kept saying.

It was. Khamsin had her face in his hands. He was going to kiss her. He was taking a very long time to get to it.

"Do you want me?" he asked in the softest voice in the world.

"We can't," she said again.

"Do you?"

She nodded between his palms. It was nothing of her doing. "But I *can't!*" she cried desperately. "There's too much hate. One of our fathers will kill the other, and mine will almost certainly kill you, and—"

"And for what? They bought your life with the promise of a truce. If they break that promise, you are forfeit. And I won't allow it." He wheeled upon their fathers. "I won't allow it! I'll die first, or go back to the shape I wore when I was hers."

"Are you—" Al-Zaman choked on it. "Are you asking for my daughter?"

"I ask for nothing," said Khamsin, stiff and haughty and all perfectly calculated to enrage al-Zaman. "This is a free woman. I will not have her used as a counter in your games."

"You will? You will not? What right have you even to touch the hem of her garment?"

"I love her."

Al-Zaman snarled. It was the Hajji who caught him before he sprang. "I think," the magus said, "that this has gone on long enough."

He waited, stern, until they had all sat down. Khamsin was as far from Zamaniyah as the circle, and the emirs, could contrive. Abd al-Rahim was close to her. Uncomfortably close. Nor could she move away: her father was there, rigid as a wall.

The Hajji folded his arms and surveyed them all. At last he said, "This was not wholly of my contriving. Allah is greater by far than I, and subtler. Let us say that I hoped for such a consequence as this. That—yes—I knew how my magic would end, if it did not fail."

"Why?" Khamsin dared to ask, with more heat than courtesy.

"I have a certain interest in the matter," said the Hajji,

which quelled Khamsin into white-faced silence. "And I am averse to enmity among princes; and I am my sultan's servant, and he has need of you all."

Khamsin was upon him, but not before Zamaniyah was. Not touching. Simply facing, bristling, searing him with soul-deep anger. It was she who said it. "You have bespelled us. You want us mated. It is tidy. It is unforgivable."

"Tidy," said the magus serenely, "yes. But there is no spell upon you beyond what won you from the black angel. Whatever is between you is yours alone."

"Swear to it," said Khamsin.

The Hajji raised his hands. "By the Hidden Name of God, it is so."

Her eyes slid. Khamsin's eyes were sliding likewise. Suddenly she was excruciatingly shy.

"I will not have it."

Both their fathers spoke. Both at once. Concurring in enmity, as never in a thousand years could they concur in amity.

Laughter bubbled. Khamsin's eyes had sparked, though he bit his lips until they bled. Her hand moved to meet his. It had been just so when he was enchanted. One will. Very nearly one body.

It terrified her.

He was trembling.

"What can we do?" she cried.

"Whatever you will," said the sultan.

"But I don't know— What do you want of me? What does any of you want of me?"

"It doesn't matter," the sultan said. "I said, whatever *you* will."

"I can't do that," she said.

"Why?" Khamsin demanded. "What do you want to do?"

Her teeth clenched. She wanted—she wished—

She had always done what she was told.

They were telling her to do what she wanted.

What she wanted—was—

Abd al-Rahim sat lost and stricken and stunned. She willed him to rise, speak, claim her. He never moved.

None of them would move. Khamsin least of all.

She spun to face the Hajji. "If I told you that I want my stallion back, would you do it?"

Even that could not shake his calm. "The gentleman might object," he said.

"I don't think," said Khamsin slowly, "that I would." He was steady under all their stares, even before his father's sudden, piercing pain. "What am I fit for here? I know how to carry a rider in battle. I can dance the Greek dance, a little. That is all. Unless you count my mastery of tavern-crawling."

"You're worth a little more than that," said Zamaniyah. "I trained you once. I could train you again if I had to."

"You wouldn't need to. I remember everything."

"Not as a horse, idiot. As a man."

She had shocked even herself. She had told him—a man—a prince—a sharif—

He was the only one who did not seem taken aback. He nodded as if it made sense. As if it pleased him to contemplate her insolence.

She forsook the last feeble remnant of her wits. She faced him. She let him see her exactly as she was: bare feet, borrowed cloak, hair loose and tangled and falling down her back. No beauty in it, and little enough dignity. She said, "I want you." The light of him nearly felled her. She held up a hand that struggled not to shake. "If," she said, "and only if, you want me as I am. I won't take the veil. I won't live in the harem. I won't stop riding to war. I won't ever be like other women."

His eyes had drifted past her. Despair settled leaden in her middle. Its claws were cold. Even he could not accept that she could not change.

He seemed to be exchanging glances with someone. But there was no one there. Only shadow.

His head bowed, rose. The corner of his mouth curved upward: a small, wry smile. It was certainly not for her. Was he mad, after all?

His eyes found her again. She gasped with the force of them. With grace that she had only seen in dancers, he sank to his knees. It was not submission. It was high and royal pride that chose, of its free will, to lay itself in her hands. He bowed; he kissed the carpet at her feet.

If he became lord of the world, he would never honor her as greatly as he honored her now.

She pulled him up. "Don't be ridiculous," she said roughly. "You've got yourself a soldier, not a queen." She faltered. "If anyone will let me soldier for him again."

"Let you!" cried the sultan. "With Syria to settle, and Egypt to see to, and a certain matter of Assassins, and a Holy War to wage? How could I let you go?"

Her throat hurt. She had not known how much it mattered, until she thought that she had given it up.

She faced her father and his enemy. But first she faced Abd al-Rahim. "I'm not the wife you need," she said, "nor the one your heart is wanting. But I would be your friend, if you would have me."

She held out her hand. He stared at it. At the man for whom she had forsaken him. At the sultan whose servant she was.

He was a nobleman. He bowed before he turned his back on her.

Khamsin's fingers laced with hers. It made the hurt a little less. It steeled her for the worst of it.

His father seemed almost resigned. Hers . . .

His eyes were fixed on their hands. His face was drawn as if with sickness; or with grief.

Her heart twisted. She left Khamsin, whose presence was a bolster at her back. She went to al-Zaman. She did not bow. She dared not touch him.

He breathed deep, shuddering. "I tried," he said. "I tried to set you free."

"I am, Father. Free and glad." His face had set. She stormed it with sweetness. "If the emir had had me, I would have vanished into his harem. Now you'll never lose me."

"I lost you long ago," he said.

"Isn't that a father's lot? But all that he loses, he gains back tenfold." She moved a step closer. "Father. I'm not asking you to love your enemy. Only to accept the war's ending."

"I accept it," said Ali Mousa. "I accept you, O my daughter. I give you my blessing."

Easy for him, al-Zaman's glare said. He owed her his life. She had no such name as his son had, which al-Zaman must endure, and must accept, if he was to bless their coming together.

Khamsin slid past her. He kissed the carpet between his hands. With deep humility he said, "My lord, I know what I have been. I have sworn never to forget; and never to return. Your daughter is my surety. I do not ask you to bless me. Will you, for the love she bears you, bless her?"

Al-Zaman looked down at him. The silken coat; the ruddy braid. The price it cost his pride to bow until he was granted leave to rise.

"I will never," said al-Zaman, sweeping his hand toward Ali Mousa, "embrace that man as my brother."

"I do not ask it," Khamsin said, still patiently, still humbly, though his hands had fisted on the carpet. "I am your daughter's servant, my lord. She asks that I be her husband. She has trained me to obedience. Would you have me break that training?"

"You would surrender your will into the hands of a woman? And you call yourself a man?"

"Hardly yet, my lord. Through a mage's art and a woman's wisdom, one day I may become one."

Al-Zaman's jaw flexed. "Get up," he said.

Khamsin obeyed. He did not conceal the glitter of his eyes.

Yakhuz al-Zaman was anything but blind. He knew the difference between obedience and submission. He had learned it exactly as Zamaniyah had, from the Greek who ruled his stables.

He bared his teeth. It was rather more smile than snarl. "I've never liked you," he said. "Now I know why. God has chosen you to rob me of my daughter."

Her anger flared, sudden and fierce. "I said that he would not—"

They both waved her to silence; which did nothing for her temper. They were doing it. Being men. Colluding in it. Shutting her out.

One of them laughed. She could not even tell which one it was. "If you harm a hair on her head," her father said with perfect amity, "I will have you shot."

Khamsin's head inclined a royal degree. "Ah. The old bargain. I'll hold to it. My lord."

"See that you do." Al-Zaman raised a hand. "Within that binding, O prince of stallions, take my blessing."

Khamsin took it as he had been trained to take all great gifts, with grace and gratitude. But his eye rolled back to Zamaniyah, and that eye was pure Khamsin. Bright, wicked, and altogether unrepentant.

Training, she thought. Indeed.

It was going to be a very pleasant war.

Author's Note

I. Saladin

The facts which underlie this fantasy are both extensive and complex; I have taken liberties mainly in the direction of simplicity. The campaigns of Salah al-Din Yusuf (whom westerners call Saladin) in Syria in A.D. 1174-5 were rather less coherent than I have shown them to be, with much shifting about from fortress to fortress and from battle to battle. I have conflated the deaths of Ayyub and of Nur al-Din and the taking of Homs and of Hama, and simplified the siege of Aleppo.

The Assassins did indeed attack Saladin at the instigation of Aleppo, at the common meal as I have described, but I have set the date rather later in the year than it actually was. It was the Turkish emir, Khumartekin, who died in giving the alarm, and a second emir who prevented the attack on the sultan's person. A second attack took place a year later, in 1176, when Saladin was again fighting against Aleppo. One of the Assassins succeeded in reaching the sultan, piercing his cuirass and wounding his cheek. Saladin, angered, marched on the Assassins' stronghold of Masyaf, not far from Homs.

The siege failed in considerable part because of the army's fear of their enemy; and because of renewed threats to the sultan. He withdrew before his siege was well begun, and left the Assassins to their intrigues. They, in return, did not attack his person again.

After the battle of the Horns of Hama, Saladin marched to Aleppo. He celebrated the Id al-Fitr, the feast of the end of Ramadan, outside the city; there he concluded a pact with his onetime enemies. Mosul agreed to a truce and a withdrawal. Prince al-Salih Ismail retained Aleppo and a portion of the north of Syria; he died in Aleppo, still resisting Saladin, in 1181. He was not yet twenty years old, and much beloved of his followers.

Saladin, for his part, was now *de facto* lord of both Egypt and Syria. In 1176 he took to wife Ismat al-Din Khatun, the widow of Nur al-Din. He spent the next decade securing his power and sparring with the Franks. At last, in 1187, he destroyed the massed chivalry of the Kingdom of Jerusalem in the battle of the Horns of Hattin. Before that year was ended, he had captured Jerusalem. No Crusade thereafter succeeded in winning it back. The sultan died in Damascus in 1193, leaving his realm to his son al-Afdal.

I should note here that Saladin did not actually take the title of sultan. He was *al-Malik al-Nasir,* the king, the protector. His biographers, however, including those who knew him, refer to him as the sultan. Since the title of king bears strong and perhaps misleading connotations, I have followed the biographers' example.

Of the voluminous literature on Saladin and on the Crusades, I am most indebted to M. C. Lyons and D. E. P. Jackson, *Saladin: The Politics of the Holy War* (Cambridge, 1982). For wealth of detail, for rigor of research, and for precision of presentation, no other single volume compares with it.

II. The Art of Horsemanship

There was not, to my knowledge, a hidden school of horsemanship in Greece or in any medieval country. There was, however, a very old tradition of equestrian training, exemplified by the treatise on the art of riding by the ancient Greek historian, Xenophon. His principles were revived in the riding schools of the European Renaissance and refined by later masters into the high and complex art which is called, aptly enough, classical dressage. Its most noted modern representatives are the Lipizzan stallions of the Spanish Riding School in Vienna.

Although the tradition—as in this novel—is primarily oral, significant portions have been set down in writing in, for example, Colonel Alois Podhajsky's *The Complete Training of Horse and Rider in the Principles of Classical Horsemanship* (New York, 1967).

There was, further, a Muslim tradition of equestrian art, oriented, as was classical dressage at its inception, toward the training of horses for war. The basic principles are remarkably similar. I have been interested to note that the snaffle bit, which Zamaniyah uses on Khamsin and which modern teachers favor for all but the most advanced horses, seems to have been in common use in the West in the very early Middle Ages; the more brutal curb bit—though not quite as brutal as the ancient Greek bit, which was a straightforward instrument of torture—was introduced from Asia, probably through Islam, for use on warhorses.

The Arabian breed is renowned as the oldest continuously domesticated breed of horses. Its origins are shrouded in legend, but are said to go back at least to the second millennium B.C. The pedigree of a horse who is *kehailan* or *asil*, of the pure blood, will vanish into the desert, into the oral history of the Bedouin; it culminates in the *Khamsa*, the five mares chosen (some say by the Prophet, others by a much older authority) to be the foremothers of their breed. My *saqla* mare has no place in the legend, but one very like her gave her name to one of the nobler lines of Arabian horses, the lineage of the Saklawi Jedran Ibn Sudan. Judith Forbis, in *The Classic Arabian Horse* (New York, 1976), details concisely and completely both the legends and the facts of the breed, and most particularly of the breed as developed in Egypt. Forbis notes that the horses of the Pharaohs as depicted in ancient art often bear a remarkable resemblance to the animals bred in Egypt in this century. As, no doubt, to those of the time of Saladin.

ABOUT THE AUTHOR

Judith Tarr is the author of a number of novels of high and historical fantasy, including the award-winning trilogy THE HOUND AND THE FALCON. She holds a PhD in Medieval Studies from Yale University, and for the past six years has been studying the art of classical horsemanship under the tutelage of the riding masters Alex and Galina Vukolov, whose Arabian gelding, Sheik Nishan, is the original of, and the inspiration for, Khamsin. When not in the riding arena, she is completing a new novel of historical fantasy for Bantam Spectra. She lives in New Haven, Connecticut, and has close connections with Auburn, Maine, and Melbourne, Florida.